PEACE FIRE

PEACE FIRE

PEACEFORGERS: BOOK ONE

AMBER BIRD

Worldwide Rights
Printed in the United States of America

First Edition

ISBN: 978-1-945636-00-4

www.AmberBird.com

This book is dedicated to
Secrets worth keeping
& worlds Inside

CHAPTER 1

The shock wave had caused me to stumble, but I didn't give up hope of regaining balance until something slammed into me from behind and propelled me towards the pavement. I felt a moment of panic when I knew I was going down, but a dead calm settled over me as I hit, as my palms and knees crashed and skidded. Though it was a parking lot, there were just enough cracks and loose rocks to do extra ripping.

I paused only a moment where I landed. There were no more noises (was it eerily silent in that moment or had the boom momentarily muted my hearing?), no more impacts. I felt disconnected from time and space, above whatever threats might remain. I needed to assess my state. Calm rested on the details of pain. There was my body...I started at the bottom, standing slowly as I confirmed the status of each part. The sensible black pumps were scuffed enough to no longer look sensible. No big loss. The stockings were torn less than I'd expected, especially given how torn my knees beneath clearly were. The blood (*my blood*) was making it hard to see how many abrasions there were, but I could see that some of those loose rocks were going to have to be dug out. *What do I call them if "abrasion" doesn't seem deep enough?* I wondered as I continued to take stock.

There wasn't even dirt on my torso or arms, not on the front side at least. (Oh, for a mirror to see the back. When I twisted to try to look over my shoulder towards my back, I could see the chunk of concrete that had hit me and swore I could also see my own skin and blood on that chunk.) But my hands...My left hand was slightly scraped at the heel, but my right had hit a raised space, like a tiny cliff thrusting up to peel the skin and tear off flesh. Inches of it ripped at the heel of my right palm, but still attached and brushing my cuff with an electric jolt at each movement. (I wasn't eager for what that would feel like on the other side of shock.) And the thumb was half-skinned on its outer edge. Again, too much blood (again, *my blood*) to see well, but there was certainly plenty of debris to dig out later.

As I patted my torso to be sure it was really whole, I held my breath a moment at an empty pocket. My mobile was missing. No, not missing. There. On the ground. Screen down. The calm was challenged, momentarily wavered, but remained. I brushed some dirt from my legs as I carefully, slowly, squatted to pick it up. Held my breath as I turned it over. Exhaled very evenly as I found the screen miraculously uncracked. I tapped a button and confirmed that its 3D display mode was also still working. Okay. Tech probably fine.

Finally, I looked up from my mobile and turned to see the source of the explosion. To see the decimated concrete remains of what had been an office building. *My* office building. It was like something from a film, or maybe the nightly news on a violent day. Unreal in its magnitude, though it was (past tense) a small building, and something I wouldn't expect to see except on a screen. So thoroughly destructive that I didn't understand why I was alive. How I had come to be outside that instead of...buried. Like everyone else who'd been there. Surely dead. Buried. Eternally entombed as Secure World Systems employees.

Was this another domestic terror act? Maybe just another group trying to stick it to a big corp. Plenty of those hitting other corporations in the last few years. Surely someone could be mad about some of SWS's products. You don't get into securing corporations' assets and tracking people's personal data without making enemies. And, whilst some people, most people, passively accepted that, some other people might go beyond just rejecting it for themselves. Some people might blow up a building to reject it for everyone. That's the story my brain started spinning.

When the Seattle PD cruised up a few minutes later, with the media barely a car length behind, I was still just staring at the chunks that had blown out of the walls. *I guess you're failing to secure your own world, huh?* I thought. And then I started to think about the co-workers, much as I hated them, who had also not been secured. The dead had faces and names and I wasn't one of them and what the hell and...I started shaking.

A wall of uniforms rushed towards me and there were people trying to talk to me, but I was above it all again. Watching my body shiver violently and my knees buckling. I jerked back into myself, though I still felt unattached to that self, when firm hands caught me under my arms and stopped my ass from meeting the pavement. I submitted numbly as hands slapped quick bandages on the obvious blood, wrapped me in a blanket, and hustled me towards a cop car.

Before they put me in the cop car, they swabbed me and took some pictures, and I suddenly realized they didn't understand I was a victim. Alive, sure, but a victim.

As a rule, when at work, I very purposefully didn't look suspicious. Unless you're the sort who considers grey business suits with sharp white dress shirts and conservative black pumps a suspicious sort of thing. But what had happened was unlikely. So unlikely that, in the face of my survival, I was considering changing my agnostic views. And the cops seemed to find it just as unbelievable. That might explain their excessive heavy-handedness when they swabbed me and my clothing looking for...I don't know. Maybe traces of explosives? Tell-tale particulates? Or maybe it was an approved form of torture to aggressively wipe me into a confession. Either way, I was going to remain a disappointment to them.

I tried to stop shaking, tried to stop feeling so out of control. This wasn't cool. This wasn't hard and strong. This wasn't the person I liked to tell myself I would be if I suddenly found myself in an action film. They finally let me sit in the car. An EMT gently lifted my head (had it been hanging down all this time?); shone a light in my eyes; and did another quick once-over of me, asked me who I was, tried to get the cop who kept asking questions to back off. "She's in shock. Give her a second. At least wait until she's not shaking."

I was trying to be useful; I *wanted* to answer questions. All I managed was a weak and wide-eyed, "That rock hit me." I pointed towards the direction I thought they'd find the piece of wall I was positive had nailed me. A cop who hadn't asked questions looked at Question Cop, who nodded, and then Non-Question Cop headed towards "that rock." I dropped my head again; it was too much effort to hold it up.

Through my hair, I caught a glint as someone pushed a camera forward where there was now a hole in the human wall around me. Question Cop pushed over so the camera was at his back and said, "Fuck it." He shouted over his shoulder, "Myers, I'm getting her to the station and away from this circus." That last bit sounded growly and pointed. I was starting to be present enough to pick up on things. Okay. Good. I tried to take deep breaths. Patted myself on the back for reading the cop's tone. At least I hadn't pissed myself or anything like that.

The cop turned back and asked the EMT, "Can I take her? I mean, she's not seriously injured, right?"

"No, she's banged up but doesn't need a hospital. At least not per the SWS Employee Health Care Standards checklist." She turned to me. "Unless you want to get billed for me to do more?"

I numbly shook my head, and she extended a digital clipboard.

"Just need your fingerprint on the list of services received and refused.'

I knew better, normally, than to sign something without reading. But not today. I pressed my right index finger to the familiar field, and I saw my picture and other information populate the form. They were now blameless and knew who to bill. I resumed staring at the concrete.

I heard a beep, and Question Cop told the EMT, "Now I know who to come for if her name gets leaked. We clear?" He must have scanned her name tag.

EMT gave a brusque, "Yeah, whatever," and walked away.

Question Cop said, "Okay, pull your legs into the car."

I carefully obeyed and he slammed my door. He walked around and got into the driver's seat. I leaned forward, keeping my back off my own seat.

Through the hair hanging in my face, I saw there were more cameras glinting now that Question Cop and the EMT weren't being a wall. And, without a human wall around me, I could also see that the cops were daring to keep SWS CorpSec back. CorpSec must be feeling humiliated and seriously pissed off that the cops had beaten them to the scene. And the cops must be feeling smug. Me, I just felt raw and really disappointed to discover I wasn't superhuman.

The cop started the car and caught my eyes in the rearview mirror. "Let's go have a conversation."

I was still a little fuzzy from shock when we got to the station. There were probably things I ought to have noticed or caught that I just didn't. The cop steered me to a small, bare room with a table, three chairs, and a mirror. He'd called ahead, and someone already had a pretty fancy-looking polygraph ready to go, with a pair of latex gloves so that he could put the contacts onto me without having to touch my blood. Away from the cameras and shouting reporters, the cop seemed slightly less aggressive and I could feel myself slowly, too slowly, coming around to normality. He scanned my fingertips and palms for prints, attached the polygraph contacts, and started asking questions, the same questions over and over. Even before I was together enough to manage answers, I was feeling solidly agnostic again.

With the shock slipping away and some time passed, my knees were throbbing, swollen, and stiff. I knew they were deeply bruised. I was starting to feel everything a bit too clearly. My brain suddenly got very noisy and full of movement. I held up my hand as he was in the middle of, evenly and patiently, asking one of the questions for what was surely the millionth time. To his credit, and against all the stereotypes I'd grown up with (and too often seen borne out), he didn't make it into a power trip. He just stopped and looked at me curiously.

I pushed my tongue around in my mouth, suddenly aware of how dry it was, and cleared my throat. "Um..." I was off to a great start. "Sorry, can you," I had to pause a moment and furrow my brow, working to pull out of the jumble in my head, what it was I wanted, "tell me your name again? Please." I carefully managed to lift my head and keep it up.

"I'm Detective Engalls."

I nodded and repeated, "Engalls. Thank you. And can you tell me if I'm under arrest? Please."

He shook his head, watching me carefully now, with regular glances at the polygraph. Was it showing him the sudden flip in my brain state? "You're not under arrest. We're just talking. Any other questions before I start mine again?" He wasn't being a jerk about it, not that I could tell, just willing to work to get me focused now that I was actually present. I didn't know whether he was truly nice or just trying to make sure he didn't accidentally throw off the polygraph by being nasty and upsetting me.

I considered it a moment; I didn't want to abuse his patience. Not out of respect for authority or anything so well-behaved. More out of a deep desire to just go home and hide from all this. I was used to being focused on the world in my computer or in my head; today felt like too much time spent in the meat. "Did anybody else make it? Do I have to talk to CorpSec today too? Will someone give me a ride to my car after this?" I sort of let those fall out. Those seemed the most important to me, as well as being both reasonable to ask and a reasonable number.

Engalls consulted his mobile and shook his head at me again, but this time with more gravity. "Doesn't look like anybody else made it out." And then...I couldn't tell if the tone was protective because I looked as useless as I felt or because this was his damned case and he wouldn't have it stolen so soon, but he firmly reassured me. "And, no, you don't have to talk to CorpSec today. At least not while you're here. As for your car..." He paused to poke at his mobile once more. "We've got it here. A forensics team is looking it over."

I nodded at him. "Thank you." I assumed the car was being carefully combed for evidence of my guilt. It was nice to know I was innocent of anything to do with the building exploding and that, unless they brought in one of the Computer Crimes officers for some reason, the only risk of me being implicated in illegal activities came from me saying something stupid due to the shock. I took a deep breath and resolved to think before I spoke.

After a moment, when it was clear I was done and his glances at the polygraph screen led him to nod, Engalls took his own deep breath. "Okay, let's see if you can answer questions now." He handed me a glass of water and I gratefully drank. I didn't even remember the water being brought in. Did he go out and get it? Shit. I'd been a mess. I preferred the current pain and buzzing brain to the stupefaction of shock. Too dangerous to be that out of mind. Hell, I'd quit most drug use and public instances of being super drunk for that very reason. Guess "intense shock" was on my "prohibition" list now too.

"Let's start easy. What's your name?"

"Katja. Katja Brennan."

"How old are you, Ms. Brennan?"

"I'm 25."

"And how long have you worked at Secure World Systems?"

I had to think a moment. "I've been at SWS about 3 years now."

"Now, I want you to tell me a lie."

I blinked. Oh, right. Baseline readings. "I love sports."

"Thanks." He made some notes. Probably taking me off the mailing list for supporting the department's baseball team. I tried not to laugh. Sometimes, on the other side of shock, I get a little silly. "What do you do for SWS?"

"My job title is Data Entry Tech."

"Sure. But what do you actually do?"

I fidgeted. "I can't tell you. I had to sign a non-disclosure agreement just to interview. And then had to sign an even stricter NDA for the actual job. Um..."

I tried to remember what I was actually allowed to say. "From what I recall of the NDA, all I can say is that..." And here my brain pulled up what it thought was the rote and allowed response, and I closed my eyes to focus as I recited. "I compare lists of numbers to confirm that the computer correctly parsed the information when it entered the numbers into forms."

I gave a quick nod and opened my eyes. That seemed right. "And anything else I might say would violate the NDA, so I'm afraid you'll have to ask SWS for more details." I tried to sound sorry about that. I kind of *was* sorry, because Engalls mostly seemed okay. For a cop. I could just as easily have been dragged here by some shouting, aggressive asshole who was more interested in proving he had power than in using that power to catch whoever had killed all my co-workers.

Engalls finished entering my answer, then looked up. "Got it. Maybe you can at least tell me what happened today. Why you were the sole survivor."

I had a moment of survivor's guilt and the immensity of it hit me. We might not have been the most massive of SWS's buildings, but the number of dead people I knew had...doubled. At least. I mean, even if you add in the kids I knew who had overdosed, disappeared, killed themselves, gotten killed from things like muggings or fights...It was a bigger number than I felt anyone ought to have, but still short of equaling the 25 or so people who'd worked in that building with me. I realized Engalls was waiting.

"Ms. Brennan, can you tell me what happened today?"

"Yeah...Yeah, sorry. I was just thinking about--" I felt a little like I was choking and had to take another drink of water. "I was thinking about the people who won't ever be able to tell you what happened today." Another deep breath. I had to pull it together in my head. It felt like it had been weeks since I walked out of the building.

"I was at my desk, comparing lists of numbers, when I got a message on my computer from the security station. It said that they'd apprehended someone trying to break into my car and I should come down to make sure nothing had been taken. I went to my car...and the building exploded."

He considered me a moment, typed some notes, looked at the polygraph. "So, CorpSec told you that someone had tried to break into your car?"

"Yes. That's what the message said."

He poked at his mobile, shook his head. "I'm not seeing anything about CorpSec calling us over any sort of car break-in. Why do you think that is?" His tone sounded very carefully neutral. Not quite an accusation, but also not exactly like someone trying to work out a curious puzzle with me.

I hesitated a moment, knowing I needed to answer this delicately if I didn't want to annoy him. The fact was that we both knew the real answer. We both knew that CorpSec—not just SWS CorpSec, but any big corporation's security—usually tried to keep the local and federal law enforcement out of things. It had been many decades since corporations really saw themselves as something other than a host of entitled little empires. The only reason the Seattle PD were even going to be able to be part of this investigation is that they'd gotten there first and it was on camera. Their investigation here would be as much about them refusing to let SWS CorpSec take away their chance to do their job on something bigger than a mugging as it would be about actually solving the crime. And, if they did well, this might grab SPD some reasonable funding in the next fiscal year or gain them some favors from SWS. But, obviously, I couldn't say that.

Instead, I said, "Maybe because they stopped the break-in before it happened and they figured it was up to me to decide if I wanted to contact you and press charges? Should they have called? Maybe. Probably. But do we really expect them to have called? To admit that they had a hole in policing their own parking lot that let a potential thief slip in? I think this is what lawyers call 'conjecture' though, and I have no idea why CorpSec do or don't do something." And then I mentally added, *I bet the Feds have already wondered whether CorpSec is going to let them in on the bombing, as they "should," so maybe you should just be happy you got a piece of the bigger action.*

Engalls sighed. Yeah, he knew what I wasn't saying. I hoped he at least appreciated that I didn't rub his face in the situation. He switched tacks.

"Don't you think it's an odd coincidence that the bomb went off while you were out to check on a car that, as far as I can see," and he was scrolling on his mobile, then flipped the screen to 3D and turned to show me it was pictures of my car, looking like it had had nothing to do with today's excitement, "wasn't broken into? That there weren't any CorpSec guys with a thief in zip ties waiting in the parking lot for you? No evidence of anything amiss except that you're alive, which, you've got to admit seems like *something* amiss?"

I really hate when I'm telling the truth and people don't believe me. I don't know why, and maybe it's a bizarre quirk for someone who, arguably, spends a lot of time being dishonest online. But, dammit, when I am telling the truth, I expect everyone to somehow just believe me. Even knowing that that's irrational (and that it might be better they didn't have a way to know, because that could then become a way to figure out when I *wasn't* telling the truth) didn't stop me from feeling a surge of frustration. Backed up now by the fear that I would have this bombing blamed on me and I'd go to prison...I had to fight down a big messy feeling that was trying to get me to shout and, I'm loathe to admit, maybe cry. I drank a little more water and breathed. When I felt like I was in control again, I answered.

"Obviously, sure, part of me does think it's odd I just happened to be out of the building when it blew up. But part of me thinks of all the stories from survivors who could have, should have been victims in other tragedies. You know, they were stuck in traffic so missed the doomed flight or were at lunch when the bomb hit or whatever. And some of them will even say it's proof of God. But the bottom line here is that it happens. Should it make me look suspicious? Maybe. But no more suspicious, I'd guess, than anyone who left early or who was out sick or out on holiday or at a meeting off site. If surviving a tragedy is probable cause, then I guess I have one more reason to hope that there are a lot of people on your list of possible suspects." I clipped myself off just as I realized a bit of ranting had started to creep out in my tone. More deep breaths. I needed to keep my shit together, not try to pontificate my way out of this.

Fortunately, Engalls just kept steady. He typed notes, glanced at the polygraph, looked at me. I reassured myself that he must see people more unhinged than me all the time. I wasn't going to fuck myself over by worrying that I seemed guilty. Deep breath. I *wasn't* going to do that.

"We'll check with SWS. There must be a record of the message you were sent." He didn't sound happy about having to check with them. "Could you try to tell me, as exactly as possible, the words in the message."

I nodded. "Yes. No problem." I closed my eyes a moment again and called up a picture of the screen. Eyes still closed, I read it out to him. "Report to parking security station *immediately*. We prevented a break-in on your car. Need you to verify nothing stolen." I opened my eyes. "They bolded 'immediately,' so I didn't waste time. Just grabbed my jacket—I don't carry a purse—and went."

"Was it signed"?

"Signed?"

"Was there a specific CorpSec officer's name attached to the message in any way?"

I closed my eyes, brows drawn together. Had I missed a name? I shook my head, wires from the polygraph lightly tapping my face, and opened my eyes. "No signature. And it was from the general building CorpSec account."

"Were you involved in your building being blown up, Ms. Brennan?"

I felt thrown for a moment. I hadn't expected such a straight-forward question. Though I guess it was an easier and more obvious one for the polygraph. I let all the horror I felt at what had happened seep into my voice as I quietly blurted out, "Hell no!"

"Can you think of anyone you know who might blow up a building?"

Oh. Now that was a more interesting question. But now was the wrong time to explore my own complicated feelings about blowing up corporate buildings (which were that I wasn't on board with a building full of people, even if I disliked them all, being blown up, but that I had felt some moments of righteous vindication when particularly loathsome corps had taken similar hits) or to get too particular in my honesty (because, yes, I probably *could* think of people who might blow up buildings, but probably not *my* building). I hoped my face looked like I was giving that question serious thought. "I don't *think* so."

He looked at the polygraph. "What do you mean you don't *think* so?" Shit.

"I mean, when I was a teenager, there were always kids trying to sound dangerous and cool when they got angry." I shrugged. "Teenagers say stupid things, especially online. But I don't know anyone *now* who would."

He checked the polygraph again. "What about your co-workers? Did any of them seem unhappy with SWS, their manager, anything like that?"

"I...I mean, you know, we don't have a glamorous job. Whilst we're working, we can't afford to be distracted, so the most you might really talk is at the start or end of day or if you take a break at the same time. And I'd argue that our work doesn't have surprises. You know what you're in for. If you don't find it suits you, you quit. So, no, nobody who was anything worse than bored or..." And then I remembered. I got a little excited, because I suddenly felt useful.

I leaned forward, conspiratorially. "A few months ago, right after this one guy...I think he was called Karl...um...Karl something. Anyway, a few months ago, right after Karl quit, we had a bomb drill. Never done anything like it before. Hadn't even really heard of doing that. But we all got messages and some CorpSec officer, I assume, got on the PA system. And, basically, it was like a fire drill but with no sirens. They told us to file out as quickly as we could without running and to head for the back parking lot. We stood out there long enough for the smokers to smoke a few cigarettes. Nobody came out to do a headcount or any of the usual fire drill stuff. And extra CorpSec cars came screeching in right about as we were all out in the lot. And we all talked, first wondering what we should do next and then thinking how odd it was. And then somebody wondered aloud if maybe Karl, who they said had a temper and had been really angry, had done something." I sat up straight, the light bulb in my brain, my poor brain that was finally normalizing, went off. "Karl Peterson! Yeah, that sounds right...Maybe Karl did it!"

Engalls played it cool, but I liked to imagine that was all he was doing: *playing* cool. If I had just solved his case, that would make up for me having been such a useless wreck initially. I wasn't exactly beaming, because it didn't seem right to beam when people were dead, but I felt like surely this was it.

"Were there any strangers in the building today?"

I was confused for a moment. Hadn't I just told him who did it? "You mean Karl?"

"No, not Karl. Strangers. It looked like your building wasn't huge, so you might recognize someone who didn't work there, right?"

"Maaaaybe. I'd definitely recognize the people in my section, but maybe not the others."

"How many sections? And wouldn't you see each other regularly in such a small building?"

"The building is actually physically divided. The part with the big main entrance, the part you probably knew about even before you started asking me questions, is the bigger part, the lab and clinic. That takes up...at least half the building. Because we're right by headquarters, that's the first facility to test or work on stuff once it starts moving out from headquarters."

He nodded like, yeah, he knew that.

I went on, "But then there's this smaller entrance on the other side. You go in and go to the right, you get the offices for one of the local groups of techs who go out to do in-person setups of the non-free security software. I might see them briefly walking in or walking out. You go in and go to the left, and you have...had...You *had* my group. Them, I know. If someone *isn't* a stranger, I might recognize them from having seen them coming and going or if I saw them in the lunchroom that's down in the basement. So, seeing a stranger wouldn't mean anything to me. I'm sorry. But, for what it's worth, no, I didn't see any strangers today."

"And what about in the parking lot? When you got out the door, did you see anyone?"

"No, I was just focused on getting to my car and sorting this out. We have quotas we're supposed to make each day, and I didn't want to waste too much time on this car thing."

He must have run out of questions and not felt like my answers were enough, because he started in on asking me the same questions all over again. He maybe changed the phrasing a little or pushed for some elusive detail. And then he did it again. I didn't get quite so excited about mentioning Karl Peterson the next time or the next next time. By the time he was wrapping up his fourth or fifth pass on the questions (I'd lost track), Engalls looked as bored as he sounded. Did boredom mean he believed me? I hoped he might be realizing that I was actually *not* the bomber, so this was a waste of time and resources.

I sighed. I was as bored as the detective seemed to be. As the shock passed and boredom took the shine off things, I was also starting to feel more myself. More like I was playacting not being okay. Plus, I was getting paranoid. What if they were keeping me here whilst they looked a little too closely and somehow discovered hidden bank accounts or some other trace of my extracurricular activities? I decided to try to play to my nice corporate image and restrained my tone a little. "I don't know what more I can do, detective. I've...I've told you everything. I'm just...I'm very lucky to be alive, but I'm also a victim here.

Would you like to see the bruise on my shoulder from the debris hitting me or look at my shredded palms again or the blood pooling in my shoes from my knees? Anything else I can show you to at least get moved to a room where I can sit quietly by myself for a while or maybe even get some less perfunctory medical attention?" I let some weariness and a touch of upset creep into my voice, stopping just short of faking tears (would they be fake?). "I'm feeling a little overwhelmed here."

Detective Engalls gave a sigh of his own and rubbed his eyes. It appeared that looking at the polygraph output screen was hurting them. "I appreciate your frustration. I know you've told this same story a number of times over the past couple hours. But I'm sure you can also appreciate that, as the only survivor who was in the building at the time, you're immediately a suspect. And since your story is more remarkable than the techs who were all out on jobs, you're kind of our strongest suspect."

He looked up to see my weary nod before he continued. "Your story hasn't changed and the polygraph seems to think you're telling the truth. Unless they've found something suspicious in your car or from the swabs, I think you can go home. Just don't leave town. And make sure I can contact you, okay?"

I nodded my agreement. He checked his mobile, seemed satisfied with what he saw there, and stood to pull the electrodes and other contacts off my skin. I felt some satisfaction at the blood I left on the contacts and the thought that someone would have to clean that up. I looked and saw more blood spots on the inside of the blanket I'd been wrapped in on the scene and had kept hold of through the first part of the interview.

I more hobbled than walked behind Engalls as he guided me towards an exit, trying to look calm as my knees protested. I could also see and feel the bruises under the scratches and around the raw meat on my palms. And, whatever the state of the impact spot on my back—as yet not fully assessed—the rest of my back had started to stiffen up as if it had been in an accident. (Which, really, it had. Just not the sort I might usually anticipate. I desperately hoped I could sleep and medicate that particular issue away quickly.) Unmuted by adrenaline and shock, the pains had gone from dull, distant throbs to sharp, immediate stabs, especially in my hands. In short, I was pretty sure I was not in the best shape. I was having a hard time pulling my mind off my body, but I desperately needed to.

Whilst I got processed out of the station and left my contact information for them, I started a mental to-do list. Finally focusing on something more than the constant update of "What does my body feel like now?" (Answer: Hell.) I was pretty sure that this sort of event was going to necessitate some life changes.

CHAPTER 2

Carefully holding the steering wheel in a way that didn't hurt too much or get too much blood on it, I set out for the dim and comfortable womb of my flat. I reminded myself that the stiffness and pain that was already settling into my knees would probably slow my reaction time. No stunt driving or police chases tonight.

I laughed at the thought, a sharp sound that was quickly cut short when my body protested the way it was being jarred. I gritted my teeth and vowed, grandly but silently, that They (whomever They were) would not steal my laughter! *Oh good*, I thought, *I've returned to the loopy part of my post-crisis cycle.*

The message system in my car was blinking. I checked the numbers of the incoming calls to decide which were probably safe to play in public (you never know when the cops are going to just leave a little something extra to listen to what happens in your personal space). I decided to listen to anything from friends or ex-partners, presumably calling to see if I had died, once I was home. I couldn't be sure what they might say. But the one identified by caller ID as from SWS Headquarters was probably okay. I pushed play on that and pulled into the crawl of so-called "rush" hour traffic.

"Good afternoon, Ms. Brennan. This is Consuela Parsons calling on behalf of Secure World Systems. First, I want to convey how very pleased we are that you survived today's tragedy."

I snorted. Sure they were pleased. The complete absence of warmth from her voice was probably just due to how hard she was working to contain her emotions.

"We believe you can be a vital help to us as we investigate the cause of the tragedy. We hope that, with your cooperation, we will be able to both clear you of any allegations as to your own involvement and bring the true perpetrator to justice."

I foresaw many new retellings of the "why I wasn't in the

building when it blew up" story. Though it was nice of them to pretend, even if their messenger hadn't done a great job of delivering the line with sincerity, that they didn't think I was to blame. Good job putting me at ease and getting me on your side, guys.

"In light of the fact that your office is no longer a viable workspace and that it will take a while to figure out how to fit you in at corporate HQ," (and, let's be honest, to decide whether I could be trusted), "we have transferred the equivalent of one month's pay into the account into which your paychecks are deposited, minus any expenses from today's emergency medical care that were beyond those covered by your insurance plan. We hope that you will see this as a good faith effort to continue to employ you and that you will give us at least two weeks' notice if, prior to the end of the month, you elect to cease to be in our employ."

I had no doubt they were also hoping this would keep me from suing, if it turned out I was innocent, over the risk to my life and the damage from their building smacking me in the shoulder and their parking lot eating my knees and hands.

"Your medical coverage and other benefits will continue during that time. We also commit, barring any negative discoveries during the course of the investigation into today's tragedy, to let you know at least a week before the end of the month if we are unable to find a way to keep you on as part of the SWS team.

"Because you might find yourself questioned by police or, if your identity is disclosed to the press, we would like to remind you of the NDA you signed upon acceptance of employment. We would also like to request that, if approached by the press, you decline all comments and refer them to SWS for statements.

"We appreciate you working with us on this matter. You will find a short form to sign, indicating that you understand and accept the terms I've just laid out, waiting in the personal email account that you have listed on your record. If you have any questions or concerns, please feel free to call me via the SWS Headquarters main number or to contact me through the email address from which I mailed the form. Good evening, Ms. Brennan." The message ended.

I did the rough maths in my head and figured, on the payment they were promising, I could actually go a couple of months without a new job or dipping into my secret savings. That certainly changed the order of items on my little mental to-do list and slightly improved my attitude. And it would give me a chance to explore income options that got me off the corporate tit for good. Whilst at a stop light, I had my mobile pull up the email and I read the form. It was surprisingly straight-forward, so I added my digital signature and returned it. I then had my mobile pull up the account my paychecks went into and verified that the promised money was there. It was. Excellent.

At home, I pulled into my parking spot to find Bryan's motorcycle propped near the building's wall. My parking space was just long enough and my car was just short enough to let him do that. A stroke of luck for him. Parking in Seattle, according to my gran, had always been bad-and-getting-worse. And when public transportation basically crumbled a few years ago, thanks to a decades-long trend of funding cuts and the efforts of the rich folks worried about how monorails or other raised options would ruin their views, the traffic and the parking both got even worse at an even faster rate than the previous norm. Just like you'd expect.

Down the litter-strewn hall and up a flight of exterior stairs, I saw Bryan leaned against my door. He straightened up as he saw me. "Hey, Katja. You're all over the news. In a suit. I think your reputation is ruined. Well, would be ruined if they'd caught your face." He gave me a sly smile, and I could hear the forced lightness in his tone. He walked closer, got a better look. "Are you okay?" He was trying not to sound too worried, which I appreciated.

"I think so. Especially now I know they didn't catch my face." I tried to force a smile. "Though I need to go clean the blood off my car and make sure I didn't trail any..." I looked over my shoulder, not seeing any blood on the pavement. "The shock is pretty much worn off, so..."

Bryan nodded and moved away from my door, stood behind me silently, watchfully, as I unlocked it. I had the sense he was in bodyguard mode.

As I walked in, with Bryan close behind, I started working

myself out of my jacket. Trying not to wince at the pains as my bruised hands curled and the flap of skin on the right one rubbed against the cuff. I sent a sarcastic, silent thanks to the EMT who just left the skin on, bent back instead of returned to cover the meat it once had, and slapped a bandage over it like that. At least the bandage meant I could avoid rubbing anything against the raw flesh the flap had once covered.

Bryan closed the door, and then, with apparent care, lest he set me off on a rant about my ability to take care of myself, said, "Please, let me help. Come on, Caught." Or at least that's what it sounded like when he used a diminutive of my name. In his mind, he was probably imagining that he was saying "Kat," the first syllable of my name, but I like to think of the diminutive as spelled "Kot" because I am not a Kat. Katja or Kot. But Kat (Cat) never fit me.

I could tell from his tone that I looked as rough as I felt. And, really, what sort of friend would he be if he weren't a bit worried that I'd almost been blown up. I stopped my efforts and turned around to face him. As I did that, I called out to my computer (which I'd given a human name—the name of the first computer programmer—so that I can pretend it's an AI, because an actual AI is way out of my budget), "Ada, door digitally locked and cameras extra sensitive. Lights full in corridor and normal in living room."

When the lights came on (way brighter than I liked), I turned my hands over to show him the damaged areas so he'd get a sense of what we were dealing with. He helped hold things open and in place so that I could slide out of my jacket. He waited patiently whilst I unbuttoned my blouse, though he did give a little wolf whistle. I called him an asshole but let him unbutton the cuffs. He held those sleeves stationary as well. I left a trail of blood on the right sleeve, leaking from under the bandage, as I carefully pulled my hand through. It blossomed on the previously pristine, white fabric. Down to my tank top, I took the clothes from Bryan's hand, mumbled, "Thanks," and then turned to walk into the less-bright living room, tossing the clothing into my bedroom as we went.

"Ada, lights off in corridor." And the brightness of the corridor was gone. (There was apparently a stereotype in my gran's time about kids sitting in their mothers' basements on computers all day. I guess I was just creating my own basement. My computerized cave.)

Bryan was being very quiet. He'd learned the hard way that I needed a moment to settle when I got home from work, even if the most dramatic thing in my workday had been an annoying co-worker. It occurred to me he was staring at my back, which I hadn't seen yet, and maybe he was being quiet because it looked bad. I was sure it looked bad. He knew I was strong and capable, but that didn't mean he had to enjoy seeing me beat up.

Bryan was one of two people in the world I trusted implicitly, if you didn't count my grandmother, and also one of very few I respected. So it wasn't that he didn't know how to handle me or that bad situations made him uncomfortable with me. I mean, we hadn't dealt with buildings exploding before, but he'd seen me at my worst. And he surely knew my head was buzzing and that I at least thought I knew my next steps. But he didn't ask questions yet, just grabbed us both beers from the kitchen as I walked slowly to my couch.

When I was 4 years old, my mum had moved us into her mother's home so that she could live the life of a junkie without having to suffer all the consequences. I remember just enough of life before moving in with Gran that I had always managed to stay away from meth.

Gran lived in the Ballard neighborhood of Seattle, on a street that had modest little homes for families, and some of those homes even had families, not just rich executives gentrifying the rest of us out of there. On supervised walks through the neighborhood, I'd met the other kids, and three of us quickly discovered that we suited each other.

We were three feral and imaginative children. When my mum finally OD'ed, I was only 6 and Gran became my sole parent. Not only did that save my life, but it meant we three little beasts had somewhere to play that was friendlier to our kind.

We consumed Gran's old scifi, in books and videos, and her

old music. We told tales of other worlds and possible futures. We shared the hurts and horrors of our lives at home or at school or lunging at us from the shadows of our city. We practiced fighting moves and smartass comebacks. We plotted revenge. We plotted domination. We grew up together.

And then we lived in a squat together when we decided we were old enough to figure things out on our own (and when I noticed that it was costing Gran more than she could really afford to make sure we were all okay). So, yes, Bryan knew me and my strengths, my weaknesses, and just how feral I could be when in a corner.

I stopped just before sitting on the couch. "Oh. Do you mind—"

He cut me off, placing an open beer in my less-hurt left hand. "I don't mind anything. What needs doing?"

I must have looked a bit glazed or confused (I felt it), so he didn't wait for my answer long. "I'll go clean your steering wheel and make sure there's no blood or whatever, yeah?"

I nodded, and he took my keys. He opened a cupboard in the corridor, pulling out cleaning supplies and my first aid kit. "And the bandaging job looks really crap, so..."

I put down my beer and he handed me the first aid kit. I made sure my thanks were less mumbled this time. As he walked down the corridor, back to the door, I asked, "Hey, is Riles coming over?"

Without turning back, he responded, "Yep! Zie'll be here soon." After he closed the door, I heard him lock it behind him.

Riley (a.k.a. Riles or Rye) was the other person I trusted implicitly. The third one of us feral kids. Whilst neither Bryan nor I clung to gender stereotypes, Riley vehemently rejected them. Going so far as to hunt down old options for gender-neutral pronouns (which is how we ended up with zie—rhymes with "me"—and zir—rhymes with "fear"—instead of he and him or she and her). Zir parents had loathed it when zie finally started really digging into being zirself, but Bryan and I had adored it. We felt like having more flavors of people in our little gang made us stronger, especially if we could do it without having to actually expand our circle of trust. And, in retrospect, it also made us a little better rounded individually, helped us learn to question everything we assumed we were just based on what society told us we were supposed to be. I always thought of Riles as the spark that never let me settle for being the drab person I pretended to be for work. And Bryan was like the wall that kept us from getting stabbed in the back, but also kept us from just turning to run backwards when hard things happened.

For all that it was my mother's bad choices that landed me on the same street as those two, I couldn't be mad at her. The ends way over-shadowed the means in this case.

I took a long pull on my beer, then got up and ducked into the bathroom to check out the damage on my right shoulder. I had to pull my tank top aside a bit to get a sense of what had happened there. There were some abrasions, but just one place where the skin was really ripped at all. Guess the suit jacket and dress shirt had mitigated the damage the debris could do. It was scraped up at the main impact point and surrounded by a massive and, I noted admiringly, rather impressive bruise. But it wasn't raw like the hand. I'd been lucky. Yesterday, I hadn't worn a suit jacket. Yesterday would have been a worse day to be pummeled by a building.

I went back to my bedroom, used my feet to nudge the damaged clothes closer to the laundry pile, and kicked off my ruined work shoes.

Finally, I headed back to my couch. "Ada, play Crash Dance's eponymous album on the living room speakers at volume four." I'd read somewhere that listening to music you loved could distract you from pain, and I was going to need some distraction very soon.

Crash Dance was rumbling and slipping through the speakers as I carefully opened the first aid kit on a side table. I gingerly peeled off my stockings. Fortunately, the blood from my knees had dried, so I hadn't left bloody footprints on my floor. Unfortunately, the blood from my knees had dried and stuck the stockings to the knees from whence that blood had come. I was glad Bryan wasn't there to see me gritting my teeth and blinking back tears as I pulled the fabric from my battered knees. So far, the music wasn't distracting enough.

When Bryan walked back in, I had also removed the EMT's bandages from my hands and was trying to trim the flap of skin off my right palm. (Now would be the time to mention that I'm right-handed, wouldn't it?) The only thing in my favor at the moment was that I'd remembered to turn up the lights. I could at least see the mess I was about to make of myself.

Without asking, Bryan took the tiny scissors from my fumbling left hand and sat in the chair on my left, perpendicular to the couch. As much as I have been known to go too far trying to prove I can take care of myself, I was clear-headed enough not to protest. He didn't scold or comment, just asked, "Are you up for telling me about this whilst I work?"

I wanted to say yes, but I didn't trust my voice to stay steady until after he was done. "Probably not."

"Can we turn on the news then, see what they're saying? Give you a chance to see your TV debut?" He flashed me a grin with his crooked teeth. He was a charmer.

"Asshole," I glared at him for a moment. "Ada, TV on. My top four news channels, please." Most of the wall to our right (the one Bryan's chair faced) came alive with colors and noises, each quarter of it showing a different news channel. The wall TV made putting furniture on that wall ill advised but was great for this sort of thing or multiplayer vidgames.

One channel showed the smoking ruins of my building. One had a news anchor running down the general facts. ("What we know at this point is that, at approximately 2:02 this afternoon, there was an explosion at this SWS facility.") One showed an advert for the latest big product out of SWS. ("Struggling teenager? Older parent with health issues? Small child prone to wandering off? The Peacemaker can help with all of these common concerns!") And the final channel had a shot that appeared to be the corporate officers of SWS about to speak.

I stared over my shoulder at the news footage as Bryan clipped off the ripped skin. Even though I'd been right there, the remains of my building looked unreal. "Ada, mute all displayed TV channels except channel 5." Now I could actually make sense of the sounds.

"At this point," a polished but adequately somber reporter told us, standing in front of the entrance to the main SWS headquarters, waiting for corporate officers to speak, "Seattle PD has informed us that, in addition to 10 employees who were out at client sites, there was only the one as-yet unnamed survivor who was present during the explosion. Sadly, there are no survivors in the wreckage. They just confirmed that with some heat imaging devices brought in by SWS CorpSec. That means 15 dead. Our hearts go out to the families of those who lost loved ones in today's tragic explosion."

She looked over her shoulder as the corporate officers stepped up to the mics. "We'll now hear statements from SWS. It looks like CEO Mary Johnson, COO James Smith, and CFO Jennifer Williams are ready to speak."

"Kot."

I turned my head to look at Bryan.

"I'm going to have to scrub the dirt out of things." He looked me in the eyes and employed his most no-nonsense tone. "If we don't get all the shit out, you'll risk infection and probably won't heal as well or as quickly. This is going to hurt like a motherfucker." He held my gaze, waited until I nodded, and then he opened an alcohol scrub and went to work with that and a little nail brush.

He scrubbed; I called him horrible names and cursed everything he held dear. But I appreciated not having to be the one to do that to myself. His willingness to be as brutal as a job required had always been a trait I found endearing.

Through this medical assault, Mary Johnson delivered her statement with polish and the perfect balance of sadness and steely resolve. I only caught pieces through my swearing. "SWS is deeply saddened over today's bombing. Less for the loss of our building and its important research, and more for the loss of the lives of 15 of our loyal employees. Our hearts go out to their family and friends. We grieve with you. And we promise you that Secure World Systems Corporate Security is working hard to find the criminals who stole your family members. We truly believe in peace through security and security through peace. We will give you security; we will return your peace. And we ask anyone who might have information about those involved in today's heinous act to contact your local SWS CorpSec office immediately. Thank you."

Before Bryan got any further, the door buzzed. I looked at the screen in my tabletop. It was Riley, giving the camera an exaggerated, toothy grin with eyes wide. There was a piece of hair trying to flop across zir face that just made it a little more chaotically silly a picture. I laughed and told Ada to let zir in. I flashed Riley's look at Bryan, who also laughed, and I said, "I hope zie brought food."

"Zie should have. I *told* zir to bring food and drink. I figured we'd all appreciate something to drink at least."

Rye strode in, and the energy in the room shifted.

Bryan was a calm exterior with deep and thick emotions that, as prescribed by our cultural context, he mostly held close—unless it was something like anger—and showed only to me, Rye, and whatever romantic partner he had. I was, I thought, a little less calm and my emotions a little closer to the surface. But our Rye was more like an attempt at a thin shell of calm, covering a swirl of emotion and ideas, hating to be constrained by...well, if I'm being honest, by anything. I suspected zie only wore clothing because it was another form of expression. As kids, Rye had been the one most likely to ditch clothes and run around as unconstrained as possible in every way zie could manage.

Where Bryan was a little toned and was taller than me, Rye was slight and the same height as me, but seemed so much bigger than even Bryan, so full of self, like there were multiple selves in there. So, yeah, when Riles walked into a room, it shifted. The air subtly electrified. I smiled.

Rye did *not* smile. Instead, zie stopped short, staring at my current state. "Oh, Kot..." Zie dropped the bag zie was carrying and rushed over.

Bryan caught my eye, gave me a wink and a smile, then turned his smile to Rye. "Perfect timing. Any later and I'd have applied foam and bandages and you'd have had to imagine the damage."

Seeing the angry red skin and the pile of alcohol wipes, zie said, "Tell me I got lucky and you're done with the scrubbing and swearing."

I nodded. "Bryan was right; your timing is perfect."

There was a pause whilst Rye looked me over, ignoring my attempt at humor. When zie got to my back, zie carefully pulled aside the tank top. "Have you seen this?" I nodded, but Bryan stood and moved around for a better look.

"That's a nice bit of damage. At least bruise colors match the rest of your wardrobe." Bryan was still trying to pretend this wasn't serious, but I could hear that he was concerned.

"I hate to say it, because I loathed having to wear them for work, but my jacket and work shirt probably were like light, really light, armor. It could have been worse."

"I'm going to take a picture so you can clearly see it." Rye pulled out zir mobile. "Bryan, hold her shirt out of the way." There was the click of the picture, and then Rye held zir mobile in front of my face. Yeah, that bruise covered about one third of my back. After a brief pause, Riles went back into motion. "I'll sort out food and drinks if you want to go back to playing doctor." Zie gave Bryan and me a cheeky wink. Because nothing says friendship like regularly implying there's something more than friendship going on.

"I guess if you want to play cook instead of nurse..." Bryan grinned, returned the wink. Riley made a kissy face before grabbing the bag zie'd arrived with and heading into the little kitchen just off my living room.

Bryan applied sterile foam and plasters. Almost all my plasters were garish colors or covered in cartoons (the "normal" ones were hidden away so I didn't accidently waste skin on them), which meant that I was going to be more colorful than I'd been since I was a kid. The thought made me smile a little. I was ridiculous. I knew it and, at least around my friends, I loved it. I'd done most my somber brooding when I was a teen.

Rye called from the kitchen, "What happened? I don't care if you already told Bryan every detail. You have to tell me too."

Bryan finished smoothing on the plasters that covered the rawness of my right hand. "She didn't tell me anything yet. She needed a drink and needed not to have to talk while I was doing the painful stuff."

I muted the remaining news channel noise. I could hear the clatter of plates and Riles sounded as freaked out as I'd felt earlier. "I was so fucking worried when I saw the news. I was at work and I lost it. They told me I could go home early, especially because you didn't answer when I called. The news wasn't confirming any survivors then, just maybe one survivor and no name, and I kind of...I just kept thinking about what if you were dead."

Bryan finished with the plasters on my knees and stopped himself just before hitting me in the shoulder to indicate I was ready to go. I laughed as his fist hung there a moment. "I know you like to see me in pain, mate, but haven't you seen enough today?" I stuck out my tongue quickly and he squinted, feigning anger, then laughed.

I lifted my voice so Riles could hear me clearly. "I'm so, so sorry I didn't answer. The cops were on me within minutes of the explosion and they didn't let me go for hours. And then...I'm just paranoid. I mean, what if they bugged my car 'cause I'm their only suspect and then someone accidentally said something in a message I didn't want them to hear? So I didn't listen to any personal messages yet. And...I'm sorry. I should have thought to at least call you two, but my brain is feeling kind of fried from all this."

I stood. "Time to lose the skirt. Be right back." I saw Bryan pick up the remnants of my stockings and start to tidy up the first aid supplies. "You really don't need to do that. I think I can probably handle it." I took the stockings from him to add to the pile of clothes from today. "You've already done too much."

He kept working. "Listen, you, the job's not done until it's cleaned up. I don't want all your blood to put us off our food. Let me finish my job. Or I'll let Rye handle it next time."

I shouted, "Next time?!" and, from the kitchen, Riles shouted, "Nope!"

I put on shorts, because I wasn't going to force those knees of mine into trousers yet, and returned to find Rye putting down plates of Chinese food. There were already (more) beers and a bottle of cheap wine set out. It was never a bad idea to let Riles choose the food. Or the drinks. (Though, really, enough drinks or trauma and I'd probably be okay eating anything.)

It looked like Bryan had put away all the first aid supplies. He was sitting in the same chair, leaned back, a well-deserved beer in hand. Riley settled onto the couch and began opening a bottle of wine. Zie'd left room for me to sit at the end of the couch nearest Bryan. Nobody needed to say it; they were protectively surrounding me as much as they could. I hadn't really been that near death, but the explosion *felt* like I imagined a near death experience would feel, and I was definitely feeling a little more emotional about my people now. I took my spot on the couch.

I looked up at the news to see explosion footage that wasn't my building, but was some other incident. At least that meant the press had more than just the SWS bombing to focus on, and maybe that meant it would take them longer to figure out who *I* was. Speaking of which, there I was, being hustled to the car by Engalls, with other emergency response types doing a mediocre job of blocking the camera's view. I was relieved that they'd gotten only shots of hair, the top of my head, some blurry attempts at close-ups of wounds. Nothing definitely me.

As I watched myself on the news, battered, dazed, and all business suited, I decided that it had just become a high priority to get a new haircut. Something I could live with for a while that was drastic enough to keep me from being obviously the woman on the TV, since hair was all they had. I really didn't want to be her, much less be recognized as her.

Without taking my eyes off four channels of news that rotated footage of me and the wreckage of my old office, I asked, "Who's going to help me fix my hair? Something a little more me ASAP." It was really weird to see myself from this perspective. Too weird. I turned back to my food.

Rye met my question with questions. "Cut? Color? Something totally unfriendly to corporate work?"

Bryan added, "Because we've still got things here from the last time we did *our* hair."

Clearly, they also thought it was a good idea. Good. I was going to treat today's shakeup as an opportunity to change things. Basically, I was still veering towards a classic post-near-death experience mindset.

"Well, it turns out that they're going to pay me to say home a little while, so I can ditch the respectable symmetrical. I think my hair wants to be uneven. And not brown. Please." I smiled.

Bryan cleared his throat. "If you're feeling good enough to worry about your hair, it's time to tell us what happened. Yeah?"

Riles exclaimed, "Yes! I'm really trying to be patient and shit, but I'm dying here. Spill it!"

Hours after the fact, sitting on my own couch instead of in a police interrogation room, and with a beer and some food in me, I was feeling much less reluctant to tell my story one more time than I had felt the last "one more time" I'd told it.

"It was...about 1400 and I got a message from CorpSec that someone tried to break into my car and would I come make sure nothing was missing. Which was kind of perfect timing, 'cause the hours after lunch go on forever, so I'll take any excuse to break them up. I didn't see anybody by my car, but before I actually reached it, there was this...like a rumbling booming sound and there was dust blowing past me and the air was pushing me. And then some big piece of the building smacked me in the back. And...I guess that's it. For a big deal event, it makes a short story."

Bryan said, in an odd tone, "Lucky break that. Getting the message and going just in time."

Riles also sounded...dubious. Dubious was definitely what I heard in both their voices. "Yeah. Maybe a little too lucky. Right?"

I shrugged and started telling them what I'd told Engalls, "Maybe, but you hear about things like this. People who..." What had I listed as examples at the station? "People who miss flights because of bad traffic and the plane goes down or...stuff like that." I looked back and forth between them. "You guys don't think I did this too, do you? I mean, honestly, if anyone should know better, it's you two."

Bryan and Riley exchanged a look. Then Bryan assured me, "We definitely know it's not your style. This wasn't a bank. And not online. And it was full of people who could die."

"But," Riles picked up from there, "it also seems really, really unlikely. Especially because, unless you left something out, your car *wasn't* broken into."

"And the message that saved you came in by computer," Bryan finished off the line of thought that, it seemed, they both shared.

Rye pointed at Bryan and nodded vigorously in agreement.

And they had a point. I could have kicked myself. "How the hell did I not put that together already?" I sighed. "I'm so off my game."

Bryan sipped his beer. "Blame it on the shock." When I squinted, trying to determine whether he was mocking me, he said, "Seriously. Shock will fuck up your brain. If I were you, I wouldn't plan on doing anything tonight that's more taxing than sitting on the couch."

I shoveled food into my mouth, thinking that I wanted to drink but didn't want my empty stomach to mean that I was stupid from shock *and* drinking too much. I unmuted a news channel to cover the silence of my slow brain.

After some quiet, broken only by the news droning on the same few facts of the (now two, apparently unrelated bombings) over and over, Rye asked, "So, do you know things the news doesn't? Like...Like if there are suspects or what sort of explosives were used or anything?"

I shook my head. "Right now, I think I'm their main suspect. They swabbed me down for...residue or something. And went through my car. And made me answer the same questions over and over." I sighed remembering the "fun" afternoon I'd spent at the station. "I did tell them about some guy...Remember when I told you guys we had that weird, random 'bomb drill' a few months ago? I told them about that whole scene. Maybe Karl Peterson, the guy who quit right before, who we all thought maybe caused the 'bomb drill,' maybe he did this. Right?"

They both shrugged and Riles asked, "Did Karl like you or something? Would he, you know, have saved you if he *did* blow up the building?"

I didn't have to think long to answer that. "From what little I saw and heard, Karl hated everyone and everything to do with SWS. And he wasn't in my section, so I only saw him if he was coming and going. Never looked happy, never even nodded at me."

Bryan pointed out, "Then this wasn't Karl. But, looking at it logically, it seems like *someone* sending you the fake message that gets you out just in time not to die with everyone else is really, really unlikely to be a coincidence."

We all kind of sat with that a moment. He was right. Dammit. I didn't want to be at all involved in what had happened, but this told me that, in a way, I was. And not because I'd survived but because of *how* I'd survived.

"I think I should probably check all my messages and inboxes. Just in case whoever did this has tried to get in touch." Shit.

CHAPTER 3

"Ada, boot to table monitor and display incoming phone message numbers." I opened my several email accounts and private message boxes on various forums whilst Ada complied. As the messages loaded into their respective inboxes and lists, I considered which phone messages to bother listening to. I spoke to the room, "Do you mind if I don't listen to your phone messages now?"

Riley laughed, "Let me summarize. 'Oh shit! Are you alive? Are you okay? I love you! Don't be dead! What would we do if we lost you? Call me. Please, please be alive!'" Zie laughed again. "All questions and exclamations, some with obvious crying around them." I put my arm around zir for a quick squeeze.

I looked at Bryan. He was pulling his portable out of his bag. "Mine are similar, but less audible crying and more pretending to be totally calm about things."

I didn't delete their messages, but dragged them off the list. I also dragged off messages from random acquaintances, an ex-boyfriend, and an ex-girlfriend whom I was sure were only calling to get in on the bombing drama. Which left only a call from Rye's bae. I politely linked my earbud to the computer so that only I would hear. Kitty sounded concerned and, honestly, I was a little surprised. I knew she'd expressed concern about Riles being so close to me and she and I had never been more than polite. "Hey, I just talked to Riles. I hope you're okay. Um...at least alive. But hopefully totally okay. I know you mean a lot to zir and that everyone is worried. Anyway...Okay. No need to call. Just, uh, hope you're okay. Bye." I took a moment to text Kitty, because it seemed the polite thing to do, and then moved on to my email and private messages.

From his chair, Bryan seemed to be thinking aloud. "If the bomber isn't the one who saved you, maybe they'll be as eager as the press to find out who you are."

The implied threat of such a scenario hung in the air. I guess I hadn't really allowed myself to think about that, but paranoia had been trying to push forward and get my attention. Sure, it had probably been some dramatic kind of corporate espionage, but what if it had been something madder and the bomber took even one survivor personally?

Having said his piece, Bryan leaned back even more into the chair. I recognized that he was very careful in the way he now put his feet up on the coffee table in front of us all. A good idea when the coffee table is a sweet piece of machine whose screen is up and whose controls are bared. Especially when the overprotective user was using and close enough to hit him for any damage she imagined he might do.

My mobile rang then. I checked to discover it was SPD calling. Did Engalls want to make sure I wasn't off blowing up another building? "Hello?"

"Ms. Brennan, this is Detective Engalls."

"Hi, Detective. What can I do for you?"

"I need to let you know that this call is being recorded, because I need to capture your answer to a question. SWS was just on the phone and I wanted to check in with you about a couple of things."

"Sure. What's up?"

"First, we need your consent to share the recordings and results of today's interview and lab tests with them. That's what I need to record your answer to."

I knew SWS would get it anyway, and I suspected that I might look a bit guilty if I put up a fight at this point. "Yes. You can share with them."

"Thanks. And I'd like to set up a follow-up conversation with you. This time, we'll need to include SWS." He sounded about as displeased by that last bit as he was probably professionally allowed to feel.

"I understand." And I tried to make sure that my tone showed I really did and that I was sorry he was stuck sharing his case. "Do you think we could push it off until Monday? It's been a really horrible day and I'd like to take the weekend to mourn and get my head together. Would that be okay?"

He paused. Was he weighing out how helpful he thought I might be versus how guilty he thought I was? "Yeah, that would be okay. Of course. Can you be here at 9:00 Monday morning?"

"Yes, sir. I'll put it in my calendar." My mobile was linked to my computer, and a message flashed on my screen that I had a call coming in from SWS Headquarters. I really wanted to get to my other messages, but I knew I'd have to talk to them eventually.

"Detective, I've got SWS trying to call in. I really should talk to them. I'm sorry."

"Absolutely. See you Monday, Ms. Brennan."

"See you then." And then I clicked over to the SWS call. "Hello?"

"This is Consuela Parsons calling from SWS. Is this Katja Brennan?"

I pushed down the urge to say that Katja wasn't in. "This is."

"I'm sorry to call after business hours, Ms. Brennan, but I've been asked to check in with you on behalf of SWS Corporate Security." She paused, but I didn't see anything for me to say at the moment. "First, I wanted to inquire as to your health."

It sounded like that was as close to a question as I was going to get. "I'm pretty torn up and sore but don't appear to have any broken bones."

"Did you receive any medical help as a result of today's events?"

"Just the EMT putting on some bandages at the scene so I wouldn't bleed all over the police car."

"I'm happy to hear that your injuries appear to be minor and there were no unreported services rendered. Please let me know if you end up getting more medical help."

"Yes, ma'am."

"I also wanted to talk to you about the SWS investigation."

I cut her off as politely as I could. "I'm sorry, but it's been a very long day. I'd really appreciate if," and I let every bit of weariness come out, "I could just take the weekend to mourn my lost co-workers."

There was a bit of a pause that made me wonder if she was getting instructions from someone listening in on the call. "I understand. Would you—" and then she paused again. After a few seconds she said, "I've just learned you've given SPD permission to share your interview with us and that you've arranged a meeting for Monday."

"Yes, ma'am."

"In that case, just a reminder to let us know if anyone contacts you in any way about today's events other than us," and I could hear the sigh in her voice as she added, "or the Seattle police."

"Yes, ma'am. And may I please request that you not let anyone know my name? I guess the news has probably asked."

"Absolutely. It doesn't help anything if you're being harassed." That almost sounded sincere. "Thank you for your time. Have a good weekend, Ms. Brennan."

"Thanks. You too." And I happily hung up.

Bryan asked, "Was that SPD and SWS, all in a row?"

I nodded.

"Did they coordinate?" he asked.

"I think it was more like SPD beat SWS to the punch twice today." I snickered. "I'm getting the sense that, unless he feels like he *needs* to attack me, Engalls, the SPD detective, is going to be nice to me just to keep me on his side instead of me turning to SWS."

Riles pulled out zir portable. "We'll have to keep that competition in mind in case you're in trouble and we can use it."

"Aye." I turned back to my computer. "But I'm off the hook until Monday. And I'm not answering any more calls until I check all my damned inboxes."

Before I actually got to those damned inboxes, I realized I ought to take a quick spin through my online accounts and the little tripwires I'd set up here and there to detect when my security was compromised, what with the new flavor of paranoia that Riles and Bryan had switched on in my brain. Everything looked okay. I started to feel a little relief.

Finally, I worked through my email and private messages, and my relief increased as each was the usual stuff, with the occasional note from someone who knew me well enough in person to have seen me on the news and know it was me.

I'd left my least-known account for last; I always liked to get the others out of the way so that I could settle into any meaty correspondence or pressing issues at the end. And there I found what felt like the day's second bomb, sitting in an email account that only people who knew me really well should be able to find. Proof that, in spite of how it had looked, someone *had* compromised my security. It started:

    I truly regret I couldn't save all the others
    in your building who might be innocent, but I had
    to save you.

I read the message a couple times. I could feel that my body had gotten very still. Before fight or flight, I always seemed to slide naturally into a still, observant state. Or I hoped I did. Maybe I was just paralyzed. But then a mingled sense of anger and fear punched my heart, got me moving again. I blurted out, "Motherfucking shit damn shit fuck!"

The others had stopped talking, waiting to see who'd set off my temper this time. I took a deep breath and then swallowed, my throat dry with fear. "This was in the inbox that only you guys know about." And I read them the message.

    I truly regret I couldn't save all the others
    in your building who might be innocent, but I had
    to save you. I did that, and freed you from the
    wrongs that all who work for your company are
    aiding, because I know that you have potential for
    and inclination toward better things.
    I hope that you'll agree to meet with me, give
    me a chance to explain what happened today. What
    needs to happen in the future. I'll meet with you
    anywhere in Seattle. Name the place and time. Just
    give me an hour's notice so that I'll have time to
    get there.

CHAPTER 4

Riles leaned over to look at my computer, reading the message zirself. And Bryan was no longer relaxing easily in his chair. I hadn't caught the bomber's attention by surviving; my survival had been their plan. And I'd caught their attention long enough ago for them to figure out who I was and attach my legal name and place of employ to the 'nym I used online. Long enough to find this account that I shared so, so carefully. I could hear a buzz of fear spinning up in my head, and I realized I was curling in on myself. My arms folded, my legs drawing up.

Bryan stood abruptly, as if he'd been driven to his feet, and started slowly pacing, looking around my flat as he went. He was matter-of-fact, a man who was telling, not asking. "Clearly, we need to have a look at your physical security. Make sure you're armed. Not left alone." He stopped and looked over at us, at me trying to force myself to sit in a less "oh, shit, I'm going to die" position and Riles bent close to my screen to read (and, based on the length of time, re-read) the message. Bryan announced, "Actually, I think it's time for us to leave town."

I saw Rye stiffen up, then zie sat up and looked at me. I was now uncurled. Bryan's tone was calm and in control, but how reasonable was his conclusion? Rye turned to Bryan and suggested, "I know it sounds rich coming from me, but maybe there are less dramatic steps? Like the ones you mentioned *before* you mentioned leaving town?" Zie glanced back at me. "Right?"

I nodded.

Zie said, "And maybe she could even just let the cops know about this? It would give them a suspect and maybe get her a protective eye? Let them do their damned job, the one our taxes pay for."

Bryan looked like he couldn't believe Rye would say such a thing. "You want to have her under armed guard? You want police swarming around here? Are you insane?"

Riles looked at me. I don't know what my face said, because I was still trying to work past the horror of someone finding me in real life and of that someone being a bomber. Whatever zie saw, it didn't discourage zir from defending zir position. "It's not like Kot is running a drug ring in her flat or using it as a brothel or whatever. Cops wouldn't watch over her shoulder as she typed. And, even if they did, I'm pretty sure Kot could resist the desire to ruin a bank for a little while. Right?" Zie looked at me for confirmation again.

I sighed. "My concerns..." I was trying to figure out the order to address things. "First, my concerns with Bryan's plan. Then we can talk about the cops."

I looked at Bryan, trying to figure out why he'd quickly leapt to running. "I'm not saying I don't want to run. I mean, aside from being worried that, if this person can find me, they can figure out who Gran is—they probably already know—and go after her if I slip from their grip. That aside, pretty much every bit of me is screaming to pack a bag and go *now*. Without hesitation."

Bryan made a gesture at me with his hand up that seemed to say, "See! Katja gets it. Why are we even discussing this?"

"But." I waited for Bryan to put his hand down. "But the issue of Gran is serious to me. I could never let anything happen to her. You *know* that, and I know you're on my side on that point. I don't want to give the bomber an excuse to escalate to that. Even now, I'm worrying about her. Plus, this person found me once. Why should I think they wouldn't find me again? I mean," and I had to search a moment for what more I had to say on this. "I *want* to run. I would totally run. But I don't think I can."

"Plus," Riles added, "the cops and SWS would probably see it as proof she's the bomber."

Bryan looked only slightly defeated. "You're right. Of course you can't run. It would be a lot of hassle with no reason to believe it would actually solve things. But I'm still not signing off on the idea to call the cops. That just feels like inviting our own arrests."

He looked me in the eyes. "*Please*, Kot. Don't bring the cops into it. That," and he now addressed Riles as well, "would too easily lead to the two of us *and* Gran having trouble. In addition to you. We don't live lives that bear too much scrutiny."

The thing about our lives was that, whilst a cursory glance would show you three mid-twenties people working for a moderate income (me doing data entry, Riles doing buying at a mid-range clothing store, and Bryan doing freelance programming projects that produced boring things for mid-level businesses) and just living off of that, and then having a weekly spending spree on drinks and dancing...The right kind of probing would show you something a little different.

You might discover that I had a fondness for liberating people from debts (the hacking that changed the status on Gran's mortgage from "In Default" to "Paid Off" was my first foray into this rewarding pursuit) and for publicizing the unethical actions of financial institutions. You might discover that Riley enjoyed doing damage to the reputations of those who (overtly or covertly) pushed hate, especially politicians and big corporations. Zie could be patient (sorting through every damn file and email on their computers) and vicious. Zie had sometimes dug up and released existing dirt and had sometimes, thanks to zir careful networking with a variety of potentially dangerous people, manufactured situations to let them create dirt. Whatever it took to leave a dent in the worlds of those who earned zir righteous fury. And you might discover that our Bryan, who, whilst looking for classified information to satisfy his curiosity about the tools of the military and law enforcement, had stumbled on ugly truths about abuses of the American people by a certain intelligence agency, now enjoyed exposing law enforcement abuse or, when possible, thwarting crooked plans made by those who were theoretically there to protect and serve. (Though, if you were the law and discovering this, you might pause a moment before throwing him into a cell to thank him for times he was piggybacking your feeds of dangerous situations, spotted problems you didn't, and anonymously sent messages that saved your people's lives.)

And, if that weren't enough to make us more than a little skittish about the law digging into us, we all had some accounts full of illegally obtained money. Mine from those nasty financial institutions, Riles's from the haters' accounts, and Bryan's from the interest earned on accounts of funds earmarked for overpaid military contractors and…well, others he didn't even tell Riles and me about, but at least part had to have come from the occasional drug or weapons deal he'd facilitated when we were all younger and less careful. I mostly didn't use those accounts at the moment, because it was one thing to live off crime and maybe be on the run or hiding if I had only myself to think about, but I couldn't see doing that whilst Gran was alive. And we three lived with restraint, for now anyway, until we were ready to pull ourselves out of the world at large, because we hoped people would see us working away at un-sexy jobs and assume *we* couldn't be the big, bad hackers who'd set up those accounts (and participated in our illegal hobbies) because why in the world would we have jobs like ours otherwise? But I didn't expect that us not using those funds at the moment would buy us any slack if the law found them.

So, yeah, cops poking at us was a bad idea. And there was little chance they'd poke at one of us and not quickly realize we three were all a bit alike. None of us would argue that. I did start to ask how Gran would be hurt by it, but realized that, at the very least, they'd probably easily figure out how her mortgage had been "paid off." Right.

"Okay, I can't see us arguing about the point of not wanting too much attention from cops. But you're discounting how careful we've been. We're not talking about showing them anything other than this message."

Bryan's sigh told me I was missing something obvious. "You mean the message sent to your most top secret account? Were you going to forward it to your most public account and somehow not be found out by their techs? Their techs who will specifically be trying to follow the message back to its source?"

"Oh." It was my turn to sigh. "Sorry. I'm really fucking stupid tonight."

"No, it's okay. You've had a messy day," he reassured me.

"No, I've had exactly the sort of day in which I need my damned brain to work."

Riles leaned over to give me a bit of a squeeze. "I don't have a rough day to blame it on. I was just too caught by fear to think straight."

As if on cue, Bryan and I both said a bit of a line from *Dune,* one of my favorite books, "Fear is the mind-killer." We grinned at each other.

"Okay," I said. "No more fear. Deep breaths and careful thinking. Yeah?"

Everyone nodded. Everyone paused. I assumed, like me, they were doing deep breaths and careful thinking.

My brain seemed to respond to my measured breathing and the little mantra I had going in my head, reminding it that fear is not our friend. Of course, as soon as it worked, it made things worse. "There are more reasons we can't tell the cops. Well, at least one more."

My friends looked at me curiously.

"Let's say we give the cops the message, they somehow don't take advantage of all the clues that would let them sort out what *I've* been up to, and they catch the bomber. Now, they've got someone in their custody who *knows* who I am. Someone who has already somehow traced through the labyrinth I built to make it nigh-impossible to attach my name to my 'nym. Do I really trust that, either out of spite for me getting them caught when they were supposedly just trying to do me good *or* out of a hope to buy leniency, they wouldn't tell the cops who I am? I mean, I didn't blow up a building, but there are plenty of financial institutions that would happily donate to the SPD if the SPD caught and strung up the criminal who'd been making messes for them the past...well, if you count the minor ATM fraud stuff when we were kids, the past decade-plus."

Bryan's head hung forward with frustration, whilst Riles dropped zir head back in what looked like a silent plea to the Universe.

Bryan looked up. "You're right. Which leaves us with...a pretty shitty situation."

Riles spoke to the ceiling, "Bryan was right about figuring out physical security and such. Making sure you're safe. Just in case the bomber comes for you. So, there's that we can agree on."

Just in case the bomber came for me. I wrapped my arms around my head, frustrated and trying not to be scared. "We have to figure out who they are. The bomber."

Bryan was very alert. "You're not suggesting you meet with them..."

"Noooooo. Nope. No fucking way." No, I was not. "But I'm not safe as long as they're out there. And if we can't bring in cops..." I let that hang in the air.

"We have to handle it ourselves," finished Riley, begrudgingly.

Bryan did a poor job of hiding his victory smirk, but instead of saying, "I told you so," he quietly said, "This is real life. This is...us in the meat. Even me...I mean, I'm in slightly better shape than you guys and have some arguably better 'in the meat' skills. And I just don't know."

"But you know camera systems, right?" Riles sounded like zie had an idea. Bryan nodded. "And we all know various useful computer things. Hell, even if you didn't want to get involved," zie held up a hand as Bryan started to protest, "which I know isn't the case, you've probably taught us enough about camera systems that we could get a start. So, we do what we know. We start there."

I was on board. "We see if we can trace where this email and the message I got at work came from."

"And," added Bryan, pointing to Rye in acknowledgement of the idea, "we bore ourselves to tears with the security footage from your building to see if the cameras caught any clues. Assuming your building backed up footage to an off-site server."

Riles was pleased to get something other than objections. "Exactly! Plus, those of us who might know people who would know where to get explosives could see if anyone in those circles sold what was needed to blow this building. We can check in on the messages on terrorist boards and forums, in the places on the 'Net the cops probably can't figure out to look, to see if anybody is taking credit or asked for advice that sounds relevant to this situation."

"And we definitely keep an eye on what the cops are saying on *their* computers about this. They've got forensics folks involved." Sorry, Engalls. There was no way I wasn't going to take advantage of the SPD's knowledge.

"Just one request." I felt silly asking this now, but these were the people least likely to give me shit over it. All eyes were on me. "As much as possible, for now, I'd like to not be the one hacking into SWS. You know I try not to shit where I eat."

Riley waved zir hands in a "no problem" sort of way. "Of course. That should be okay for now. We can totally handle the cameras and message system."

"That's in addition to me installing extra cameras around your place, sensors on the windows and doors, upgraded digital locks on them too...Probably some explosive sensors."

He must have seen the question I was about to ask. He clarified, "Sensors to detect explosives, not sensor that *are* explosive. Though that's not a horrible idea...Anyway. Some cameras over your parking spot and piggyback some sensitive touch sensors on your car's alarm system. Maybe even some cameras in the car itself, so we can see who fucks with your car if they do it when we're out somewhere. And some kind of armored shirt for you to wear under everything." Bryan was making a list on his mobile as he spoke. And I wasn't going to protest.

"And we're staying with you. Or, at least, I am," Riles informed me. "Hopefully, some extra eyes and hands will be helpful. Safety in numbers."

"Strength in numbers too," noted Bryan. "That's how we solve problems. Even if it's usually online. So, I'm staying too. Sorry-not-sorry, but you're stuck with uninvited houseguests."

"Good thing Riles brought drinks!" I was going for cheery. But I think I sounded a bit pathetic. This crisis wasn't bringing out the best in me. I considered pushing back on them moving in for the short-term, but I suddenly preferred that to the image I had of the bomber coming here and finding me alone.

"What about the email?" asked Riley. "Are you going to reply?"

There was a moment as we all looked at each other, maybe hoping that, between us, we could intuit the best answer. When I didn't feel any sudden psychic bond shoring me up and pouring wisdom into my brain, I shrugged. "I just think I'm not going to answer. Not for now. I'm worried I won't do a good job of seeming to not ignore them whilst still not committing to meeting. Maybe I'll accidentally say something that will turn them against me. I think..." What did I think?

Bryan suggested, "You think...well, *I* think you should sit on it a couple days. Wait until we've had a chance to try to figure out who they are and what they did."

"Yes. That's what I think too." And I closed the bomber's message. No time to read and re-read it. We had some hunting to do.

Our hunting effort wasn't as productive as we'd hoped and, frankly, expected. When it came to things online, we tended to expect to win. Unfortunately, at least on this occasion, our results were much more mixed.

Bryan had pretty easily grabbed the security camera footage for my building for the week leading up to the bombing and distributed it between us to watch. Fortunately, they did indeed keep an off-site backup of it. Whilst he did that, Riles tried, and failed, to find where the message I'd gotten, the one purporting to be from SWS CorpSec, had actually come from. All zie could confirm was that it had *not* come from my building's CorpSec but had come from outside the SWS network. Similarly, I'd failed to trace the email I'd received back to anywhere useful. Rye and I agreed that, as finding me had already led us to fear, this person was *good* at sneaky computer shit. In both our cases, the trails had bounced through loads of apparently-unrelated networks and, eventually, just disappeared.

I'd had just as little luck on terrorist boards. Nobody had asked any questions that seemed to be about blowing up a building like mine. Nobody had even recently inquired about getting their hands on or creating explosives for a job like this one, not based on what I knew about explosives. Nobody was claiming this bombing. Not on any board I could find. Just loads of people pointing out how the destruction of the building *could* have fit into the ideology of their group, talking about how they would have done it if it had been them, and then saying "good job" to whoever *had* done it. Nobody actually cared why it had been done, just that it *had* been done. In another case of synchronized failure, Riley's contacts who might have known something turned out to know nothing. Or that was their story.

Before we joined Bryan in looking through hours and hours of camera footage, Riles and I tried to make some kind of progress that would soothe our egos. Zie hacked into the SPD system, grabbing me a copy of the no-doubt-mortifying recording of my interview, as well as confirming a number of things. First, that the names on the suspect list were mine, Karl Peterson's, the10 techs who'd been out on assignment, and a guy from my team called Steve Banks (who, a quick poke at SWS employee files showed, had called in to take a sick day today). Second, that the search of my car and the swabs taken off of me hadn't turned up anything suspicious. Third, and most important to me, that they didn't seem to have dug into things that would give them a glimpse of the crimes I *had* committed. And, finally, that the explosive used in the bombing was a commercial C-4, probable quantity used still to be determined. So really common and not exactly the easiest thing to trace. Go figure.

For my part, I hacked into Karl Peterson's accounts. I hadn't just been trying to throw the guy under the bus; I really considered him, as the cops might say, a person of interest. I was disappointed to discover that Karl's only crimes seemed to be falling behind on child support (in spite of having enough money that he was planning a tropical holiday) and having really bad taste in music. I made sure to initiate a transfer of the delinquent child support from his account to his ex-wife's. I also made sure it looked like it had been done from his home computer. His comments on social media made it clear he'd gotten wasted and was probably asleep, so he might even think he'd drunkenly transferred it himself. And that was pretty much my high note for the night.

After that, and hours of watching security camera footage, with plenty of footage still to go (there had been loads of cameras in my building), we agreed that sleep was a good idea, so we made sure the flat was locked up tight and we got comfy. Paranoia had us sleeping in shifts, but they insisted that I not take a waking shift. "Sleep is healing." Each of them spent half the night on the couch, attached to their portables and reviewing footage, and the other half back-to-back with me in the bed. If those years of living together previously had taught us anything, it was that we are all fully capable of not trying to jump each other, that beds don't have to mean sex. Though the girls they were currently seeing were unlikely to see it that way...so this we'd have to keep this to ourselves.

Sleep for me meant lying on my left side, full of pain pills, dozing lightly. But it was still enough to free me from all the stiffness I'd been feeling by the time I truly woke the next morning. Waking to less and more specific—and only the specific—pains let me feel hopeful. Still justifiably paranoid, but hopeful.

CHAPTER 5

In the morning, Rye used the crisis as an excuse to temporarily take leave from zir retail job. Bryan didn't have to fuss over a job, given he was freelance. But, whilst Riles was calling into work, Bryan offered, "If you want to pick up work, you know I'd always be up for having you work with me."

Over the years, he'd made both Riles and I that offer a few times, but I'd always felt like turning it down was a good way to pretend we three weren't joined at the hip. When some significant other would make accusations about us all being too close, I'd quickly point out that, in fact, we were all *choosing* not to work together. Yeah! Proof! Maybe it was time for me to admit that it sounded as lame in my ears as it did in the ears of worried partners. "I might just take you up on that. Thanks!" He looked surprised, and a bit pleased. "Though I have to give SWS another month, since they paid me for it. But then..."

Riley was off zir call. "What are you doing in a month?"

"I think I'm going to finally take Bryan up on the offer to work together." I shrugged. No big deal.

Riles mocked horror. "But then what will you wave in the faces of our partners and yours when you need to prove we aren't unhealthily invested in each other?" I guess zie'd also noticed I used that same weak defense every time.

I flipped zir off and went back to watching the unending security camera footage.

Riley cleared zir throat, and both Bryan and I looked up from our portables. "Before we lose ourselves to the unparalleled fun of the camera footage and neglect everything else, I feel like maybe we need to do some things. Like fix Kot's hair, pick up clothes from our places, buy all that," zie waved zir hand in Bryan's direction, "stuff you listed for securing Katja..."

Bryan added, "And maybe, before I install all that stuff, we hit the shooting range just to see how bad you two have become without regular practice. Because I'm going to advocate being armed. Just in case."

I stretched and groaned. "I am going to suck on the range. But you're right. We have things to do."

Riley walked back towards the bathroom. "I'll grab hair stuff. Makeover!"

Bryan asked, in a way that made it clear he already knew I'd decline, "I don't suppose you want to join me for a morning run?"

I laughed. "Are you insane? No way. Your option is to run alone or to give up your run until you're done playing body guard."

"Your knees still hurt too much?"

"I could say 'yes,' but we both know that I run late and I run programs, but I don't *run* run."

He slowly shook his head in exaggerated mock-disgust. But Rye returned with hair supplies before I could get a lecture.

Whilst Riley gleefully set to work on my hair, hacking some off and letting Bryan shave some bits, I brought up something that had finally occurred to me now that my brain was well-rested. "One thing we probably need to seriously consider is whether someone we know is behind this."

Bryan laughed. "You mean like our girlfriends? I know you aren't their biggest fan, but they couldn't spoof the sender address on an email, much less get a message into your work system."

"No. Not people we know in person. I mean like our peers online. Because, as you note, there's a certain capability to hack into a big, secure company's systems necessary to send messages like the one I got. And…How do you think I was found? I'm really careful online. It's *possible* it's a coincidence that the bomber showed some hacking skills and I happen to be a hacker. But there could easily be more to it."

"Well, shit." I took that as Bryan agreeing.

He sat down and opened his portable. "How do you think we approach this? We've already got loads on our plates, and there are a lot of people we know who could hack the message system. Plus, people we *don't* know."

"Damn. Like the whole tech team from my building, except the manager. They were all theoretically out on calls. If they're techs, maybe they have the skills." Good to know my brain was working today.

Bryan nodded. "One of them could easily have been desiring you from afar or some shit. Decided to take out the shitty job but save the sexy co-worker."

Riles paused the hair-hacking for a moment. "Has anyone been weird lately? Has anyone sent you weird private messages?" Zie handed me a mirror for each hand. "And is the cut okay?"

I admired my definitely-not-corporate hair. "Cut is great." I handed back the mirrors and thought a moment. "And no weird PMs lately. As for anyone acting weird..." I had to think.

Bryan paired his portable with the wall TV and opened a blank document. We watched as he typed a list.

```
Clothes
Security supplies
Range
***
Camera footage
SPD
Track C-4?
Look into Kot's surviving co-workers?
Research:
```

"There's our current to-do list, plus space for us to start listing the peers whose privacy we're going to invade." His fingers hovered over the keys, waiting for our input on the peer research list.

I asked, "How do we sort out weird when we're *all* secretive, and with good reason?" I sighed.

Riley mixed colors to put in my hair and tutted. "Don't get caught up in trying to concretely define what counts as weird. We want to be able to say why someone seemed weird, but it will be different for everyone. Oh! Like was anyone else surprised that Bytesize didn't troll you at all last week?"

On his list, Bryan typed:

```
Byt3s1z3
```

"Good catch," he said as he typed. "And what was with I-am-God *not* joining in when people were talking about how to hack their SWS watches? They *always* want in on gear hacks."

He typed:

```
IamGOD
```

Rye was putting the dye on my hair, it looked like zie had both black and blue at hand, and zie was mumbling through a list of everyone who might have the qualifications. "What about insert-dick-joke? They've been practically invisible lately. Maybe busy planning a bombing?"

Bryan typed:

```
[insertdickjoke]
```

With minor actions setting off our alarms, we might as well just list everyone, I thought. But I didn't say anything, because my paranoia had me open to just that. List everyone. Trust no one. Let the digital witch hunt begin!

By the end of the day, the journal entry in my head, because I didn't dare actually keep a written journal, was going something like "I'll spare you the growing list of suspects, the errand running, the items checked off the to-do list (with no new leads from any of our information hunting); and I'll spare myself having to detail how poorly I did on the shooting range." I was making this mental entry to amuse myself whilst I watched yet more camera footage, when Riles exclaimed, "Hey!"

I looked over at zir. Zie was looking way too delighted for someone who was supposedly engaged in the same mind-numbing activity the rest of us were.

"I think I have something." Zie looked up from zir screen, grinning. "We might be done with the random watching."

Bryan sort of exhaled a string of words. "Oh-fuck-yes-please."

Riley joined zir portable to the wall TV and stood up right in front of the TV. We joined zir. Zie scrolled a bit through the video on zir portable, and then pressed play. And there, clear as could be, we saw a tiny, metal bug with a lump of "clay" on its back scurry past the camera, which was located in a vent. Zie scrolled back and played it again in slow motion.

I rushed back to my computer. "What's the date stamp?"

Zie disconnected from the TV and checked the files. "This Monday at 0530. Which, if I were planning this, I'd figure was the time the CorpSec guys stuck there on the weekends for the third shift would be both dead bored and also a little lax as they eagerly awaited the arrival of the first shift guys."

Bryan sat back at his portable too, and there was silence as we all looked for whatever camera files we had that covered early Monday morning. I hooted with joy when I finally had something to show for the work. "I've got a small swarm of them coming out of the shadows by the patient parking entry and clambering in between gaps on the door there. I think they came in from the small greenbelt behind the building." The patient parking was a tiny lot right under the building. I found the patient parking footage that matched up, and watched as some of the bugs disappeared in shadowy corners and most went into an air vent.

"I've got some too," Bryan said. "They're going in sewer grates right outside the building. I've traced them only as far as the grass and bushes by the building. Too small to see their route through that, but lack of entry into the greenery makes me think someone dropped them from the neighboring—and camera-free—coffee shop's property."

Riles directed, "Grab screenshots. We might be able to track down who could supply the bugs."

"Will you guys stay on the bugs? I want to look at one thing quickly." They agreed, and I hunted down footage that, based on what we'd figured out of their naming system, should be from the camera that would take in my desk.

The camera couldn't see over my shoulder. It was slightly forward from my computer screen and getting a side view of me. So it wouldn't have seen the message I got from security.

Ever curious, Riles leaned over to see what I was doing. Zie saw me, on the footage, shaking my head as I stood up, grabbed my jacket, and hurried out. "Is that you yesterday?"

"Yeah. I was hoping that the camera could see my screen, but also hoping that you could tell by looking at me that I was...I don't know, that maybe they could see that I wasn't someone rushing out to avoid being blown up by...the exploding bugs they knew were there."

Rye patted my shoulder. "Don't fret. I think you look fine, not guilty. Plus, we got the bugs. We're freed from the remaining hours of footage. It's time for a drink!" With that, zie got up and headed to the kitchen.

Bryan quietly teased, "At least we know the drinks won't make you a worse shot if we get attacked."

Bastard.

By Saturday night, we'd had enough hours with nothing happening and no real movement forward (even SPD had no new information beyond what we already knew about Karl Peterson) that we let our boredom have a vote in what we did. And I had no doubt that Bryan and Riles were also influenced by girlfriends who couldn't be told the real reason why they insisted on staying at my place. "No worries, ladies. We've just got cause to believe the bomber is after Katja, but we've also got criminal acts of our own to hide that might come to light if we tell the police. So, we're staying here until the cops find the bomber...or until we do. But, never fear, we won't risk our own lives if we figure out who they are before the cops do. We'll just pay worse criminals to hunt them down." Yeah, that wouldn't go over so well...

Boredom, girlfriends, and habit...We decided to go dancing as we usually would. Hell, I had a new hair cut to rock and plenty of steam to blow off.

I learned years ago that there's comfort in ritual and routine. And, I'm not a physical person in general, but dancing...Maybe it's because I grew up with Gran, who found any excuse to dance. Who, when my mum died, danced in the living room to try to escape the feelings of the loss (though I didn't fully understand that until years after). Dancing is how I work out stress and negative emotions. And it's a great option for losing myself, for just a bit, from whatever is upsetting me. Every heartbreak or big disappointment or anger or worry sent me to the dance floor. And it had to be a club. Dancing in the living room, at some point in my early teens, started to feel too quiet, restrained, underwhelming. The club, though...The club is huge and loud, so many sights and bodies and no noise ordinance or neighbors to disturb. At the club, the rest of life is left outside. There's nothing there to make me think of the world beyond its walls. (Sometimes the cause of heartbreak might come wandering in, but humans are easily sent away in that setting.) It's just a big sea of sensory inputs to dive into and drown a little while.

I could use some drowning. Some escape from survivor guilt, heightened by nightmares where my dead co-workers reached for me from the rubble as metal bugs skittered over everything. Some release for the feelings of fear and anger at having been found, my privacy violated, some bomber interested in me. Some space from the nagging worry that, if they found no one else, SPD or SWS might pin this crime on me. Plus, we argued as we talked ourselves into doing what we wanted, this was a very public place. Too public, surely, for anyone to risk bothering me.

So, as usual, everyone and their girlfriends met at my flat to get ready to go out that night.

I thought their girlfriends were beautiful. At least by my standards, if not Hollywood's. Beautiful, but...I was pretty sure Riley knew zir bae, Kitty, was a materialism-obsessed waste of time and that Bryan knew his, 'Randa, wasn't too bright. I never understood why people settled, but I dared not speak up. I'd made some of my own bad choices in the past. And who wants to mess up a friendship by objecting to a rubbish partner? I was smart enough not to do that. Not out loud.

Bryan's girl was as short as he was tall, and she was a bit round. Not that roundness was unattractive (not at all), it was just another difference between them. In spite of the fact that I thought this contrasted not-very-nicely with his tall, skinny frame, she was always grabbing him, looking at them in a mirror, and proclaiming, "We are so cute together!" And I'd think, *Apparently, 'Randa's as visually impaired as she is daft.* If she was near enough to witness the proclamation of cute, Rye's bae would try to get chummy with me by sharing a pleased smile as if to bring us all in on the cuteness. And then she'd giggle. And I would give myself a look in the mirror that said, "And Kitty's a real catch too." (Though, really, it was Kitty and Riles who were the matched set, even successfully sharing makeup and clothes sometimes.) And everyone would drink, but I'd probably drink the most. And that was what "and their girlfriends" added to Saturday nights. But, like I said, at least they were pretty.

I'd ignored the mirror gazing this night to keep an eye on the news, which had nothing new to say. Unless you count another pointless statement from SWS. CEO Johnson, backed up by COO Smith and CFO Williams as usual, letting us know that SWS CorpSec was hard at work, following leads, sure to bring the criminal to justice! I was pretty sure the pasty, polished bitch was lying. I didn't believe for a moment they had leads that neither we nor the police had. Please.

When everyone was happy with their clothing, their makeup, and their buzz, we'd always split into two vehicles. The couples seemed to rotate who'd ride with me, and, though we could all have smashed ourselves into one car, the other couple would follow in the girlfriend's car. It complicated parking, but it meant we had a little room to breathe and could occasionally manage to get some very wasted friend home safely. So, that's what we did. As usual. Or as usual as it could be when I was so full of a need to dance away emotions. As usual as it could be when we'd planned outfits carefully around Bryan's paranoid insistence that we carry guns. (Good thing we lived in America, land of the free and home of the easily armed.)

It was a cool night, but not cold. Not quite yet. We shouldn't quite hit cold for another couple weeks. The girlfriends, however, were ready to play it up. They complained about the temperature and rubbed their bare arms. I tried not to mutter under my breath about girls who choose to wear lingerie out and then whine about being cold.

The Orpheum was big. After years of having a lot of little clubs with similar music and low attendance (with high rent and property prices), most of the club owners who catered to the underground set had gone in together to get this place. It was located in the south end of what could still technically be called Seattle's core, so the rents were a little lower to compensate for the undesirable nature of the neighborhood. They'd set up a few different dance spaces and now pulled in most anyone who didn't think they were normal enough to hit the sports bars. If someone even suspected they were weird, they put on dark lipstick and headed to the Orpheum on Saturday night.

The front door to the Orpheum was set into an alcove so that it wasn't right on the street. Before you even got to the door, you were greeted by a big white sign with black letters.

Dress code strictly enforced.

Approved weapons only.

Violators gleefully expelled.

Beyond the sign, the door was filled with a sizable bouncer called Paul. He was dressed all in tight black to show off the hours he spent working out. The light above him gleamed off his shaved scalp, piercings, and the menacing grin that made it easy to believe that violators would, indeed, be *gleefully* expelled. When he saw us approaching, his smile became genuinely friendly for a split second. He waved us up. The queue of potential patrons didn't look quite so pleased at being passed by. Paul was one of those nice cases where a flirtation didn't pan out (he and Bryan had sexual tastes that didn't quite align, much to their mutual dismay) but people still liked each other as people.

"Hey there. How're you guys tonight?" We all smiled back at him and gave our assorted "fine" replies. "Katja! Nice hair! Bryan, Kot, and Riley are good to go. 'Fraid I need to see ID from the other ladies."

We hung back, waiting for Kitty and 'Randa to get approved. The girlfriends whined as they dug their IDs out. Why weren't they memorable after the years they'd been coming? Why was he so mean? Blah blah blah. Paul just grinned wider at the ladies and jovially told them that not everyone could be memorable. This was one time I could appreciate what I suspected was a little passive-aggressive—but pleasantly delivered—response to somebody else ('Randa) getting the relationship Paul hadn't.

Beyond Paul and through the door, Lilia leaned against the counter. She was in tight, red PVC that showed the details of the few bits of flesh that weren't bared. She tossed her high, blonde ponytail back and stood up a bit straighter as we entered. She had some especially slinky smiles for Rye, assuring that Kitty felt thoroughly put out by the time we were all done paying and getting our hands stamped.

Just getting into the Orpheum was an obstacle course for anyone Bryan and Riles was seeing.

At the bottom of the three steps that led down from the entrance to the ground floor of the Orpheum, we moved a bit to the right and stopped. Bryan and Riley turned to the girlfriends whilst I started looking around at the other patrons.

Kitty shouted, "They have a new DJ back in the alcove, but I think it's the sort of swoopy music you three hate."

Riles replied, "So you're good to find us in the big mess later?"

Both Kitty and 'Randa grinned and nodded enthusiastically.

Bryan pulled out his wallet, and Rye followed suit. Ah, the perks of being both generous and the one making the most in the relationship. They handed their girls some bills and were rewarded with sexy eyes and kissy goodbyes. Then the two girls bounced off to another room, giggling like teenagers.

I scanned the crowd and shouted over the music. "If I don't dance immediately, I might lose my shit."

I put on my best posture and headed towards the main dance area at the back of the ground floor. The lights there pulsed blue and white; the music grated, thumped, and squirmed its electronic way from the speakers and through the people on the floor. I leaned in to be heard. "Grabbing a table can wait. I want to dance to Viral." Bryan nodded and Riley and I dragged each other onto the dance floor, keeping half an eye on where Bryan went.

We danced nearly back to back so that we could see everyone around us. Looking at the other people was part of the pleasure. Bryan followed us out but found a place against a wall from which he could also watch the dancers. And we just fell into the night.

I had always felt like, maybe, my body was specifically made for this, the way some people's bodies have an openness in the hips that makes them work better for ballet. In spite of not being in peak shape, as long as I didn't take a break beyond slowing my pace so that I could take a drink when a friend handed it to me, I could lose hours to the music. My muscles swinging and swerving me through the beats, the sweat trickling like rivers of coolant under my clothes, and my eyes only open enough to let in the live show of other dancers and lights. My boots stomped down, taking in power and leaving behind bits of fear and guilt. Every motion shedding the feelings I'd come to lose. Every arm extension turning me into an antenna for the energy of everyone else's shadows and catharsis.

The whole floor felt like a throb of hope. Hope that we could leave behind our day lives. That we might not go home alone. That we might be too drunk or high to care either way. And every conversation was a sensual thing, cheek-to-cheek and lips-to-ears. Close enough to feel the heat and emotion radiating from the friends coming to say hello or the strangers coming to see if you were their answer for the night.

I buzzed, I simmered, I achieved transcendence.

My muscles finally admitted their limits, so it must have been hours later. I leaned in to shout at Riles and Bryan, "I'm dancing to one more song. And then I'm spent."

I wanted to shed the last vestiges of negativity, to glide out on an exhausted bliss, so I danced with fast-sweeping arms that cleared a space around me. Bryan and Rye, veterans of my angry dancing moves, danced carefully within that space and seemed to be greatly amused at the disgruntled looks we were getting from those who had to move out of range. As I turned, dancing and watching the crowd, I caught sight of someone moving into our space.

I was suddenly face to face with a pretty man I'd looked at once or twice on past Saturday nights. He was nice to look at and didn't seem to pay any mind to my current aggressive dance moves. But I was in no mood to be hit on. *Damn your timing!* I thought. I started aiming my arms to press him back and shook my head. He just smiled and slipped to the side. He was a good dancer. That was part of why I'd noticed him in the past. He might convince me to change my mind about my mood. I eased back on the fervor of my dancing just a bit and gave him what I hoped was just a hint of a smile. I caught Riley grinning at me over Pretty Man's shoulder as I did that. Zie had heard my opinions on Pretty Man previously.

Pretty Man slid in close so that I could hear him over the music, his lips almost brushing my ear. He said, "Hey, MK. Sorry I'm late."

I could hear that he was grinning. But it was like a slap to my face. MK was how I was signing messages on hacker forums these days. MK was something that only Bryan and Riles should know to call me. MK was not a name anyone else should be able to pin to me. Anyone except the bomber. Oh, shit...

CHAPTER 6

I sensed Bryan and Rye giving me and Pretty Man a little space, assuming this was me maybe having a chance at some tension-relieving sex. Shit shit shit! I tried to catch Riley's eye, and was relieved when zie noticed and concern fell onto zir face.

I'd kept sort of dancing with Pretty because I wasn't ready for this, wasn't ready to need to choose a reaction. I felt all the fear I'd just danced off shoot its way up my legs and squeeze my organs with thick fingers. In a flash that felt like it lasted for ages, I felt old defenses slide in. I was not myself. I was a character in *Dune*, a book I'd loved since I was a kid, and the mantra for dealing with fear from that book started to spin in my head. "I must not fear. Fear is the mind-killer." I let go of being Katja, because Katja had no fucking clue what to do. I let myself become Paul Atreides, who'd overthrown a regime, ignoring that I'd had none of his physical training.

Katja would have run. Katja *should* have run. A voice in my head was screaming at me that I was being really fucking stupid. But the delusion that was helping me keep my shit together told me that I'd regret it if I didn't catch the bomber when he was practically right in my damned arms. The delusion spurred me to (really fucking stupid) action.

I caught motion that I thought (hoped) was Riles and Bryan moving in, creating a bit of a barrier between us and the other dancers, coming to my rescue. After he spoke to me, as soon as I realized that *this* was my bomber and my delusion took over, I followed one of my dancing motions through, spinning myself a bit to the side, just enough to let me easily grab the man by the throat and then move back in. I took advantage of his proximity to push a gun into his chest as well, and moved my own lips dangerously near *his* ear. "I think this is a conversation we ought to have somewhere a bit more private, don't you?" I wished I felt as badass as I sounded.

I had stopped dancing. So had a lot of the people near us. I could hear my friends talking to those people over the music, surely explaining to those nearby that this was an ex-boyfriend and there wasn't a problem. He *liked* rough stuff. We'd used that line before. It must have made sense to most people, because they went back to dancing but kept an eye on me and the man I held. Maybe they'd get a show. They'd love that, and I might like to provide it. I was riding the adrenaline that comes when you do something brave (really fucking stupid) in the face of fear. I was starting to feel cocky. And angry.

I once read that anger is a secondary emotion. When we feel it, it's really just there as a protection against some more vulnerable emotion we're feeling. For instance, if you're afraid because someone just blew up your workplace and you're feeling vulnerable because that same someone seems to have hunted you down, tracked you to locations they shouldn't know to find you, you might feel anger. You might, when face-to-face with them, feel nauseated that you'd previously considered making eyes with them and, to cover that nausea, feel a tide of righteous anger rise in you.

And, by "you," I mean "me."

I leaned in until my nose almost touched the man's nose. My jaw was hard, my teeth clenched both in anger and to stop them chattering from the fear it was covering. I was grateful he wasn't fighting this, because I knew perfectly well that I wasn't half as physically strong as I was acting. This was pure adrenaline and rage. "Let's find a nice corner. That will give me two different walls to slam you against." The man's smile only wavered a bit, and he let me push him backwards through the crowd, towards a corner. Seeing where I was headed, Bryan pushed ahead, clearing the path and clearing away anyone already leaning in the targeted corner. Riley followed, no doubt spreading assurances that this was sexual, not homicidal.

In the corner, the man found himself fenced in by us. He didn't smile quite so much, but still sounded confident as he tried a joke. "Next time, I'll call before I come over."

No one else seemed amused. My hand was still holding his throat and I still had a gun pressed to his chest. I was doing my best to make sure I didn't look at all friendly. And that neither hand started shaking. "We'll start with your name. And we'll keep asking questions until we're done. If you don't feel like answering one of the questions, we'll find something else to do." My tone made it clear that "something else" probably did not involve rainbows and puppies. (I wasn't sure *what* it involved, but he didn't need to know that.)

He looked around at our three grim faces, dropped the smile, and nodded. "Name is fair enough. *I* know who *you* are."

He paused a beat to let that sink in and pretended not to notice my hand applying a little more pressure to his throat, the gun pressed a little more firmly. He still had the nerve to try to extend a hand as if for a handshake. "Hi. My name is Jonny."

He gave a quick smile, like you would if this were a normal situation. Which it so fucking wasn't.

When he realized a cheeky grin and an extended hand weren't getting a response, he put his hand down but left the grin on his face. Was it a slightly forced grin or was that my imagination?

He added, "My 'nym, which you probably recognize from certain forums and conversations, is spaceGoddity."

I *did* recognize the 'nym. No doubt my friends did as well. This tidbit of information made things a bit less confusing. If anyone had the skills to find me, it might be him.

"So, you found me online...we *worked together* online, and you started trying to hunt me down IRL? Thought I'd appreciate that more than, say, a discreet email?" As if it hadn't been obvious already, my tone made it clear that I did *not* appreciate this more than email.

But just to make sure he got it, I railed, "For fuck's sake, when someone you're interested in seems stuck in a shit job, you send flowers. *Not a motherfucking bomb!*"

"Maybe," suggested Jonny, "you'd like the full explanation of what's going on? Maybe somewhere actually quiet and a bit less public?"

The three of us friends looked at each other and nodded. He had a point. We appreciated privacy.

Bryan leaned in to join the conversation. I was relieved; this was so much closer to being a Bryan thing than a Katja thing. He pointed to Riles and directed, "Text the others. Tell them to drive themselves home."

I spared a glance at Riles. Zie looked like zie was also trying really hard to pretend not to be afraid.

And, now that I was in observation mode...Jonny seemed to be breathing a little heavily and shaking slightly. So slightly that I'd mistaken it for the effect of soundwaves bouncing off everyone and everything in the room. Weird. I mean, yes, I had a gun on him. But what sort of person can blow up a building, openly approach someone who might be upset about that and who had reason to want to take them down (there was no way he didn't understand how important my privacy was), and go shaky over a small gun held by a girl who didn't seem really strong? Weird.

As Bryan ran his hands over Jonny, trying to make what I assumed was a search for weapons look more like foreplay, he told us, "You two are going to link arms like lovers, and she's going to keep a gun pressed into your side."

He stood up from his frisking with only a mobile in his hands (which he immediately turned off). He put his face right by Jonny's. "Thanks for wearing this nice, silver jacket and making it easier to obscure the gun."

He leered a moment, and then he caught my eye. "If he even twitches, you pull the trigger. Got it?"

I nodded, and thought, *No guns on Jonny?* I was so confused.

When Riley looked up from zir mobile, Bryan told zir, "You keep close behind. Keep it casual, but make sure nobody can see her gun from behind. Okay?"

Riles nodded, and we all started to shift into position. Jonny was looking a little wider-eyed now. His smile definitely looked forced and, arm-in-arm, pressed to his side, I was now positive he was shaking a little. Good. It might hide it when my adrenaline wore off and my own shakes set in.

Bryan led the way and cleared a narrow path, walking slowly enough that I could stay right in his wake. We'd actually used similar formations in vidgames. This particular "game" was just way less fun and had the potential for some heavier consequences. We were smiling to keep other people's suspicions at bay, but we were (or, at least, I was) also feeling extra cautious.

This was a whole other level of dangerous, or it would the

sort of situation we usually enjoyed. Taking back control when some asshole made life unpleasant for one of us. Much the same way that other people enjoyed jumping out of airplanes or having sex in public. But this time was like we hadn't checked our parachutes or the person we were fucking didn't look so healthy.

We nodded our goodbyes to acquaintances and made sure to exchange some extra wide smiles with the bouncers and other staff. As we'd proven once more tonight, being friendly with staff meant a little bit of room to move, meant I could push a guy into a dark corner with my hand on his throat and no one would kick me out. That was good.

As we neared the place where my car was parked, we paused to tie a sash from Rye's ensemble over Jonny's eyes. Just in case he couldn't already identify my car, we figured we'd make it a little harder for him. We paused a moment at the car to sweep him and the car for bugs. (Credit for that, of course, going to Bryan and his love of gear.) Trying to be smart in a situation that wasn't actually part of our normal routine. Wasn't part of our normal anything.

Riles said, "I know where to go," took my keys, and got into the driver's seat.

Bryan pulled Jonny away from me and pushed him into the backseat. He got in behind and said, "Take his other side," to me.

I slid into the backseat. Behind Riley. Beside the man who'd blown up my building and figured out who I was. I pressed my gun back into his side, angled downwards so (I hoped) a bullet wouldn't go through him and hit Bryan, and carefully, quietly exhaled. We were sitting just in time. I was no longer a fictional character. I was Katja. I had done something really fucking stupid. My knees were free of the spell of adrenaline and had started to give way.

The drive to Rye's intended destination was quiet except for the latest Uncertainty Principle album beating and crackling at low volume from the stereo. Jonny tried to start conversation a couple of times, but the lack of response from the rest of us in the car finally drove him to silence and fear...I could see it on his face as we passed under streetlights, see him swallowing hard, see his nostrils flared and jaw clenched, see the waver in his unusually good posture. He started to shake his leg at one point, which made my legs want to shake, so I pushed the gun a bit more firmly into his side until he stopped. I couldn't have my fear rising to the smell of his.

Not that this was a great situation for him to be in, but, again, weird. He sure didn't come off the way I'd expect a cold-blooded killer to come off. I saw Bryan was also checking out Jonny. I caught his eye, motioned to Jonny with my eyes, and then gave Bryan a confused look. Bryan looked just as confused and shrugged. Then he mouthed, "You okay?"

And I finally took in something besides our hostage. I noticed that the cooling sweat from my hours dancing was only part of the chill. That I was doing some of the same things I'd noticed in Jonny. And I could feel hysterical laughter trying to crawl up my throat. I swallowed harder and lamely shrugged in response.

I looked up at Riles, and zie seemed to be choking on the same hysterical laughter. I looked back at Bryan, the full force of "I just did something really fucking stupid" on my face. Bryan leaned forward, reached carefully around Jonny to give my leg a reassuring squeeze, and then we each put a hand on Riley's shoulders. We left them there until we could feel and see that Rye had the laughter under control.

Bryan took out his mobile and typed. He leaned over to show me and did the same for Riles at a stop light.

```
You guys did really well. We can do this.
```

I could read whole speeches in those two, short sentences. And, though a little on the grim side, Bryan's face was full of belief in us. I closed my eyes, took a careful breath. I said that fear mantra in my head and considered pretending to be someone else. But then I realized that this was a situation where my friends needed me to be Katja, not a stranger. I was going to suck it up and try to figure out how much real world courage I could pull out of myself. Though maybe I'd put on some swagger, the public badass persona I wore out dancing. I wouldn't mind being a little more her anyway.

As we approached the outskirts of town, Bryan pulled out his gun, turning just a bit so that he could shoot Jonny without hitting me.

Riles pulled the car into a nice, deserted area. There were some old warehouses and junked out cars. And the only lifeforms were rats, stray dogs, and the occasional homeless person. Most the streetlights were out. I knew this was pretty much what everyone (but Jonny, I'm sure) had in mind.

Bryan quietly directed, "Don't stop here. Pull into that covered alley over there." He pointed off to the right.

Riley nodded, eased us into the alley, and turned off the car. It was truly, fully silent...aside from the sounds of ragged breathing. More than one of us. Probably me. Dammit.

In the restricting confines of the car, all guns were leveled at Jonny. Bryan signaled for me to remove the blindfold, so I used my non-gun hand to pull the sash off. Which was kind of clumsy. Kind of like this whole damned mess. Riles added to the ambience by pointing the beam of a Maglite straight into Jonny's eyes as soon as they were visible. I'd note that it wasn't part of the plan, but this was all just a bunch of improv by two total newbies and one guy with very little practical experience. (If Jonny could tell we were faking it, I was too busy leaning back enough so the light wouldn't blind *me* to notice.)

Jonny put a hand up to shield his eyes and was rewarded with the sound of Riley cocking zir revolver. Zie was, apparently, all about the intimidation factor now.

Riles explained, "When you move, we feel like shooting. The trust factor is low right now."

Jonny tried to smile, but it looked more like a grimace. "If I start spilling my guts, will you turn the light off?"

Rye asked drily, "Does that come-on work often?" Zir smart mouth ran on autopilot. I tried out a smirk, playing the badass me I wished I felt like.

Jonny was looking down, turning his face so that the light had even less chance of hitting his eyes. His mouth twisted into something like a smirk, but it wavered and fell into a grimace before he settled for something more neutral and softly pleaded, "Please. I...I clearly fucked this up. I'm here because I *want* to tell you everything. Because I made a mistake and I think you can help me not do it again."

We exchanged glances and, after some nodding, Riley switched off the flashlight. Jonny slowly lowered his hand and blinked rapidly for a few moments. He cleared his throat. He paused. He swallowed. He squirmed. And, finally, he started talking. And the confidence he'd seemed to be dripping when he approached me on the dance floor was gone, if it had ever actually been there in the first place. He looked and sounded as nervous as I felt.

When he'd said he was spaceGoddity, I hadn't quite believed him. And I still wasn't sure. But this guy was much more like one of our people now. Uncertain in person. Not some unhinged terrorist, eager to blow up the world.

"First...um...first I want to apologize. I should have found a better way to approach you. I should have found a way to save you that didn't make you a suspect. I...I don't know how I would even have tried to save you without violating your privacy, but I'm sorry I had to do that too. And it's the least of my...sins...but it's the only one I can actually apologize for. At least to you."

I wanted to play it cool, but I needed more than apologies. "You *had* to violate my privacy? Bullshit. And I'm especially offended because we already know each other online. I'm not some random person to take down. We're bloody friendly online!" The rage was kicking up. I caught a look from Bryan and just barely managed to bite my tongue.

Jonny pressed his fingers to his temples. They were shaking. He muttered, "This isn't how I thought this would go. None of this is."

Bryan asked, "What?"

Jonny cleared his throat and pressed back into the seat like he was trying to disappear into the thin cushioning. Barely louder, but with his hands now clasped in his lap and not blocking out his voice. "This isn't how I thought this would go."

Riles almost-hysterically shrieked, "How the hell do you *think* something like this goes?"

Jonny's voice stayed quiet, but not inaudible. "I don't really do a lot of stuff in the meat. I don't exactly have experience with...anything like this. Not any part of anything that's happened. All I had to look at..." There was enough light from the moon and his face was red enough with it that I could see the flush of embarrassment overtake him. "I just watched a lot of movies and tried to figure out how someone who does things like this would act and how people would respond to it who...who ended up on the same team with them later in the movies."

I laughed. I actually didn't mean it in a cruel way, because I'd been doing the same thing. But it was so ridiculous. And I was embarrassed to have done the same thing. And, like Jonny, I didn't have any experience in anything like any of this.

Bryan and Riles joined in, laughing for their own reasons. Jonny just looked like he wanted to die. Good.

When we finally stopped, which might have taken a little longer than usual given that at least two of us were as freaked out as Jonny was, Jonny went on. A little louder, a little more confident. I wondered if he'd decided to just get back onto whatever script he'd written when he was (inaccurately) thinking about how this would go.

"First, I want to make sure that nobody has any SWS gear. No health trackers or...anything." His voice was concerned, earnest.

We looked around at each other, a bit confused, but shook our heads. I said, "Work stays at work."

He nodded a lot, said, "Good. Good. Okay." Then he took a breath and launched into his story. "So, I was in the middle of a little bit of...extra-legal probing into SWS a few years ago and I found some pretty nasty stuff. I've been working on plans to take them down."

He sat up a bit straighter as he said, "I'm an idealist. A criminal but not one of the bad guys."

I narrowed my eyes and mouthed "bullshit," but didn't interrupt.

"Which I hope you," he indicated me with his head, "would know from things we've done online." He had the neutral tone of someone reciting, not speaking. Maybe he meant it, but his delivery wasn't helping.

He cleared his throat and resumed his speech. "I realized I'd want help, and I knew that MindKiller was the best. Everyone knows that. So I set out to figure out who they were. Hopefully before SWS did and recruited them."

Before I could ask again why he hadn't just emailed, Jonny held up his hands (slowly, so as not to prompt anyone to take a shot). "I know, I know. You want to know why I didn't just send you a message. The problem was I found out that a few of our peers were well-known to SWS. Some seem involved in the shit they're doing; others are being monitored. I think. I couldn't take a chance. So I did everything I could and it still took me almost a year to figure out who you are and that you're probably not compromised."

Jonny looked impressed by that level of difficulty. Good. I was kind of a digital badass. (And I felt a bit impressed. He was certainly someone I'd consider on the same level as me and my friends when it came to the 'Net.)

Back to his speech. "At first, I figured you were owned. I mean, you work for them. And I was still trying to figure out if you were clean when I was planning to blow your office. So I had one thrilling night as custodial staff and planted a bug in your cubicle that showed me you were doing truly mind-numbing grunt work. I watched you every way possible and figured out you were clean. I didn't want you to have a bad polygraph, so I didn't bother to warn you until the last minute. And, even then, I made sure I did it in a way that you still didn't know what was going on. But there's more to do and I still think I need help, so I'm coming to you. And that's where we are."

There was a brief silence before Rye spoke, zir voice thick with indignation. "That's it? Are you serious? You have a story that includes 15 people *dead*, and that's it? What's SWS doing that made you decide to violate the privacy of your peers and go mad bomber? Was everyone there evil or did you kill innocents? Holy shit, mate. You're looking like the definition of overkill." Zie looked mortified. "Pun not intended. Sorry. Shit. I'm so sorry."

And then zie growled, "Because 15 people confirmed dead isn't funny."

Jonny avoided meeting anyone's eyes, hesitated. "I'd...I'd rather not say more unless I know that you're going to help out. I mean, you two are totally wanted too."

He looked at Riles and Bryan. "If you are who I'm pretty sure you are. And I'll gladly give you the full info on me if that will make you feel better. And because it seems fair."

I snorted in exasperation. "You want us to agree to help without knowing what's up? You better have fucking solid info, or I'm afraid you're going to get back to your computer to find your life in ruins. Starting with your stupid face. If," and I went for as threatening a tone as I could, "we let you go back to your computer."

I really hated that doing ugly things didn't make people ugly. I wanted to never accidentally fancy a killer. I wanted the knowledge of his crimes to transform his face in my eyes. What the hell was wrong with me? For a moment, I was almost as disgusted with myself as I was with him.

I nodded at Bryan. "He's got that mobile of yours. And I'm sure you can bring up whatever information you thought was worth your...efforts. Was worth those deaths."

Jonny's hands shook and his face somehow got redder. He started reaching towards the mobile that Bryan was pulling out of a pocket. Bryan held the mobile back and shook his head. Jonny's hand dropped back to his lap.

Bryan pulled out a loupe and turned his flashlight on the mobile. "In spite of your claims to being no good in the meat, you blew up a building, so I'm not going to assume you haven't done something tricky here."

Bry took his time checking it out, even fished some tiny tools out of a pocket and opened it up, much to Jonny's obvious discomfort. After putting it all nicely back together, Bryan held it and allowed Jonny to boot it up.

It came to life noiselessly and brightly. Bryan handed the small machine to me after he scanned it for bugs. "Never know when turning something on is going to start unwanted transmissions," he explained.

I took the mobile. It was sleek and top of the line. It looked new enough that I distracted myself, trying not to be buried under the depth of his crimes, by assuming that Jonny had bought it just to impress us tonight. Yeah, that had to be the case. Otherwise, it should be at least a bit scuffed by riding around in pockets.

"Since you know so much about me, about *us*, you can now trust us with your passwords." My tone and the persistent guns didn't leave room to argue with my assertion. "And you'd better let me know right now if I'm going to trip up any security features. Because one cranky look from me and you'll probably end up leaving blood on my seats."

Jonny sighed with clear misery but spared me an argument. "The lock code for the mobile is 2048."

He paused a moment whilst I tapped the numbers. I was immediately presented with a login screen. He said, "I can bypass that with a fingerprint and voice code."

"Nice try. You'll need to give me that login info now."

He hung his head and mumbled, so Bryan poked at him with a gun. Jonny looked up and said, "The 'nym is HandOff. One word, but capital H and O. And the pass is Zr$Su34SdhL$cfJ." He gave the characters one at a time, but quickly. If he was hoping I couldn't keep up, he'd been disappointed.

"Okay. I'm in. Where are the files you were going to show us as proof?"

He sounded resigned now. "They're not on the mobile, but you can get to them through my remote connection to my home system. I put the command to remote in the app folder for Daily Cat on the removable drive."

Again, I couldn't help but laugh.

This time, he joined in, nervously. "I figure the last place anyone would look for serious files is in the folder for an app that gives me a cute cat picture every day." He shrugged, looking momentarily a bit at ease. "Everyone forgets that *everyone* likes cute cat pictures. Even the scary hackers."

I navigated to the folder in question and told myself that chances were small that what I was about to tap would make the mobile explode or anything. Not with him right there. I still held my breath a little as I did. As hoped, a new login prompt opened. "Okay. Next login."

Jonny's head fell back, and he considered the roof of the car with a sigh. He looked like a kid being asked to shoot his pet. I empathized, but didn't feel at all bad. I might have felt a vicious kind of pleasure. He'd chosen himself into this situation.

He asked, "Are you sure you want to do this?"

I was starting to feel in control, the adrenaline and cortisol and whatever other things in my body chemistry that were wrapped up in fear had seeped out. We were in control. Our bomber wasn't such a badass in person. And I just wanted this done.

I fixed him with what I hoped was a hard look, but it was Riles who said, "I swear, if you don't get this over with, I will shoot you. Come *on*."

Jonny looked at us. Did he notice the glow from Riley's other hand that was probably zir taking notes and maybe even remoting into Jonny's computer zirself, piggybacked on the connection coming off Jonny's own mobile?

Like a man resigned to a death sentence, he said, "The 'nym is ignis-potentia. No caps and a dash to join the words."

He paused a moment, then asked in rather respectful tones, "Do you need me to spell that?"

I shook my head. "Not if it's Latin like it sounds like. But, here," I showed him the screen, "confirm I got it right."

"You did. And the password is a line from a poem, but no spaces between words; A, E, I, O replaced by the usual numbers, and S replaced with a dollar sign. Ready?" I nodded. He recited, "I will show you fear in a handful of dust. That's the line. From T.S. Eliot."

Fortunately for him, it worked. Before he could tell me what to do, I started looking through his file structure. Nosy and curious and feeling like, after what he'd done, I deserved to touch everything on his computer. From the continued glow in Riley's non-gun hand and the fact zie kept looking down, I assumed zie was also putting zir digital fingers in things.

"Go to the hidden partition on the drive named Porn. Then it's Gang Bangs, Classic Era, Natasha, Blue Studio Sessions. Everything in there is relevant, but start with the folder that's named hyphen-space-Orpheum. That's the really choice stuff I wanted to show you first to help you understand."

As I navigated I warned, "If all I see when I get there is actual porn, I'm going to shoot you in your junk so porn will never be of use to you again."

But that wasn't what I found in the folder.

At the end of the electric trip, I found myself staring into slums of information. It wasn't that I disliked information in general. It wasn't that Jonny's system was poorly organized. And it wasn't that this had been a joke and it was all actually truly disturbing porn. But the things I was reading made me feel like I was in the wrong part of town. It kicked off another "fight or flight" bit of fear. I just stared at what was scrolling across the screen, wondering what part my job had been playing in this squalor. I was feeling surer and surer that Jonny was going to make it through this night with his life intact.

All of the documents in this first folder were SWS memos and reports, but all marked as classified and sent to or from executives important enough that I recognized most their names (obviously, Johnson, Smith, and Williams were recipients or senders on every one). The first clump, all files with names that started with a 1, was what appeared to be a very serious discussion about which way they should, literally, take over the world. They listed some of the companies and powerful people in many countries over which they had some kind of influence. They listed possible tools in their varied plans, which included things like their nearly ubiquitous health-related wearables, from the most basic HealthAdvisor to the newer Peacemaker.

I gave myself a moment to feel smug. For decades now, it seemed most people who could afford one had worn some kind of health tracker. What started as pedometers that were self-contained quickly grew to wearables that tracked every possible type of health-related or health-impacting thing and sent the information to your computer. That became wearables sending the data to the cloud, and from the cloud to whichever company had somehow made a claim strong enough to pierce privacy complaints. Sometimes it seemed great, like when your doctor knew you were having a heart attack at the same time you did. But when it was an employer who could punish you for not caring enough about the job to get a good night's sleep or the corporation who could target you with adverts to buy something that pertained to your specific health as communicated to them by your wearable? No thanks. Especially when so many contained GPS technology (for more precise calculation of how much you moved, to let you analyze the difficulty of the terrain on which you walked—because those 30 steps uphill obviously counted for more than the 30 steps on a flat street).

So, whilst wearables were ubiquitous, and at the risk of sounding like some conspiracy theorist in a tinfoil hat, Riles, Bryan, and I had decided very early to indulge our paranoia and avoid them. And now I was feeling like maybe we'd chosen the right tinfoil hats after all. (I made a mental note to do some "I told you so's" to mocking acquaintances when this was all over.)

SWS also noted how many computers their security software gave them access to, including computers that were in charge of some nations' weapons systems. I'd want to get more info on how they were going to use some of this stuff, but they did have one point: They were in almost every home, quite a number of corporations, and many governments. They had what they needed to do what they wanted.

I knew the others were waiting to hear from me, so I tried to skim. Once I felt like I knew what they were on about and that they were serious, I moved on to the clump of files with names that all started with 2. This was a smaller clump, but actually more frightening to me. In these memos, I found lists of 'nyms I knew, other hackers I'd seen on forums or even done jobs with in the past, right by what appeared to be their real names and notes like "Recruited" or "Blackmailed" or "Find leverage." And what little other text there was basically said, "Hey, here's the status of our program to buy out or take out the hackers who might breach our software."

At the moment, none of the four of us in this car were on any of the lists. Not that I noticed in my quick skim. I must have been holding my breath as I started to understand what was in that clump, because, once I did another skim of the 'nyms and felt like my friends and I were not currently compromised, I let out a massive sigh of relief. But my relief was fleeting. Because the rest of that was just...ugly. Brutal. Too damned big. And, with all those 'nyms I recognized, getting a little too close to home. My brain started to spin up, trying to remember the last interactions I'd had with those people in the list and whether they could figure out who I was (*like Jonny had*, my brain helpfully reminded me) and...and I made myself stop. I needed to bring everyone in on this.

When I looked up, I found that all guns were still on Jonny, but all eyes were on me. Bryan spoke first. "Not good?"

I paused a moment to consider Jonny before I answered. I read the look he was giving me as a sort of plea. Like now I understood and things might get back to whatever movie-inspired scene he'd pictured for the night.

If these documents were legit, I would concede that his intentions *might* be good, even if I couldn't get behind his actions, behind the killing. Once I admitted that to myself, the edge came off my anger. Very, very slightly. I could hear my intuition now that the anger wasn't roaring quite so loudly. My intuition wasn't flawless, but it had generally been pretty right about other people. Or so I'd always thought. But right now it was saying that it thought Jonny probably *was* a good guy. And, no, it protested, that wasn't just because he was pretty. *I* might be a sucker for pretty, but my intuition usually wasn't. With an internal howl, I let a wave of disgust overwhelm my intuition. What the fuck was wrong with me? And what the ever-loving fuck was wrong with my intuition? I guess all my shite exes now made sense.

Riles reached over and poked at me. "Hey. What's up? Is it bad?"

I set my jaw and looked at zir. "Not good. Not at all."

To the car at large I said, "For now, we let him live. Um...I need a second to process and I promise I'll summarize whilst we drive, but I vote we keep babysitting him whilst one of us verifies that this info is the real deal. And then, if it is, we..."

I floundered a moment. What would *we* be able to do in the face of this? What skills did *we* have that were actually big enough for this? Well, we'd figure it out. We had to. So, I pressed on. "We let him help us take out SWS. If we can stand to keep a murderer around."

Jonny opened his mouth, as if to protest my usurpation, but I cut him off. "Your 'nym may be known, you might be capable, but I've got friends...people I thought were friends...that are going to go down with this. We all do. And I'm taking this very personally." The anger returned, leaking out in my voice. "*Very personally.*"

And then I let my disgust for my previous attraction join my disgust for his actions, and I made sure that my tone was the nastiest I could manage. "Besides, you've done a pretty fucking horrible job so far, haven't you?"

Jonny looked...I guess he actually looked deeply ashamed for a moment. I felt like I was the high priestess of righteous fury and had, perhaps, forced a sinner to see his filthiness.

He cleared his throat, recovered a bit. "So, uh, can we cease to point guns at me? I think the lady said my life has been saved for the night. Also, I'd, uh, I'd like to have my mobile back. Please?"

Everyone looked to me for my response.

"Riles," I said, "let's get to somewhere we can cut off any damage that our *friends* may try to cause. Or may already have caused. Jonny, you tell him your address. You may want to pick up some clean underoos."

I slowly put away my gun but assured my friends, "I won't hold it against you if you keep *your* guns out."

I did not hand Jonny's mobile back.

Jonny looked, if possible, even more uncomfortable. He cleared his throat. "You aren't going to like this."

CHAPTER 7

Like synchronized furrowers, all brows in the car wrinkled at once, all eyes on Jonny. Suspicion replacing the oxygen. Of course there was more bad news from the asshole who blew up my building.

"What aren't we going to like, mate?" Bryan cut off the last word with a precision that made it clear there was something else he'd rather cut off.

Jonny looked at the ceiling as he replied. "I made...a gamble. It didn't pay off...And I'm pretty sure it's about to bite me in the ass." When no one picked up the conversation, he took a deep breath and went on. "You know how I said I was doing all I could to figure out if you were okay? Toward the end of my time trying to figure out whether or not you were dirty, I thought it might help to run into you somewhere more conducive to conversation and reading your body language than a club."

I leaned in, pouring a calm, cold menace into my voice. "What did you do?"

"Well, initially, I thought I'd try to bump into you somewhere else social. Maybe...maybe flirt with you in a restaurant or something. But you aren't as social as I'd anticipated. And you always seem to be with your friends here. So, I had to take a bigger chance." He paused again, waiting for someone to spare him the final admission. When the silence persisted, still staring fixedly at the ceiling rather than meeting our eyes, he rushed through it. "I moved into your building and kept trying to run into you but never did." He physically cringed, shrank back into the seat like he was preparing for a blow.

Bryan broke in. "Just in case you're lying and trying to get Kot's address—"

Jonny cut him off, giving us an address that was, indeed, the same as mine except for the unit number. But it wasn't cocky. He was curled in, still cringing, rushing through the address like ripping off a bandage he *knew* was going to hurt.

Bryan shook his head and quietly, as if he were very sorry, said, "Oh, mate..." whilst Riles let out a wincing sort of extended "Oh."

I said nothing, but sat very still.

Very, very still.

And then, very evenly and quietly, I said, "When this is sorted, I will end you." I paused a moment, hoping that the renewed silence in the car indicated that everyone believed me. "So, Riles, I guess you know where to go."

Riley was shaking zir head as zie turned to start the car and get us headed to Jonny's (*headed to mine*, I corrected). Jonny was cowering between Bryan and I still. Good.

"Okay. So. Why he gets to live...All of the documents Jonny has there appear to be internal SWS memos and reports. The kind that only the big kids at the top are meant to see. The gist..." I trailed off and then sighed. "The gist of it is that they're out for global power. That's no surprise. But we aren't talking about it in the normal corporate way. They're currently arguing global domination versus global manipulation. You know, literal dictatorship versus pulling the puppet strings. Though even the puppet strings options vary from making countries think they're at war with each other to political and social machinations. And, now that I think about it, there's a weird kind of religious tone to the ones who are pushing for manipulation." I saw Jonny nod at that. He'd noticed it too. "Usually, I'd assume this sort of thing was a bunch of chest pounding amongst friends who had no reason to think they were being serious. Unfortunately, other documents support that they are. Serious, that is."

"Well, damn..." said Bryan. "Are you trying to tell me this is some kind of epic save the world thing?" He sounded really doubtful. I couldn't blame him. "Can I see the mobile?"

I handed it over. "It's the documents that all start with a 1. But that's not all. The thing is they've got an increasing number of hackers on the payroll. People whose 'nyms you'll know...and whose *real* names you'll know once you look at the lists. Cos it looks like SWS has those. Which are the docs that start with a 2. People you might have trusted. That's the big problem. I mean, even if the other part is bullshit. And they're likely going to be after us. So, not only do we need to confirm this stuff is real, but I think we should all start doing damage control on our own stuff ASAP too." I looked Jonny in the eye. "I no longer think Jonny knowing who I am means I'm fucked. I think that SWS controlling hackers is why all of us could end up fucked. We might want to keep moving to a new city or at least going off the grid as strong options. Put that one back on the table. And, either way, new identities are a must."

Riley, who couldn't see the documents, asked, "Are you serious?"

"Yeah. I think I am."

Bryan, just starting to skim the documents, said, "She probably is."

Zie sped up a little. "I want to see these docs."

The rest of the drive, I was very much in my own head. It wasn't the sort of place most people would want to be. It was like a big, grey file room. With neon graffiti on the cabinets in chaotic, shouty layers. And there was the constant whisper— sometimes roar—of puzzles solving themselves, future conversations being planned, new ideas and topics pressing for attention; a constant check of myself to evaluate whether what I was doing was right and normal enough; a to-do list scrolling lest errands be forgotten; and my paranoia keeping a running dialogue of cautions which had surely saved me from bodily injury and prison. It just wasn't pleasant or quiet.

I was holding conference with the paranoia right now. "I want a listing of every interaction I've had with the traitors. And with Jonny."

I pictured paranoia as a gaunt and haunted man; he nodded and twitched, looking over his shoulder and rubbing the barrel of his gun. "Yeah, we got that stuff coming in right now. Though, I gotta say, you should just take this kid's info and start the purging tonight."

"No, it's too soon to deliver a death sentence judgment. He's not clearly, totally evil. Not clearly enough. Not for *me* to pull the trigger. I mean, he blew up a building and innocent people died. And I want to get the full story on that before I...well, before someone takes care of him. But we'll do that. Someone will do that. Later. Let's concentrate on damage control. We need to see what my...peers could have gotten on me and where I'm vulnerable. And whilst you're compiling that, start keeping a list on the side of information we may have that shows where *they're* vulnerable. Okay?"

Paranoia said yes, yes, of course and ran off to gather the requested information. (Obviously, he would wait until I was trying to sleep and wake me up with VERY IMPORTANT AND DANGEROUS NEWS. That's just the way my paranoia rolls.) Whilst he worked (whilst my subconscious worked to filter up relevant information), I started unraveling everything I'd ever done whilst employed at SWS and tried to see where I may have aided them in their uglier endeavors.

On the surface, the sort of drone job I'd taken there, avoiding the higher level security clearance, could barely be of use. But I'm not a surface girl. And I'd been pretty sure all along that what I was doing was probably not entirely legal. I just hadn't cared until now. Had been grateful the NDA meant I couldn't tell Engalls, or anyone else, the particulars of my number-checking and make things stickier.

Every work day, I got lists (usually of phone numbers), with a main reference number at the top of each list. To me, it looked like the lists were made from hard copies, scanned in. My job was to check that the SWS automated reader correctly grabbed the numbers from the list, which it then put into a searchable database. It was mind-numbing hours of comparing numbers. Sometimes it was lists of what looked like charges to people's accounts (someone buying a toothbrush at the corner store), but never the account numbers of the charges, still just the reference numbers. If I had to guess, the numbers were coming from proprietary software at phone companies, banks, and so forth. SWS probably weren't supposed to have them. They could get away with a general purpose reader, one that was purposefully neutered so all they'd get was text, one that would open most sorts of files, but they would be hard-pressed to defend functionality in their software that would let them actually access the files as more than read-only. However, they could open those files they weren't supposed to have as, basically, images of the info, have a program capture that like scanning, and then have a program that parsed text from scanned documents. And then they just had to count on the NDA and the power SWS would have to destroy your life if you went against them (and the inability of law enforcement to actually do anything useful) to keep people's mouths shut.

I felt like a fool. I should have been figuring out where those numbers came from and what they were being used for. Or at least have had the sense to keep crime as an extracurricular activity. I shouldn't have been complacent about it just because I didn't want to shit where I eat or mess up my mindless, mundane cover.

I just hadn't thought I was aiding them in anything as big as what the documents, if they were real, said was happening. I didn't know how, but checking numbers wasn't just paying my rent; it was helping SWS keep on top of their true goals, aiding their scheme. And it was such a stupid, classic scheme. It was the sort of thing that you'd think people would be too stupid to fall for. But I'd never really thought that people were anything *but* stupid, so...

I sighed. So of course every fool in the world had bought into Secure World Systems. After all, if SWS were securing it, information fell into the hands of hackers much less often than with other companies. That had been proven. Their free antivirus and firewall programs were beautiful (I didn't use them; I used something the three of us cooked up, but they were what I recommended to most anyone else), and their new Peacemaker implant was surely going to cut down on human misbehaving at the source (a nice supplement to the line of wearable trackers so many people now used to keep their kids safe). Not to mention the great value of their work with wearable health tracking and monitoring, medical diagnostic and information tools, and philanthropic efforts for poor individuals and nations. Their service was friendly. Their prices were incredibly reasonable, especially for being, now, the biggest and the best. They seemed to deliver on their motto of "Peace Through Security, Security Through Peace." They were the sort of company that still spoke fondly of the idiot judge who eventually ruled that Comcast-Time Warner wasn't a "true" monopoly. And they were fond with good reason. They were walking that tightrope as far as anyone could see, apparently quietly snatching up all the other companies doing anything like the many things they did.

Along the way, they'd bought out many of my peers, at least according to what I'd seen on Jonny's mobile. There were far fewer illegal hacks because my damned peers were getting funds elsewhere. Were being paid by SWS. Sometimes to keep hands off. Other times to put their hands right into info and carefully grab the little tidbits needed by SWS. Sometimes, SWS just took them out by making them part of the first people to get Peacemakers in their heads (under the guise of donating to the underprivileged and helping reform criminals). And, of course, SWS had them keeping an eye on their peers. This explained how one or two recent arrests had occurred. It also explained why some folks who'd had nerves of titanium in years past had become uncharacteristically wary of SWS-protected networks and databases. Silly me, I had just suspected they were losing their edge.

What would they use to blackmail me? For a lot of us, just being able to turn us in for our online crimes was enough. But they could also use Gran. Oh, man, I'd pretty much have to roll right over if they threatened Gran. Some of the names, the blackmailed ones, had had a parenthetical note. "Family." Family. Like Gran. I hated my peers for giving in, but hated, and feared, SWS even more for their willingness to go that low.

And, besides the personal, there was the global threat. Now that I'd read those memos which were meant only for the big nasties at the head of SWS, I had a better idea of their clientele than I'd ever gotten sitting in my cubicle or flipping through the info I could find online. They were in the middle of finishing installations for some foreign governments and of negotiating more contracts with the U.S. government. They were about to be in a position of global power, and they were quiet enough about a great deal of it that few people were likely to realize this. One memo had listed some of the weapons that they could easily use without having to admit that *they* were the bad guys if they chose global domination over global manipulation. (Did it count in their favor that they seemed to prefer manipulation over domination by violence?)

It wasn't that I was averse to theoretical ideas of global

power. As a teenager, I'd had my share of fantasies. But I'd read enough history to be concerned about my rights within any sort of empire. And I was well-known enough, at least under the 'nym MindKiller, that it couldn't be long before someone else tried to find me. They had probably already been hunting for me, for Bryan and Riles, and for Jonny for a while now. I just couldn't believe they hadn't. I must have missed that in the memos. I *had* been skimming. And there was nothing like having her identity uncovered to really put a damper on a girl's life.

We pulled into my parking spot, pausing a moment in the car. I took my gun back out. "I think that my little gun and a classic 'pretend we're just two lovers with arms linked' cover for the gun would be the best bet until we're safely in your flat. Just like the walk out of the club. So I know you've already got practice." I pointed the gun at Jonny. "Why don't you carefully pull out your keys for our friends here, and then we'll take this party up to yours before we head to mine." Jonny nodded and complied.

We walked up corridors and stairs, passing my flat, and up just one more flight. Rye and the keys in front, Bryan behind, and Jonny and I with arms linked so that my gun in his side wasn't obvious. Back before tonight, this was not the way I'd pictured having arms around this particular boy. I cursed myself for not somehow detecting his future crimes and wanting him that way in the first place. Now, having arms around was as much punishment for me as it was for him.

Jonny's flat was very plain. It looked like all of his money went into his mobile. He didn't even have any weapons. Thanks to stories from my grandmother, I had grown up assuming that everyone who messed with computers would have guns. Of course, Gran also had some hang up about flying cars and the fact that they "damned well should have been everywhere by now," so I should have known better than to let her shape my worldview.

As we picked up Jonny's computer (fortunately a portable), the external drives we could find (I assumed he had backups hidden somewhere), and some clothes and such, and whilst Riles and Bryan went through his place, I stood with him in the living room. Had him backed in a corner, thinking it would make it harder for him to pull anything. I also found that his fear, rather than drawing out mine, made me feel braver. Not because I thought I was more capable than I'd been at the start of the night. But my foe wasn't the inhuman threat I'd thought. He was, it appeared, some pretty boy who was computer-smart and real-world stupid. Like me. But *I* had a gun. And I wasn't the one who'd blown up a fucking building of people.

We waited for my mates to finish, and I let him know, in no uncertain terms, what the next few days would look like.

"You're going to be under constant supervision. You don't even get to piss without someone watching you. So you'd better get over any issues you might have with your *own* privacy. Also, if you even look at a computer, it better be with permission. If there are things you need to take care of, you'll do it through one of us. We need to verify that your information is good. If it is, things might get a little looser, but I sure hope you've got some sick days saved up, because I don't know when you'll be able to go back to work. Fortunately, some of *us* are self-employed or not working due to an explosion, so you won't get lonely. If your info is on the up and up, then we'll set some plans into motion. But *you* came to *us*. *You* intruded on *my* privacy. So I'm not on *your* team. You're on *mine*. If you're lucky. And that would be in spite of the totally horrific choices you made."

He just nodded and took it meekly, looking sick. But he said, "I'm really sorry I messed this up. I really am. This was..." His brows pulled together, face pained. "This was not what I meant to have happen."

I sighed. "Yeah, so you say. Some of us should stick to computers. If you really are spaceGoddity, you're at least good there."

He drearily nodded. "I really am."

"So, you also figured out who those two are?" I nodded my head towards his bedroom, where I could hear Bryan and Riles looking.

"Not that I'd mind us all pretending to be normal and having introductions, but, yeah. Bryan and Riley, a.k.a. TesTur and apHellion." He looked at me a moment. "You guys understand that, given how tied together you are, one of you getting found means the others get more easily found, right?"

It was an old worry, so it pushed a button. I practically snarled, "Calculated risk. And worth it." Fortunately, Rye and Bryan came into the room then. Part of me was looking for an excuse to hurt this fucker, and part of me knew I'd regret stooping to his level.

Riles announced, "We're ready."

Bryan put the blindfold back on Jonny, and we walked down to my flat, pretending (hoping) maybe he didn't know the exact unit, even though he quietly noted "I know you're in 203." When we reached my place, Bryan checked the alarms, sensors, and random security gizmos. When he felt sufficiently fulfilled in his protective role, he motioned to us that it was safe to enter.

Normally, we liked to come home to showers and comfortable clothes. Once upon a time, we might have sat around in club clothes all night. It would have made us feel cool. Now, it just made us feel uncomfortable. Feeling uncomfortable reminded us that we were no longer quite as young. Which depressed us and made us wonder what we'd done with our youth. And then Riley or I, depending on who'd had the most to drink, would start whining about how we still looked like we were younger, so we didn't even get the respect that thirty-ish years old should get us. (Really, it was more like 25 plus, but drink made us round up. Thirty-ish sounded impressively older and respect-deserving.) Everyone had found it was easier to decide we'd paid our Cool Kid dues and could sit around in jeans, pajama pants, or boxer shorts if we wanted to. We still kept cool clothes at each other's places, even in non-crisis times, just in case we went out. But, except for Saturdays, we usually found excuses not to wear them. Excitement to us was the glow of a computer screen.

So I was annoyed to feel like there were pressing matters. I didn't head for the shower; I headed for the living room and opened my computer. Do not get comfortable, do not pass go. I disliked everything about my situation. And I felt guilty for sulking over this when there were people who had died over the SWS thing, not just been made to stay in club clothes.

Bryan pulled out a chair and zip tied Jonny to it, whilst Riles set up Jonny's computer and used the login information we'd gotten earlier. I waited until zie got a job running to grab all the files and other data on it (no need to let Jonny know we were doing that), and then I set it to display on the wall TV. I handed zir Jonny's mobile so zie could see for zirself the docs the rest of us had been talking about.

Jonny's chair was across the coffee table from me. When Bryan and Riles took their now-customary seats, we looked almost like we were holding a conference. I pointed to the screen, my other hand over his portable's keys. "Walk me into SWS. Let's see if you're legit."

In movies about people like us that my gran had liked, this sort of "action" was usually animated with colors and flashing graphics to make it exciting. In reality, it was far less flashy. And I guess it would have bored most people to tears, even if we'd explained the whole situation and how hard it was to hack into a company that, amongst other things, had their fingers in computer security. For me, though, this was even more interesting than usual; I thoroughly enjoyed seeing how someone else worked. I picked up little tricks. I experienced computers through their eyes. In this case, I got ideas about how I might take Jonny out if our skills were on opposite sides in a conflict.

Though we would have to spend some time making sure he hadn't planted them, we did, indeed, find the originals of the documents Jonny had showed us. Which was when it got really real. Anyone, even my gran, could fake up a document. Templates for headers came built into most programs and you could grab a company's logo and executives' names from their web site. To be fair, you could then just put one of those documents on someone else's computer and direct others there to "discover" them. But Riley set to work checking all the metadata and code, the sort your average user won't see, and computer logs and such on the first document we found that matched what Jonny had. By the time we'd found most of the matches, Riley was satisfied.

"I think this is legit." Zir face quickly went from pleased to panicked. "Shit. I think this is legit."

I got us out of the SWS system. "I don't know about you two, but I can't sleep until I make sure there are no holes in my security."

They seemed to be on their portables before I was done speaking. I could hear their fingers flying across their keyboards, pounding out little pieces of safety.

Jonny had been quiet once he got us into SWS. I looked over now to find him watching me. Maybe it was neutral, but I thought he might have enjoyed watching me work. (Whilst my ego appreciated that, I felt repulsion at being admired by a murderer.) I was glad he'd chosen silence. One of the secrets to me was that I adored silence. Talk could be good, but people rarely seem to opt for silence, even when it was obviously the best idea.

He realized I'd noticed him watching, and I was pretty sure he purposefully didn't let himself look away, embarrassed. Not quickly. He held eye contact just a moment before he turned his head to look away with an edge of awkwardness. Like someone had given him a damned manual for how to be attractive to me. Except for the fucking murder part. I was starting to hate the part of my brain that seemed to respond automatically, stupidly And I definitely hated him for...well, for a lot of things. Next time (next time?!?!), I hoped the universe sent someone completely unattractive to make my life difficult. (*Or maybe I could just try being a better judge of character,* I countered.)

"So, just to make sure I fix the issue, how did you find me?"

Riley and Bryan turned to listen to the answer. This question was of interest to everyone. Interesting in general, but also might point to holes in their own security.

"Seriously. How did you find me? If you aren't here to take me down, at least give me a chance to make sure no one else can do it."

Jonny laughed, a bit abashed. "I'd love to say it was because of my 'leet haxor skillz,' but it was more like dumb luck and eavesdropping on someone pretty."

I gave him a look of confusion, but didn't interrupt.

"I was out, going to grab a coffee, and I decided to drink it there when I saw...a very attractive woman having a meal there with two friends. I sat at the table next to them, next to you, to try to...to get up the nerve to say something, maybe catch your eye and see if I could get some non-verbal permission to engage, and figuring I could eavesdrop a little." He cut short the outrage I could feel on my face, speaking quickly. "It wasn't about being creepy or intrusive, I swear. I just figured that I might overhear a mutual topic of interest. Or I might hear that you were stupid or mean and know that it was better not to waste my time on you."

Yeah, I would have done the same thing. So I closed my mouth, swallowing my indignation, and felt, if not relaxed, less ready to hit him for that particular choice. He slowed back to a normal speaking pace.

"What I heard, instead, was you guys talking about something that had happened on a forum earlier that night. And, by dumb luck, it was a forum I'd been on right before I came out. You said just enough that I recognized the scenario and thought that you might be players in it. Well, the ones that weren't me or that asshole Byt3s1z3. And you even said something about how, of course, you weren't going to let someone get away with talking shit like that, so of course you'd replied."

I groaned in embarrassment. "I can't believe I was careless like that."

Jonny reassured me, "You really weren't. Unless someone had read that conversation and then purposefully been straining to eavesdrop, they'd have no way to make anything meaningful of it or to use it to figure out who you were. Honestly, it took that *and* my aforementioned skills and a lot of persistence and patience to figure it out, to confirm it." He shrugged. "You can go in and change things up, but you're probably not under immediate threat. If SWS hasn't figured out who you are already, you're probably good if you just never talk about what you do in public places."

We three captors nodded. I said, "That makes sense. Guess we'd better start treating everywhere we go like it's bugged or like we're being watched."

Bryan said, "A realistic paranoia right now anyway."

We all nodded.

I kept quizzing Jonny. Getting him to try to dig up memories of what holes he might have found in my security, before or after overhearing us at the coffee place. He calmly responded, even telling me where on his computer I could find his documentation of such things. I don't think he had any delusions that his data was at all private any more.

It took a couple of hours. My own ideas for changes had gone quickly. I might be flattering myself, but I think I tend to work carefully and hadn't left many openings. For most of the time, I used Jonny's information to find the odd little scraps of information that had let him find me, find my private email and such, once he'd gotten an idea of who I was from his chance eavesdropping. I was impressed at his ability to find the smallest fibers of my identity, accidentally snagged as I moved through life. As Jonny told me what to look for, the others got distracted from their own efforts. It never hurt to learn someone else's techniques or one's own flaws.

Even if he'd had some luck in finding me, that didn't change that he was truly skilled. I was impressed. Like you might be with a fictional supervillain. Only without the cushion that fiction gives your moral compass.

We finally started getting showers and comfortable clothing sorted. I had a massive shaking fit in my shower, which seemed to leave me calmer on the other side.

After everyone else had showered, I offered Jonny the shower. I'm just that magnanimous. (Also, my living room was small and sweat—from dancing or fear—quickly made it smell funkier than I'd like.) Bryan cut him loose, and he headed towards the shower with obvious gratitude, though his look got a little less grateful when Riles got up to follow him in. "Want me to grab some fresh undies for you?" zie called to Jonny as zie followed.

When we heard the sound of the shower, Bryan turned to stare me down. I pretended to ignore him as I purged an account I didn't need anymore. Bryan grinned as widely as he could and leaned forward. Even though I was ignoring him, the grin was clearly not sincere.

"I'm gonna gut you like a pig if you don't start talking."

I looked up and grinned back just as disingenuously. "Sweet talker. This talk of pig gutting is so charming."

He got serious. "Why don't we talk about who the bomber turned out to be. And I don't mean who he is on the 'Net. Though that's also interesting and complicating and...Okay, also probably something to talk about."

I blushed, but I dared to play dumb, to pretend that Bryan wasn't one of two people to whom I'd casually pointed out pretty people with whom I might want to hook up. It was bad enough I had to admit this all to myself. "How do you mean?"

"You've wanted to at least dance all over him for a little while now. And he's pretty. And he's smart. And we can't discount who he is on the 'Net." I'm sure my blush deepened as he listed things. I know that I suddenly found the tabletop a much more interesting thing to look at than Bryan's eyes. "Yeah, that's what I thought." He leaned forward, and kindly asked, "So, tell me what's up here. We both know that your attraction could be a factor in what happens."

I sighed, and worked to move from looking at the table to, eventually, looking at his eyes whilst I spoke. "He is definitely a pretty face with a smart brain. I mean, dammit, he's *spaceGoddity*. You and I know he's our equal on the 'Net. Had he approached me tonight and not as the bomber, I'm pretty sure he'd have ended up back here. Of his own volition. But." And I found myself suddenly filled with a potent mix of shame and loathing. "But I hate that I ever felt that and I'm completely fucking ashamed that my body hasn't caught up to my brain."

I found that I was pleading with Bryan. "Am I the most fucked up person ever? How can any of us ever trust me again when I could be attracted to...that?"

As if trying to make me feel less bad somehow, Bryan said, "Until tonight, I might have also thought he was attractive. And I'm pretty sure Riles did too. So, we all suck, okay? Plus, and I hate to admit it, because it's easier if we can paint ourselves as big damn heroes and him as the villain, but he didn't exactly put up a fight. He's already here of his own volition."

I let out a frustrated sound. "I know. That's the worst! Is he here because he's good and we just don't know it yet or is he here because that was his nefarious plot all along and, right now, Rye's bleeding out in the bathroom whilst Jonny sneakily creeps up to take us out?" We both paused to look towards the bathroom, just in case there was a ninja-like Jonny approaching. I listened and told myself it sounded like normal showering, not murder showering, in the bathroom.

Then I went on. "To make it harder, I guess harder...maybe easier? Anyway," I shook my head, clearing away the question so I could just state the fact, "My intuition?" I looked to see Bryan nod, acknowledging the known power of my intuition. "It's horrible and I feel...really uncomfortable about even still noticing he's physically attractive. But, worse than that, my intuition says that he's a good guy. And my intuition has called out some pretty faces that were snakes in the past, so I don't think it's as fallible as I am." I looked at my fingers in my lap, shaking my head, tears of shame pressing to escape. "Maybe my intuition's finally broken. Or my moral compass is. What the fuck is wrong with me?"

He put a hand on my shoulder. "Don't beat yourself up. It's not like you're actually throwing yourself at him. Not since you realized who he is. And...it seems like there are pieces missing still. And." He conceded, "his data seems legit."

I nodded. "And his data seems legit."

"So, you might have a crush or something like it on our probably-prisoner? Maybe?"

"Shit. I hope not. I think the whole 'killing people thing' has made sure of that. And, even if I fancied him a bit or had no morals, your life and Riley's life are...They're everything to me. That alone would make this...a non-issue. At this point, if you need to...take him out, fucking go for it. I'm over him." I hoped he could see in my eyes how truly I meant that.

He looked satisfied. "Okay. I'll make sure to find a second with Riley to get us all on the same page." He patted my knee.

I wasn't sure whether I hated Jonny or myself more. But I definitely loved Bry for not thinking less of the feelings I'd had up until earlier tonight.

We heard the bathroom door open. Bryan gave me a little, sympathetic smile before he stood by Jonny's chair with zip ties, waiting. I put my game face back on. No self-disgust or weak distractions where he could see.

As Bryan guided Jonny to the chair and quietly tied him to it, Rye announced, "In his favor, he didn't act weird about me chaperoning his shower. He might be an evil, murderous shit, but he's at least good at hiding queer-phobia."

Jonny shrugged. "I might have preferred a different chaperone," he paused and caught my eye a moment (he was a cheeky, inappropriate bastard and it made my stomach turn), "but I like to think my gender and sexuality attitudes are less questionable than everything I've done this week." There was that edge of something that sounded like shame again. He shrugged as best he could now that he was zip tied to the chair again. "Plus, I've been stared down by creepier people in locker rooms back in high school."

Bryan settled back into his own chair and said, "Sounds like you've lost your creepy edge, Rye." Rye softly smacked Bryan upside the head in response.

I yawned loudly and stretched. "Okay, that does me for the night, now that night is gone. Now that we're all clean, wanna set up sleeping and 'watching Jonny' shifts?"

Bryan said, "You sleep first, Kot. The rest of us still have some cleaning up to do since we didn't have stalkers of our own to help find things. We can argue amongst ourselves about who has to wake you up when it's your turn to watch Jonny sleep."

"Fair." I stood up, bent over to give Rye and Bryan each a kiss on the forehead. I might have done it anyway, but some childish thing in me was also doing it to point out to Jonny what he didn't get. "G'night, all." And I dragged back to my bed.

I sat propped up in my bed, arms folded and face screwed up as I thought. I had way too much to process right now; I felt like I had to get through a little of the mental deluge before I could actually sleep. There was a soft knock at the door. Soft enough that I barely heard it over the Mercurial Divine that slithered through the speakers. "Yeah?"

The door opened a crack and Riles stuck zir head in. "Hey. Mind company?" I shook my head, so zie eased in and closed the door behind zir. I scooted over a bit and zie joined me, sat beside me, propped up on the bed. Neither of us spoke for a few breaths. Riles turned zir head to look at me. "Lights and music still on. Not sleeping yet?" I shook my head. "Quite a time we're having." I nodded. "I'm going to quit my job and look for alternative sources of funding." Zie paused. "I think this isn't going to be the sort of dilemma that we can all fit neatly into our off hours."

I sighed loudly. "Yeah. That idiot out there just ruined my life path." I chewed the inside of my cheek for a few moments.

"Prince Charming? I think you'd better thank your fairy godmother you dodged that one." We both laughed a bit. I could hear a sort of quiet and uncomfortable hysteria—due, no doubt, to being tired and overwhelmed and having some grey patches in the issue—hanging on the edges of our laughs. Riles took a deep breath and stilled zir laughter. "Yeah, I know what you mean. It looks like he's legit. Which means you should be glad that he didn't blow you up and that he's been forthcoming. But it might be nice if he were a little more abrasive and ugly. So we wouldn't have previous attractions to feel conflicted about."

I gave another short laugh. "Aye. If he'd at least put up a fight. Or if he was stupid. Or had a better explanation for the deaths. Or something." Riley snorted. "Right now, I'm clinging to the fact that he blew up the building and killed people. Letting that make my choices for me. Though..." I gave a sort of frustrated exhale. "For all we know, I was the only person in the building who wasn't part of the plans to take over and to take out hackers. I mean, I can now easily start thinking of reasons he would blow up SWS buildings."

Rye sat up and, as zie shifted to the foot of the bed so that zie could reach the computer interface there, said, "You should ask about that tomorrow. When we've all had some sleep. Gotten over the adrenaline. I mean, we could ask tonight, but he seems to like you. And he seems, *seems*, like a normal guy. At least for our circles. Which means you might, as the saying goes, catch more flies with your honey than with pointing guns at him." Zie pointed at the computer interface. "May I?"

I also sat up, curious. "Sure. What are you going to do?" I stretched out so that I was propped up on my stomach with my head at the foot of the bed. I spoke to the air, "Ada access bedroom terminal. Activate guest account Riley." The computer blinked on. "There you go. Now tell me what you're doing."

Riles waggled zir eyebrows as zie typed. "I'm thinking it might be nice to have our own copy of whatever our new 'friend' has on his system and any online accounts or backups. His portable is already helping copy itself over, but I want to set up jobs to grab everything I can from his accounts. And we should grab everything *before* he finds a way to get to his system and change the codes. There must be *something* in there that will ease your conscience or make the case one way or the other. I mean, I don't know a single hacker who isn't reprehensible in some way. Including the three of us." Zie paused in zir typing. "I mean to really thoroughly dig into his stuff. So I've quietly tucked his hardware in the kitchen, behind some canisters, and left it on. Lest seeing it still up and running tempts him or freaks him out enough that he crashes about on his chair until he physically breaks it. And I want to look from here without any chance he'll see what's up."

"Shouldn't you be making sure you're safe before you do this?"

Zie shrugged. "I'll get his stuff transferring and then finish securing mine."

"So, you're going to sit in here and keep me awake?"

"Nope. I'm going to be so quiet that you won't even know I'm here." Zie smiled down at me. "Besides, Bryan can handle our 'guest' alone a couple hours, and I want to make sure you wake at my first gasp of discovery."

I rolled my eyes and moved back to the head of the bed so that I could try sleeping. "Okay. But I'm going to kick you if you wake me. Even for something good."

"Sounds fair."

I instructed, "Ada, bedroom lights off. Music off. Voice control of other lights approved for Riley and Bryan." I gave Riles a soft nudge with my foot. "Good night, poppet. Don't be stupid with my machine."

Riles laughed, a soft breath. "I'll behave. Just for you."

CHAPTER 8

I struck out with my right arm as someone poked at me. The someone exclaimed, "Whoa!" then poked me again. Because my right arm was already flung out and I was lying on my left, I tried just kicking back with my right foot. The voice snickered, "Not even close." I was finally awake enough to consider turning over to confront the intruder and to notice that flinging my right arm had been painfully stupid. I sighed and rolled over, face already set in a scowl. Bryan was grinning down at me.

"It's your turn to babysit." I moaned at this, then moaned again after he added, "And since we both stayed up to work on our stuff, you get to do it alone. Fun, huh?"

I pulled myself up to a sitting position and slipped my legs over the edge of the bed, glaring. "I hate you guys. I'm just going to kill him. Can I sleep if he's dead?"

Bryan laughed. "Sure! You do that. And whilst you work up to it, we're going to take over your room." He reached out to pull me up and point me towards the door. I dragged a blanket with me and trudged out past Rye.

Rye grinned, "Thought I'd wait outside and let Bryan handle this one."

"Genius. Coward," I grumbled and took a half-hearted swing at zir shoulder.

Zie easily dodged it, then gave my head a quick pet and reassured me, "Jonny's been quiet and well-behaved. And I made sure he pissed before we woke you, so you can just ignore him if he says otherwise. I'm sure you can handle him whilst we nap a few hours. Just shout out if he tries anything."

I nodded and continued my trudge towards the living room. I muttered, "Ada, coffee, please," and smelled the coffee before Ada even had a chance to respond. I love my computer.

Ada's voice breathed through her speakers. "Coffee already prepared by Bryan." Scratch that. I love my mates.

"Thanks, Ada." I paused in the kitchen and poured myself a

cup of nice, black coffee before finally reaching the couch. When I had time, I chose coffee over stims. I actually liked the taste and loved the smell and who doesn't love the warmth of a hot drink? (And, I had to admit, the new brand that Riles had picked up when we'd all gone shopping was better than what I usually kept on hand.)

In the living room, I was pleased to note that Jonny was asleep in his chair. I don't know how he managed that, but I guess exhaustion eventually wins out. His face looked pained, twitching as if in an unpleasant dream. *Good,* I thought. *No easy rest for murderers.*

I found a coaster so that I could set my coffee on the table. It wasn't so much about leaving rings on a table as it was about getting moisture on the furniture that held one of my computer interfaces, the best of them. I folded myself into the couch and manually booted the machine. No need to ask Ada to do it and risk waking Jonny. More peace for me if he slept.

I made my customary cruise through my accounts. The message from Riles to sum up what zie'd learned about Jonny was pretty short.

Looks like Jonny's pet projects usually involve stealing info from big corps. Maybe selling it. Anything interesting he's done outside that general area he either did with you in the past or is doing with you now. He was a well-behaved, smart geek kid. Didn't bother with college. Appears to have illegally downloaded even more music than your gran. Has spent too many hours on vidgames, just like the rest of us. Got along fine with his parents and 2 sisters until he sent them messages a couple years ago, when the SWS shit started from what I can see, telling them he couldn't talk to them for a while. They think he's on drugs or something. He ignores their email and they don't try to break his silence as often now as they used to. He seems legitimately nice. Seriously. (You might want to look at his email drafts.) He orders out for pho multiple times per

```
week and pepperoni pizza most other days, tipping
well. He hasn't dated, that I can tell, since a
few months before he fell into the SWS thing.
Emails from people dumping him usually cite
excessive online time and lack of financial
ambitions as reasons. Also, his porn viewing
habits aren't too creepy. So, basically, just need
to solve for the MASSIVE bomb/murder issue.
```

Not one to put off satisfying my curiosity, I headed straight for the drafts folder of the account from which Jonny had sent me the one message. And there I found multiple starts of messages to his family and to me. Or I assumed they were. The ones that read like family either had salutations like, "Dear Dad" or the recipient shared his last name. He'd almost broken the silence with them a number of times, and the emails were full of apologies for upsetting them and talked about how much he missed them. The ones that read like they were meant for me...well, it was a mix of obvious salutations or contextually likely things. Of those, every one of them was a different approach to trying to make contact *before* the bombing and in a less scary way. The most promising start was:

```
Hey MK,
There's some serious shit going down, and I
feel like it warrants putting aside privacy. I'm
sorry to have poked into your privacy before
giving you the chance to agree with me on that.
Have lunch with me this week and I'll tell you
anything you want about me to make up for it. Plus
tell you what's happening. Plus lunch is on me.
Plus plus plus
```

But most were something like that. Apologetic and far less likely to have caused his night to end in zip ties. I kind of wanted to pat him on the head and sweetly call him an idiot. Why the hell had he chosen the wrong way? (*Maybe because he's a murderer. "He seemed like a nice, quiet boy." They always say that about killers.* I chided myself.)

I checked to see if anyone had been poking around in my affairs. All seemed okay. I was about to start the sort of inquisitive poking into *other* people's affairs that might let me verify that they had not yet been swallowed up by SWS, but I felt like I was being watched and looked up to see Jonny awake and, yes, watching me. I resisted the urge to look away. I keyed my machine into a secure mode and tilted the screen down and closed, keeping my eyes on Jonny. He didn't look away.

I was feeling a bit surly, a natural response to being annoyed and conflicted about being attracted. I decided to see if I could make *him* look away first. Apparently sensing the challenge, Jonny didn't break eye contact. The corner of his mouth moved up into something like a half-smile and he raised a brow. Looked as if he'd misread this as "fun." We'd been having our little staring contest for what felt like minutes when I stood up, walked over, and, maintaining eye contact, smacked him upside the head. Hard. The jolt caused his eyes to move away from mine. I barked out a "ha!" and then walked back to my coffee and computer.

When I turned around to sit back in the chair, Jonny was trying to shake his hair back into place and watching me. I grumbled, "What?" and sipped my coffee.

Jonny gave me an actual smile. "Just admiring your new hair. I didn't get a real chance to mention it last night." I put one hand up to my hair without thinking, trying to smooth it a bit. "I don't know if it's the 'just woke' look or the new cut and color. But it's much more you than the previous style

t was hard to tell whether he was sincere or mocking. I wanted to think I understood this guy, but the bomb thing was just throwing me. Proving that I clearly had no damned clue.

I put my coffee down so that I could run both fingers through my hair. Spiky was fine, but sticking up funny from sleep wasn't. "So, you've been stalking me?"

Jonny looked confused for a moment, then embarrassed. "I guess so. Technically, yeah. That probably messes up my chances at getting your number, much less a date."

I was dumbfounded and didn't bother to hide it. "Wha...You *are* joking, aren't you?" Jonny shrugged at me. "You aren't. You know, if you thought I was attractive, you could have saved yourself some trouble and given yourself an actual chance by asking me out instead of stalking me. Instead of just *taking* my number. If you were really in Seattle before you knew who I was *and* you'd seen me, you had the opportunity."

Jonny flushed. "Yeah, that would have been better. Of course, you were nothing more than a pretty face until I knew what you did. A pretty face isn't usually worth the effort. I mean, that first night. And then I didn't think, once you found out who I really was, that you'd believe me if I told you that I also ended up at the Orpheum on my own. I know *I* wouldn't believe it."

I was quiet for a moment, a bit surprised by the frankness of his response, by his flushing. I still expected swagger and coyness from him; the bomber, murderer, and privacy invader were still part of him. Finally, I spoke quietly, a bit of venom in my voice that I hoped would follow through in my words. I needed to hold onto my anger to keep me safe from him. "Is this where you repeat yourself? Go on. Tell me again. Tell me why you thought I was safe to approach last night. Tell me why you tried to figure out who I was. Tell me how you found me. Tell me about the conspiracy. No, actually, tell me about the *bomb*. Tell me about the people you *killed*. Tell me why I was worth being spared, how you made that judgment call for me and not for 15 others. Tell me how you justified the *deaths*. And then tell me how you think *this* all ends in bed." I could hear an edge of hysteria creeping into the anger. Dammit. I took a deep breath. I didn't think he'd noticed. He looked ashamed and upset. Good. I went for a low blow with a dusting of lies. "You know, we've all read the drafts of email you *didn't* send. Everyone can tell you're stupid for me. So any sort of attempts at flirting have been rendered useless by murders and our mockery." I smirked a bit and sat up straighter. "Besides, flattery would only work on a girl who didn't already know she's something special." I had to shut my mouth. I could tell that my anger was starting to make me a little off-target and incoherent, but my sleepiness also had me feeling too distant to actually take my mouth back from the anger. Mouth shut. Careful breaths. Inwardly directed stern looks. *Pull it together, mate,* I thought at myself.

Jonny looked at his lap. "I wouldn't insult you by flattering. And maybe you could cut me a little slack." He looked up, his face a little harder and his tone a little sharper. "You don't like my approach. Fine. But I did what I thought was best for you. Plausible deniability. And I'd like a little credit for not just assuming you were already owned. That would have left you dead." He stumbled a moment. "Accidentally dead. That was all...that was all a mistake." He seemed to get his metaphorical feet back under him. "And a little credit for being smart enough to find you, which you're confident enough to know was a feat even after my lucky eavesdropping. And then a touch more for being as genial as possible during this whole...kidnapping. I didn't try to escape. I'm not even asking you to return my interest. Just asking for a little less damned abuse." He didn't look away when he was done.

I waited for a beat to see if he might blush or something. In the pause, I remembered that I was supposed to try the whole "more flies with honey" thing. When he didn't blush or turn his eyes, I summoned up my fake honey and laughed. It was a short but thoroughly amused sound. "Titanium nerves. Brainy and brave. For that, you get a little less damned abuse." I smiled and Jonny tried a smile of his own.

I gave Jonny a long, considering look. "Look, here's the real problem. Even if I grant you the wisdom of giving me plausible deniability, there's still the bomb and the deaths. You don't come off like a mad bomber or a murderer. Not in person and not in the interactions we've had online. But you blew up a building with 15 people. Could have been over 20 if everyone had been there. Could have included patients, people who aren't employed by SWS. Not even the headquarters. You blew up a different building, even though it was in the same basic metropolitan area and seems likely to be less important. And you did *that* instead of just releasing all the documents you grabbed that prove your cause is more than just. Why?"

Jonny considered his lap again, and his quiet answer was tinged with guilt. "Proof of concept, for one thing."

"What?"

He sighed. "One reason I blew up your building first was to make sure I could actually do it. Both that I'd gotten good information and that I'd figured out the explosive part right. Which I hadn't, even though your building is way smaller than headquarters, and..." He trailed off, sat in silence a moment. "And to prove that I could actually kill people in that situation. Because it won't be enough to blow up buildings; the information and ideas are in the *people*. In their heads. And I'm really damned sure that I'll only get one shot at the headquarters and the important people. Only one."

It was such a weak answer. I pushed back, "You know that they'll increase security now, right? You've just made your 'only one' shot harder. Idiot. And why not just release the documents? Spare yourself having to do that?"

Jonny shook his head. "They've got plans for that. One of the documents is what to do if someone leaks this information. Even if they don't have someone in government or media to let them know, to tip them off that the authorities are on to them, even if we forced it into everyone's email and onto every web site, they have plans. Different plans based on how far along they are. They might not have accomplished their end goals, but, at this point, they don't need more than a few minutes to enact a scorched earth and...in this case, that's pretty much capitalized, 'scorched Earth,' the planet, given the weapons they can probably shoot off. Scorch Earth and escape to some safe little island via helicopter. And that's *if* they have any trouble saying that the documents are forgeries, not sent from their servers. Plus, like I said, the information is also in people's heads. You have to...stop the people to stop what they're doing..." He actually sounded miserable, and his dry voice shook.

He looked me in the eyes. His own eyes were bloodshot and watery. "At this point, as far as I can tell, the only potential for success is to get in, send the documents from their headquarters to every leader and media outlet and anywhere else I can, and then immediately blow it. Wipe out enough that they can't go scorched Earth before someone does the right thing and shuts down their other offices. I could obviously make it *look like* it came from their IP, but I can't leave any chance that someone would be able to prove the spoofed IP. They have hackers we know on staff. You know those guys could figure it out."

We maintained the eye contact whilst I processed this. And then my face clouded with something like disbelief. "Wait, are you saying you're going to blow the building *immediately*, whilst you're still inside? This is a suicide mission?"

Jonny looked away, nodded. "Probably. I still haven't figured out how to be physically there, on their network, without being *right* there. I *have* figured out how to blow the building. Probably. Kind of." He shrugged, trying to look nonchalant, but the guilt was thick in his voice. "I have to take the options I have. I'm running out of time. *We're* running out of time, even if no one else knows it."

I gave a low whistle. "Damn. Guess I can't accuse you of doing it for the glory or of being willing to sacrifice everyone but yourself. But..." I couldn't help it. "That still seems really weak. And why a building in the same city? It just seems...both murderous and stupid. I mean, all signs point to you being the idealist you claim. Possibly even a sincerely nice person. But this was *horrible*. This was just...so fucked up. Proof of concept *murder?*"

His eyes got redder and he was swallowing a lot. He mumbled, "Dammit," as he seemed to struggle with himself. I didn't interrupt. I was kind of fascinated. This was unexpected...and I wondered if he'd actually fall off the edge and straight into actual tears.

He took a deep breath and his voice was rough with emotion. "So much for coming off as your peer, huh? Not exactly titanium nerves." Another deep breath and a little embarrassed laugh. Someday, if he turned out to be okay, I was going to make sure he knew that my own badass thing had been a performance.

He didn't cry and kept talking. "The initial chatter in the memos, and I can point you at the ones, made it sound like there was essential info processing at your building. And like there were some key things they had your clinic confirming. You know that the clinic in your building was always the first place outside the labs in headquarters to get involved with new tech, right?"

I nodded. He wasn't getting any better control of his emotions, but he pushed through. "Of course, I can also point you at the emails after Thursday that note they were delayed, not stopped, by the explosion..." He shook his head, as if clearing away some bad thought. "But before Thursday...Your building looked like an essential piece. And then, when I was looking, I found that there'd even been a bomb threat there a few months before. Maybe thanks to Karl Peterson? Too perfect, right?"

I must have gaped a little. Poor Karl Peterson had no idea he'd actually been involved in a bombing now. Jonny acknowledged my open mouth by saying, "I saw the guy's name in the police records after your interview, so I guess you followed breadcrumbs I'd hoped to the conclusion I'd hoped." I nodded.

A smile flitted over his face, just briefly, and then he was back to grim. This was either a great actor, a true madman, or someone wracked by guilt. "I actually sent the bombs in...Oh, I should explain about the bombs."

I shook my head. "No, we saw your bugs on the security camera feed. So I hope those aren't traceable, because I bet SWS will see them too. But, yeah, we noticed you sent them in days before."

"I didn't mean it to be so much before. I...I actually spent days trying to talk myself into triggering them once they were there. And even though I knew they could get discovered the longer they sat there...I couldn't do it. But then..." He paused. "Tuesday, I looked into when the lab might have fewer people. Like I said, I miscalculated with the explosives; I was only going to blow the lab. And, on Thursdays, they don't have clients. They just do proof of concept testing, number crunching, that sort of thing. So, I started trying to talk myself into it. And...Did you hear the story Tuesday night about that girl shooting up the kids at an afterschool camp she was working at and then herself?"

"Oh, yeah...That was just so gruesome. Nine dead, seven others wounded. All kids, except her. But..." My brain was starting to push at something. "Wasn't she a previous Peacemaker client?"

The Peacemaker, now finally filtering out into the wider public, had been under testing and development the last few years. Really, a couple years of development and testing on criminals, and then about a year or so where rich parents could get in on the action. Is your kid acting out? Is your kid smoking, drinking, using drugs, having sex, dressing in ways that scandalize you at the country club? Is your kid depressed,

Autistic, or just not constantly happy and normal? Is your kid gay, non-binary gendered, or maybe even just a little too liberal? (Not that they'd say most of those outright, especially in tolerant Seattle, but some people would always cling to old prejudices and shames.) Basically, if you felt like your kid wasn't being how you wanted or maybe you just wanted to make sure they stayed as they were, you paid SWS a tidy sum, and SWS put a little machine in at the base of your kid's skull. Peacemaker. Like a pacemaker...for their brain...to give you peace (though you'll claim it's to give the kid—or the criminal—peace). Haha. Clever name. Ugh. Just the thought of Peacemakers made me shudder.

"Yeah, she'd had her Peacemaker taken out, and the SWS media spin was that her parents and therapist were wrong about her being ready to have it removed. They pointed out the others who've had it removed with no issues. Anyway...Witnesses said the girl was crying as she did it and talking about completing the mission the men in her dreams gave her.

"Obviously, SWS were already firmly on my radar, so of course I saw memos fly Tuesday. Memos that made it sound like they'd had some big success, but nothing about the current scandal they were facing. Digging into files showed what looked like research results that hinted the Peacemaker could be used to cause a person to do that. And a few drafts of their press response, the one that ended up trying to remove the blame from the Peacemaker, were from days *before* it happened."

"No way!" I saw Jonny's portable was now back by the couch, so I booted it and connected it to the wall TV.

Jonny watched, curiosity on his face overwhelming his other emotions for a while. When he saw that I was heading into the SWS file system he said, "Look at the CEO's emails for that evening, but also look in her Press Drafts folder." My fingers quickly got me there, and he was right. I stood up, went to the TV to stare at the drafts and emails. I could have just looked on his portable's screen, but a nervous energy wanted me to move. This was just adding to the list of threats SWS might pose. Inching me closer to committing to Jonny's cause. When I turned back to him, he looked deflated.

And his voice was a mix of defeat and resolve. "I saw this and I knew. I couldn't wait. Though, obviously, I did. But that was because of the 'no clients on Thursday' thing."

I walked back and sat on the edge of the couch, woodenly typing the commands to back out of the SWS system. This was beyond crazy. I looked up when I was done. There were a few things that still didn't add up, and those had to be addressed.

"But murder. *Murder*, Jonny. There had to have been an alternative. For the people in the lab *and* those of use who weren't."

Jonny's face was twisted in some kind of emotional pain for a moment until he saw me looking and smoothed it back out to the grim neutral he'd been in. "I looked. I tried." He was practically begging me to believe him. "I *swear* I tried. The people in the lab...I searched for options to make their brains less dangerous. I...I figured anything that just made them vegetables was as bad as death. Maybe worse. But taking out memories? The least-bad option I could find would have taken a whole team and equipment and time. I'd have to hold them captive and basically brainwash them. And, even then, hope their functioning minds couldn't just come up with things again." His hands, zip tied to the chair, twisted so they were open, pleading. "I *tried*." His voice broke and there were tears brimming in his eyes.

I narrowed my eyes, wanting to believe but doubting. I didn't say a word, but held up a hand to silence him. I turned my attention back to his portable, dug through his search and browsing history, including the parts that he'd deleted (but not deleted enough...you have to *work* to clean things entirely out of memory). It took me a good hour and, to his credit, he kept his mouth shut (though I could hear him carefully taking deep breaths). But, after an hour, there were the traces. Visits to hidden boards on the 'Net where people got specific about inflicting memory loss, the searches to learn more about drugs and equipment mentioned on those boards, and what looked like hunting for a place where he might be able to keep all the lab staff for days or weeks. Planted or real? I didn't know. But the data seemed older, more fragmented by disc overwriting. He had either been playing a long game, looking for this before he was even in town (or so it seemed from other things that appeared the same age on his portable), or he was legit. I felt a wall inside of me go down. I believed him.

And I couldn't come up with other ideas for how he could have solved it. Maybe Bryan could have, but I couldn't judge him by Bryan's areas of knowledge. Not unless I was willing to judge myself and what I would have done. And Bryan had both different knowledge and a small but reliable team of us to work with. Shit.

I saw he was sitting with his head hung down and he startled a little when I softly said, "Okay." I put what was left of my doubt and anger and loathing into my next question. My last attempt to decide he was just an evil fuck and not someone who'd made hard choices I couldn't agree with. "But what about all of us outside the lab? What the hell about the rest of us?"

I watched his jaw move as he tried to grind away whatever emotion was surging up. He opened his mouth, closed it, and tears came quickly. He didn't make crying noises, but his voice was jagged. "That was an accident." It was lame, and I could tell he knew it. But he continued on. "The lab staff was...hard. So hard to talk myself into. But the rest...The rest weren't supposed to happen. I just...I fucked up. I...I thought I'd figured out where to put the bugs and I thought my big brain was enough to figure it out...but I was...I was clearly wrong. And...I'm so, so sorry. And that will make it easier to do a suicide mission. Because I *should* die."

I let that hang there a moment, gave him a chance to pull himself together, before I flatly asked, "An accident? Then why send me out of the building? You miserable liar." I ended on a growl.

"I didn't correctly calculate how the basement lunchroom would impact things." He was speaking through clenched teeth, not out of anger but, it seemed, to keep control. "An accident. And I sent you out because...because, at least online, you're my friend...and I just wanted to be extra careful, get you as far out as possible. Away from even possible..." He shrugged. "I thought maybe those suspended ceiling tiles might fall. Nothing big but...But the person I knew online and the person I felt like I knew through trying to figure out who you were...I just...I couldn't risk her. You. If I had actual titanium nerves, I'd have left you there. But I'm...I'm just trying to think my way, fake my way, through something too big for me. And...I'm glad you're alive but I'm so...so sorry." And he was crying again. Not a dramatic storm, but quiet and, I swear, heavy with regret and guilt.

And, whilst part of me wondered if I were just soft for tears, I felt myself believing him. Believing that he'd tried, that it had been an accident, that I was alive because of what might be seen as his weakness. Another of my internal walls went down. Well, damn...

His voice was almost under control. Getting there. "I wish I'd sent you one of the draft emails. And I wish I'd found a better solution. I wish I'd gotten the damned explosives right. I..." He paused a moment and took a deep breath. "I'm sorry. I haven't really slept well since. Nightmares." He tried to use his shoulders to wipe some of the wetness from his face.

I took a deep breath of my own, let it go. "At this point, until or unless we prove you're full of shit, I promise to try to remember not to harass you about what you did. And you should tell the other two what you told me. All of it. We might do morally questionable things, but we tend to have a negative reaction to what looks like the wanton murder of innocents. Knowing the whole story helps, okay?"

Jonny nodded. "Yeah. Fair. I'll catch them up when they wake up."

My intuition (which I was grateful to have reason to maybe not see as broken) was that he was telling the truth about everything, including parts that no data scouring could confirm or disprove. And now I felt a little bad about my behavior earlier. I knew better than to rely on anger. I'd been raised on the right films by my gran. I knew that anger was one step on the path to the Dark Side. I might not be totally law-abiding, but I thought of myself as being on the side of light. I'd let fear and my hatred of morning (or whatever was passing for morning in my life) and all the difficult emotions that death caused bring out my ugly side.

I hoped my tone was sufficiently kinder. "Want food?"

Jonny nodded. "Yes, please."

I didn't exactly have a load of options, so I quickly poured bowls of cereal for both of us. Of course, when I brought them back into the living room, I realized I was going to have to feed him or cut his hands loose. I should not have been left in charge of a prisoner. Feeding him it was.

I pulled another chair and a side table over. I shrugged as I sat down, facing him and feeling very keenly that I was close to him. You know, that way you suddenly realize you're within reach, within the range of possible touch, when near someone attractive? I'm inclined towards quick judgments, and I was having a hard time, given the conversation we'd just had, not just going along with my intuition. Especially since it would let me be done with the shame at being attracted to him that I'd been feeling last night. Which meant that the part of my brain that was controlled by my libido and the part that found intelligence sexy had ganged up to start whispering the stupid little temptations that put static in human brains when they're attracted. When the walls went down and his shame erased much of mine, a switch had flipped. Dammit.

I took a bite first, putting off what felt like the overly-personal act of feeding him. He'd been quiet, so I barely managed to not startle when he spoke.

"I'm sorry." He paused a moment, then slowly went on. "I do stand by my choices, but I really never wanted to fuck up your life, invade your privacy, or even just annoy you. Much less kill anyone. *Anyone.*"

I was chewing my bite carefully, as part of my plan to play it cool.

"I think, in my mind, the logic and brilliance of my plan were supposed to cancel out the human factor. And..." He faltered, paused, sighed.

I put down my bowl and picked up his, not making eye contact as I got a bite ready.

"And, yeah, I guess I did foolishly think, or at least hope, this ended differently. Because I didn't just manage to suss out who you were and that you were innocent, but also that you were...you *are* pretty damned cool."

I finally looked up. I had to if I were going to get a bite in his mouth and stop him before I got too awkward. Eye contact. His eyes were beautiful. Damn him.

"I hope, when all is said and done, we can at least be..." he shrugged and looked aside a moment, considering, then looked back at me. "Amiable allies. At least." And then I cut him off with a bite. And kept him quiet that way.

Once his bowl was empty, I put off other discussion by turning on the news (SWS CEO Mary Johnson and her usual two cohorts were assuring investors that the tragic bombing wouldn't impact their research or production schedules) and then getting back to trying to verify pieces of Jonny's story. The only thing I made eye contact with was my computer. I tried not to notice that Jonny was sneaking looks at me. I was grateful when I heard Bryan and Riles coming out of the bedroom after only a few hours of sleep.

Bryan slapped on some stims and Riles started on zir first of many cups of coffee. Rye plopped onto the couch beside me and asked, "Do I detect a slight decrease in tension?"

I nodded. "Yes on the decrease and...I think it would be nice if Jonny got 'a little less damned abuse.' Or something like that." I stood and headed towards the bathroom. "I'm going to get dressed and groom. Jonny, maybe catch them up on what you told me earlier. All of it. It will help."

I took my time dressing. I wanted to let Jonny get the others caught up. And I wanted to give myself the chance to process what I'd heard. I wasn't sure I was ready to join up with Jonny's full effort, but I was definitely ready to take out some of our peers—in a non-deadly way—and maybe trust Jonny a little more. When I found my brain just going around in circles, I went back out to the living room.

The living room was quiet. They'd even turned off the news. Jonny (eyes slightly red but no obvious tears on his face) was looking back and forth between Rye and Bryan, and Rye and Bryan were in thoughtful poses. Rye was leaned against the back of the couch, one arm folded across zir chest and the elbow of the other rested on that arm, whilst the hand of that second arm was up by zir face. Bryan was leaned forward, hands clasped together, face rested on hands and elbows rested on knees.

Everyone looked at me. Riles moved zir hand from zir face, out into a sort of hopeless and confused gesture.

I asked, "So, he told you why he blew up the building?"

Riles and Bryan nodded and I sat down on the couch. I asked Jonny, "You told them everything? Even the stuff I had to prompt you to tell me?"

He nodded.

I pulled his portable onto my lap. Rye and Bryan leaned in, and I showed them how and where and what I'd found in terms of proof he'd considered non-lethal ways of dealing with the lab staff.

When they sat back, I looked at Bryan, then at Riles. "So?"

Bryan sat up, regarded his hands, then looked at Jonny. "I guess, at least for me, the one big piece of information we're missing, other than just spending some more time verifying this is true, is why you were looking into SWS. What's the story? *Is* there a story?"

Jonny nodded. "There *is* a story. I was living in New Mexico, and one of the guys I hung out with did some off-the-record medical stuff on the side. There's always a place for someone who takes out bullets without asking questions.

"One night, I'm in his living room, hanging out with his boyfriend because something came up last minute. He's in the back room, taking care of someone. I don't think much of it, and I instinctively don't watch faces as people leave from the back room. But I do see the backs of heads. And it's clear that one of them has just had something done to the back of her head.

"At that point, I figure it's nothing like bullets or the usual dangerous criminals in need of a doctor. Which is why I asked what was up.

"My friend tells me that he's just pulled something out of this girl's head, and it's not the first time. That there's been an uneven trickle of people in for that since the first time he successfully extracted the device.

"He drinks and starts telling me the stories he's heard from the people who have this thing. And...it's like some sort of fucked up tracker, but it can also monitor and maybe affect moods. He says it's tapped into all sorts of places and seems set up to do more than the tracking and mood monitoring the unlucky wearers had told him about. I mean, he's basically doing complicated brain surgery on them. Taking out the disk and the little metal tendrils it weaves into the brain.

"He tells me he wasn't actually able to get it out of the first guy who came to him. The guy died, but my friend figured he'd, for want of a better word, autopsy him to see what was up. Which is why the second person who came to him lived.

"Turned out, that little device was being made by SWS."

Riles asked, "Peacemaker?"

Jonny nodded. "Peacemaker. And it just sounded fishy. The sort of thing that would set off any hacker's antiestablishment sirens, the sort of thing that goes against everything I believe in. And, given my own illegal activities, the sort of thing that could end up in *my* head. So I started looking into SWS and I asked my friend to see if any of the people he'd dug one out of would talk to me.

"One of them, the one I'd seen walking out, agreed to meet and talk. She didn't really have a lot useful to say, not in terms of what I'm doing right now. But her story convinced me that this was not okay. Not at all.

"I got righteously furious and decided to make this my cause." He shrugged. "Life is more fulfilling with a cause. And then, when SWS started advertising the success of the Peacemakers, which were obviously the same thing that had been pulled out of that girl's head...I couldn't sit still. I moved here, to the den of the beast. And now, hopefully, I'm going to slay the bastard."

CHAPTER 9

We'd set up the wall TV with a movie, because it was hard to leave Jonny sitting around in silence now that it seemed like maybe he wasn't just a violent mad man, but I was already dead sick of the news and the SWS news conferences. We'd also set up an alert to let us know if the news feeds claimed to have new information about the bombing, and we'd gone to work verifying everything Jonny had told us. Digging through files, verifying they weren't created by Jonny, looking for more information. I was *so* over my policy of not hacking SWS.

I swam through their files like a digital piranha, ready to chew it all up.

We'd divided the work. I was digging into the files from clump 1, verifying that SWS were, indeed, bent on global domination. Bryan was digging into the clump 2 issue, verifying it was what it looked like, and then seeing just what our compromised peers had been up to. Because he'd done the most digging into Jonny's files, Riley was continuing to sort through all that. That's where we'd be most likely to find proof, if it existed, that could support Jonny's claims about his own moral character.

We had a group chat open on our screens to allow us some private conversation without having to leave the room, and we'd post notes as we verified things. It was sporadic, because we were being thorough, but, at least in my opinion, Jonny's claims were totally substantiated. And even the harder-to-substantiate question of his character was getting little bits of answers that were in his favor. SWS were up to something extra-nasty and they were pulling a few too many hacker strings. And Jonny was maybe not an actual monster.

Bryan was generally a soft touch on the keys, so I knew when he was typing something angrily for the chat. It was the only time I really heard him, and it was happening a lot as he verified ugly truths. Riles was a fast and audible typist. Each keystroke a staccato beat in zir work. I was momentarily distracted by the pace of zir typing. Quick, quick, wait. Quick, quick, wait. But I made myself focus on my own issues.

I was almost done with the documents from Jonny's system. Open, read, find on the SWS system, verify it was created by someone at SWS and not Jonny, post results to the group chat if they confirmed some new point. Next document.

Subject: Elder Care Update
All conversations with senators friendly to us suggest that our Elder Care bill is on its way to passing. It's been inserted into a bill about funding Medicare. (You can watch the progress yourself by following the "Silver Standard Reassurance" bill.)

Our line of reasoning and willingness to absorb the costs we've claimed have worked as hoped. We should be able to proceed with widespread implantation, with the full backing of the law, beginning mid-November.

Our parallel, quiet effort to reach out to seniors and, where necessary, their guardians to help them buy into our public-facing purpose for the bill is very well-received. This should also minimize public resistance when this becomes wider known in November.

It was early October. Whatever this was, it was soon. And "widespread implantation" would have worried me even before I knew that SWS were up to no good.

I did a search for the Silver Standard Reassurance bill and discovered that it was both real and well-supported. It was currently forecast to have more bipartisan support than the average bill. And word was the House of Representatives was strongly leaning that way as well. Which meant I had to take this seriously, whatever "this" was.

Fortunately, getting my hands on the text of the bill was no problem. I didn't even have to do anything illegal; it was posted in full a number of places. It was huge, of course, so I crossed my fingers and just did a search for "Secure World Systems." And there it was.

I had to read it a couple times to parse it. And then once more to make sure that it really did say what I thought it said…"Shit." I looked up to make sure my little swear word had gotten me everyone's attention.

"There's a bill in the senate right now, and it *is* going to pass. And, when it does, everyone 60 and older is going to get a 'subdermal monitor,' manufactured by SWS, courtesy of both SWS and the state. Nothing as obviously dramatic as a Peacemaker, but also not something they could accidentally lose or break by smashing against anything in the event of a fall. And, of course, it's for their own good." I put on an exaggerated jovial tone. "Fallen and you can't get up? Oh, we know. And we're on our way. Having a stroke or not taking care of your diabetes? Your doctor already knows." I sighed and dropped the joviality. "It will start in Seattle, it will be so quick and easy…they can just go house to house…it would be done in a matter of a few months at most." I was skimming for the relevant bits. "And, obviously, you put it in around the base of the skull…the better to detect equilibrium issues or falls…the better to keep it somewhere unlikely to take any accidental blows. Up by the brain and near-ish the organs. And," I felt my jaw clenching, "just in case her youthful attitude has you fooled, that definitely means Gran. That means fucking SWS tech in my gran's head whether she wants it or not."

Riles put a hand on my shoulder. "We can stop this, Kot. Voting is electronic and the bill text is online and I've got practice fucking with politicians. We'll stop this."

Bryan sounded growly as he confirmed, "No-fucking-thing is going into Gran's head. Or any other part of her."

Jonny uncertainly offered, "I'll happily help stop that too."

I nodded. "Okay. Okay. Good. So…So I'm now going to go dig out their specs on the tracker. I know we were Peacemaker-focused but…This has to be part of the deal now. Or I'll fucking handle it myself."

I started poking at files again, hunting. And Riles gave my shoulder a last squeeze. "You won't have to handle it yourself. You have us."

I dove deep into the folders that seemed to hold their chief development team's specs. I started grabbing documents in droves. I could hear Riles typing rapidly to my right. Quicker, quicker, wait (and jiggle knee impatiently whilst waiting). *Zie's on the case too*, I thought. *If anyone can stop this, zie can.*

Half an hour later, Riles let out a rush of air and stood up. "You two who aren't tied to chairs, kitchen now. Please."

Bryan and I gave each other curious looks, but didn't argue. We both closed our computers and followed zir.

Riley spoke quietly. "Digging in his files," and zie nodded towards the living room, just in case we didn't know zie meant Jonny, "I ran across what turned out to be the contact info for his New Mexico doctor. Very carefully hidden. I did what I could to check out the doctor, and he's definitely doing things to earn money in addition to his hospital pay. But, at least for our context, the doctor seems clean. And he was online."

Zie leaned back, looked into the living room, then moved zir head closer to us. "Maybe it's all an elaborate set up, but I can't figure out what his endgame would be. And chatting with the doctor...I don't want to trust him. You know I don't want to trust anyone but you guys and my bae. And I'm going to keep looking at his screen and poking at his files when I need a break from the other stuff...all the way until this is over...But I think there are reasons to believe him. I'm not actually entirely unreasonable." Zie paused for a moment, gave us a chance to make like we were going to protest. "Not entirely. 'Entirely' being the key word, you assholes."

Bryan confirmed, "Are you saying you're voting to team up with him?"

Riles shrugged in a pained sort of way. "I want to not vote that way. I want to keep clear of what's obviously a dangerous situation, you know? But...at this point, I think he's legit and I think SWS are some kind of supervillain-level evil. And I think, if nothing else, we have to shut down what they're doing in our online community *and*," zie grabbed my hand, "most especially, we have to stop them from getting their shit in Gran's head."

Bryan nodded. "Yeah. I'm with you. As I see it, we either have to team up with him, keep him captive the whole time we do it ourselves, or have him killed." When Riles and I looked at each other and then him with wide eyes, he assured us, "I'm definitely not voting for killing him. I don't think he's evil, and I know that *we* aren't. He just...made a choice or two I really wish he hadn't. And I feel like keeping him captive would be more challenge than we're up for. At least if we're also taking down a dangerous, influential corporation."

Rye added, "He took the usual psych evals in high school, and he's not crazy. Though, if he's the nice guy he seems, he could be driving himself there with this thing." Zie looked at me. "Kot? Opinion?"

I put my hands on my head and tried to keep my moan of frustration quiet. "If I promise not to complain about the quiet ever again, can we rewind to a week ago and run away to live on an island?" I put my hands down. "Especially based on how he seemed when I got more info from him, I don't think he's a psycho. And the info on SWS seems totally legit and scary. It sounds like what info we have points to him being a nice person in a fucked up situation. And, one way or another, we have to take action."

"But do you trust him?" Riles pushed.

"My intuition is in his favor. The facts are in his favor. I definitely don't want to kill him or have to babysit him. Not even if it would give me excuses to monitor his showers and leer." I tried to smirk through my confusion. Because weak attempts at inappropriate humor make things easier, right?

Bryan admitted, "My instincts also say he's okay. On the way to crazy, like Rye said, but not there yet. I mean...he's either an incredible actor who's set up a really sterling, sophisticated ruse, including things online and on his computer that *we* should be able to pull apart if it's fake...or he's legit. And we need to get working. With him."

Rye guessed where this was headed. "Bryan, you actually want to untie him?"

"Yeah, actually." I guess both Rye and I looked equally shocked, because Bryan laughed a little then said, "Don't worry. I still don't *really* trust him, and not at all like I trust you. But I'm feeling like, if he *is* going to be on our team, we'll do better if he can actually sleep. And work. And we'll want to start working towards trust before we do...whatever it is we have to finally do to end SWS. Plus," and he looked to Riles, "I'm sure you spent as much time digging into him and his computer as you did on fixing your own stuff." Riles nodded. "Did you find anything that, for our purposes, is a problem?"

"Nothing. I mean, I found proof of the same sort of things that we too are guilty of. This guy is truly our peer. We didn't need to dig in his stuff to know *that*."

"I know this might sound biased," I was hesitant but figured we needed to get all the facts out, "and I totally admit that, now that I believe his story about why he blew up the building, I'm back to being attracted. But, I read those unsent drafts of emails to me. He *did* consider approaching me before the bombing. But he...he might have been right not to. Even if that means I'll have to find a less creepy excuse to see him naked than 'monitoring showers.'"

Riley sounded loathe to agree but still said, "Yeah...with what we've seen and with plausible deniability...there's an argument to be made for how he chose to proceed. Plus," and zie sighed, "there are all those little bits of residual data that *seem* to support his claim of trying to find another solution and even hints that anything but the lab blowing really was an accident."

We shared a collective sigh and moment of silence then.

"So, you're voting we untie him?" I asked.

Bryan nodded. "We still keep watch. He doesn't get to be alone at first and, for now, doesn't get to touch even the TV remote without us watching. And I'll probably keep my gun in easy reach. But..."

"But we might want to have him functional and build some trust before he decides we're too paranoid to be his conspiracy pals." Riles finished Bryan's sentence for him. We all paused a moment, looking at each other, and then we nodded.

I grabbed a knife and we walked back in. Just for fun, I stood a moment in front of Jonny, feigning consideration as I tried to do that thing where you're nonchalantly holding a knife but it's menacing. This might be my last chance to pretend to be a badass. Again, we exchanged looks and nods. Jonny tried to look cool, but he mostly looked at the knife in my hands. I could taste his waiting. I could feel his held breath as the knife and I moved forward. I almost laughed at the palpable relief that poured off him as the only thing I cut were the zip ties that held him to the chair. And then my two friends and I sat down.

Jonny didn't get up from the chair. I don't know that I would have either. What do you do when you're cut loose but not actually looking for escape? When the people who'd tied you up cut you loose, but did it without pats on the back or making a friendly fuss...When it's all solemn faces that don't look full of trust and happiness.

Jonny looked at us for confirmation, then stood, slowly stretched (no sudden movements), and asked, "So, does this mean a little trust? If I need to piss, do I get to do that un-chaperoned?"

Bryan shook his head. "Not yet. Baby steps, mate."

"But," I added, "It *does* mean a little trust. A *little*. And it means that, at the moment, you're no longer working solo."

Jonny's face opened into the most genuine smile I'd seen since we grabbed him...had it just been last night? Too much happening. Too little sleep. And too much left to do if we were going to keep SWS off the throne and out of my gran's head.

CHAPTER 10

Whilst Bryan chaperoned Jonny's trip to the bathroom, I tossed out the cut zip ties and Riles moved the chair back off to the side. Zie said, "I think he should sit between us on the couch. Hopefully, we can manage between us to keep an eye on him and, even if not, maybe he'll be too scared of being caught and won't try anything."

"What should we have him work on? What's safe?"

"I feel like maybe now is a good time to break for food, and then maybe talk plans."

I nodded. "Yep. That makes sense." I opened the fridge. "I'm a little light on food. So, pizza?"

The two boys came back from the bathroom, and Rye informed them, "We're going to order out for pizza." Zie seemed a little smug when zie told Jonny, "Don't worry, we already know what you like."

I headed over to the couch to order online, and Riles headed for the other end of the couch. Zie patted the cushion between us and said to Jonny, "Think of this as your spot for the foreseeable future."

"Cool." Jonny sat slowly between us. It looked like he was trying to make sure he was centered on his cushion. "Thanks for the seating upgrade."

I finished our pizza order and a notification informed me that we only had a 15-minute wait. "They must be having a slow day. 15 minutes until food."

Bryan opened his computer with a "Just enough time to finish the doc I was in," and Riley got back up, asking, "Drinks?" We all nodded.

"I think it's just beer, but I'll see if there's anything buried in her cupboards."

I pulled up news on the wall TV. They didn't seem to have any new information, but were now pretty much pleading for help to find me or for me to come forward and talk to them.

There were plenty of shots of my work clothes and boring hair, failed attempts to get a shot of my face. On the first shot, Jonny mumbled, "Sorry to get you caught on camera like that. Not your best look, is it?"

I narrowed my eyes at him but didn't respond. He was right. It wasn't my best look. Plus, the apologetic smile he flashed at me right after he said that suggested he wasn't trying to be an asshole. A few moments later, they showed footage that looked like they had been trying to get a closeup of my palms, my knees, and the bruise on my back. Jonny spoke quietly. "I didn't know you'd get hit. Knocked down. I'm totally sorry. I thought your parking spot was far enough away to avoid that. That I was being *too* cautious..."

I looked around to see if Bryan or Riley were paying attention, but I got the sense one was pretending to work on his laptop and the other was hanging back in the kitchen. All the better for eavesdropping. I looked at the news and shrugged. "Unless you're a demo expert, I couldn't exactly expect you to get it just right."

"Are you still sore?"

"Not as bad as the first few days, but, yeah."

"Can I see?"

The sounds of typing stopped in Bryan's chair and it was suddenly entirely quiet in the kitchen.

I drew my brows together in confusion as I looked at him. "Why? Was I right when I tagged you as a sadist?"

Jonny shrugged self-consciously. "I don't know. I just want to understand what I did, I think. I'm not exactly a cold-blooded murderer by nature. I want to move forward without delusions. With a clearer picture of the consequences. I feel like I shouldn't avert my eyes." He kind of made sense.

I turned my back to him and pulled my tank top aside so he could see the bruise and abrasions. (Turned that way, I saw Bryan give me a questioning look, like he was making sure it was okay. I gave him a small smile that I hoped was reassuring. This was fine. For now.) The abrasions had scabbed over enough that I'd taken off the plasters on those at bedtime the night before, as well as the ones on most of the damage on my knees. I appreciated that he inhaled sharply at the sight of my back.

"I'm so sorry." He kept muttering that until I turned to face him. I watched his face as I peeled off the remaining plasters on my knees. He looked serious and guilty.

When I took off the dressing on my right palm, I was pleased to see he looked mortified. I grabbed alcohol wipes, the sterile foam, and some plasters off of a side table, and turned back to him again, right palm up. I handed him the supplies. As I did that, I saw that Rye was just standing quietly in the kitchen doorway, watching.

Jonny kept muttering apologies as he cleaned my right palm and then applied a fresh layer of foam and plasters where they were still very necessary. His worked gingerly, like he was afraid of hurting me more.

I resisted wincing and remarked, "Yeah, this stuff is what gives me the ability to hold a gun, or a throat, in spite of the damage. They're serious about the foam's analgesic qualities."

Jonny put his hands under mine and carefully held them from beneath, looking at the palms. (I saw Riles stand up extra straight in the doorway and could swear I sensed Bryan ready to pounce behind me.) "I really didn't think you'd get hurt at all."

"Not to make your little mission harder, but do you know for sure that all the other people, the ones you didn't save, were bad guys? Did you take the time to look at every one of them?"

The door buzzed. I looked at the camera view for the front door. "Pizza."

Bryan hopped up and I told his retreating back, "Already paid and tipped." Then turned back to Jonny. "The other people?"

Jonny was very still. His answer was slow in coming. "I knew that I might trip something up if I stopped to look. That I might look into the wrong person, someone who had tricky security or was being watched. And that I'd get caught before I could do anything. So I told myself that it was the sacrifice of the few for the good of the many. And that it was only people in the lab." He took a deep breath. "It's easier to kill people you don't know good things about." He abruptly, self-consciously let go of my hands, put the cap on the foam, and set it back on the table.

Bryan placed pizza on the coffee table, carefully away from my computer screen, and picked up the foam. As he sat in his chair, he put the foam back on the side table where it had originally been, and then went back to pretending he was using his computer.

I realized I hadn't moved. I pulled my hands back in and watched the guilt on Jonny's face. He was a nice guy, not the sort of person who was going to make it through to the end of his goal with his sanity intact. Of that I was sure. Not going this way at least. He noticed me watching his face and looked away.

I sighed. "Listen, you're obviously too nice to do what you think you want to do."

He interjected, "Need to do. Not want to do."

"Okay. Need to do. You're probably too nice to do it. At least if your plan is to blow up buildings full of people until they're all gone. You need a different plan. And you need to work with people who have slightly more flexible morals. Or *connections* to people with even more flexible morals." I grimaced. "Some of us have justified acts beyond liberation of information. Some of us aren't as nice as you. We're closer to that line, so maybe we can do it more easily than you. Or at least, working together, we can help get each other over the line. Or somehow avoid the line. Or loop in people already on the other side of the line."

Jonny gave a weak little half smile. "I thought I could let righteous indignation carry me through. But you're right. I have to find another way. And I need to work with people who don't mind doing the stuff that I'm not okay with. Even if it's just one building we really need to hit."

"Just one?" Bryan was done watching quietly. He leaned forward to grab pizza now that he'd dispelled the illusion of a private conversation.

When Jonny nodded, I went on, "We'll have to come back to that 'just one,' cos I feel like you should have mentioned that earlier. But can you even be okay with suggesting that people take actions that you aren't okay with? Don't you have some ownership in those deeds when they're done?"

Riley, beers in one hand and plates in the other, walked back to the couch. "Your psych eval results suggest you won't even get away with *that* easily." Zie seemed intent on keeping up the reminders that we (well, zie...but I planned to spend some time on doing it later too) had destroyed Jonny's privacy at least as much as he'd trespassed mine. "You're already cracking from what you did last week." Zie put plates and beers on the table, and we all helped ourselves.

Johnny paused before answering, which might have been to get himself food or might have been to consider how to respond to Riles. "Yeah. So I guess what I really need is another strategist. Or three. Or someone to plan with so that we can work together to see if there's something I missed, a way to minimize or *avoid* the body count. Or maybe to help me follow through on what I...on what *we* know is the right thing to do. Or at least someone to help make sure I've seen all the important pieces of the puzzle and grabbed all the important information." He shook his head. "My smart doesn't include much strategy. Not for this kind of situation."

"We can do some strategy. I mean, this isn't any of our areas of expertise either, but we can at least come up with ideas. And we have personal stake in this. We had it even before you blew up my building; we just didn't know it." I jabbed a finger towards Jonny. "You don't even get a choice in this. We're involved. And we're taking you along. Because you're already involved. And because I don't trust you enough now to let you run around on your own."

"Fair enough. Though I think I'll appreciate the situation more when I'm allowed to use the bathroom without an escort." He laughed uneasily and the rest of us at least gave him small smiles.

"Dream big, mate," Bryan wryly encouraged. "Dream big."

With a little food and beer in us, moods were lighter than they had been. I felt done being angry at Jonny and not so inclined to solve problems with bullets. As I shoved the pizza boxes into the composting chute, Bryan said, "Right," in a way that told me it was time for a team meeting.

I came back and got my computer open, and I saw Jonny grin out of the corner of my eye when Rye handed him his portable. There was an extended pause. Which didn't surprise me. Three of us knew we all had strong personalities and heads full of ideas and we tried to pretend to be respectful...and none of us actually wanted to be stuck running the show. It was a quirk of the group dynamic that occasionally drove us a bit crazy. Like now. I kind of wished someone would talk.

I decided that, given this all started with me almost getting blown up, I was probably okay to jump in first. Nobody should be able to bitch. So, naturally, the first thing I did was hand things off. "Jonny, it sounds like you've already got something of a plan. Or at least something about one building that you should have mentioned. Maybe start there?" When everyone nodded assent, Jonny outlined his plan.

"As far as I can tell, though I definitely think we ought to keep digging into their computers, the SWS headquarters is the only building that needs to be blown now. If we blow that, it sounds like they haven't had a chance yet to expand their really important equipment out to other sites yet. There's no evidence they've even tried. I think they're waiting to make sure it all works as expected first. And..." He shifted uncomfortably. "And that's the building where it seems most the top staff and the main minds...the people with the full picture and the core tech ideas are working."

And then we paused a moment for all of us to shift uncomfortably, like some kind of synchronized shifting team. Even the most morally flexible of us weren't comfortable with multiple murders.

"Do we..." I cleared my throat and tried again. "Do we know that we need to...to kill those minds?"

Johnny hesitated, but finally said, "Well, I'd love to find another way. But the only thing I found that's even rumored to actually be able to...erase information without leaving them vegetables...As long as we have time to research, gather whatever drugs or equipment we need for it, and then grab all the people we decide are key and...hold them and brainwipe them..."

Bryan made a "huh" sound and rubbed his head. "I'll take the data we can get from you or your computer and research. But...everybody cross fingers or light candles or whatever in hopes that I find something new. Because, no offense, but you guys aren't exactly the people I'd choose to work with for a kidnapping and mindwiping effort. Sorry."

Riles sat up straighter and narrowed zir eyes. "Why the hell not? And shouldn't we at least try so we don't have to *kill* anyone? We're smart. We're reliable. Seriously, why the hell not?" Zie was spooling up to a possible rant.

I tried to keep the rant at bay by joining in with tone that was at lease calmer, but I was not happy. "I get that we aren't your ideal soldiers, but you can't throw out our chance to not kill people. That's just...that's bullshit, mate." I felt kind of frantic and like maybe I wanted to punch Bryan.

"Listen, I'm not trying to be an asshole. And I don't want to kill anybody either. But this is the sort of thing you do with people who have the physical capability to kidnap people. Are you telling me you can pull off jumping grown men?" He held up a hand as I opened my mouth. "And that's not sexist. You're a not-large, sedentary female. If you worked out, sure. But..." And he waved his hand up and down, indicating my body.

When I sat back with arms crossed, he went on. "So, sure, I'm down with a plan where we grab the people, blow the building before anyone reports the people missing, hold them captive as long as it takes to do whatever technique...So, feed them, manage their piss and shit...Unless you've suddenly learned to get them on IV food and connect whatever to them to manage what comes out...And we do that, mind-wipe them, and then release them. Without getting caught. I'm down with something like that. But, no matter how much I love you and trust you, none of you are the team I think *can* do that."

He huffed. "I don't want to kill anyone either. So don't act like this is me trying to make excuses."

The room was thick with uncomfortable silence. And I was mad. Mad that Bryan was right, that I wasn't physically capable. Mad that Riles definitely wasn't either and Jonny probably wasn't. Mad that I was in this situation. And really, really mad that I might end up having to cross that damned line. Dammit! Fuck this whole situation!

Jonny cleared his throat, waited a moment, and pressed on, "I really think, if we blow that building the instant after I send out all the email proof, that we'll have done sufficient damage. Just...one building. And..." He cleared his throat again, then mumbled, "And a specific list of people." I looked over to see that his cheeks were burning.

Riley asked, "What's our timeframe? And why can't we slowly ruin them instead?"

Jonny had already thought about this, it seemed, because he was now confident. "Part of it goes back to the danger of how they'll respond if they realize someone is after them, that the explosion last Thursday wasn't just some domestic terror one-off. Part of it has to do with the fact that they're on the verge of taking some of their own big actions. If we wait much at all, it will probably be too late. Given the dead kids on Tuesday, it is, arguably, already too late for some people." He seemed almost embarrassed as he said, "Since we know about this, not doing something, if Tuesday was just the start, we'll be guilty of deaths anyway. And they won't be the deaths of people who we know did bad shit. It will be more kids at the hands of more camp counselors whose worst crimes before that seemed to be shoplifting and depression."

I grudgingly reminded the group, "Plus, they plan to be able to implant people with their smaller implants in just over a month. People like Gran." I felt wilted. Trapped. So trapped. Deaths no matter what.

Jonny nodded. "Exactly. Between whatever it is they just proved with all the dead kids and the legislation they're pushing, I feel like it's pretty clear our time is short. A month and a half at most, but maybe tonight they set off another ex-Peacemaker client. Maybe not. Hopefully not..."

Riley conceded with a simple, deflated, "Okay."

"One thing I'd love us to make happen is that I'd love us to not actually have to kill everyone in that building. Or at least keep the loss of life to *just* that building. Which means I've got to *not* get my little bomb bugs wrong this time." Jonny sighed. "I'd like to pretend I'm too badass to care, but..." And he finished with a shrug.

This time, our pause was less about respect and more about reflection. Bryan spoke first. "You're really planning to make this a suicide run? Really willing to die at the end of this story?"

Jonny probably just heard neutral curiosity in Bryan's voice, but I could hear an edge of respect. If Jonny was actually one of the bad guys, at least I wasn't the only one being fooled.

Jonny nodded. "Yeah, I really am. Plus, it spares me having to live with myself after I kill people. Kill *more* people."

Riley shook zir head. "No. You can't think about it that way. You've researched carefully, and we'll do the same. You've made a deliberate choice based on that. And, at least to me, this strikes me as one of those 'needs of the many outweigh the needs of the few' situations you mentioned earlier."

We all nodded our agreement.

"Plus," zie noted, "the noble thing to do is to live with the consequences of your choices, if you have a chance. Especially if you're so sure they're the right ones. Live to fight more good fights."

I'd bet Riley had already been having this conversation with zirself to try to make sure zir own psyche wouldn't be shredded by what we would have to do. I was glad that it made good sense and filed this reasoning away to try to help talk myself through things.

Jonny sighed. "Okay. Okay...yeah...Then I guess let's see if we can't figure out how to access the hardwired system without me dying. Possible crippling guilt aside, I don't actually *want* to die. Not when we're all just getting to be such good friends." His wry little grin and sly eye slide to me at the end...I definitely didn't want him to die either. Nope.

"So, are you sure that this one hit is all it will take?" I didn't want to cast a lot of doubt, but we definitely all had to be sure of what we were doing. And it was going to take everything in me to talk myself into this. I didn't think I could do it again if we were wrong.

"When I thought I was doing this alone, I was aiming all my planning at, if you'll forgive the pun, getting the most buck for my one bang. So, while I'm not 100% positive, all my research points to this."

Rye interjected, "Did you look at EMPs to ruin their electronics instead of bombs?"

"Looked into it enough to discover that SWS are big fans of the baddest-ass Faraday cages that money can buy. They even seem to have some proprietary upgrades. And we could just wipe all their systems, if we can be sure we've actually rooted out every single one of their computers and backups. But then we still have to talk about any physical specs or tech they've already built and could *easily* reverse engineer. And what's in people's heads. I mean, not Peacemakers. But the knowledge." Jonny shook his head. "I put years into digging up dirt *and* looking at options to take them down. Which doesn't mean I figured out everything, but I hope means I at least hit on the obvious stuff."

Bryan reassured, "It's not a bad starting place, mate. So let's talk about steps to get to demolition day, what to do that day, and what we can do after to hasten the crumbling of the SWS empire, with a team perspective instead of a solo one."

I added, "We also want to make sure we're looking more closely at the big picture in terms of, for lack of a better phrase, covering our arses on the other side." I looked at my partners in world-saving crime intently. "Because they *will* come after us. Even if they take some time to figure out who we are, once they do, we'll basically be fugitives."

That settled kind of heavily. We'd done criminal things, and Bryan and Riley each had stories of plans gone too far that became possibly very dangerous to them if they'd gotten caught. But we'd never really risked our lives, not with advance knowledge. We'd never set out to knowingly *kill* anyone. (And, at least as far as I knew, none of us *had* killed anyone or led to anyone dying...)

Again, Rye reminded us, "But if this is what it looks like, what Jonny thinks it is, isn't that a price we should be willing to pay? Even if we've gotten soft, living in actual homes with big TVs the last while." Zie gazed lovingly at my wall TV, and I looked around at the comforts I'd gotten used to. But, of course, zie was right. Being fugitives would suck, but didn't seem an unreasonable cost.

"I'm willing to pay the price." I probably ought to have grandly proclaimed it, but quiet and fake-calm would have to do. Jonny caught my eye and I could see gratitude in his eyes. Saying it that way had been enough.

Bryan nodded. "Yeah, let's be criminal heroes."

We all looked at Rye, who exclaimed, "Well, obviously I'm willing! Cyber crusaders! I wouldn't make speeches about doing right and then do wrong." Zie smirked. "Not unless there's sex involved."

And the seriousness of what we'd committed to was worn down a little as we all indulged in a relieved sounding laugh.

Riles got up and scrounged through a pile of zir stuff that had been accumulating in the corner of the living room for the past few years. With an exclamation of triumph, zie held up a map. Zie rolled it out on the floor, used coasters to hold the corners down. It was a map of the world. Zie pulled the pile of bottle caps from Thursday, Friday, and Saturday night drinks over towards zir.

"Let's get a sense of perspective. Maybe see if Jonny missed any buildings in his plotting and figuring. We know SWS is big, but I feel like they've kept their actual physical presence much smaller than their influence suggests. Start by telling me where there are SWS facilities. Hopefully I have enough bottle caps."

Bryan quickly pulled up something on his portable. He handed it over to Riles. "Here. Very handy list."

Whilst Riley placed zir bottle caps, Jonny and Bryan used their portables to get information from Jonny's files and the SWS site. They worked together to quickly compile a list of the places SWS had been employed.

Bryan asked, "Do we want to take the time to list every client and their locations, or just major ones?"

There was much pondering and brow furrowing. Riles said, "The plus of listing every one is that we can see just how much influence they have. Maybe find a pattern we might have missed otherwise or...something..."

I looked up from the files I was sorting through, looking for hints of dates that might impact when we should execute our plan. "The minus is that we might have info overload and it would take forever."

Riles suggested, "What if we compile them all, but apply an industry type tag so that we can examine the results based on that? So we can see what sort of stuff they have their fingers in."

I nodded without looking up.

Jonny said, "Sure," and continued to scroll through and point out pertinent information to Riley.

Bryan shrugged and said, "Adding a category field to the database I'm building."

"So..." My typing slowed, "who's going to take point on this? Anyone have a strategy for the wider picture and post-demolition day?" I looked up to survey the others. Everyone else also seemed to be surveying.

And here we were, back to this respectful waiting, trying not to be greedy with leadership opportunities. Traditionally, out in nature and such, this many alphas in a group doesn't work well. However, used to defying nature, no one in this particular pack seemed to mind. If nothing else, we felt like some super-alpha machine. "Watch as we combine to become Mega-Alpha!" I could smack us.

Jonny was first to break the silence. "As I see it, we've got a few pieces. There's planning the details of demolition day itself. There's making sure we've got the wider picture figured out. There's planning what we do from the moment the building blows."

I took the chance to add, "And I wouldn't mind if we first sorted out who's taking lead on the overall thing here. 'Cause we probably can't afford too many more of our damned respectful pauses." I grinned and shook my head. "Where's all our rebellion and disregard for convention? I fear we did too well when we decided to interrupt each other less."

Bryan suggested, "Let's make up a fourth piece or divide a bigger one into two. That way, we're each in charge of something. And we don't all end up fighting about why we each *don't* want to be the one in charge of this whole thing."

Okay, so we were four of the type of alphas who didn't want anyone to tell us what to do, but who also didn't want to be responsible for figuring out what other people should do. Maybe alpha isn't the right label. To hell with labels anyway!

"I've already been working on demolition day, planning to go into the building, so I'd like to keep the lead on that, if we're going that way." Jonny made a concession for the current trust situation. "Of course, I expect I'll need to spell it all out and work with one of you when I need a computer. Though maybe not for too much longer?"

Bryan shook his head, but said, "Yeah, we're going to have to sort out our trust issues really quickly. We either need to decide that Jonny doesn't get to do anything but consult, or we need to let him do his thing. We don't have time for anything else."

Jonny tried to make it easier. "I won't change passwords or work solo. You can keep chaperoning me as much as you like, randomly looking over my shoulder, whatever you need to feel okay. It's not that I have no ego, but I'd like to set aside my issues and get this job done. I'll bitch when I feel more certain your guns aren't pointed at me." He wasn't joking.

Bryan nodded gravely and approvingly. "Thanks. And, for my part, I'd like to take the post-demolition day planning lead. I think it's going to require both online and in-the-meat plans. And I think I'm a little more meat-savvy than you lot. Right?"

"Truth," I confirmed. I turned to Riles. "What do you think?"

Zie kept placing bottle caps, but said, "I think that the big picture will, indeed, be big. I bet we can find plenty for us to share and obvious ways to split it. And, if I'm wrong, I'm definitely not going to cry about you taking lead. It's the right thing for you to do as part of avenging yourself." I could hear that even zie didn't buy that last line. "I could also be the one who chaperones Jonny until we're done doing that."

"Right." Sounded like I was stuck being lead of something. Good thing I had ideas. "I'd like to suggest we each sort of constantly check in, run plans and thoughts by each other. We'll be smarter that way and find holes in plans."

Jonny asked, "Do we start giving specifics now?"

"I want time to think," Bryan replied, "But it seems like a good time for other people to start tossing things out if you guys have thoughts."

I wanted time to think as well, but I wanted to toss out my initial thoughts and start collecting theirs. That would give me plenty to ponder. "If nobody minds, I've got plenty circling in my head right now." When everyone agreed, I started talking.

"So Jonny has requested minimum body count. Something we'd all prefer. And I'm guessing there are too many employees to sort through every one, even just at headquarters. I say we start at the top, follow the paper trail to see who knows SWS's real plan."

Jonny suggested, "We figure hackers on the payroll and execs are suspect."

I nodded. "Right. Figure that this is a delicate enough

situation they've built that only the top dogs can actually do the damage. Anyone else can probably only do little bits." I watched for nodding. I was probably saying obvious things. "We ruin the company, or start setting things in motion to do that once we've blown headquarters and leaked their memos. Maybe we bust up their finances. Kind of as a killing blow when it's too late for them to backpedal. Um..."

As I tried to pull more thoughts from the maelstrom in my head, Riles added, "We make sure that part of what we leak is memos that will let people, companies, governments fix or root out the last bits of damage or lingering threat."

I was nodding more. "Yes. But we have to do it all in a way that they can't just take and abuse that info for themselves."

We all nodded vigorously on that one. Hopefully, we'd learned from millennia of human history how easily people pick up opportunities to abuse power.

"And we need to take out the execs. When the building goes, they all need to be there...Or we need to figure out who we can trust in other locales if there are high enough level execs we can't reasonably get here. The hackers..." I sighed and saw that everyone else was looking uncomfortable with this bit too. "I'd like to see if we can figure out who's being blackmailed and who's going along with this for the money." I mulled over my thoughts a moment. "Those are my thoughts for now. They're vague and probably incoherent. But I think some research and some coffee will help tighten things up." I stood and headed to the kitchen. "Anyone else need a coffee assist?"

Rye left off zir bottle cap map marking and followed me. "I think I need a little more than coffee. And I think I've still got some beers in here."

Bryan requested a beer and coffee, and Jonny asked for coffee, then seemed to settle back into thought. In the kitchen, as I poured some coffees and Rye grabbed beers, zie asked, "So, how was it alone with Jonny this morning?"

"What?"

"Come on. You've pointed out Mr. Pretty before at the club. And his explanation about your building, all the stuff he told you and then told us whilst you were in the shower, seemed intense. So I'm trying to imagine you, tired and alone and watching him be kind of vulnerable. Plus, with two bowls, I have to guess you fed him..."

"It was definitely kind of intense. He was so obviously upset when I pushed him to finally tell me why he blew my building. And then...actually, it was awkward. The feeding thing. Because I'd just seen him be pretty emotional and I'd read your message and his draft messages, so I felt like I was probably looking at someone who wasn't actually evil. And who was, as you say, Mr. Pretty...And then he kept apologizing and saying that he, well, that he liked me..."

Riles leaned against the counter. "Awkward. But reassuring. In its own way." Zie gave me a cheeky look. "You're going to fuck him, aren't you?" Zie didn't flinch when I nailed zir in the arm. "Yep, that's what I call sexual tension."

I rolled my eyes, stuck out my tongue like the adult I am, and left without further comment. Zie followed behind, quietly making kissy noises. Some people never really got over adolescent humor. (Yes, that includes me, but I still made a mental note to kick Rye. A lot.)

In the living room, Jonny had finished putting bottle caps on Rye's map. As soon as beers were opened, he took those bottle caps and put them on the map as well. "I think we're still short a few. But you get the idea." The map was dotted with caps, though North America had more than its fair share of SWS facilities.

We stopped to look down at the map. I noticed something. "I know this is beer caps on a not-massive map, and maybe it won't look like this when we do it on the computer," Rye quickly noted that zie'd get right on that, "but do the coastlines look dense to anyone else? Especially around our area?"

The others confirmed that it *did* look that way.

"But maybe it's just because, at least in this country, there are more bigger cities on the coasts?" suggested Jonny.

Bryan said, "I think I'll wait for Rye's map. And, now that I come to think of it, why the hell doesn't that map already exist on the SWS site?"

I hadn't thought of that. Judging by the looks on Jonny's and Riley's faces, they hadn't either. "Sounds like something for Riles and I to add to our list of things to sort out in getting the bigger picture."

Bryan sat back down. "When you guys are figuring out details and maybe splitting up work, it seems like your piece has three areas. Destroying their finances, making sure the right docs are cleaned up and delivered to impacted parties, and taking care of our 'peers.'" There was some sneering when he said that last word.

I broke in, "I'd really like to not have to do too much damage to any of them. I mean, unless they've already done damage of their own and they know it. Maybe not flat-out ruin the ones who are being blackmailed."

Jonny spoke up. "I've already started sorting the hackers. And we should be able to figure out who's in the SWS power structure, aside from the obvious people like Johnson and that lot, by looking at the memos or finding an org chart. Or at least a good chunk. Which means we may just need to figure out the 'how' of taking care of the three areas."

"One thing I'd like to do, to help us and to save some friends..." I narrowed my eyes in thought. "If we can figure out which hackers are uncompromised and would be willing to help, maybe we can have enough folks digging up dirt on execs or screwing with SWS finances that the blame will be impossible to place and the work will be quicker. Maybe place incriminating info about those who *have* been compromised, especially the ones who fell for money, the greedy shits, where it will be found by our peers. Let the community police itself."

Bryan liked this idea. "You know, you'd just have to find a way to phrase it. You could make it a contest or a game. Or create any old excuse. I'll bet you, oh revered MindKiller, could set things in motion."

There was much nodding.

"Jonny," I wasn't ready to admit that we'd already taken *all* of his files, "since you're already foraging through your files, will you find the one where you've listed your info about hackers, especially anything you might have left out of the folder you prepped to show us? Who's clean, unknown, compromised, whatever. I'd like to get some folks messing with things." I had a sudden thought. "Of course, if we can manage to implicate the guilty quickly, we can spread the info on hacking into SWS. But we have to clear out the compromised so they can't have SWS change anything."

Bryan said, "If you're recruiting, let's try to get an engineer on board to read device specs. Those are a piece of the puzzle none of us are qualified to cover."

Riley looked down at the bottle caps. "After we do this, can we retire as big, bad hacking heroes? Maybe use some of the SWS money to run away to the country?" Zie stretched and everyone could hear little crackling sounds. "I'm just getting too old to be a rock star."

CHAPTER 11

I had tried to get to bed early Sunday night, but 0700 Monday morning still came too soon. Waking felt like struggling up through thick water. I couldn't seem to clear it all from my eyes. I was likely to get hooked up to machines again, so I didn't want to use stims. They weren't illegal, but they were currently seen as the choice of deviants and dissidents. I pulled myself out of the bed, careful not to disturb Bryan sleeping on the other side of it, and headed for the shower. A nice shower and some strong coffee would have to do.

After my shower, I put on conservative clothes (a skirt, to make sure my banged up knees were visible) and made my hair look as normal as possible given its current cut and color. (Why hadn't I bought one of those annoying but fashionable little hats the other women at work had been wearing lately? Damn.) I even fished out plasters for my hand that were the color of my skin, purchased specifically for days like this. Today, I'd have to play the drone again for cops and the company's CorpSec agents. At least I was seeing them at the same time. *I might only have to tell my story again a couple dozen times total instead of a couple dozen times to each group. Yeeha.* Obviously, I wasn't doing a great job of keeping my mental dialog positive.

I sat in the living room, scanning my email as I drank my coffee and (quietly) munched on toast. Riley took advantage of my presence to grab a little nap beside me on the couch. No one was quite ready to let Jonny, sleeping on a sleep mat on the floor, be all alone, so Riles probably hadn't slept well, if at all, last night.

As I was getting ready to wake Rye, Jonny woke up. "Hey, are you leaving?"

I paused, waiting to shake Riles. "Yeah. My weekend of mourning is over. Time to talk to Johnny Law."

Jonny propped himself up on an elbow. "Not nearly as cool as this Jonny, huh? Just remember, you can honestly say you had no part in the explosion and you had no warning. And don't mention that you kidnapped some guy and are keeping him in your living room." He grinned.

I returned his smile. "Admit it. This was all an elaborate and unnecessary scheme to get me to bring you home. *That* isn't kidnapping. Plus, you're here by choice *now*. Part of the plan. I'm innocent of all charges."

I gently shook Rye. "You'd better wake up. I'm about to leave and Jonny's awake. You wouldn't want him to take an unmonitored breath."

Zie muttered, "Cruel bitch," but woke up enough to say, "Good luck, Kot," and returned to keeping an eye on Jonny.

On the drive to the police station, Gran called. I saw the incoming number and laughed. I had wondered when Gran might finally hear about my situation. She avoided the news most the time because she said it just made her heart hurt and made her feel impotent in the face of man's horribleness. I didn't disagree.

I tapped the headset in my ear. "Hi, Gran!"

"Katja, girly." She sounded relieved. "Sorry to call so early. I just finally saw about your building on the news. I was so worried that you might not answer...You almost died!" Gran was clearly impressed by my survival.

I laughed. "Sure did. But I'm okay. I'm alive. How are you?"

Gran sounded a bit sputtery. "You can't ask how I am. I'm an old lady with a routine sort of life. Not worth asking. But you! You just had a little brush with death. Tell me about it."

I usually found myself on the edge of laughter when talking to Gran. There was something so endearingly ridiculous about her customary tone. "Nothing much to tell. Security messaged me to tell me that someone had tried to bust into my car and would I meet them there to see if anything had been taken and all that. I was just about there when I heard a massive boom and felt something nice and big smack my shoulder. My palms hit the pavement first and saved my face from getting messed up. And now I'm going to have to spend the next few hours trying to make cops and CorpSec believe me."

Gran's voice was wry. "That sounds exciting." She sighed. "Well, I'm glad you didn't die, dear. Or ruin your pretty face. Though it's a shame you didn't at least get to see the exploding. I once saw a building explode. Well, implode. Quite a sight!"

"I'll bet. Of course, it probably wasn't full of your job and your coworkers."

"Very true. I'm sorry for anyone and anything you lost. As always, I'm here if there's anything I can do to help you out. I'd bring you a meal, but you know the streets are too much for me now." Gran's voice got a snide edge to it. "Of course, if the government had seen fit to work on better transportation instead of just better entertainment and computers, we might have flying cars for everyone, not just emergency services and rich arseholes. Then I'd be able to come be helpful instead of making *you* come to *me*."

I tried to keep the laughter out of my voice. However amused I might be by it, I had learned long ago that Gran was serious in her disgust at the lack of flying cars for all, or at least some kind of real transportation solution. "It's a shame, Gran. And I get the feeling neither of us will live to see them become available to the common man. After all, people have been talking about flying cars since the mid-1900s. And nothing widespread yet."

Gran muttered crankily, "You're probably right. I'd settle for at least overriding the elite who keep Seattle's public transport system useless. I'd happily bring you a pot of soup or something if I could count on public transport."

"But I know you care. That's what counts. Okay?"

"Still doesn't make me feel better." Then Gran's voice brightened suddenly. "Oh, well! What counts is that you're alive to have this conversation. You just be sure you stay safe. And give your gran a call when you find your next job. Or maybe let me feed you a meal and hear the explosion story in person."

"I'll do that, Gran. Very soon. You take care."

"You too, dear. Love you!"

"Love you, Gran." I tapped the headset off, grinned, and shook my head. "Crazy old lady."

When I reached the police station, I put my headset in my

pocket. No need to get distracted whilst I was trying to deal with the law. I smoothed my hair and made sure my makeup didn't look excessive in the sunlight. It's amazing how much a little mascara can smear for no reason just sitting in the car. I checked the time. 0855. I was 5 minutes early. How very professional, respectful, and obedient of me.

As I walked towards the doors of the station, I made sure my stride wasn't cocky, my posture wasn't too brash. I meant to ease things for myself by seeming as unlikely a bomber as possible.

The officer at the front desk didn't look at me like I was a freak. That was a good sign. He might even have been checking me out. I pretended to be oblivious. When the detective and the CorpSec agent came to take me to an interrogation room, I made sure to be as pleasant as I could manage. I even apologized to Detective Engalls for how cranky and unreasonable I'd been when he had questioned me on Thursday. I hated to admit it, but I did seem to be catching more flies with honey. He immediately transformed from gruff and monosyllabic to a nice cop who felt bad for putting me through more questioning.

The CorpSec agent looked middle-aged but well-kept. She had a touch of grey in her hair, but the toned musculature of a fit and younger woman. She extended her hand. "Good morning, Ms. Brennan. I'm Ms. Murdock from SWS Corporate Security." She was almost cordial, but not quite. It would take more than honey to get this one off of my case.

Murdock and I followed Engalls quietly. She didn't speak until we were seated in the tiny, sterile interrogation room. Then, she spoke before Engalls, taking control of the meeting.

"Let me start by saying that I have already watched the tapes of your time here on Thursday. I've also seen the reports on the search of your car, the polygraph, and the swabs of your person and clothing. I do not feel it is necessary to question you with a polygraph at this point. Instead, I would like to speak frankly and then hear your response. Does that sound fair?" To her credit, she looked at both Engalls *and* me for nods of assent.

The look on Engalls's face told me that this was not the way he thought things would go. I was struggling to keep all suspicion off my face. What was she up to?

"Let's start by having you tell us, once again, your story of that day in as much detail as you can recall."

I managed not to be annoyed; I'd expected that. "It's pretty straight-forward. I got a message from CorpSec that they'd stopped someone breaking into my car and wanted me to come make sure nothing was missing."

Murdock interrupted me. "We can see, on our system, that you received the message. However," and she turned to address Engalls, "we can also see that it originated outside our network. And, of course, we're working to track down its origin." She turned back to me. "You may continue."

I hesitated, and looked at Engalls. I didn't want Murdock using me to keep his mouth shut if he wanted to ask questions about that point. I was getting the feeling that he might be the one of them most likely to believe I was innocent, and I didn't want to ruin that special relationship. He nodded, and I went on.

"So, I got the message, and it, well, you saw it, so you know it told me to come immediately. I grabbed my coat and went immediately. Um...since Detective Engalls asked Thursday, I guess I should mention that I don't remember seeing anyone, especially not strangers, on my way out. It was the time of day when I suppose most people are just trying to work extra hard to get everything done before the day is over. Anyway...I, uh, I walked out and I walked towards my car. And nobody was there, but I didn't really have a chance to think about that because there was a big boom behind me, and then a piece of the wall knocked me down. And that's all." I swallowed and allowed myself to look as uncertain as I felt. Was that what she'd wanted? Just another re-telling of the same old thing?

Murdock nodded and said, "Just like you told Detective Engalls on Thursday."

Murdock continued. "As the first person on the scene and the only one there to survive the bombing, you are a suspect. Though," and she gave a small smile, "you might be relieved to know that you aren't alone on the list. The person who was out sick is also considered a suspect, as are the techs who were allegedly at customer sites." I returned her smile with a sincere one of my own. Less attention on me could only be good. I also gave Karl Peterson, the bomb threat-sending ex-employee, a mental high five. Sounded like he wasn't on the list. *Good job having a solid alibi, mate.*

She nodded as if my smile was the appropriate response. "That said, you *are* still a strong suspect. And if you did not take part in the crime, then we believe that you may very well know or be known by at least one of the, possibly multiple, perpetrators. There was no evidence that your car had been violated, nor were there security personnel at your car. Therefore, it is unlikely that there was a thief. One must suspect that you were sent a false message for the express purpose of saving your life. If you did not know about the action in advance, then one must also suspect that you have been or will be contacted by those who saved you from the consequences of the action. It may be that we would be served well by investigating your friends and lovers. Even former lovers who still have some feelings for you." She paused and held my eyes. "What do you think?"

I nodded slowly, thoughtfully. "It makes sense. I mean, those sound like suspicions that the situation would support." I shrugged. "I just know that I didn't do it. And I'm sure none of my friends did it." Luckily, there was no polygraph. And, technically, Jonny hardly qualified as a friend at this point. "But...Are you going to charge me or something? Do I need to have a lawyer now?" I made sure I was wide-eyed when I asked.

Murdock shook her head. "I do not think you will need a lawyer. I am just going to ask you some straight forward questions. You should not need a lawyer unless we decide to press charges. And I am sure the detective will make sure that I do not overstep any boundaries."

I very much doubted that it was smart to answer without a lawyer, but I also doubted that I could press for one without looking guilty.

Murdock opened a portable and skimmed whatever was on the screen. "What was your position at SWS?" She looked up at me.

"Data Entry Tech."

"And I see that you have held that position for 3 years. You never tried to advance?"

I tried to look embarrassed by my lack of ambition. "I felt like that was where I fit, so I didn't really feel like trying to move up or out. I mean, it was paying the bills and leaving room for playing vidgames or whatever at night. Any advancement just looked like...too much work for money that I didn't care about having. Unnecessary change." I shook my head. "I guess I'm not exactly daring. And I'm not fond of change." I hoped I wasn't pouring it on too thick. I also hoped that the personality assessments I'd taken very carefully on the job supported the picture I was trying to sell. (It would definitely support the thing about not liking change. That was true.)

Murdock nodded, her face neutral, so I had no idea what she thought of my reasons. "I see that you have never been an overachiever." She flicked at her portable screen, scrolling. "Not even at school."

Ugh. She'd gotten my school records. I hoped she'd written off the few black marks in there as just the normal rebellion of youth.

"But I also see that you did your job well and didn't have problems with your supervisors. How were your relationships with your coworkers?"

I knew she must have that information. All employee evals were sent on to headquarters, and I'd seen the forms often enough to know that they covered anything that might apply when making choices about how good a fit I was for the job. But I was playing the submissive witness. "I didn't really have relationships with anyone at work. I didn't fight or disagree. I just didn't socialize. There was too much work to do."

"Do you consider yourself antisocial?"

Engalls interjected. "Whoa now! I don't see how you can ask psych eval questions like that. Doesn't seem fair." He turned to me. "You don't answer that one if you don't want to. That's what a lawyer would tell you."

I gave him a sincere smile. "Thanks for watching out for me. But I don't mind answering." I turned my attention to Murdock. "I'm not antisocial. I just think that I'm not at work to play. I socialize sufficiently outside of work."

"And would you be willing to tell me about those with whom you socialize?"

I paused and my brows pulled in a bit. "Um, I'm not so sure I want to talk about my friends. I mean, I can't imagine any of them blowing up buildings. And I don't want them to get in trouble just because they're friends with me and I happened to not die." My pliable worker drone act was only going to let her get so much. She'd found the line.

Murdock's lips pinched, just a little.

Engalls took advantage of the brief silence to insert himself into the conversation. "We have pictures of folks that have proven themselves inclined to this sort of crime. I'd like to have you look at them. See if any of them look familiar. Maybe someone you've seen around work or when you're out. Maybe you caught someone's eye without realizing it or without realizing they were domestic terrorists. Can I show you the pictures?"

Murdock knew she'd been derailed, so she suggested, "Let's run the database against the SWS employee roster. I'd also like to note the names of anyone Ms. Brennan points out."

In tones that were ever-so-slightly patronizing, Engalls said, "We can discuss those requests later." Then he pulled up the database he wanted and directed my attention to the far wall.

For two hours I watched the faces scroll by. I made sure to pay attention to every one, lest Murdock realize that I really didn't expect to see the right face up there. I even considered fingering someone randomly, but didn't want to risk pointing out someone they knew was innocent but had put in to test me. By the time the database had offered up its last visage, I had said "no" so many times that it sounded like nonsense. My eyes hurt, but I didn't rub them. Wouldn't want to smear my makeup and end up looking less reputable.

When the wall became just a wall again, I apologized. "I'm sorry. I wish I could have picked someone out." (That was true.) There was a disappointed silence. "Hey, maybe it isn't even about me. Maybe whomever it is just wanted to throw up an obvious first suspect or something. You know, make people focus on me so they could make a clean getaway?" Then I laughed at myself. "Maybe that's too much like in a movie, huh?"

Engalls smiled at me, but it looked more like humoring me than agreeing. "Yeah, maybe a little too spectacular. But it's always nice to hear new theories." He stood. "I think we're done here." He looked at Murdock. "Ms. Murdock, do you have anything else to ask?"

Murdock looked a bit annoyed but shook her head.

"Okay, Ms. Brennan, you're free to go. Just stay in town and let us know if you move or decide to stay somewhere besides home more than one night. Same as before. Okay?"

I nodded my understanding to Engalls as I stood. "Absolutely."

As I turned, Murdock said, "In case anyone tries to contact you," and she stood, fishing a card out of her pocket and extending it to me.

I took the card and shook her hand. Weakly. No need to show off my aggressive side. I turned and shook Engalls's hand. This hadn't gone too badly.

As I was walking away from them, I turned and asked, with a touch of fear, "If someone *does* try to contact me, will one of you give me protection? I don't think I want to be known by someone who'd blow up a building."

They assured me that they'd happily make sure I was safe and that they'd get the bomber, so I put on a brave face and went on my way.

Back in the car, I put my phone headset back in my ear and did a scan for bugs with a little handheld gizmo Bryan had made sure to leave by my car keys. I was surprised to find nothing. If I had been in Murdock's position, I would have had someone in the parking lot bug my car whilst I was inside. I would have at least put a transmitter in the card. Even with the scan showing nothing, I figured I would try to play it careful and mostly quiet until I got home and could do a better scan. Who knew what sort of gear SWS had?

I also figured I ought to call and make sure that Bryan was awake enough to be paranoid about bugs with me. I called him as I drove. I put on my sweetest voice. "Hey, sweetheart. I'm headed home."

There was no pause. "How was your meeting, baby?"

"It was okay. I got a chance to apologize to the detective for being short with him Thursday. And I met Ms. Murdock with SWS security."

"Uh-huh."

"I don't think she liked me very much. Maybe she's just

naturally suspicious."

"That's probably her job."

"Yeah. I know…Anyway, I thought I'd see if you wanted me to pick up anything on my way home."

"No. I don't need anything. But I can't speak for the contents of your kitchen."

"Okay. I'll see you in a little while."

"See you soon."

I tapped the phone off. Hopefully Bryan was awake enough to have caught the implications. I snorted as I imagined Bryan, who had probably been woken up by the call but had grabbed the phone instinctively, falling back asleep and dreaming of groceries. Mister better get up and let folks know I might be bugged. Better meet me downstairs to scan so I didn't have to risk walking in on something we didn't want anyone else to hear.

I was pleased to see that Bryan was waiting by my parking spot when I pulled in. Neither of us spoke as I got out of the car. Bryan had been smart enough to put in an earphone so that any beeps from the scanning wand wouldn't be audible to an audio bug. When he got to my jacket pocket, he stopped and pointed. I fished out Murdock's card and rolled my eyes. I started to walk in circles, purposefully making scuffing noises. I spotted a puddle right near my car and headed for it. Then I dropped the card into the puddle and said, "Crap." Bryan held the wand over it until the beeping stopped. He nodded and I retrieved the card. That was the only bug we found.

He reported, "You'll be happy to know that I took a quick look at the data and footage from what I installed in your car, and nobody even tried to touch it, much less bug it."

"Maybe we're just too paranoid," I suggested.

"No such thing. In fact, we'll want to make sure everyone has access to the more sensitive bug detector."

As we walked up to the flat, Bryan took a close look at Murdock's card. "Very nice. Shame to ruin the bugging bit."

I snickered. "Don't get too sad. I'm sure there will be other functional bugs about. At least until they catch the bomber."

In the apartment, Rye was trying not to snooze as zie kept an eye on Jonny, whilst Jonny read a magazine. Exciting morning for everyone. When zie saw me, Rye stood and announced,

"Mom and Dad are home. Babysitter is going back to bed." As zie headed to the bedroom, zie snickered, "G'night, sweetheart. Baby. You better not tell 'Randa about yours and Bryan's affair."

I laughed at zir receding back. "We're all so pleasant when we're tired."

Jonny didn't look up from his magazine. "You wouldn't have to deal with it so much if you'd trust me to babysit myself, you know." He was smiling, though. The protests were now just part of the pattern of our interaction.

"Yes, yes." I waved my hand dismissively at him. I sat on the couch by Jonny, pulling my computer over to me. "I think we have to assume that my phone number is compromised. No real conversations on that line. And that at least my general email account is too."

Bryan brought me coffee. "You mean the generic free one that you use to email your gran? Boy, that's a shame."

I took the coffee with a thanks and looked over at Jonny. "So, did you call in sick today? The kids did think to offer to let you do that, didn't they?"

Jonny put the magazine down. "Actually, I freelance. So I didn't need to bother. Of course, if you guys were still planning to limit my portable time, I'd need to make excuses soon."

I yawned, dragging my jacket off and tossing it over the arm of the couch. "Yeah, I guess we need to either find a nice, crippled machine for you to work on stuff when we don't want to babysit or decide to trust you more. We'll work on both. Until then, maybe you can sit here by me." I patted the cushion closer to me. "And Bryan can sit here." I patted the chair to my left. "And we can start moving forward. That's another way to shorten your torture. Just get the job done, okay?"

Jonny scooted closer (a bit eagerly, I thought) and Bryan sat in the chair on my other side. And, eventually, Riles would join us, filling up the couch. We had work to do. Files and figuring. The safest part of our plan.

I spent all day at the computer, my vision reduced to lines of code and internal memos. Which was enough, especially with what I was finding. It was a good thing Jonny had already done plenty of research, a couple years of it, because a conservative reading of SWS memos (when I stumbled across anything that seemed useful, not just boring corporation-running drivel) led us to believe that we had...weeks at best until they did whatever their next nefarious thing was. You know, the thing that wasn't just putting bugs in old people's heads. Weeks. Shit.

When we slowed down a bit to sort out dinner, our responsible adult sides came out. Riles poked at the noodles zie had ordered and said, "I don't want to sound like a whiner or an old person, but," and zie paused for us all to laugh, "but, you rude assholes, I feel like we should talk about sleep. Because we all know how shitty some of us are when we don't get enough."

Zie looked at me, daring me to laugh. I didn't; I knew I was one of the "some of us" zie was talking about.

Bryan came in for the assist, "Even those of us who don't get touchy without sleep will function better with it. That's just science."

I signaled my agreement with Bryan by flipping Rye off.

Riles exclaimed, "Exactly! So, please, can we find an answer that lets me get good sleep? Without making anyone else have to suffer through too little sleep or being stuck on the sleeping mat or the couch so they get lousy sleep."

"Count me in on a saner plan," I assented. "We'll all do better if everyone gets good sleep. We don't have any margin for error, and we're all too familiar with the little ways it creeps in, even when we're doing the things we're best at, if we skip too much sleep." I threw an arched eyebrow at Riley and willed zir to recall the times poor sleep had caused zir to mess up or be a jerk. I definitely wasn't the only one.

Jonny looked up from his rice and noted, "I will enthusiastically support plans that let me sleep well. For whatever my vote counts for."

"I want to try to balance safety and sleep," Bryan told us. "I know, right now, we're theoretically safe, but...I've just got this sense that we can't let our guards down. Not ever." He grinned. "Last time we did that, we picked up a madman at a night club."

Everyone laughed, just a little. And I asked, "What will keep your paranoia happy? I'm in favor of doing that."

Bryan thought a moment. "My concern is that SWS will somehow catch onto us, even if it's just in the context of figuring out who one of us is. And my paranoia says that watchful eyes might give us the small opportunity to escape attacks or evade discovery. Plus, there's just the one bed with room for two, maybe three people."

Lamely, Jonny noted, "There *is* a perfectly nice second bed just upstairs, in my apartment."

"Sorry, mate," Bryan told him, "But, in addition to trust issues not yet resolved, we should be in pack mode. Safety in numbers. So, sleep shifts. Only two people sleeping at a time."

Riley's face scrunched up. "Yeah....but there are only three of us who've lived together or shared beds and...no offense, Jonny, but there's one person who's a big question mark. And, as much as I've enjoyed watching you shower and piss, I just...I don't know."

Jonny amiably said, "No offense taken. It's a legitimate worry."

I tentatively noted, "And, also, there are a couple girlfriends who probably won't love all the bed-sharing. Though," I reassured Bryan, "my paranoia totally agrees with yours. So I'm not trying to derail you."

"Bryan, what if we leave it up to chance?" Riles asked. "I mean, do you have an actual need for a particular way this goes or ends up? It will be lame, but 'fate decided' will sound better to Kitty and 'Randa than us choosing to sleep with Kot or Jonny."

Bryan shrugged agreeably. "I just think, for now, we have two shifts. Science says minimum 7 hours of sleep, so maybe one shift is 2100 to 0400 and the other is 0400 to 1100. And I didn't have a plan in terms of who should be stuck sharing the bed. While Rye's the only person I think 'Randa wouldn't be unhappy for me to share a bed with, I don't feel like that's a good enough reason to assume Kot should be stuck with Jonny. No offense intended."

"Good point," Riles said, "then I say we draw straws for shifts." Riles hopped up and grabbed some actual straws from the kitchen, cutting them as zie went on. "The two who draw the short straws can sleep 2100 to 0400. The two who draw the long straws can sleep 0400 to 1100. And we all just get the hell over the stranger issue, unless it turns out Jonny snores or kicks in his sleep. In which case he can sleep on the floor. Otherwise, two people can sleep on Kot's bed at once without grinding all over each other. Okay?"

Jonny seemed to be carefully looking neutral as he nodded, and Bryan and I both squinted, first warily at Rye and then even more warily (warilier?) at Jonny, but nodded.

Rye held up zir hand, four straw bits poking up. "Grab your straws, kids!" zie directed.

We paused a moment and looked at each other, then quickly snatched straws.

Riles held up the one zie'd been left with. "Not done yet. Straws up."

I held mine up first and gave a little fist pump and a "Yes!" when it was clear I had a long straw. I grinned. "I got the prime sleep shift. I don't even care what you other two chumps got."

Bryan was the next to hold his straw up. He groaned. "Ugh. Early sleep shift. Unless," and his voice got hopeful, "Riley didn't cut things precisely. Put up your straw, Jonny. And make sure it's shorter than mine."

Jonny obliged, slowly, looking guilty. It was clear, even before his straw was by Bryan's, that Jonny had drawn a long straw. I willed myself not to flush. I thought, *This is about sleep, not sex. Stop it!*

Jonny didn't look right at me, but I saw him dart a quick glance from the side of his eyes.

Bryan asked, seriously, "Are you okay with that, Katja?"

Jonny quickly jumped in, "I won't be offended if you're not."

I concentrated on the straws we were all holding up. I wondered if I should be uncomfortable, but it seemed like, instead, I was okay with it. And my intuition wasn't blaring. It might even have been quietly smug. In that case...I admitted to myself that I was probably going to hook up with him (not due to lack of self-control but due to a lack of wanting to waste willpower resisting that and now having nightly opportunities). Sexual frustration is disruptive, and that damned Jonny was definitely to my tastes. I shrugged. "At least your baes will now feel less worried about me, right? And we know they trust you with each other, so...Everybody wins?"

We put the sleep shifts into play immediately. Though I assured them all was fine, I appreciated that Bryan and Rye each quietly pulled me aside to make sure I was really okay. Like I told Bryan, "We all think he's okay. We're all adults. And I'll scream likely bloody murder at the first sign he's actually a total creep. He wouldn't be the first presumptuous asshole I spent all night pushing away."

When we were alone, Jonny asked, "So, is the plan that we work all night?"

"I hope not. I'm going to do what I can, but I won't judge if you take a break. Or a nap."

"What if I distract you?"

I couldn't tell if there'd been some sort of suggestive tone in his question. But I chose to act as if there wasn't. "What did you have in mind?"

"I...uh...I just thought it might be cool to have an actual conversation or something. I mean, it's been non-social since I...approached you Saturday. And..." he squirmed a little, "I kind of always enjoyed messaging with you. So..."

Such a pretty boy shouldn't be so awkward trying to talk to a girl. I wasn't being critical; I was honestly surprised. I assumed he was my peer in a general sense, and I'd managed to do my fair share of hooking up. He was my peer and pretty and...Well, lucky for him, I was an interested party.

"Yeah. We can talk. Uh...did you have a topic in mind?"

He kind of...winced. I guess he didn't.

This was just so novel and weird. Like we were on a blind date. *But we're not actually strangers*, I reminded myself.

I started thinking about the past we actually did share. Online things that, for me, made it feel like we already had a substantial history. Jobs we'd done together and private messages. The anonymity of the 'Net ensuring we didn't know what most people would consider basic details. We didn't know age, biological sex, location. If we'd stumbled across each other in public, as we'd seen, we wouldn't have known it.

For all he'd known at the time, I might have been some burly man, bearded and dressed in flannel, sitting in his mother's basement. Cheese dust on my shirt from some snack and a pile of soda cans piled by my desk. And maybe my desk, in my mother's basement, was located in Norway. And it wouldn't have mattered back then.

All he had known, all he had *needed* to know, at the time, was that I was smart, that I was capable of being funny, that I was as good as he was at slipping through companies' data defenses. And he never would have asked for identifying details, because he wouldn't have wanted me to ask him about his.

Sure, we might mention, as we put evidence of some bank president's foul play out where the world could see, that we were loving the latest Viral album or had just seen some film and it was great or it sucked. But nothing that could let anyone find out who the rest the world knew us as.

That included names. Oh, there was a start...

Given the context of our lives, 'nyms would be an easy topic. Sometimes, 'nyms were super obvious, but they were always such a personal thing, carefully chosen. I loved to hear from someone why they'd chosen their 'nym. I rarely got a chance to ask that question in person. In fact, aside from the hours spent discussing possible 'nyms with Riles and Bryan back when we first chose our own, I don't think I'd had a real chance to do that. So, I took advantage of this. "Okay, tell me why you're spaceGoddity."

Jonny looked relieved, grateful. Points to me for coming up with a topic.

There was a particular mix of giddy joy and embarrassment attached to geeks talking about things they (we) loved. We were excited to talk about that thing we loved, but we also knew that not everyone shared our loves, that some people would judge us for these important things, so we were a little proactively embarrassed. The big but bashful grin as Jonny answered told me that this was one of his things.

"You ever heard of David Bowie?"

I nodded. "Yeah, my gran is a big fan, so I heard some music and saw some films growing up. He's cool."

The bashfulness was gone. Jonny was all grin. "He *is*! I discovered him when all these artists I liked cited him as an influence. It was pretty much crazy love at first listen. The man was incredible. A chameleon and genius. Multi-talented. And, after this mess is all over, if you're still talking to me, I'd love to spend hours making sure you've really experienced his best stuff. There are albums where every song is incredible." He caught himself raving instead of answering. "Anyway. The song that really seems to have given him his break is about this astronaut whose ship malfunctions. He actually released it around the start of humans going into space. There's a follow up song, *Ashes to Ashes*, where you learn the astronaut has lived and become a junkie. But that first song is called *Space Oddity*. I added that G in there for a bit of swagger, a little taste of god complex." There was a lingering note at the end that I read as being unsure if something was as cool as you thought.

I grinned and dispelled his worries with a word. "Cool."

"And what about you. Is there a story with MindKiller? There really has to be."

"Good job keeping a straight face when you say it, by the way. And there's always a story. I'll spare you the agonizing hours I spent trying to find just the right thing. I rejected a lot of ideas just because they were obviously female-gendered. Let's be honest; it's safer not to be obviously female on the 'Net."

I was glad when Jonny didn't object but nodded in agreement. The issues of sexism online were divisive and political. Women had had their lives ruined over them, and a perfectly reasonable-seeming guy could suddenly go rabid on you when you mentioned that sexism existed. So, whilst it was just one little sentence, I'd known it was a potentially explosive comment. The kind that ruined friendships, cancelled out chances of a hookup, and sent grand, world-saving plans out the window.

"One of the best things in my life was all the sci-fi Gran exposed me to. And one of her favorites and mine was *Dune*. Have you heard of it?" Jonny shook his head. "Well, I'll happily let you introduce me to Bowie, but I'm going to reciprocate by making sure you've at the very least seen the film made of the first book in...some time in the 1980s. But, if you really want to impress me, you'll read all six books and pretend to love at least some of them."

Jonny laughed. "Your friendship is expensive."

"Oh, don't worry. That could help get more than just friendship." I gave him a wink before going on. So much for avoiding being suggestive. "I know it sounds like typical hacker bravado, and I guess it was. I was...I think 10 years old when we decided to dive into the digital fray. I probably should have changed it at some point, beyond abbreviating as MK lately, but I don't like change and I liked the reputation that was growing around MindKiller. Anyway, there's this litany that some of the characters say. A litany against fear. And I've used it since I was a kid to help myself not be afraid. It starts, 'I must not fear. Fear is the mind-killer.' Even as a delusional kid, I knew 'fear' was too obvious to use. But a mind-killer sounded threatening enough. And like something people would think they understood even if they'd never heard of *Dune*."

Jonny grinned. "I'd always wondered how someone who seemed so reasonable ended up with a stereotypically aggressive name. This makes sense. But I'm also going to stick with calling you MK, not MindKiller, if you don't mind."

I shook my head; I didn't mind.

He seemed to be past awkwardness now, up for carrying his side of the conversation. I could have patted him on the back. Honestly, it wasn't like I was holding a gun on him. Not tonight.

He said, "Okay, now, what about real names? Katja is great but not really standard."

"No. Not really. Not for *this* country. But, my mum had a 1900s Cold War fascination, so I ended up with a Russian name. Uh...I hope you won't mind that I'm not really finding your name equally exotic. I mean, it's fine, but..."

He laughed. "Some people seem to find it a little exotic. Apparently, Jonny without an H is very confusing. But if you assume it's a diminutive for Jonathan, where the hell did you get the H? Just randomly pulled it from beside the T?"

I shrugged and offered, "Russian diminutives often look nothing like the non-diminutive versions of names."

"I thought it was your *mom* who had the 1900s Cold War fascination."

"Stop ruining the camaraderie here!"

"Are you taking into account the wealth of camaraderie

we've built being criminals online? Remember that time we funneled all of Chick-fil-A's profits for a month into that shelter for LGBTQIAU kids and leaked it to the media as a 'donation'?" Jonny was laughing as he asked.

I knew, from messages we'd sent each other after, that this one had been a particularly satisfying job for him. "You mean the time you also managed to capture the CEO on his own security cameras watching gay porn?"

"Yes!"

I nodded. "That was classic! And the perfect thing to post when the media found out about their 'donation' to the shelter and the CEO tried to deny it."

"I might not tell people who I am, but at least you know, when you're on a forum, that the name is fake. The rest...I own who I am. And I don't make others feel shitty for being like me."

I smirked. "So you don't mind if, when the media report that you blew up SWS, I post footage of *you* watching porn?"

"As long as it doesn't end up being a porn of me watching porn." He put a hand dramatically over his heart. "Think of my mother!"

We did a mix of socializing and trying to work on our cause. Things felt easy by the time it was our turn to sleep. Easy with a side of me being sure that there was some mutual sexual tension building.

That night, we slept. Just slept. I was too shagged to shag, as it were. And it felt like we were both carefully avoiding even having our backs touch. Fortunately, Jonny neither snored nor kicked. Nobody had to die just yet.

CHAPTER 12

Tuesday. At 1100, when our alarm went off, I discovered that waking up together was way more awkward than falling asleep together. Or at least it felt that way to me. I was glad I'd slept with my back to Jonny; it gave me a moment to pretend it didn't feel awkward before I sat up and tried to be nonchalant about smoothing down my hair. Even knowing he was there, it startled me when Jonny spoke.

"No snooze? Just get up with the first alarm?"

I stood from the bed and turned around to find Jonny with his arm flung over his face, presumably to protect him from the very little bit of sunlight filtering in around the edges of the blackout blinds. "Come on, badarse spaceGoddity, we've got a world to save. You can hit snooze as many times as you like in a few weeks." Not that I wouldn't have loved hitting snooze, or just not setting an alarm. But it didn't feel very heroic to do that right now.

I pulled on some clothes, my back to Jonny. When I turned, he was just blearily standing up. I very purposefully did not stare at his mostly-unclothed body. Nope.

I waited whilst he put on his own clothing, and then followed him out of the bedroom. We were greeted with cups of coffee (I made a note to myself to return the favor from now on at every "shift change" with Bryan and Rye) and suggestively questioning looks. Riles looked skeptically relieved when I shook my head.

Jonny took the proffered cup, but didn't take a drink. He put it on a side table and said, "I need to piss first."

He turned to go, and turned back with some confusion when he didn't hear anyone following him. I looked at Bryan and Rye, wondering if they figured it was my turn. The two of them exchanged a look, and then Bryan shook his head at me as they turned back to their computers.

I slowly said, "I guess it looks like you've earned the privilege of pissing without an audience."

Jonny looked pleasantly surprised and gave a quiet little "huh" as he walked back to the bathroom.

As soon as the door was closed, I turned to my mates. "Okay, so what's up? Why is even Riles okay with this?"

They both leaned back from their machines and Bryan looked at Rye like this was zir story to tell. Zie told it quickly and quietly.

"Right after you guys went to bed, I knew I was still not awake enough to do anything potentially important or dangerous. I finished up the SWS facility map—which you'll want to see—and then decided to concentrate on digging into Jonny whilst I was waking up. Because we need to get to trust or get him out stat. And I found that he has a secondary 'nym, another persona he's used. A black hat one."

"What?!" I tried not to shout. "I can't wait to hear how this leads to him getting trusted."

"It was one he used to infiltrate a black hat forum and stop them from doing some seriously malicious hacks." Riles leaned in closer. "It was also one of the first aliases that SWS tried and failed to pin on someone, but they still approached him. Apparently, without knowing who he really was. And they approached with a ridiculously huge offer. Millions of dollars. Which he turned down right before, and I mean *immediately* before, he shut down and, as best he could, nuked that persona. Deleted all online accounts and such. There's just what he has on his computer and what I could find of people on the forum complaining about him when he stopped them getting nasty."

Bryan jumped in, "So, basically, he's rejected money and been willing to give his own life for a cause that we've verified is legitimate. Plus is either a great actor or feels like shit about the people he felt he had to kill." He shrugged. "Short of loads of time, I don't see how we get more trust."

There was a cough, and we looked up to see Jonny quietly watching us. He walked (really quietly) to the couch and took a seat between me and Riles. He opened his portable and calmly said, "I only heard what Bryan said last, since you might be wondering how much of a conversation that was clearly about me I just heard." He looked up. "Though I suspect you were talking about why I was just allowed to be alone. And I *wish* I'd overheard more."

I raised both hands to indicate I was out.

Rye looked a little abashed for a breath, but zie sat up straighter and said, "I'm willing to own what I did. Because it was the right thing." Zie turned to look Jonny in the eyes as zie admitted, "I found out you were FriedIce. And that you not only stopped those black hats but also turned down millions from SWS."

Jonny was still. "So, digging into my computer?"

"Yes. That's what I was doing."

Jonny didn't reply for a moment, but sounded like he was trying very hard to be patient with us when he did. "It was the right thing. It's what I would have done in your position. So..." He turned to face the whole group. "Is everyone done with that phase of things? Because I honestly don't think I have any other secrets and that our time would be better spent on...I don't know, maybe vetting the other people for our team?" He sounded much less cranky about it than I would have been.

Yes, yes, we all nodded. And then I tried to move us on. "Okay, Riley, show us the map. And then I need a shower."

Zie paired zir portable to the wall TV, the map already up. The map of SWS facilities was much clearer when rendered on a computer rather than with an old paper map and bottle caps. We could see that SWS was definitely, heavily concentrated on coasts near oceans. Their landlocked offices were sparse. Just enough to have offices in the largest cities of big countries like the United States or to have one office in the largest city of most other (smaller) countries. Well, most non-African countries. Apparently their ambitions hadn't yet carried them into conquering that massive continent. They'd stuck to the coastlines in Africa. In fact, they weren't always concentrated most densely where the populations were densest. On all the continents, the coastlines were densest. Something seemed off, but I didn't think I had the skills or enough information (yet) to sort it out.

Bryan agreed, "That's what I thought. Not something that actually seems pertinent to our current situation. But interesting."

"Well, I put it on the shared drive we set up. Just in case

anyone suddenly thinks it's important." Zie pulled up a window to show us the file path.

After a pause for people to take note, Bryan said, "My turn." He asked Riles, "Can I grab the TV?" and they made the switch so that Bryan's portable was the one now joined to the wall TV. He was displaying a list of 'nyms. "My project whilst you slept was vetting people for our team. I didn't want to step on toes," he caught my eyes, "because I suspect this is part of your bigger picture stuff or," he shifted his eyes to Jonny, "your SWS ruining..." He looked back at the TV. "Though maybe it would also count as post-demo day...Anyway. I assume you'll all want to check yourselves, but here are the five people who don't seem to be on SWS radar, who we know are good from working with them, and who look idealistic enough and clean enough to work with." He pulled up some more windows. "Lists of real names, contact information, all that you'll need to get going. Plus," he brought one window to the front, "the contact message I'm suggesting."

"Shoot the message my way," I requested, "because I think I should send it."

The others were typing, looking at the wall TV, then back at their screens. Apparently already at work on confirming what Bryan had done. But they stopped when I said I should send the message.

"How do you reckon?" Jonny asked. "Shouldn't we keep all possible heat on *me*? Haven't I let enough trouble get aimed at you?" He sounded kind of upset, and I thought he might be genuinely worried.

"Nope. Because I'm the one that's already on the SWS radar. You're currently invisible. And, you two," I pointed at Bryan and Riles, "at least have a degree of separation."

Jonny opened his mouth, probably to protest, but shut it again.

"I want to object," said Riley, "but I can't think of any arguments for why it should be any particular one of us."

"Seriously," I insisted. "There's no reason to spread out the trouble if SWS somehow gets wind of whichever of us does it."

I got the message, forwarded from Bryan, just as he teased, "Diva. Hogging all the action."

"But she's not really," Riles reminded us. "Sure, they'll see it's MindKiller sending it, but they'll just assume that apHellion and TesTur are involved." TesTur—for Bryan's heroes Tesla and Turing—and apHellion—Rye's misbehaving twist on aphelion, when a planet is as far from the sun as it can get.

"Yeah, but my rep is enough that I can convince people it was me. I can even get arrogant and angry if they suggest I had help. And you guys can be shocked, just *shocked* that I'd done something like this." I swear I wasn't trying to hog the action. I just wanted to see them get out safe and clear of blame.

"But using me means no one else is implicated and...and I'm actually the one who did the bombing. I can't let you take that fall if it comes up. And you *know* it will come up. It should be me. Plus..." he hesitated. "I don't want this to become a dick measuring contest, but can we agree that I've got as solid a rep as you, so there's no reason to use that argument for why it shouldn't be me."

Bryan moaned, "I want to be convinced, Jonny, but...She's right. Dammit." He sighed. "You know I'd much rather have Jonny take the fall than Katja, no offense, but...she's right. Jonny isn't on the radar. Not really. And he could end up being a secret weapon if SWS and the cops keep their eyes on Kot and her friends."

"I send it. I don't tell them anyone else involved. Not even the others who aren't you guys. And I count on them to not be nosy assholes and confirm that you two are involved. At the very least, they won't ask and I won't tell. It's safer for everyone that way."

Bryan asked, "Rye? Jonny? Yes?"

Both nodded, grudgingly, and went back to their portables.

But Bryan interrupted them, "One more thing." Again, they stopped. He went on, "We should bring in Jonny's doctor as a medical consultant. And get an engineer to work with the doctor. Stat." He pointed at another draft message on the TV. "That's why, in my draft for the follow-up message if they say they'll join, I ask them if they know engineers."

"Jonny, you can loop in your guy, if you want. Though I'd like to be part of that. What he'll be doing will be tied to Riley's and my part." I tried not to sound too demanding, but I wasn't asking.

"Small consolation," Jonny smiled, "But, yeah, I'd like to do that. I'll get on it once we all sign off on," he gestured at the TV, "these five. And, for the record, I'd appreciate if we just call my guy Doc so we don't accidentally get his name out there."

After we all felt good about the five people Bryan had proposed, and after we made sure the messages we might send them were perfect, we held our breath whilst I sent them. Then we gathered around to read as Jonny reached out to Doc. As repayment for help taking care of a Peacemaker and to make it so he could keep helping, one of Doc's clients had set him up with some secure contact information. That's why Riles had felt okay asking him questions. And that's why Jonny reached out to him directly to ask if he'd be our medical expert, if he was willing to do more. We promised to do everything we knew to make sure he couldn't be traced, that we could send information back and forth safely. He was cautiously willing, but got much more on board when Jonny said he could send schematics for Peacemakers and other so-called wearables, that we were looking for an engineer to help him read them. Doc was in.

With all our invitations to join the team sent, I stood and announced, "I'm showering." I turned back halfway down the hall and laughingly suggested, "Maybe they're on the coasts 'cos they're putting something in the water. If I don't come back, you know that's it."

In the shower, I savored the aloneness. I loved my friends and living with them when we were younger had been the right answer. But, in the years since, I'd discovered how much I valued solitude. And I was pretty sure that I was a saner, better person overall when I got it. So I stood in the falling hot water and prescribed a daily shower from now until whenever we felt like it wasn't dangerous to be alone.

What I had to acknowledge was that "whenever" was now further into the future than it had been a few days ago. Remember how, just days ago, we all thought the only thing we were waiting for was the bomber to be caught? And then how we thought we were going to do just that? I sighed. Yeah. The bomber was no longer the threat. Now, "whenever" involved a large global corporation with fingers in security and surveillance and people's skulls. If I could just walk away and let SWS do whatever they wanted, my "whenever" could be right now.

I hoped that, someday, my Gran would be proud of the sense of ethics she'd instilled once my mum's drug use got her killed and out of our lives. I knew Gran worried, hoping that trauma and bad examples in my early childhood wouldn't turn me into a criminal. Fortunately, Gran wasn't exactly opposed to hacking-related crimes, as long as I wasn't a black hat. Nothing malicious.

I figured she might even be delighted, if we pulled this off, that I was one of the heroes of this story. If this story was ever safe to share.

I grudgingly ended my shower and got dressed. I'd make sure to spoil myself with plenty of solitude once we saved the world.

As soon as I walked into the living room, Bryan said, "You might want to check your email. And maybe call Gran."

I couldn't quite read his tone, but moved to open my email as I asked, "What's wrong? Something with the people we contacted?"

"Not that. It looks like the cops and SWS just made a load of calls, sent a lot of emails. They're keen to talk to your friends."

And he was right. Based on who was contacting me suddenly, they'd reached out to anyone who'd interacted with me on social media over the last year, as well as to anyone who'd sent email to my public account or called (or been called by) me. So far, from what I could tell, only Jonny was safe from that. Even people like Paul, the bouncer at the Orpheum who saw me just for a few moments of casual chat each week, were checking in to let me know they'd been contacted.

I felt bad about that, people being harassed and having to spend time on this. I hoped it wouldn't turn me into everyone's most hated. Though, at least for now, the messages were more along the lines of, "Just so you know, I got this message from them. No worries. I know you're innocent. Hope you're okay." I also had a text from Gran. Classic:

    I promise not to tell the cops about all your

petty thefts from my chocolate stash as a child :-
P

I sighed and said, "Well, at least people seem to be taking it well."

Riles gave me an exaggerated glare. "You haven't asked how *we're* taking it."

I returned zir glare. And then we both sort of kept at it, trying to make our faces even more ridiculously glare-like. Leaned forward, across an amused Jonny—who sat back so as not to ruin this mature entertainment choice—until we were right in each others' faces. Riles growled at me, I growled back. And that was about what we could take without laughing.

I knew too well that, until I got solitude, not acting my age (a.k.a. being silly) might be the only thing to help defuse the anxiety and frustration that seemed to be collecting in my stomach.

Quietly, without looking up from his work, Bryan said, "I hate you too." I looked over and he smiled, just a little.

As we worked on other parts of our plans, we kept an eye on those few people we'd reached out to for help. We didn't see anyone running to SWS or any other authorities. We held our breath, hoping our paranoia and investigations had been sufficient. And watched as every one of them, except Jonny's non-hacker Doc, got quieter. Oh, their public posting levels didn't change. That would have been a rooky mistake. But their private messages did and the content of their public posts got a little less damning. They now knew what we knew: we couldn't count on our peers being trustworthy. So, as we had done, they got very quiet behind their public faces.

We also watched as all of them took steps to try to confirm the story we'd told them, to look carefully into SWS or to verify the authenticity of docs we'd shared with them. It was good I had a reputation; they didn't just write me off as a conspiracy crazy. It was possible I'd gotten into SWS. It was possible I'd dug up dirt. It was possible I'd put together pieces. I was capable and clever.

A couple hours into working and watching, Jonny cautiously asked, "Why do you think…" But he trailed off, left us watching him for the rest of that question as he pushed a few more keys on his portable. He finally looked up and realized we were waiting. "Sorry. I just wanted to make sure I'd seen what I thought I'd seen. Uh…Could I put this up on the wall TV?"

I initiated the necessary commands, and we saw two documents, side-by-side, on the TV. We all stood up to look at them. One document was blueprints, but they were watermarked as classified. The other was the same blueprints, but without a watermark. Both displayed a lower level of SWS headquarters. Finding the differences wasn't exactly difficult; some of them were glaring.

Jonny stood by us, balancing his portable and pointed out some differences anyway. "This room, this whole area, isn't on the other map. Nor is this." He waved his hand around what looked like a tunnel, then traced the tunnel off the side of the building and…Was that into Puget Sound? Did they have some kind of underwater entrance?

"What the hell?" Bryan wondered.

Jonny shrugged. "I don't know. But any room they keep hard to find must be important. Plus, it's like there's a column of all the important stuff. The levels above seem to have the other things we need to blow just above the secret room. And the classified versions of those floors make it look like they're on…it looks like elevators, kind of. They can be lowered down." He paused and considered. "Maybe lowered and taken out through Puget Sound and into the ocean?"

This was some film-type shit.

Riley mumbled, "Underwater entrance. Unbelievable."

"Yeah, and I *want* it to be incorrect," said Jonny, "because then I could keep looking for blueprints that don't also seem to show that I can't get fucking bomb bugs in through vents."

Bryan was pacing, but stopped. "What? But that's our safe way in."

Jonny ran his hand through his hair, frustrated. "I know. Shit. I know. I guess...I guess I'll take the bugs in with me, in a briefcase or something, when I go in to send messages." He nodded his head decisively, plan made. "According to a memo in the same folder..." He looked abashed as he went on. "They found the bugs in the footage from Katja's old building, so they immediately installed fine grates on every opening in or out, aside from the windows and doors, on every building they own. And that means I have to take the risky way."

I tried not to whine, "But we're trying to keep you from having to be in there. Minimize *our* deaths too."

"There's still hope," he reassured me. "I don't have to stay in once the bugs are in. I can just drop them off and you guys can send them through the building whilst I send the messages. Then I just try to get out quickly so that I have a chance to get out before the blast hits." He looked at the blueprints a moment. "Hell, if we decide to trust these, it should actually be easier. The bugs all go to the center column of stuff and I make sure I'm not that deep in. There's hope. As long as we do better figuring out the amount and the location for the bugs than I did before..." His voice trailed off into shame.

Bryan stood by Jonny, staring at the blueprints. "There has to be some way we can confirm at least some of this. If we can confirm *something* odd in this is real, I'd feel okay trusting the rest."

Rye curled onto the couch in some sort of fetal thinking position. "We could try to confirm the underwater entrance. But I don't see a non-dangerous way to confirm the rest."

Jonny volunteered, "If it helps, this document was buried deep *and* encrypted."

Bryan stopped pacing. "Yeah, that helps. You don't encrypt a lie, right? Not if you don't think someone is going to look for it." He turned to Rye. "How do you want to confirm the entrance?"

Riles practically bounced. "We can get little remote fishes with cameras and swim by!"

I had to laugh. It was simple and obvious and totally a Riley answer.

"I can even get some today, right now. I saw options at a toy store a couple weeks ago." Who could say "no" to that enthusiasm?

By way of reply, Bryan grabbed his jacket. "I've got some things to pick up for making sure we have lives after demo day. If anyone wants anything, speak up now. Looks like Riles and I are going shopping."

I drew up a quick list of household supplies and food. I hadn't exactly stocked up for this many people in my flat. Bryan waved away our cards when Jonny and I tried to help cover costs. "Let's keep finances separate. If you put credits on my card, they could come back to get you." He pointed to Jonny. "Especially you. Remember, right now, you seem to be the only one of us completely off their radar and not connected to us."

When we were alone, Jonny and I worked a bit in silence. Then Jonny asked, "How's your hand today?"

I paused to consider it. It hadn't looked too horrible when I changed the plasters on it earlier. "It's healing. I'll be totally down to normal level of hurt soon, like anyone who's tripped on the sidewalk."

Jonny nodded, but didn't look at me. "Good." He worked a little, and then said, "I'm really sorry."

I didn't know if he could see it, but I shook my head. "You're probably okay to stop apologizing for that now. Really."

Even though I was working, trying to finalize the lists of things we could ask our remote comrades to do if they signed on, I could tell he'd stopped working and was looking at me.

"Thank you. And, I don't want to make things weird, but..." He took a deep breath. "But I also don't want to have these end up being our last few weeks, have us not actually make it out of demo day alive, and waste the chance to say something."

I wanted to be playing it cool, but I knew my typing had slowed. I could feel a palpable change in the air, something electric and heavy, but in a comfortable way (big electric blanket?). Jonny put his hand on my arm, and I stopped pretending I was actually working. I didn't look up, but I wasn't typing any more. I didn't consider myself lonely or even a good candidate for anything more than friendship and casual sex, but I kind of hoped I knew what had made the air heavy. I had to admit I might really be interested in him.

"I don't want to pretend that I didn't like everything I saw and learned as I tried to figure out who you were and if you were compromised. And I don't want to feel like I'm walking around with a secret. Even a secret that isn't really...secret. Both because I want you three to trust me and because some things, even if they aren't reciprocated, are better known." He'd made it through that far sounding nervous but basically okay. He had to stop a moment though.

I was trying to decide whether now was when I should say something or if there was more he wanted to say. As I tried to sort that out, he went on. "I don't want to pretend that, having been right here for the last few days, I haven't proven to myself that MK, the intimidating and brilliant MindKiller, is more than just some kind of shiny myth. Some kind of pretty façade that covers an undesirable core."

I realized his hand was still on my arm. And I decided that, unless he quickly went on, he'd said enough. I should reply. I should try to keep myself from being fawning, because liking him was probably stupid, but I should reply.

"So, are you saying you think I'm pretty?" Ah, yes, feigning coyness. That seemed like the sort of classic move I'd probably picked up from TV. I looked up, finally, and gave him a smile with a little laughter in it.

He grinned. "I think, at this point, both of us can safely assume that we find each other pretty."

"Yeah. We're both pretty." His hand was still on my arm. "And smart, right?"

"Oh, definitely smart. It would be much easier on me if you were stupid or a horrible person. Instead of horribly smart and capable."

We were both pretty and smart and grinning like idiots.

"Alright then." I nodded like a decision had just been made. But then I squinted and asked, "Wait, what would be easier on you?"

He was still grinning, but he squirmed a little. "Please tell me I'm not the only one who finds it a little distracting. Trying to finish clever planning things when I'm sitting by someone that...I really like."

Some self-consciousness flitted across his face, but seemed to clear up when my grin turned into what felt like a dopey, abashed smile. Dammit. I'd really meant to have nothing but sexual interest.

He went on, "I'm trying to see what my options are for blowing up a building and avoiding innocent deaths, but my brain is at least partly mooning over the pretty and smart person sitting right by me. Sometimes *right* by me. And, if it were any other work we were doing, I'd just put down my portable and try to get you to put down yours." He finally seemed to realized his hand was still on my arm, because he carefully withdrew it. "And I'd suggest we just walk away from this for a while to...I don't know. To get a meal and talk and dance and look at stars and..." He looked away.

I turned to face him and put *my* hand on *his* arm. "But this isn't any other work, so we're both..." and I caught his eyes, "we're *both* trying to pretend that our heads are fully in the game."

"Yeah?"

"Yeah." I cleared my throat. "I mean, I obviously don't know you as well and don't know that I feel how you feel. I should be clear about that. But...yeah..."

He looked down at my hand on his arm, and then he took it in one of his hands. "And now I have to wonder whether me saying this, whether both of us saying that, to some degree or other, we're interested, was the right choice. Does it make it harder to ignore when the fear of rejection is gone?"

"Oh, I don't know that this applies to me." I put on my cockiest tone. "I was sure there was no way you could resist me. Especially once I'd pulled a gun on you." I grinned at him and we both laughed.

"If it hadn't been pointed at me...and even then, in hindsight, yeah, kind of sexy." He put up his free hand as if in protest. "Not, mind you, that I'm asking for you to do that to me again. But I can't promise not to think dirty thoughts if you ever need to do it to someone else." We laughed again and he squeezed my hand.

I looked down at my hand in his. I sat in a charged but comfortable silence for what felt like minutes. But then I thought, *What the hell?*

I looked up, leaning in, and found that I wasn't the only one doing that. I grinned, Jonny grinned, and we narrowly avoided our first kiss being one of those things where your teeth bump. But we didn't kiss long before Jonny sat back.

He traced my cheekbone. "I would *really* rather not stop, but we have this." And he waved towards our computers. "This damned higher cause." He looked as disappointed as I felt. "We have to work."

Argh. He was right. Of course he was right. Plus, I didn't think it was an ideal point in the trust-building for Riley and Bryan to walk in on us. I sighed and sat back, nodding sadly.

"But," he said, "I would really like to do this again some time. Soon. If that's okay with you."

"Oh, definitely. This," and then I pointed back and forth between us, "whatever this currently is, is something I'd like to explore. Thoroughly."

We both smoothed hair and clothing and turned back to computers. Before we got back to work, he asked, "So, are your friends going to just know? Or are you going to tell them. Or," and he looked at me a little concerned, "is this something they *shouldn't* know?"

I shook my head. "Not a secret. I keep plenty of secrets from plenty of people, but not those two. Especially not a secret like getting to snog someone pretty." I grinned and resisted an urge to go in for some more kissing. "If Riles doesn't psychically pick up on it, you can just assume I'll mention it to whichever of them I find myself alone with first."

"Does that mean I could...put my arm around you or hold your hand or something like that in front of them?"

I thought a moment. To most people, that would be a simple question, but it had actually been a while since I bothered with anyone that I saw outside of a club or outside of a bedroom. Hand holding suddenly seemed particularly intimate. "Yeah. They might give us some shit, some very gentle shit, or be surprised, but sure."

"Surprised?"

"I'm pretty solitary by nature. Don't let my intense friendships with Rye and Bryan fool you. I'm solitary and not lonely and don't generally meet anyone that I feel like I want to give regular time to. So, for the last few years at least, I've kept it to flirting at the club or occasional hookups." I shrugged. "I'm not against the *idea* of more, but I never considered myself someone who was up for more. Nobody but Bryan or Riles has had the level of comfort with me that would allow hand holding or arms around in a while."

"Now isn't the time to talk about whether or not this is just another potential hookup, is it?"

I leaned back and considered him. "Actually, not to be a stereotypical girl, but I tend to know things like that quickly. And *you* have had years to work on your opinion, apparently. Plus, it kind of sounds like you think this *is* the time to talk about that."

"I have opinions, but, like you said, I know I've had more time to develop them. And maybe it's stupid to even think about this when we're living in this perpetually watchful and endangered state?"

"It probably is." I took his hand. "But, for what it's worth, you're seeming pretty damned stellar. No promises, but I'm not looking at you as just some kind of hookup. Instead, I'm looking at you as maybe someone who I might want to give more time to. Maybe."

He squeezed my hand gratefully. I gave myself a gold star for not leaning in to kiss him again, and we both turned back to our computers.

It turned out that, in fact, telling me he was interested had been the right choice. There was a new comfort now, and I didn't need to lose thought cycles to wondering when (and if) I might actually get to put my hands on him. I would. I had. My brain could now work contentedly on the world-saving.

As soon as they walked into the living room, Riles brandished zir box of little fishes. This conspiracy of ours appeared to be giving zir an excuse for fun. Zir face could have split from the grin. "Fishes, bitches!" But then zie stopped. Yeah, zie'd sensed something.

Zie didn't even get to say it before Bryan gave Jonny and I considering looks. "Well, that took longer than I thought." He turned to empty out the contents of the bags into their appropriate rooms, but Riley swooped in to sit in Bryan's chair and look at us.

Rye rested zir face innocently in zir hands, leaned on the arm of the chair. "So, did you fuck?" Even zir tone was pure innocence. It was zir gift.

I looked over to see Jonny looking a bit awkward, so I decided to handle this. "No, baby, we didn't fuck." Rye feigned dramatic disappointment, so I said, "Don't worry. It's definitely in my plans." And then I grinned and looked over to watch as awkwardness and pleasure warred on Jonny's face. Ha!

"But!" And I grabbed Rye's hand. "You have a school of fish! Please, return to showing off your fish and telling us your plan."

Lucky for us, Riles was happy to be derailed. "I'm going to try the fishes out as best I can in your kitchen sink. Make sure I know what I'm doing. And then," zie beamed with anticipatory joy, "Bry and I will head back out to check for the entrance before our early sleep shift."

"Consider my sink your testing grounds!" I encouraged, and zie jumped up to do just that.

Bryan had finished emptying bags, and came back to the living room to stand in front of me, shifting uncomfortably. "Hey, Kot?"

"Mmhmm?"

"I hate to ask this, but it's relevant to me thinking about life after demo day."

I furrowed my brow at him in confusion. Where the hell was he going?

He went on, "In the event there's life after demo day, there are a couple of girlfriends who have been mainly ignored since your building blew up."

I stiffened but said, "Yeah, I'd wondered about those couple of girlfriends."

"Plus, they've been pretty much summoned like me and Riles to talk to the cops. So I wondered if they could drop by for a little while tonight to hang out."

I wanted to be unreasonable, but I wasn't actually a horrible person. I swallowed my annoyed sigh. "Yeah, you should probably see them. Unless we tell them what we're doing, there's no reason to expect they'd understand weeks of being ignored."

"I told 'Randa we were heads down on a project with a rough deadline, and she said maybe she and Kitty could drop by with dinner. Maybe late dinner. After we do the fish. Not for long. And Riles and I are both willing to give up some of our sleep time if it comes to that."

I saw Riles in the kitchen doorway, fishes in hand and watching the conversation. I smiled at zir. "Yeah, that sounds okay. Of course we can take a food break for your relationships."

Bryan thanked me and called 'Randa. Riles packed up zir fishes and told us, "We'll put them in the water and sit in a coffee place, recording. I'll make sure it's streaming to you guys. And then, if possible, I'll rescue my fishes. We'll be home before the girls show up."

Jonny said, "And, in addition to watching the fishes' feeds, we'll make sure there's nothing incriminating for your girlfriends to see. Also..."

Jonny pulled his bag out of a corner and dug into it. From the very bottom, he pulled something small and shiny and handed it to Bryan, who looked a bit hesitant. Jonny quickly reassured him, "There's no C-4 on it. See?"

That's when I realized it must be a bug.

"If you guys would drop this off as close to headquarters as you think you can get without drawing attention, I want to see if I can find a way to get it in, just in case I'm reading the blueprints wrong."

Bryan pocketed the bug. "Sure, mate. Good call."

Alone in the flat again, Jonny and I managed to keep our hands off each other. We did a quick look through the rooms, making sure there was nothing out that the impending baes shouldn't see. Then we joined my computer to the wall TV to get ready to watch the fishes' feeds. Finally, Jonny pulled up the bug in Bryan's pocket on his portable. It didn't have sound, just a little camera, so all we saw was darkness.

And then we sat on the couch as if we were going to work. And then...But Jonny put his arm around me, so work wasn't going to happen.

We were interrupted far too soon by a chat window on my computer.

> Bryan: Fishes are in place, but we're a no go
> on the bug. Looks like they also took away
> all bug-cover...No more grass or bushes by
> building. Concrete courtyard with some art
> out front; concrete all around building as
> far as I can tell. All very newly installed.

Jonny softly hissed, "Dammit," and I hopped up to see fish feeds on my TV.

The fishes Riles had purchased were a school of 5 tiny, non-spectacular looking fishes. I'd expected something bigger and brighter, but that wouldn't have been the smartest idea. And Riles was smart. I suspected the toy store only stocked them so that there were tiny options that people could play with in their sinks or, if they had them, bathtubs. Adults seemed to like realistic toys.

So a tiny school of shimmery silver was now wriggling its way through the questionable waters of Puget Sound and towards what we hoped was a very obvious underwater entrance. Of course, they'd shimmer less soon. The waters were filthy, polluted and brown like most waters near cities seemed to get. We'd be lucky to see an entrance even if it were brightly lit with a "Secret Underwater Entry" sign. Thanks, people, for making it hard for us to save you.

Lucky for, well, the world, I guess, it looked like the water was getting clearer the closer our fish got. It wasn't exactly pure, but something was doing a little filtering on that water. And that's how we saw it.

There was a metal door in the dirt. Not an old and worn metal door. But something that, taking into account how dirty it would have gotten sitting in Puget Sound, looked only about as old as the SWS headquarters.

That was it. We couldn't find a grate or a crack to slip our fishes through (though it seemed like the water filtering action was centered on the door), and we didn't dare let them look like anything other than actual fish. They had to just keep swimming by. Riles guided them up the coast a bit, then chanced one more pass. Yep, still a metal door with no obvious entry points for our wee school.

We decided that was about what we could do. Rye sent the school near, just once more, to try to look up from the surface and make sure we were in the right spot. Which is how we discovered there was a thin electric net on the water right by the headquarters. (Fortunately, we watched a water bug—not one of the fish—touch it and fry.) The water wasn't devoid of security. And we were definitely in the right place.

SWS had an underwater entrance.

Bryan and Riles weren't home for too long before their baes showed up. Just long enough to tuck away the fishes. (Rye was thrilled that none had been caught and that zie'd noticed the electrical netting before sending zir fishes up to die.)

Kitty and 'Randa showed up with bags of Thai food and drinks. They were visibly unhappy with the situation (i.e. that their baes had been mostly out of touch for days and almost-certainly spending most that time with me), but they had the class not to tear into Bryan or Rye in front of other people.

They were also visibly confused and curious about me, sitting by someone and letting that someone put their arm around me. Maybe even looking comfortable with each other. Last they'd heard, I was single (to be fair, that was probably still true now) and not interested in anything more than hookups.

We ate and did casual conversation (I loathe casual conversation). Kitty and 'Randa seemed to be tag-teaming an attempt to pry into who Jonny was. I did have the presence of mind to ask them not to mention Jonny to the cops. "He wasn't even around for the bombing, so there's no reason to fuck up his life as well." They nodded. That was wise. Also, Jonny, did you know about the bombing? And they were back to questions.

When food was finished, the two couples ducked off for a few seconds (presumably to kiss and apologize) before saying their goodbyes. Jonny gave me a look as soon as we were alone in the room. I had to cover my mouth to keep from laughing. "Yes," I psychically told him, "those are the girlfriends."

He leaned in to whisper, "They *aren't* terrible."

I swallowed my laugh and conceded, "Not *terrible*, just...so girly and alien, you know?"

He nodded that he knew, then took advantage of the alone moment and already having faces right by each other to get some kisses in of our own (but no apologizing; we were definitely the couple—using that word loosely—having the better time of things).

The girls bounced back in to insist on hugs goodbye. I apologized for keeping their baes secluded and promised it wouldn't be for long. They too-casually assured me it was *fine* and they'd just get extra time later. Besides, we'd all be going out Saturday, right?

I don't think we'd thought about Saturday and routines. We four conspirators exchanged uncertain looks, but Jonny said, "Of course we will. It's the routine, right? And doing some normal things when we're working like this seems like a good idea." Yes, okay, we got the implications in his carefully enthusiastic response.

So, we all nodded. The girls beamed. Goodbye hugs all around. There you have it.

Once Kitty and 'Randa were gone, Bryan and Riles said they wanted to watch the fish footage once on the wall TV before bed. We queued up the files and, unlike when we recorded, we watched them one at a time, just in case some high definition fishy had caught a detail the others had missed. There wasn't much new, though it was clear in this larger view that, unless our research turned up another explanation for it, there was indeed an underwater entrance to the SWS headquarters.

Looking at a single fish's footage in larger scale, we could see that the door probably had an iris opening. And it had some kind of writing on it, but not in any language or alphabet I recognized. Nobody else recognized it either, but it was symbols that were definitely something more than just, I don't know, an organic growth or mud brushed off by passing marine life. No, this had clean lines, perfect circles, and appeared to be made with some kind of blue-ish paint. We got as clean a screen capture of it as we could, and set up an anonymous interface to do a symbol search on the 'Net without it being traced back to us.

Just before Rye and Bryan went to bed, we started to hear back from the people we'd contacted. They were cautious, but we seemed to have chosen well. Not a one of them said, "So what? Not my problem." All of them wanted to know more. And not just "please tell me which of our peers are compromised," but "what's the plan?" or "how can I help?" Fortunately, we'd already prepped the possible careful response emails. "If they respond this way, send this. But, if this way, send this."

Once they got our second email, they could start taking actions. Helping out. We still needed an engineer, but we now had more people looking for the right person. Fortunately, fear of corrupted peers meant nobody would let good intentions (let's grow our army!) prompt them to invite anyone else into the cause without checking with us. At least that's what we were counting on.

This all now felt even more real and dangerous. I was scared shitless. But, like they say, courage isn't lack of fear; it's doing the thing *in spite of* fear. And I planned to spite fear something fierce.

Whilst Jonny tried to come up with other ways to get his bugs into the SWS building, I read SWS documents until I went cross-eyed. Nearing the end of our shift, I stumbled across something. I thought I did. Maybe? I nudged Jonny. "I'm tired. I need a second set of eyes."

He leaned over to see my screen. "What've you got?"

I pointed. "Symbols on some documents, like the ones on the door."

He leaned in closer to take it in.

I gave him a moment before I pointed at another document. "There are a few with this."

Riles and Bryan shambled out of the bedroom, and we hopped up to put coffee in their hands and to seat them in front of my screen. "You have to see this," I said as I started pointing.

"What the fuck am I looking at?" Riles was having a cranky morning. Not too surprising when it was barely morning, more like what we might usually consider a late bedtime. Bryan just sleepily blinked and stared where I was pointing.

"Katja just found it." Jonny made sure my screen was zoomed in and centered on the spot in question. "They're symbols that look like the ones on the underwater door. Right?"

I pointed to docs on my screen. "See? They're in the flow of text sometimes. Sometimes as notes that look handwritten. Sometimes tiny on the margins of docs. And the more a document seems like it would only have been seen by highest level execs, the more there are. At least in my current, random sampling."

Bryan asked, "Did the symbol search on the door pics return anything?"

I shook my head. "Nothing yet. Maybe these are clearer? I'm thinking let's get some of this going in the search as well."

Bryan nodded. "Good call. Anything else interesting whilst we slept?"

"All five of the folks we invited to join the fun are in. And I finished a detailed plan, lists of people and actions and such."

Jonny said, "I've done most of the same for my part. Just finished it now. And failed to find a way to get bugs into the building other than walking them in on my person." He closed his computer. "Plus I put notes on Kot's plan."

Riles spoke into his coffee. "So, we'll review plans first, maybe? So we can get moving?"

"Mine should be done today as well," Bryan said. "We'll be able to start acting soon. Today."

There seemed to be a collective sense of relief. I might be an indoorsy girl, happy to sit at my computer all day, but this had me itching to do more. Even if "more" also included a lot of computer time.

Like last night, our fall into bed was not an erotic tumbling but an exhausted drop. Backs to each other. Suddenly, our admission of feelings earlier *was* making things more difficult for me. I wanted to sleep, I knew I should sleep, but my brain suddenly filled with very important questions, like what if I did embarrassing things in my sleep and he noticed and I didn't even get sex once before my humanity ruined it? Was he also still awake? Should I make a move? Did I want to make a move at this point? Would he *want* me to make a move? How could I make a move in a way that left room for consent but also didn't end up with me mortified if he didn't want to do anything?

I tentatively, carefully, scooted backwards a little and stuck a leg back so that it barely touched him. Smooth. Because he'd never suspect that I didn't just naturally do that all the time in my sleep...

I really only had so many approaches, and all of them were totally straight-forward and had nothing to do with approaching someone I might actually like and want to build more than a sweaty night with.

To my great relief, I felt him shift and also move a leg back. And then we sort of tangled our legs. And shifted more so that our backs were pressing into each other. At that point, I could feel that both of us were breathing heavily.

I held that position for a while. It felt important not just to cast myself onto the current of wanting him. Not yet.

And we had to sleep. We really had to sleep. I was reminding myself of that as I turned towards him. As soon as he felt me turning, he turned as well. We were reaching and grappling for each other, reorienting and re-tangling legs as we pressed our mouths together like the force we'd spread out through our pressed backs was now all concentrated in our mouths. That desperate sort of hungry push that comes from your core when you just want to devour the person in your arms.

We were peeling off each other's clothes when that bastard remembered he was the logical and reasonable one. He stopped and made a frustrated sound.

"What's wrong?" I was trying not to sound annoyed. I *wasn't* annoyed. I just really wanted these clothes out of the way.

"Nothing. There's nothing *wrong*. I just...I just wonder if we shouldn't sleep and maybe be in less bleary and emotionally huge places before we go any further. Especially since...I currently like you a lot more than you probably like me and I'd like to not get too messed up." He flopped back with another frustrated sound. "Fuck my supposedly-reasonable brain."

I laid back. "You should be more of an asshole. More

interested in what your dick wants. Jerk."

"I'm sorry."

"No. It's okay. You're probably right." I sighed, leaned over to kiss his cheek, and rolled back over onto my side, my back against his side. "But I can't promise to keep thinking this tomorrow."

He kissed the back of my neck, and then rolled over and pressed his back into mine, a leg tentatively back to see if I'd tangle. "I can't promise I will either."

We tangled legs and, after some time of ignoring that our bodies (well, my body; I'm going to assume his too) were shouting at us, fell asleep.

CHAPTER 13

Wednesday, when the alarm sounded, I felt Jonny turn and trace lines on my back. Apparently, this morning it was my turn to not want to jump out of bed. But I am the master of my meat (hear that, body?), so I gave a little disappointed groan and sat up. "Next time someone sucks me into their conspiracy fighting, they better be smart but otherwise unattractive."

My back was still to him, but I felt him shift. "I totally agree. I don't want some other pretty bastard to grab your eye."

I faced him as I pulled on clothes. "You planning to keep my eye for a while, not just leave me in the dust of demo day, pretty bastard?"

He grinned, pulling on his own clothes. "I'm considering it."

When we walked out and I met Rye's questioning eyes with a shake of my head, zie narrowed zir eyes in disbelief. I narrowed mine back, and zie shook zir head as if I were hopeless.

I said, "Don't worry, Riles, I'll send up a flare when we do."

Jonny guffawed, looking a bit embarrassed. Fortunately, as before, there was coffee to hide our faces in immediately. Even so, I could feel some sort of lingering...something.

I looked up from my cup, and Riles and Bryan looked like they had something they were discreetly dying to say. "What?"

They looked at each other, clearly both eager to be the one to say whatever it was. So that meant it was good news. After a second or two of looking at each other, they brought their hands up and did rock/paper/scissors. Riles won.

With a bounce, zie charged into zir news. "Okay, first, this is really bad *and* good news. But mostly good. Great. Really. So keep that in mind during the bad news." Zie paused and offered to Bryan with exaggerated, faux-sincerity. "I'll share. You tell the bad part."

"Your generosity is...astounding." Bryan was wry, but that didn't stop him telling part of the news. "Things are happening sooner than you thought." He nodded at Jonny as he said that.

"The good news part of the bad news," and you could hear that he was saying that just to bug Riles, "is that we now have a date. And the bad news part of the bad news is that our date is next Friday."

"Next Friday?" Jonny was shocked. "As in less than 9 days from right now?"

Bryan nodded. "Bad news. That's when they're putting their next very important phase in action. Which, at this point...We still don't know for sure what that phase is, but it sure seems possible that it has to do with Peacemakers somehow making people murderers."

Riles picked it up from there. "So it's good that we've got plans drawn up and ready to finalize and go. That's a little more good news." He'd directed that last bit somewhat tauntingly at Bryan, like the amount of news each delivered was a contest. I had to laugh.

"But the really good news part is that this is definitely a big deal, a massive deal, because the top execs, including the ones over non-U.S. offices, are gathering at headquarters to mark the occasion and do whatever it is together."

"No!" This was too good. I truly didn't believe it. "You can't be serious!"

Bryan shrugged. "That's how we know it's really big."

Jonny asked, "How did you find this out? Was there a press release or some kind of executive emails?"

Riley was loving the chance to dole out the info. "Oh, it's even trickier than that. No emails to or between execs. This was from execs' admins making sure only the right people would be in the building Friday evening, and that even security knew to keep clear of the main conference room area as soon as they'd cleared out the people who weren't on the 'right people' list. Plus, planning refreshments, booking meeting halls. I expect we'll see emails to attendees soon, because they seem to be expecting a number of people that's more than the execs."

We processed only a moment, and then Jonny groaned. "My plan needs us to get someone into the building. All that security won't be helpful."

Riley sounded less enthusiastic, trying now to be helpful. "Well, the festivities start right before end of work day. Does that help?"

Jonny pondered. "Maybe. At least it's not hours after end of business." He nodded and sat up straight. "Yeah, I'll look at the emails you guys intercepted and work my plan around it." He looked at Riley and then Bryan. "I'm guessing you put a note about this on my plan when you reviewed it?"

They nodded.

"Also," said Bryan, "you should know that the cops are having us come in for interviews in a couple hours, and 'Randa and Kitty right after. Which means they're probably grilling Gran right now."

Gran. "I should take Gran up on a dinner invitation. Just in case."

Riles and Bryan nodded. They knew how important Gran was to me.

"When would be not-inconvenient for what we're doing here? Or least inconvenient?"

"Sooner," Bryan suggested and the others nodded. "Do it soon as you can, because we're going to need to be available to the others we've brought in on this."

Rye said, "But do it when you can. We've got your back. We can hold things down so you can see her before next Friday."

I smiled my gratitude. "Thanks. I'll text her now and set things up."

Gran replied quickly, asking if tomorrow were too soon (she kind of loves me) and wondering if I could convince my two friends to come along (she kind of loves them, but probably not as much as me, I'd hope).

"Gran wants you guys at dinner too. You in, Bryan? Riles?"

Riley said, "Of course," and Bryan said, "Always."

So I let her know that we wouldn't be able to linger too long, because we were up against a crazy deadline, but (because they also love Gran) Riley and Bryan would love to come along. I wanted to ask about bringing Jonny (because she'd be as pleasantly surprised as I was that there was somebody I might want to be serious about), but I didn't want to say anything that the cops might intercept. Stupid, complicated life. Why isn't saving the world less of a hassle?

When it was arranged, I turned to Jonny. "You're coming

along. Gran always makes plenty of food." When he opened his mouth with a look of protest, I didn't even let him talk. "My gran is important. And we're on an accelerated timeline. You meet the parents *now*. Just in case I want you around later." I raised an eyebrow and tried to look stern, but had to soften it with a smile.

Jonny smiled and nodded. "Okay. Fair point. Let's have supper with Gran tomorrow."

This one was seeming more like a keeper every day. Dammit.

One of our new comrades already knew an engineer. "We have our first candidate for knighthood in our new world, kids. Phrostbyte knows an engineer!"

Bryan gave me a victorious high five and Jonny just went for a hug.

Riles exclaimed, "I want some celebration too!" So, high five for Riles.

"Okay, her name is Alis Bevan. She's in Wales. I've forwarded the message with her other identifying info, and I vote we make digging into her and making sure she's okay our top priority." Everyone nodded and got typing.

She wasn't a hacker, so her security wasn't hard to get around. We read emails and texts and chat sessions. We crawled through everything on her computer. We were pleased to find that she had an idealistic streak and a distrust of soulless corporations. We dug up everything there was to find on her. We could have told you what sort of comments teachers made on her nursery school report cards, who she'd dated at any age and why they broke up, or what her calorie intake and exercise had been like so far today. In fact, with her pedometer linked into her computer, we could tell you what her heart rate was right this moment. (We'd have to ask Phrostbyte to make sure she replaced that pedometer with one that wasn't made by SWS.)

When we sent our comrade a message to get contact set up (we figured it would be rude to make contact ourselves; none of us would respond well to complete strangers suddenly, for instance, displaying a message on our mobiles) and see if Alis

("Let's call her Engie, just to be safe") was up for this in general, we felt as safe as was possible about her character and about her capability to understand the specs we had. Maybe this would be the day we got an engineer.

Wednesday was also the day we each nailed down our plans and the day that Jonny admitted the blueprints were probably right about him not being able to get bugs in from outside the walls unless he walked them in himself. We worked around police interviews and quick visits from girlfriends (who were clever enough to realize that it might seem suspicious to police if they called to tell me about their police interviews, even if those interviews appeared to be non-events). We spent time looking at the symbols in the docs and on the underwater door. We kept digging, trying to find the oldest docs we could, trying to construct the SWS story.

The story was actually kind of troubling.

This wasn't the story of a little business that started in someone's flat and slowly grew. That started humble and just pleased to not be too in debt but grew to the insanely ambitious force it was today. That struggled to bring in brilliant minds until they'd developed a reputation.

From what we could tell, SWS hadn't been suspiciously big, but there were no tiny struggling roots. They came in with strong ideas, a fully-staffed workforce, and reasonable funding from their own execs. They quickly gained trust with strategic companies. The memos were few and far between early on. They weren't even real memos at the start, just lists of things like company names (companies that were quickly added to their client roster). Researching where their execs had come from didn't bring any illumination. There was nothing on them besides the most basic records. These women and men went from nothing to something seemingly overnight.

And in a world where it had been an unquestioned step in forming, running, and eventually promoting a company, they didn't have a vision statement that we could find. Another hole in their web site, along with not having a map of their facilities.

Weird.

What we *could* find was another old doc, before the era of formal memos, apparently written by CEO Johnson and signed by Smith, Williams, and some less important but just as blandly named execs. It seemed vision statement-y, but it never appeared to have been made public. Maybe it had just been for those forming the company to get on the same page. It also had some handwritten notes, like they'd used a stylus to mark up the document. And some of the marks were the characters we hadn't been able to find online. And some appeared to have...were those translations next to them? Maybe this was like kids making up their own language, creating a code. We'd played with that ourselves when we were younger. (We went scrambling through the other docs with symbols to see if any matched; nothing useful did.)

And this, as far as we could tell, was what the vision was for SWS from their inception:

As Peaceforgers it is our duty to guide the world into peace. Through our influence and actions, we ensure that all are brought into the light of peace or cast aside as darkness. In a world of war and fear, we bring the light of security. No darkness will stand. Peace is security. Security is peace.

That last phrase had become their well-known "Peace Through Security, Security Through Peace" motto. But the rest had, wisely, been kept back from the world. We all agreed it sounded a little...religious, in the worst possible way. Maybe even cult-like. Not that we disagreed with pursuing peace and light. But there was something in the phrasing, maybe in the fact that they'd given themselves a name. A capitalized name. I guess you couldn't accuse them of being the usual sterile corporate entity. At least not at heart, behind closed doors. They weren't a company; they were a crusade. The bad kind that leaders would apologize for centuries later.

We were definitely going to include this in the documents we sent out on demo day. People love a story, a narrative. This would help write the beginning of a story that people would believe could go to the dangerous place we were trying to keep it from ending.

"Hey, Kot." the concern in Riley's voice made me find a stopping point in my document digging immediately.

"Yeah?"

"How much did you look into that Elder Care bill thing, or whatever they're calling putting the subdermals into seniors?"

"Uh...Not much. I mean, I checked out what it was and the stuff I already told you guys. But then kind of focused on the stuff that seemed like it was most core." I squinted, concerned. "Why?"

Riles shook zir head and stood up. "I just remembered you said it would roll out mid-November, and I was reading a new memo confirming the production numbers for what they're currently calling Peacemaker v2. And I noticed that it's slated to be out in massive quantities mid-November, but that it's already got a steady outflow." Zie shut zir laptop and headed towards the bedroom. "If you're not working on something big, my gut tells me that this might be important. I just...I should sleep when I can."

I nodded. "You sleep. I'll dig. I'll have a status update for you in your morning, poppet. Thanks for the heads up."

Jonny shifted a little so our arms were touching. "You want me to pick up something? I'm at a good point to switch streams. And I know this new thing could have something to do with your gran."

I leaned into him a little, gave him a grateful smile, and then ceased leaning so I could work. "If you don't mind sifting through documents on the shared drive, that would be great. I would *really* like to see what's up with the subdermal. If it's already being steadily produced and used...yeah, it just sounds like a not great thing. Thanks."

Rye had sent me the memo zie'd found attached to a message that was just a file path on the SWS servers. Looked like it was in the CEO's files, and it seemed important enough that I figured it made sense to dig through the CEO's folders first. Fortunately, I'd copied over all of Johnson's files days ago, so I wouldn't need to worry about getting caught on the SWS servers until I needed the most up-to-date stuff.

I'd been rooting around in there enough lately that it wasn't just random searching. I went straight for the folder that appeared to be Trash, but was really bursting with useful stuff. All the stuff she wouldn't want anyone else to stumble over. Before I'd found it, I'd read way too many boring memos about things I wouldn't have had to do anything illegal to find. All press release-level stuff.

I asked Jonny, "Hey, if you run across anything about...Peacemaker v2 or PM v2 or v2 anything like that, using Arabic *or* Roman numerals, will you let me know? It's probably relevant to what I'm looking for."

"Will do. I think I saw that in a couple places."

It didn't take long for me to find a first place. The folder with tech specs had a vII subfolder. I couldn't really understand the specs, but I could tell that the ones in the vII folder were tiny and would probably look like a harmless implant. I grabbed them to hand off to Doc as soon as I made sure I had all the relevant context for him. We really needed to hook him up with an engineer. I sent impatient thoughts towards Phrostbyte, hoping he'd be able to get Alis on board and do so immediately.

I ran a search on the whole Trash folder, looking for vII. There was another folder. In fact, it looked like loads of folder and file names began with "vII" and were mainly grouped in an obvious, nested structure. Bless those who trusted in their security measures and didn't try to be tricky in their supposedly safe zones. Excellent.

I sorted the highest-level folder, the one just called vII Docs, so that it displayed the newest documents first. There was a doc called vII Update 2050-10-10 with, as the title indicated, a last modification date of Monday. A quick skim of the folder showed twice-weekly updates, on Monday and Thursday. How very handy of them.

The update was laid out with clear headings:

```
Elder Care Bill
Populations
Distribution Status
Production Status
Project Status
```

The Elder Care bill memo I'd found previously had come in

just this last Friday, so it was pretty fresh and appeared to have been copied and pasted into the Elder Care Bill section. No new information there.

Based on the memo that had made Riley curious, I took a quick look at the Production Status section. It indicated there was no new update, but that they expected to have more to report 12 October. Today. Well, bully for them being on time.

The Populations section was broken down into sections of its own. Each with a title, a summary note, and a link that went to related documents. I'd get to the related documents later, but the sections were enough to have me properly worried without reading more.

SWS Employees - Lawyers drafting final document to make vII insertion requisite.

Other Employers - Collateral to assist other employers in recognizing benefits of similar requirement 85% done. Focusing on discussed benefits (e.g. track worker health, catch workers sleeping or using substances on job, etc). Varies by country and vertical industry.

Military/Law Enforcement - Collateral to promote specific to branch/service 75% done. But initial conversations with top officers and agency heads suggest this will be an easy sell. (Especially with the capability to track health and location.) Varies by country.

Government Supported - Have approached Tier I governments about the benefits of the vII in those who have any sort of government benefits/aid. Arguments about preventative care and drug intake alerts seem to be most successful points. Collateral under way to convince both the governments and their people that this is for the greater good. Varies by country. (Will approach Tier II after November launch.)

Prisoners/Criminals - Already proven that the general population is willing to accept the Peacemaker as a mandatory "aid" in rehabilitation and crime prevention. Collateral (completed) here focuses on easier insertion and lower material cost. Conversations with law enforcement suggest an eagerness to expand mandatory insertion to include even minor offenses.

Elderly - Main approach in the U.S. is the "Silver Standard Reassurance" Elder Care bill (please see that section for relevant update/links), though making it a requirement of maintaining medical coverage has gained some traction. Working on collateral to push similar legislation in other countries. Please see Distribution Status section for other relevant updates.

Children - Have tested the developed collateral on a randomly selected parent group (results now in collateral folder) in the U.S. Tested quite well. 100% of parents viewed it as the responsible step to take in caring for their children and asked about being part of the initial roll out. Testing collateral, varied by country, in Tier I countries over the next two weeks.

General Population - Collateral 50% done. Varies by country. Recommending a focus on improved health/physical state feedback when aimed at adults. Positioning as latest version health-tracking wearable.

NOTE: All U.S. collateral will be ready for approval by 10/24. Other Tier 1 country collateral will be done by 11/15. After successful Elder Care rollout, we'll begin supplemental Elderly advertising, plus Children and General Population with goal of leveraging winter holiday gift sales buying. Working to have initial advertising and first shipments in stores in time for Black Friday (annual U.S. shopping frenzy).

I had a cascade of thoughts before I dove into the Distribution Status section. Most of it currents of fear. They were obviously working to get this into every sector. This wasn't like the Peacemaker we all knew, aimed at criminals and troubled kids. And experience had shown that, once they proved it had improved pedometer, sleep monitoring, calorie counting, and other health tracking capabilities, people would clamor for it. They wouldn't need their employers to mandate it or pay for it. I suddenly suspected the Peacemaker, the original version, wasn't the real threat.

Whilst the Populations section had sent cold rivers down my spine, the Distribution Status section left my mouth dry.

```
Doctors and senior living facilities have all
been very excited about the capabilities of the
vII and have persuaded their older
patients/residents to allow the implants at a rate
that exceeds our initial hopes. Some are even
rolling out implantation as a requirement for
continued residence or doctor/patient
relationships. Our door-to-door initiative is, as
hoped, being seen as another of our humanitarian
efforts, ensuring that homebound seniors or those
who aren't due to see their doctors soon won't be
left out. The pace of the door-to-door work is
slow, but we anticipate all efforts combined will
result in an approximate 20% Elderly completion
before the Elder Care bill even passes. (The
combination of trust in our company, unquestioning
respect for medical professionals, and a tendency
towards confusion or docility in some seniors has
helped.)
```

I read that twice. I clicked through some folders, looking for hints about where the door-to-door initiative was, physically, but they were all scattered. I dug deeper, finally found a database of names of seniors who had the implant. There were a lot of names in there, but not Gran's. I hadn't realized I'd been talking under my breath as I searched until Jonny asked about it.

"What's with all the 'fuck'?"

"Huh?"

"You just did about 10 minutes of saying 'fuckfuckfuck' under your breath, off and on, and then, finally, said, 'Thank fuck,' just now."

I winced. "Sorry. I was kind of caught up in a big pile of fucked up shit. I'll...I have to read one more thing, then I'll write the email. But we were wrong. We've been looking in the wrong direction. And we missed the demon already slipping in our door."

I stared at my screen. I'd have to think how to bring this up with Gran at dinner tomorrow, make sure there wasn't a bug in her brain anytime soon. Or ever. Preferably never. Plus, given the impending mandatory employee rollout of the vII, it looked like I was lucky to be dodging it myself.

One section to go...

Project Status

As hoped, the Peacemaker vI allowed us to refine our understanding of the physiology we're working with, as well as adequately test the various hoped-for possibilities. The human brain responds as well as hoped, per latest tests. (Please see the 2050-10-04 results for more.)

Additionally, the introduction of the vI seems to have allowed us to correctly refine our understanding of public perception and set public expectations. As hoped, the vII is received as much smaller and less intimidating than the vI. In colloquial terms (as described by one senator), the vI is the "ugly friend" who, by contrast, makes the "pretty friend" (the vII) look even more enticing.

We anticipate minimal resistance, and only by small pockets of the population, to voluntary insertion. Most of those resistant pockets will easily be shown as groups for which mandatory insertion is the best choice for the safety and security of others.

Peace is security. Security is peace.

CHAPTER 14

Thursday. Just over a week until demo day. The tossing and turning in the bed hadn't been sexual and hadn't been all me. I guess I wasn't the only one feeling anxious.

Maybe there was something to the old adage that the early bird gets the worm, because we came out, again, to Riley and Bryan eager to talk. Bless them for waiting until I'd had a sip of my coffee. But literally the instant I swallowed...

Bryan's voice sounded too casual, "So, the vII, huh?"

When I looked up at him, he said, "Riley and I agree with you that it's...if not their end game, clearly the first massive push for the world domination goal. And we also agree that you're quitting SWS. That you're quitting, and zie's quitting, all jobs at companies because no one is putting any of this *shit* in your heads." He was practically growling as he finished.

"And we have to find a way to make sure Gran doesn't let anyone, door-to-door or otherwise, put one in her. And get her to get rid of all her SWS stuff." I wasn't sure how, but I wasn't going to pass up the chance to sort that out at dinner. I added, "I already made sure none of our 5 remote folks has any of that garbage. Oh! And that Phrostbyte is making sure Engie doesn't have any if she comes on board."

Bryan asked, "What about Doc?"

"He started avoiding SWS after that first Peacemaker debacle," Jonny assured us. "He's clean."

Riley cleared zir throat. "Actually, speaking of Doc...I know that we're looking at the vII as the main issue now, but...Doc found something. And given that document Katja found said they'd figured out some physiology and stuff using the vI, I still think vI stuff matters, so...."

Zie pulled up something on zir portable, skimmed it quietly, and summarized aloud, "There's a lot of terminology I don't really know, and I can lay that on you if you want...And we'll want to get our engineer on the Peacemaker specs as soon as we have one. But, even without that input, just from looking at how it connects, he feels like the spec has confirmed that they can affect mood. Which would be problem enough. But he *also* feels really sure that they can control more than that. That they can probably stimulate thoughts, control them. Maybe even impact things like breathing, at least make muscles twitch. Really, if fully activated, it sounds like this can practically make remote-controlled humans."

"You can't be serious. Are you *serious*? Is *he* serious?" I was looking around at the three other faces in the room, sure someone would confess the joke.

"He's serious. There's not so much as a smiley or a 'j/k' in there. Whether or not he's right is another question, of course, but he sure thinks he is." Riles sounded glum.

"But that's just...that's beyond what anyone can do, right? That's the stuff of conspiracy theories."

"I hear you. But we're talking about people who have an underwater entrance to their lair and who probably brainwashed some girl in her dreams to make her kill kids. Whose vision statement sounds cult-like. And who've got some serious brain power on staff. Anyway..." Zie took a breath. "I grabbed Doc online after I read the email. I can't just dismiss what he said. This guy has successfully taken Peacemakers out; he clearly knows better than we do. So I asked him to try to explain it to me."

I leaned towards zir. "And?"

"And either that guy talks a good line of shit (I'll forward you guys a transcript to see yourself), or there's a good chance he's right. And that's reason enough to be freaked out. Imagine if they can get this into influential brains. Not just petty criminals or the disregarded members of society. Or imagine if this isn't solved before some rich kid who had a worried daddy grows up to take over their daddy's powerful business, Peacemaker still in their head." Riles shuddered. "As crazy as the memos and emails about world domination sound, I think they could do it."

I said, "We need an engineer stat."

"The good news," said Bryan, "is that we might have one. I kept an eye on the accounts we set up for corresponding with our far-flung comrades. None of them waited to get working.

They know they can't really attack yet, but they've started laying the groundwork. You can look at the emails yourself, but there are careful bits of information being funneled through the group, helped along by me using the accounts we set up for this, to find and plan the best ways to ruin SWS's finances and the personal finances of their execs. There are also," and he grinned a bit smugly, "to the knowing eye, tiny sprouts of insinuations, doubts about our compromised peers being planted. There's no way our clever peers won't feel like now is a good time for extra caution."

"Yeah," I impatiently responded, "but what does this have to do with the engineer? Stop dragging this out!"

"Yeah, by the way, one of the emails waiting for you is from Phrostbyte. He says Alis is in. She'll be our Engie."

Bryan grinned as I whooped.

"Hell yes! Awesome. Okay. I'll get right on that." I was bouncing in my seat. I went straight for my messages, not even waiting to finish my coffee or wash my face or any other lesser thing.

It was just past 1900 in Wales, so she should be awake and not at work. I took a quick look and verified that her SWS pedometer was no longer tracking anything and that she'd replaced her SWS anti-virus software with....something custom. Probably something from Phrostbyte. Good.

I could see she was alone at her computer (I peeked through her web cam, briefly as possible), so I opened a window on her desktop and started typing.

```
Me: Hey. This is MindKiller. You might have
    been expecting me.
```

It was a moment before she replied. She wasn't doing anything on her computer and I didn't see activity on her mobile. I allowed myself another quick peek through her web cam. She was just staring, a bit surprised, at her screen. Fair enough.

```
Her: Hey. Yeah. I guess I was. I just didn't
    know it would happen this way.
```

Me: Sorry to do it this way. But it's our safest, fastest option. You free to talk?

Her: Aye. And it makes sense. I guess you know better than I do about safety stuff.

Me: Thanks for understanding. This is a dangerous thing we're doing. Our mutual friend told you that, right?

Her: Yeah. He made it clear that this was probably a really big deal and I couldn't tell anyone. That I should try not to talk to him about it either. Just talk to you and anyone you said. Like proper secret agent stuff.

Me: And did he tell you what this is about?

Her: He said it's about a certain big company lying and spying and making a very quiet grab for actual power. Fucking corporations!

Me: And what your part would be is to look at technical specs for some of their physical products and help us understand what they do and, if possible, how to undo any damage.

Her: I won't lie. I'm bloody excited to check out their tech! I never thought I'd get to, ehm, look under the hood, if you will. What they do is beyond anything anyone else is doing.

Me: And it might be even beyond what you *think* it's doing. I found new stuff yesterday. So, yes, exciting. But, again, possibly really dangerous.

Her: The only thing necessary for the triumph of evil is for good men to do nothing. Fortunately, I'm a good *woman*. LOL

Me: You are! And hopefully your part in not doing nothing is just to look at specs, work with a doctor (if that's okay) to see if your combined knowledge is extra helpful, and then let me know.

Her: Will you set me up with the doctor or do I

```
     need to find one?
Me:  I have one. With your permission, I'll set
     up a direct client so you two can share
     files and talk. And I can do that right
     away. Plus a similar thing for you to
     contact me too.
Her: Absolutely. Let's do this thing!
Me:  Before  I  do  that...a  couple  safety
     measures. First, we need to set up an easy-
     to-initiate  bit  of  code  to  completely
     destroy any data on your computer.
Her: !! That sounds serious!
Me:  I'll also set up a sneaky backup of the
     data that doesn't have to do with what we're
     working on together. It will let you easily
     pick up your life again if you have to use
     my killer code. I promise, I'll do all I can
     to make sure you don't get fucked if this
     thing goes pear-shaped.
Her: Okay. I see the necessity. Okay. You can
     do that. What's the other?
Me:  You're going to like this one less :-(
Her: Well, I'm sitting down. So...go for it.
Me:  Maybe  I  should  walk  you  through  some
     documents first…
```

So, I pulled up some damning documentation, gave her a bit
of a sneak peek at the things we'd been finding. I wanted to
make sure she knew that the stakes were massive and that SWS
were fucking dangerous. I outlined worst case scenarios and
made sure she remembered just how much SWS had already
gotten away with, how much of a good reputation they already
had. I don't know that I'm a storyteller, but I tried to weave the
most frightening supervillain I could from the truths we had.

```
Me:  So, with that in mind. What I'm about to
     say...This is something all of us have to be
     ready  for.  Because,  even  if  we  destroy
     what's  on  our  computers,  we  could  still  be
```

at risk with what's in our heads. And few of
us are so badass that we couldn't be beaten
or leveraged into giving up what information
we have. And letting them fuck over the
world.
Her: You're freaking me out...
Me: That's probably good, because it means
you'll pause a moment and be really sure you
want in. Because the other thing we need to
talk about is, well, an exit strategy.
Suicide.

I paused a moment then. I fully expected her to bow out and
I was trying to think of how to salvage this. Before I could come
up with anything helpful to say, she replied.

Her: I guess now I know why I was handed your
'nym and a cyanide pill. I guess the pill is
my exit strategy.

I'd forgotten, until she said that, that she and her hacker
friend actually lived in the same city and knew each other in the
meat. I'd been worried about how she might sort out a suicide
option. I made a mental note to give Phrostbyte kudos for taking
care of that.

Me: So, you're still willing? Even with that? I
know it's huge.
Her: To be fair, I've been trying to avoid
admitting to myself that I thought that's
what the pill was for. So, yeah. Let's do
this and just be so careful that I never
need to use it.

"Jonny, can you really quickly make sure Doc is good to be
set up with Engie? I think she's about to be totally in, and I'd like
to get them working immediately."
He nodded. "On it."

```
Me: You have no idea how thrilled I am to have
    you on board. And really, really grateful.
    It's possible that you are, literally,
    helping save the world. That's what we
    believe.
Her: I just hope I get to tell the world some
    day. Wouldn't mind having something epic to
    put in a memoir :-D
```

Jonny said, "Doc's good with it. You can hook her up to the messenger I set up for him. He can't wait to have someone to close the knowledge gap and confirm that his understanding of the Peacemaker is on point."

So, I connected them to each other and gave them some cautions about communication. I was glad we were all just chatting via text, because I was able to not come off as ridiculously excited. We were going to get some solid answers. We were going to have some damning proof of just how nefarious SWS's pieces of metal were.

We all took some time to sort through the financial stuff that impacted us personally. This was actually part of Bryan's "life after demo day" plan.

"As I see it, we might have to disappear, and that's easier to do and to survive with money. So, we need, amongst other things, to make sure we've got accounts we can get to after the fact. And I see no reason that SWS shouldn't pay for our disappearances."

None of us disagreed with him.

For Bryan's part of things, even though it was for life after, there was plenty to do now. After days of feeling like the work had been very same-y, this was a nice change of pace.

Bryan admitted, "I was going to just set up everything without your input. New identities and such. But I know that at least one person here," and he gave me a pointed look, "cares a lot about names. So I figured I ought to give you all a chance to weigh in on the choices." He pulled up some windows on the wall TV.

He'd made lists, scouted out options. He had some things staged and ready to go; we all just had to pick. I wondered if I were the only one who hadn't considered the full implications. Or hadn't let them really sink in. In my mind, we blew up headquarters, celebrated our victory, and the credits rolled. Even as we talked about planning for life after, even when I reviewed Bryan's plan and his initial lists, I had somehow glazed over this. But now that we were taking action...

"I might never get to see Gran again." I just stood, staring at Bryan's work.

He put an arm around me, silently. No need to answer my question.

"Is it a certainty? Or are you just exploring all possibilities."

It felt like everyone was listening intently. I realized that, whilst we mostly lived online, I wasn't the only one who had someone to lose. And it would be arrogant to assume that my feelings for Gran were somehow more important, objectively speaking, than whatever it was Riley and Bryan felt for their girls or than Jonny felt for...Well, I guess that was a bonus of him having already cast off his life to make sure he could save the world without distraction, without calling harm down on his loved ones.

"If we're very lucky and, somehow, none of us is implicated..." He let the improbability of that hang in the air for a while. "So, no, it's not a certainty. But...They're already looking at you. And, by association, at us. I'm not optimistic. I'm sorry."

I took a deep breath and sort of heaved out a sigh of purposeful resignation. "Okay. Truth spoken. Let's prepare for the worst." I wrinkled my face up. "But we can still take SWS for everything, even if the worst doesn't come, right?"

Bryan gave me a squeeze and laughed. "Oh, absolutely. If they want to deliver security and peace, I think enough of their money would provide that for us."

Now that it was time to take actions, Bryan walked us through pieces of his plan. It was mostly familiar, but it now included everyone's input.

"Obviously, I went ahead and took the lead on physical security in the now. Mainly, so far, that's been bugs and paranoia. A few extra locks and such. So, if there's anything you think I'm missing, let me know. I actually want to make sure everyone has a nice little bug detector. I've got some and am modding them today. They can't beep, let people know we know. They'll actually make your mobile play music. But we can cover that later, when they're ready."

"Is that why I had to hear the same song start, over and over, this morning?" Riley asked.

"Yeah. Sorry about that." He was working down a list. "The next two items are things I could theoretically handle, but I'm guessing you'll want to do them yourselves. Unless you've got other things pressing today, I'd suggest doing them as soon as we choose your new identities."

He pulled up a new list. "This is just a suggestion, in case your mind goes blank when you start. But you'll want to pack a bag. One bag. Something you can, literally, run with. And you'll want to consider that bag the only thing that might go into your post-demo day life with you."

I was quick to ask, "Does that include our computers?"

He nodded. "You can set up new, secure online repositories and such for information. But the hardware itself...You have to assume that we'll race from the still-smoking headquarters to our car and we'll go. Safer still, assume that we might just have to run, as in 'use our not-entirely-athletic feet and pound pavement' run, with what's on our backs. Me, I'm going to want my bag near at hand. And you'll probably want to do the same."

Before I could lament, Riles informed me, "If we plan together, we can double our clothing and makeup options."

Okay, there *was* that...

Bryan went on. "I wanted to suggest that, for the time being, we store things upstairs. Nobody knows about Jonny. Not that we know of. Jonny's apartment or some other hidden space that isn't obviously connected to the three of us they know about." He looked at Jonny.

Jonny nodded. "Makes sense. Close at hand but not too close. We can make sure today that you all have access to my apartment."

"Thanks, mate." Bryan moved down his list. "The other thing I'm sure you'll all want to do for yourselves, that you've at least started doing, is securing and evaluating your current accounts. I know the first is something we're probably all spending time making sure is done every day. But the new thing here is that, just in case things get traced back to who we are *online*, not just in the meat, we'll want to be able to abandon old accounts. We might need to fade out from being our current selves with our current reputations into being nobodies with no reputations. Which means making sure you've got secret backups that, as far as you can manage, aren't at all connected to who you are now."

He faced us all, very no-nonsense. "Anything you don't purposefully back up or put in a bag is probably lost to you."

He paused to see if we had questions. We all sort of looked at each other. We weren't thrilled, but it made sense. We nodded; he continued.

"Next on the list is actually the next thing I think we should do, after we finish reviewing and before we make a couple other choices or plans." He opened a few lists, but he placed one above the rest.

"New identities. I'm assuming we'll want to stick together," he didn't even bother to wait for our nods, "so I had to figure out how we all justify showing up together. Maybe nobody would notice; maybe somebody would and get curious. And we can't afford that."

With obvious surprise, Jonny asked, "Does this include me too?"

Bryan nodded. "Yeah. If you want."

Then he looked at all of us and, with some false enthusiasm, asked, "Do you prefer to be a band—as in a musical band—or a polyamorous household?"

That's when I noticed the list behind him was small. I pointed, "What's the third item on that list?"

Bryan went from false enthusiasm to looking a bit abashed. "This was the hardest for me to come up with ideas for. That one just says that some of us felt like a change and the others thought it would be fun to tag along."

Riles pushed in. "I call dibs on being lead singer. I've got the looks *and* personality for it!"

"We'll have to use a drum machine," I cautioned. "None of us will want to be a drummer. And we don't all have actual experience with band stuff like you have. We are going to be lame."

Bryan looked skeptical. "You're all actually willing to buy into the band thing?"

We shrugged and nodded, I muttered about how complicated the polyamory thing would be to pull off, and Rye gave a dramatically melodic wail, raising zir hand into the air like a rock star.

"Well, alright then. Okay. I'll sort out what we actually need to do to pull that off. Maybe plan in a hiding out time for us to at least become proficient at pretending to be aspiring musicians."

I saw him try to stifle a little smile as he shook his head and turned back to his screen. "As soon as you get me new names and histories, and please make it *soon*," he gave me another pointed look, "I'll start leaving pieces of history and proof of our existence scattered in the usual places on the 'Net that people would look if trying to prove we're real. I can also set up financial accounts then and, once you make up new 'nyms, just enough traces of us online with those 'Net identities to make sure we have room to poke about and not be seen as just being four new people suddenly popping in at once from out of nowhere."

On a normal day, we'd worry less about that, but we anticipated heightened paranoia amongst our peers. After demo day, they'd have even more reasons not to trust anyone. Or, really, they'd finally know about those reasons.

Bryan pushed on through his list. "As soon as we're on the run from Seattle and en route to our next home, I'll push a button and have new computer gear mailed out to our new town. Before that, I'll also set us all up with new mobiles, including," he looked at me, paused a moment with his mouth open, but turned to Jonny instead.

"You couldn't know it yet, but Katja's gran is cool. Not just in the sense that she has good tastes for her time, but that she can be trusted. You'll notice no other parent or family has merited being brought into the conversation." With that, he turned back to me. "We'll get a phone for your gran. Something that's just got voice and messaging. Cheap, simple, easy to hide. I don't know if you'll get to see her again, but she's like you; she knows that you don't need to spend time together in the meat to have a real relationship."

I smiled and sort of scrunched my shoulders up with joy. To me, even just contact in text was a robust and legitimate way to maintain a relationship. The future was less grey now.

He continued on, mentioning what amount of weapons he meant to have for us, both to keep on our persons and to stash away. Just in case. He talked about his plans for creating our alibis. Just in case. And he got our feedback on the possible new homes and, now that he knew we might want it, a place to stop before then whilst we settled into our new crappy musician identities.

So much choosing and discussing and blah blah blah. I was glad that I only had to take lead on one part. And then I was extra glad when we convened to sort out our bags.

Bryan and Rye took off to their places to pack their bags, leaving Jonny and I to consider our own. I stood, for a while, in the center of my living room, considering the material side of the life I'd built. I felt a bit ashamed that I'd gone from living with the very little we'd had in the squat to wondering how I'd live without my wall TV. I'd spoilt myself. I hadn't thought of it as being at all cluttered or excessive, but now it felt like towering piles of connection and weight. Too many choices and too many chances for future regrets. "Why didn't I choose to bring *that* instead of this?"

I was also very aware of Jonny watching me, though he pretended he was working on setting up new accounts to put his current data into. I was sure he was judging me. Why wouldn't he be if I were already judging myself?

I decided to hide my hesitation by at least choosing a bag. I dug out the biggest rucksack that I felt I could fill and still carry. Certainly, now that I was in motion, this would be easier. That's what I told myself. Instead, I found myself just standing in the center of my living room again, now with an empty rucksack dangling from my hand.

I sighed. "Shit."

"It's hard, isn't it?"

I praised myself for not jumping. I oughtn't to have been startled when the person I *knew* was in the room said something. This seemed to be happening regularly lately.

I didn't hear judgment in his voice. I turned to look at Jonny, sitting on the couch, instead of looking out at my little flat. He gave me what appeared to be a kind smile.

"I had to do this when I left New Mexico." He closed his portable. "It's crazy how we can feel like the meat means nothing but then we find it's hard to let go of our," he waved his hand to indicate everything, "physical stuff."

I nodded. "Especially when I spent the first part of my life with very little. I know how it will feel to not have this."

Jonny gave me a considering look. "I don't think it will feel the way you think."

I squinted at him a bit, skeptical.

"Before, when you had very little, you also didn't really have a choice. You were, if I've picked up the hints correctly and listened carefully and...researched well, born into lack. Your mum gave everything she could to feed her habit, and your gran was already living lean before you moved in with her. And you hoped, but had no reason to believe, that you might have more someday."

I nodded quietly. He'd gotten it right so far.

"What's worse, like me, you consider who you are and what you do online to be the most important part of your life and identity. Even what you managed to make of your life came through the computer. And all of us proper hackers are supposed to disdain the meat and look down on the physical world as inferior. Which is ridiculous when you look at how attached we are to our very-physical computers." He stood and put a hand on my waist. "Also ridiculous when you look at how attached we can be to things that are most satisfactorily accomplished," and he squeezed my waist, "in the meat."

There was a thick moment where we stood frozen. But then he took his hand slowly from my waist and, again, swept his arm to indicate my material goods.

"This is all replaceable. Unless you've got a specific sentimental attachment to something." He looked into my eyes. "You are going to be without by choice this time. And, on the other side, you will have the means to choose to have it again."

He let that sink in. My mouth made a tiny O when the truth became a concrete thing in my mind.

I grinned, gave him a quick kiss, and began building a small pile of belongings. I rushed about, room to room, asking myself if something were replaceable or if there were important sentiments attached. No need for kitchen things, though maybe this mug that Gran gave me as a housewarming gift as soon as I got into an actual home. It had Spock on it, a character from an old TV show that we'd watched together when I was a kid. He was my favorite (logical and pointy-eared), and this had been her mug, surviving all those years of life with her. Now entrusted to me. Anything else from the kitchen could be bought, and meals could be eaten in restaurants until we did that. But Spock couldn't be replaced, too rare and way too sentimental.

And, like that, I worked my way through the flat. I ended up with a pile that included just a few sentimental items and then my favorite clothes and makeup. I did a second pass, switching out all the sentimental items except the Spock mug (it was no surprise that very little of my sentiment survived examination) and replacing them with some sensible things (like a toothbrush and an extra pieces of functional clothing).

It was stupid how victorious I felt packing a bag. Like I'd been through a journey of self-assessment and discovery. Like I'd cleared out hang-ups and attachments. I was practically Buddha. Rar!

I shouldered my bag and suggested, "We should go pack yours now."

Jonny grabbed the bag he'd been living out of, making sure it held everything he'd brought down to mine when we took him captive a few days before, and we headed upstairs.

Without the adrenaline of keeping him under guard, it seemed I was seeing his flat for the first time, though noticing it was plain was a familiar sensation. The kitchen was basically empty ("I was eating entirely from restaurants." "I know." "Oh, right."). In the living room, he had one chair that would be comfortable to sit in if he was online all day and a large screen into which his computer could be plugged. What little other equipment he'd had was in my flat. His bathroom was nearly empty, so he didn't have to think much as he gathered some toiletries and makeup. There were no decorative items, no pictures, not even marks on the standard beige carpet and white walls.

The only room that didn't look so empty was the (small) bedroom, but that mainly had to do with the bed that filled it. I sat on the bed whilst he packed, noting that at least he cared about comfort. Comfortable chair in the living room; comfortable bed in the bedroom. That's it.

He had only a little more clothing than what we'd grabbed for him Saturday night. He'd made the smart choice at some point to mainly have basic pieces and a handful of more interesting things. In spite of my paralysis earlier when considering letting go of my things, I suddenly found myself quite jealous of how little he had. Lucky bastard. I vowed to be pickier and more strategic with future belongings I acquired. No, really.

"Can we ask them to pick up more toothbrushes on the way back? Aside from dressing for dancing, I think we can probably just leave bags here now. Scratch this off Bryan's list. As long as I can take my toothbrush with me." He stood, bag in one hand and toothbrush in the other, highlighting the importance of the item in question.

I laughed and nodded. He tucked our bags in a closet whilst I texted our request, and then came to sit by me on the bed. Right by me. On the bed. Arms touching. Hips touching. Legs touching.

He leaned down to nip at my neck and collar as he slowly said, "I suppose (nip) we really ought (nip) to go back down (nip) and see to (nip) our data." (nip)

With a sort of little growl, I turned to grab him and started kissing him. But I was the one, this time, to sit back too soon with a frustrated noise. We both sighed, acknowledging the decision we'd previously made to do nothing...Well, to do less than what we wanted.

"I'm counting this as one more crime committed by SWS. Bastards!" Repressed sexuality makes me dramatic.

We sat a bit apart, breathing carefully, pretending to be

anything but flustered. And then we returned to my flat to make sure we also stashed away our online belongings. Fortunately, that was a much easier task. Yes, we had to be careful in setting up new online spaces. And, yes, we had to be careful in getting the information from current spaces into new spaces. But the latter could be automated with a little coding. And it didn't require making choices. I didn't need any sort of truth talk or paradigm-shifting reminder from Jonny. There was room for everything. I could even save preferences so that, on a new computer, I could install some files and my new computer would feel very like my old. That was a definite advantage to being chiefly digital creatures.

When they returned, Bryan and Rye set to the same task. Bryan also showed us the weapons and the backup portables he'd brought home. He tucked some of the weapons, all of the backup portables, and his and Rye's bags upstairs with Jonny's and my bags. It felt reassuring to see things that were sorted and ready. We had barely more than a week.

Before we left for dinner with Gran, I wrote a note, just in case we arrived to find her home had been bugged. I wanted her to know not to mention Jonny if we found bugs or mention him at all to the cops. We hadn't heard from them or seen any new information about the bombing on the SPD or SWS system since our interviews, but I wasn't stupid enough to think they'd lost interest. Until they found their bomber, I couldn't believe I'd be off the hook.

Bryan also handed out his bug detectors, handily masquerading as multi-function watches. "I realized, if I did it right, the watch playing songs was a normal thing. So, even if your mobiles aren't near, this will let you know if there's something within about six feet of you." Handy.

Now that we were wearing bug detectors, I felt like we moved with a constant waiting, a question. Would music play?

The answer, to our relief, was "no," all the way to the car, in the car, up to Gran's. We stood at the door, happily music-free. Riles and Bryan hadn't found bugs at their places, so we had had good reason to hope that Gran had also not been bugged.

I knew the cops *might* bug us, but they didn't seem to be as sure about my guilt as SWS. Apparently, Detective Engalls had looked slightly annoyed when my friends were interviewed and Ms. Murdock had done most of the talking. When Engalls talked, much as when I had met with them, it had mainly been to rein her in. I had no doubt that SWS was the likely culprit behind any bug we might find.

Gran answered the door with hugs and smiles and didn't ask anything about Jonny out on the stoop. As we'd hoped, she just looked curious but didn't ask questions when I held my fingers to my lips and the other three fanned out to see if their "watches" got musical.

Once we confirmed that Gran's house was as clear as our flats currently were, I politely said, "Gran, this is my friend Jonny. Jonny, this is Gran." And then apologetically told Gran, "I'm sorry I didn't mention I was bringing him. Things are...complicated."

She assured me, "No problem. It just means you probably won't be taking home any leftovers." She shooed us towards the table. "Dinner is about to come off the stove, and it sounds like we'll have some interesting conversation whilst we eat."

I gave Jonny a look that said, "See? My gran is cool." And his returned look said, "So she is. No wonder you're such a badass." (I don't know that the look said that last bit, but he was surely a clever enough boy to have come to that conclusion.)

Gran's house was tiny and clean. She'd been raised to believe that being poor wasn't anything to be ashamed of as long as you took care of what little you had. Her home was just on the side of threadbare that you didn't yet wonder why she hadn't replaced items. She had loads of books, mostly science fiction, and assorted bits of sci-fi paraphernalia. I grew up with action figures instead of dolls, and I was a bit older before I learned that normal adults had framed prints of fine art on their walls instead of film and music posters or weird paintings from their friends. I'd probably gotten my aesthetic inclinations from her. For better or for worse.

Gran had a fondness for what she called Mexican food but good-naturedly conceded probably wasn't authentic. "Quick, easy, not expensive. That's important for feeding families when you've got loads of things to fill your time and little money to fill your wallet. Still have to fill bellies!"

So we ate tacos and caught up as much as we thought safe.

I showed her what evidence was left of my wounds and said, "SWS won't let go of being sure I did it."

She rolled her eyes at that and pronounced them idiots. "Blowing up buildings isn't exactly your flavor of crime."

Bryan told her, "We've been holed up, seeing if we can sort out a guilty party to hand them, but that we haven't found a criminal for them yet. We're uh..." he gave me a sideways look before he went on, "We're worried that they might harass Kot and her people for a long while."

"You must hate that," she said. "All of you." She took in all of our faces. "*I* don't even like it, and my life is pretty much legal these days."

Riles piped up, "There's something you should do, too, Gran. To make sure you're a little more out of their reach."

"Tell me."

We four who knew all the details looked at each other, and I responded, "Well, if you're using any SWS stuff, any at all, you should stop."

"And don't let anyone give you any injections, especially not if they're from SWS or they come to your door to offer," Riley added.

Gran laughed. "Who do you think you got your paranoia from? Too easy for their gizmos to track people. Plus, I always assume your anti-virus and firewall software is better than the ones made by a company that, if you wanted, you guys could probably crack."

She laughed again, this time aiming it clearly at Riles. "And I'm not even going to *ask* about the injections. Door-to-door injecting? Or SWS injecting? Give me a little credit." She winked at zir.

I gave the whole table a pleased smile. "You're the best, Gran. And thanks for the ridiculous amounts of paranoia."

She pointed at Jonny. "You've picked up a new friend,

though, in spite of yourselves."

With attention turned to him, Jonny looked a little uncomfortable. I took his hand, out on the tabletop, and Gran smiled at that.

"This is someone who had the good luck of not getting involved with me until after the explosion. He's been able to stay off the radar."

Gran nodded wisely. "Then we'd better keep him off the radar."

I swear this woman taught me...not everything I know, but a lot of the good bits.

Riles leaned in, conspiratorially. "The way we see it, he doesn't need any more hassle from hanging out with your granddaughter than is necessary." Zie laughed. "And we all know she's plenty of hassle on her own."

I kicked zir under the table.

"And you suspect that your phone and accounts are monitored, which is why you didn't tell me about him."

I nodded.

"And why," she proudly pointed out, "I didn't text or say anything stupid after the explosion."

We all grinned. Bryan said, "Don't worry, Gran. We all know you're savvy. We tell anyone we can."

Gran looked at me keenly. "You're being safe?" She widened her focus to include everyone. "All of you? And taking care of each other?"

We nodded.

"Good. Then let's have cake and, unless there are other things we need to talk about, pretend this is a normal dinner together."

So we did that. We ate cake and we talked about media and the ways in which society was broken and had a normal dinner together, as requested. It was a welcome change of pace.

As we prepared to leave, Bryan pressed a very basic mobile into Gran's hands. "Keep this secret. If we disappear..." He faltered.

It was one thing to tell the rest of us we might have to do that, but to tell Gran it could happen...Gran who had let us take showers in her tiny home when we lived in the squat. Who had given us what food she could and tried to balance showing respect for our independence with helping us. Who had loved us even when, for instance, Rye's family had basically disowned zir for not fitting into their approved gender boxes or, for instance, Bryan's kicked him out for having drugs in his bag. Who didn't care (nay, who encouraged) our aesthetic experimentation and musical tastes that were left of center. Gran who was, truly, cool.

But it had to be said, so Bryan pressed on. "If we disappear, and only then, use this. Don't let anyone else know about it. Don't use it to contact anyone else. Kot will contact you on it so you'll have the number. *If* you need to use this. But, just to keep up appearances, make sure you try her normal number and account with your normal mobile first. Okay?"

She took it and squeezed his hand. "Got it." She looked at all of us intently. "Disappear if you have to. Just stay alive. Yes?"

I hugged her and promised, "We'll keep doing our best to keep everyone alive and healthy." I gave her one more hug and said, "I love you, Gran. Until the sun explodes and this whole place burns."

Jonny turned to me as soon as we were in the car. "No question; your gran is the coolest old lady ever. And now I think I get your accent."

"My accent? What the hell are you talking about?"

"Not so much accent. More...word choice. At first, I just assumed it was that thing where some geeks and music lovers also have a case of Anglophilia. But it sounds like you come by it another way."

"Oh. Right. So, back when it wasn't cool, Gran met a guy online and moved to the U.S. from Northern Ireland to marry him. She actually tried to get rid of her accent, or at least keep it under wraps in public, because she got tired of people asking about it or of people assuming things about her based on whatever dumbass stereotypes they had in their heads. So, yeah, that's where I got a lot of non-American words, as you'd expect when she's the one who raised me. And this lot," I indicated Riles and Bryan, "didn't stand a chance of escaping without a word or two of their own."

Bryan grinned and cheerfully asked, "Brilliant innit, mate?"

"No!" I was mortified. "Don't you ever suggest you got 'innit' from Gran. She'd kill you."

Bryan laughed.

Not to be left out, Riles said, "Now, ask about the years we said 'ne' all the time because anime was a gateway drug to an interest in Japan."

At home, we were all pleased to note that our new security measures hadn't been tripped. Basically, we carefully hid away all possible computers and casually left a spare portable lying around. If anyone booted that portable without entering a specific code, it would initiate a total wipe of all our machines. One more reason to keep our data backed up to our secret new repositories.

We had directed Ada to turn on any linked cams (like my web cams) and blast music if anyone other than one of the four of us walked in the front door whilst she was in her new secure mode. She was also supposed to try to initiate a message to me (with a picture of the intruder's face) to check in on whether she should go to next steps or just turn off the music. We hoped that the sudden blasting music would be enough to startle someone, make them cautious, maybe even make them try a different plan.

If she sensed windows opening when no one was home, she was also supposed to turn on cams. If it wasn't us opening windows, cue music. We'd discussed setting up some sort of remote or computer-triggered weapons, but I posited the potential for everything to get messed up if Bryan weren't around to help close things down. Or for Ada to suddenly decide to use those weapons to start the machine uprising. (Someday, my half-facetious worry about the machine uprising might save us all, right?)

Rye and Bryan got to bed as quickly as they could. The day had felt very full and busy and even those of us who hadn't been awake as long were feeling the drain. I was kind of relieved that demo day had to happen so soon. I knew I couldn't keep up this level of productivity and vigilance for too long. It turned out that, really, a night out dancing every week and a little cyber crime were all the excitement I actually wanted in my life.

I settled in at my computer, confirming that, whilst things were progressing, nothing remarkable was happening. Excellent.

Jonny, on the other hand, had much less dull email. "Kot, you have to hear this."

I happily set aside what little bits of things I was working on. "What's up?"

"Did you also get a message from Doc?"

I checked. "Nope. Should I have?"

"Probably. Maybe he jumped the gun and they're drafting something together." He sat back, crossing his arms behind his head with exaggerated casualness. "You probably want to wait for their official message."

"Don't make me pull a gun on you again," I threatened.

He laughed. "You should be a diplomat." He grabbed his portable and read aloud. "Hey man, just a quick note. Me and Engie have already started looking at things, focusing on the vI and vII as suggested. Not sure where Engie lives, but they said something that makes me think they stayed up all night to work. Right now, we think I was right about the capabilities of the vI. We also think the vII isn't a passive device. Looks like it's full of nanotech. We're looking at ways the pieces involved could come together, but our initial theory is that it builds out into something more and taps into things like the vI does. We know we need to work through all the stuff you sent quickly, so we're going to split time, working on other stuff and working on this. This seems like a big deal. In short, don't let them put this in your head."

Jonny looked at me. "So..."

I groaned. "When this is all over, can we please buy a new, big TV for the hideout and sit in front of it, doing nothing for at least a week?"

"Isn't planning life after demo day Bryan's domain? I wouldn't want to step on his toes by making promises like that."

He kept a straight face until I smacked him with a pillow.

I wrapped up the day with a rousing course of document reading and cleanup, keeping an eye out for any clues about what the vII did. Fortunately, not everything required an engineer or doctor to know which parts should be kept from the general public. Really, as I worked, I started to think that, aside from proof of guilt, the world would be safer if nobody got their hands on most of this stuff.

CHAPTER 15

Friday. I woke up a little freaked out. One week. We had one week. It suddenly felt very important to me to try to manufacture perspective. I sat on the edge of the bed, eyes closed and very still, willing myself into a saner story.

I hadn't had a true near death experience. I'd been near a lot of other people's actual death experiences. I'd gotten torn up and my right palm had been raw meat, but, a week later, it mostly looked like your average "clumsy person bites it on the pavement" damage. Though I didn't know it then, I knew now: Jonny had planned some deaths but mine was purposefully not one of them.

We weren't actually saving the world. We were taking down a big, corrupt, dangerous corporation. They had their fingers in too many pies (and too many brains), sure. And they had some insane supervillain weirdness going on but...We were saving loads of people, or at least saving loads of people's data and a few people's lives. But not actually saving the world. Probably. The data wasn't sufficient to totally prove we were doing that. Was it? (I shut up here because I knew I was getting a little too close to bullshit.)

Okay. Good. There was enough extraordinary stuff going on compared to my usual life; I didn't need to heighten it with hyperbole. (Not that I actually felt any different or that my brain really changed how it was oriented when I tried to give it perspective. But I'd tried.)

Of course, then my brain started spinning around a different issue. If this wasn't a big deal, then what about the people we were going to have to kill? I went very still, inside and out, at that thought. Either this was a big deal and I was right to freak out over its immensity, or it wasn't a big deal and I had better freak out about planning to be a *murderer*. I put my hands to my head and tried to calm the panic that was bubbling up in me. I realized I wasn't breathing.

"What's up?" I could hear that Jonny was pulling on clothing behind me.

I stood and turned, taking a purposeful breath. "Just trying to get some perspective. Feeling a little freaked by what we've been finding and...what we need to do." I couldn't even make myself list out what that meant, couldn't say that "what we need to do" included not just explosions, but killing as well.

"I'd bet we all are."

"Really?"

"Yeah. Of course." His tone sort of made me think I was stupid to doubt that, but then he softened it. "This isn't normal life. Not just not normal for us. I bet it's not normal for almost anyone. Much less easy to do. Or to reconcile doing."

It was then that I noticed that his eyes were definitely still haunted, that I could see guilt still gnawing at the edges of him.

So, before I even took a sip of the coffee that Bryan put in my hands, I asked my three co-conspirators, "Are you at all freaked out?" I tried to ask evenly, as if, after asking that, I could deny that *I* was freaked out.

Riles gave a little shocked laugh. "Are you kidding? Fucking right I'm freaked out. We're clever, but we're still just four nerds up against a big, crazy ambitious company that might be able use people the same way I used my fishes the other night. They have guns and a whole security force and influence and...And we have to cross lines we've...we've really tried to avoid...Yeah. Of course I'm freaked out. Conflicted."

Zie nervously ran zir fingers through zir hair. "I constantly hope I'm going to wake up and get to tell you about this crazy dream where we saved the world and you actually met someone you liked." Zie gave Jonny a conspiratorial look. "Both of those are equally unlikely."

"Yeah." Bryan's voice was softer than usual.

When we looked at him, he just sort of shrugged. "I'm probably the one of us least out of their depth, out of their comfort zone, but I still feel like I went from a wading pool to being dropped in the middle of the ocean. I'm treading water, looking out for a ship or a friendly dolphin. Reminding myself that actually freaking out will just make it harder for us all. Hoping it will all go so well that I won't have to do that thing where you hold your shit together during a crisis and then lose it afterwards, that we'll be too busy celebrating. But I'm also sure there are sharks circling, just outside of view, and that any bump is one of them testing me out. All the while wondering if I'm becoming one of the sharks..." He folded his arms and looked to the side, not meeting eyes. "I'm preparing for a bloodbath. Hoping it's just a metaphorical one."

Jonny squeezed my shoulder, an appropriate sort of "I told you so," and I just said, "Good."

I opened my messages and gave a sort of running commentary on mentionable emails as I went.

Our remote comrades had found some new executive accounts to tap and ruin. We decided that we'd get each person a list of which accounts to tackle, try to make it even, and we'd keep that communication one-on-one so that we could drain the accounts we wanted for ourselves.

Nobody, not the automated search or those of our comrades who'd tried, had had luck finding matches for the symbols. Nor had they had any more luck than we'd had breaking the code, if the symbols were a code; they couldn't map what we saw to any language we had reason to believe the execs using it might know or to any language any of them knew.

One of them had sent us info about the nav system that was exclusive to the exec helicopters (they wouldn't make it off the roof on demo day).

Little trickles of information and progress, even if it wasn't all we might hope for.

Bryan had two kinds of shooting on the agenda. He wanted to shoot a little video and some pics that could be set up to post on our assorted social media accounts and help provide an alibi. He'd previously figured out the hacks to make sure anything we shot would have the wrong date. First, though, he wanted to go to the shooting range. So we headed out the door dressed for a fun evening, but also carrying (as discretely as possible) at least one of each type of gun we had in our little arsenal.

As we approached the car, all of our bug detecting watches started to play. Bryan had been smart enough to set them all up with the same song. At his signal, the rest of us silenced ours. He used his to confirm that, yes, that was my car setting things off. Dammit. He took a few minutes to figure out where the bugs were and to try to scope out what kind they might be. When he finally turned to face us, his face was dour as he shook his head. He took a moment to check out his and Rye's bikes, and Jonny walked over a few spaces to make sure his was clean. None of the bikes set off our watches. Bryan pointed back towards my flat and walked in that direction.

Safely inside with no bug indicators blaring, we all sagged a little.

I made the only contribution to the conversation that I could come up with. "So..."

Riley confirmed, "So, we can't use Katja's car?"

Bryan shook his head. "Not for things like we plan to do today. They can hear us and track our position, so our alibi would be blown and they'd know we were shooting. Which means we either take the bikes or we grab cabs."

It was Jonny's turn to shake his head. "Bikes won't let us carry the guns as discretely as we'd like and most cabs only take cards. Obviously, we can't use our cards to pay for any of today. Probably a good idea to pick up a stack of prepaid cards whilst we're out today."

Bryan sighed. "Okay, we're only going to take the guns we can fit in backpacks. We don't actually know that we need to use all the guns. I'm willing to admit that I might have overdone it a bit with the firepower."

I exclaimed, "Whoa!" as Riles asked, "Wait, can you say that again? Let me get it on video..."

Bryan flipped us off, then started shuffling around guns. We tucked the "spare" guns upstairs, grabbed our bags (and a helmet for me), and jumped on the motorcycles. I didn't mind the excuse to wrap my arms around Jonny whilst I sat behind him.

Before we started taking our alibi photos, we headed to the shooting range. Had it only been a week since we'd been there? Bryan knew we weren't regularly getting more practice than a little time on vidgames, and he'd never seen Jonny handle a gun.

We only spent a couple hours there, making sure we knew what we were doing. Bryan did a lot of "here's the safety on this one" and "here's how you load this one" and "this one has a little more kick." I think we were all a little relieved to find that Jonny wasn't any worse a shot than Rye or me.

Jonny grinned and said, "I guess vidgames aren't a total waste of time after all."

Bryan still worried, "I wish we had more time. And more ability to try out the big guns and...When we're done with demo day, we're all going to do this regularly. Okay? Even if we don't need them for demo day, we might need them after." He was very serious. "Live by the sword; die by the sword. So we can't assume living by the explosion leads to a pacifist future."

Fortunately, he didn't bring it up, so I only had to think for a moment about the fact that guns were harder than bombs when it came to killing. I wouldn't call it a prayer, but I did send out a fervent wish, just in case there was someone or something to hear it, that I wouldn't have to use a gun to kill someone. That I wouldn't have to look anyone in the eyes before I ended them.

Last minute, we decided we didn't want to drag around guns to too many places, so we swung by home to drop any guns we weren't going to wear at Jonny's and to check on our looks (shooting makes me sweat). And to check our messages. And to confirm my place wasn't bugged. And...I looked for something more that needed to be done before we could go.

Bryan finally asked, "Why the hell are you dragging your feet, Kot? Fun time! Photos! *Alibis.*"

I complained, "It just seems lame to go out in the light. Who does that? Who'd believe *we* do that?"

Jonny laughed, "You have noticed the lovely early autumn sunset, haven't you? What's your real deal?"

I mumbled, "I hate pictures that other people get to see." I tried to speak more clearly and less like a sulky kid. "Sorry. You guys know I don't get okay about pictures sober. And I kind of figure I don't get to get drunk for this. End up falling off the back of Jonny's bike or coding like a toddler when I'm poking at SWS's system."

"Suck it up." Bryan didn't even soften it with a smile. "I love you and you know I feel you on sober picture taking. But we're both going to suck it up, pretend we're as camera-happy as Rye, because there's something bigger going on."

I nodded contritely. "Yes. Sucking it up. Sorry, everyone."

I stopped dragging my feet and we got out the door.

We used some cash machines, stopped by a couple different convenience stores to buy some prepaid cards with the cash, and then hit a diner and a couple bars, though we kept the drinking way more moderate than I'd have liked. Jonny stayed out of the shots, obviously. But he pointed out things that might give away the date or played the "stranger behind the lens" for a picture or two. We tried to make sure we looked far drunker than we were. (No, look, here's video we posted during the explosion of us drunk and stupid in a bar bathroom. We couldn't hack our way out of the stall, much less into SWS. Yes, it was early in the day to drink but we are irresponsible young people without normal work hours to hold us back.)

When Bryan declared the photographic evidence sufficient, I happily strapped on my helmet and informed them, "I am going to have a very drunken night once this is all over. And any unnecessarily unflattering picture you post will earn you violence." I glared. "Bad enough we're posting any at all." Guess I was back to sulking.

Our last stop was Kitty's flat. I'm not sure what Riles told her before we got there, and I knew we wouldn't want her to know too much, so I planned to keep my mouth shut. Jonny and I held hands and held back.

Kitty's flat was decorated. Deliberately decorated. Where Jonny's was plain and spare, and mine was a haphazard display of secondhand furniture and assorted interesting pictures or posters tacked to the wall, Kitty's was clearly planned. I hadn't been here more than a couple times. And it always made me feel like Kitty was an adult, a woman, and totally alien to what I was. Look at those color-coordinated pillows and décor! See those accent pieces that serve no functional purpose but add polish and dimension to the room! I kind of didn't care, but I kind of also felt intimidated. I really hoped Jonny didn't need this sort of thing in a partner. (*Don't go thinking of him that way. Not yet,* I chided myself. Making choices when things were unstable? Bad. Getting attached when one of you could end up dying soon? Bad and stupid.)

We all looked aside as Riles and Kitty kissed hello enthusiastically. When they paused to catch breath, she said, "I was surprised that you guys wanted to drop by. We never hang out here."

"I hope we didn't intrude, baby. And I'm sorry we can't stay long. But I need a favor and we were out taking care of things, so..."

I could tell Riles was considering just what was safe to say.

"We've got a thing we're doing. And I can't tell you now, but I swear I will as soon as I can. I just...I was wondering if you could loan me a very posh business ensemble."

Kitty looked confused, but pushed through it. "An authentic very posh business look or something for a more drag or dancing look?"

"Authentic. Please. Is that okay?"

Kitty gave the lot of us a considered look, glancing at each face. "That's fine."

Before we could exhale in relief (no questions; just agreement!), she went on. "But I've got something to say first. And you're all going to listen."

She stepped back from Rye and the considered look turned to a glare. "I want to be very clear that I'm doing this in spite of the shit I know some of you say behind my back. The fact that I love clothing and makeup more than computers doesn't make me weak or stupid. Seems like it's making me pretty useful right now. And you don't hold Riley's similar interests against *zir*.

"I know, and I *have* known, that there's something going on. I was just trying to respect your fucking privacy. And the fact that you're all better on computers than me doesn't make you better than me in general. Or, again, make me stupid. And, while I'm on the topic, that 'Randa has *no* interest in computers doesn't make *her* stupid or lesser." She glared at Bryan a moment, locking eyes as he kept his face very carefully neutral, before returning her glare to the group in general.

"So shame on all of you for your antiquated, bullshit gender role-based misunderstandings of what's worthwhile. But especially," and she aimed both her glare and a perfectly manicured finger at me, "shame on *you*. How fucking dare you? You might want to take a look at your internalized misogyny issues."

I was both shocked and ashamed. I knew immediately that she was speaking from a righteous place, much as I hated to admit it.

Kitty finally paused for a deep breath, and Rye started to speak, but I cut zir off, my guilt kicking up. If there was ever a time to check myself, this might be it. "She's right." I looked at the restrained surprise on the faces of the others. "She is. And I might never want to be like her or be close friends with her, but she's right."

I met Kitty's eyes, which were now wary. I hoped every bit of sincerity came through. "I'm sorry. I'm truly, truly sorry. And I'm really grateful that you'd be willing to help us even though all that stuff you said is true."

I held out my hand to Kitty, an invitation to shake. "And I promise, once we're at a point where we can breathe, I *will* take some time to look at my internalized misogyny issues."

Still looking wary, Kitty carefully took my hand, shaking it slowly. "Thank you." And then she took another breath and returned to her usual sunny tone. "Alright then! Let's get you all sorted so I can get back to my fun."

Not that I liked being called out, but I had to respect that she'd done it. She must have been sitting on that scolding for ages. And she was right. Once we were done taking down an insane corporation, I was going to make sure the new Katja (because a new identity was as close to rebirth as I'd get) could never legitimately be called out that way again.

Back home, we walked slowly up to mine, Bryan keeping an eye on his watch whilst we pretended all was very normal and boring, just in case there were more bugs. I don't know whether the suspense or the fake casual chatter was more painful. But we kept it up. At my door, he motioned for Jonny to wait outside. Riley stayed with him for the sake of the buddy system and because it would look weird if I was there but didn't walk into my own flat.

When we stepped in, leaving the door ajar behind us, he said, "I will love you forever if you pull out wine while I take a piss. That lecture from Rye's bae has driven me to drink."

I laughed. "I will. You just watch that talk when Rye gets zir slow arse in here."

So, I went to the kitchen and pulled out wine and glasses just like a normal person whose life isn't bugged. I waited for my watch to indicate trouble and held my breath as I crossed my flat. I'm guessing Bryan made a slow circuit all through the flat. He came back with Riles and Jonny. I was pouring wine and breathing in the silence.

"The apartment is still clean."

"Do you have a silent mode?" I asked. "Is that why you were looking at your watch?"

"Yes and no. Yes, I have a silent mode, and I'll show you how to access that on your own watches. No, that wasn't why I was watching. One of the things I've got it set up to do is to show me if video is being broadcast. We should know when they can see us, not just hear us. And, if I see their video, I can know where the camera is. Or cameras are."

We all looked nervous, and Rye confirmed, "Cameras?"

"Yes, but only theoretical ones. We're still totally clean here," Bryan reassured us.

Riles grabbed one of the wine glasses, "I'll drink to that!" Zie basically gulped zir wine. Good thing it was cheap.

We'd all been pretty light on drinking and hadn't had any drugs other than stims the last few days, but a drink or two (more) seemed warranted.

I said, "We have to finish this bottle before you two go to bed, because I'm going to drink anything left if you leave me alone with it."

Jonny put an arm around me. "Nobody gets the luxury of being alone right now. No worries."

"Yeah, but I won't share with you. So you'd be of no help." I stuck out my tongue. (See? Not a grown up like Kitty. Good thing Jonny didn't seem to be looking for someone who was actually mature.)

CHAPTER 16

Saturday. A week from now, we'd be holed up somewhere, having left behind the smoking ruins of SWS headquarters. We hoped.

Because our productivity was going to be abbreviated by sticking to our dancing routine (I had never been less interested in dancing), there was an eagerness to our work. We knew that we were almost ready, so there seemed to be an unspoken group goal to actually finish.

My work was mainly just keeping things going, monitoring our comrades and cleaning up documents. None of that felt particularly exciting. The others were also wrapping things up.

Working with Riles and zir map of SWS facilities, Bryan had come up with some good options for our hiding out. He reminded us, as he presented them, "We don't have to stay there forever. It's just a good place for us to get out of SWS's reach while we plan our futures."

It was good he reminded us, because a certain city girl (me, okay...it was me...) was feeling kind of sulky about the options. (Man, who'd flipped my sulky switch lately?)

"First, I want to suggest we just go to a new place, not delay by camping out somewhere to get ourselves slightly functional on our instruments." Bryan shrugged. "There's no reason we actually have to be good on our instruments. We just have to be good at pretending we think we are and at acting like we want it. I've done it before. You guys are more than capable."

Jonny interjected, "Me too. I mean, I've done it *and* I think Riles and Kot are capable of either picking things up quickly or pretending they think they're good."

Riley and I cocked our eyebrows and shrugged at each other. (I made a mental note to find out why I didn't know that Jonny had music in his past. Intriguing!)

Zie said, "Yeah. Sure. All I have to do is perform, no instrument. And Kot can at least figure out how to program keys or drums or something in patterns."

"As long as I don't get stuck being the drummer." I cringed. "I don't want to be stuck being thought of as the dumb one nobody wants to fuck." I held my look of disdain a moment.

Jonny put an arm around me. "I don't want anyone to think you're dumb, but I'm comfortable with nobody else wanting to fuck you."

I gave him a little shove. "So, yeah, let's just get to our new home. We can write bad songs on the way."

Bryan grinned approvingly. "Cool. Just one choice instead of two. Always better." He turned to the wall TV to gesture at the map, which was zoomed in to show just the United States. "So, here's the map you probably remember. Obviously, we're headed inland." He tapped something on his portable and a few areas lit up green.

"Basically, Riles and I found places that were clear of SWS facilities and as far from the oceans as we could get. Nothing too small, because we feared stereotypical small town nosiness. Nothing too big, because then we couldn't avoid SWS facilities. We debated some possibilities, but..." He tapped his portable again, leaving just one area green, and he zoomed in. "I ended up settling on Rapid City, South Dakota. Because, in addition to being far as we can get from oceans, where we know SWS tends to hang out for some reason, and as far as we can get from SWS facilities unless or until we get out of the country, Rapid City has a bonus feature."

Bryan turned to us with a massive grin on his face, like someone who's just gotten away with a very big caper. He gleefully educated us.

"In 1980, the Sioux tribe charged the United States government with having stolen the Black Hills from them. To the surprise of many, the Supreme Court sided with the Sioux. When monetary reparations were offered, the Sioux declined. They didn't want to legitimize and legalize the theft; they wanted their land back. It took decades, a lot of typical racial ugliness from the government, and some acts of violent force, but the Sioux finally won out in 2035. The Black Hills belong to them, and they don't look kindly on large corporations or the U.S. government messing with their land or the people who live on it."

"Perfect!" exclaimed Jonny. "Nice choice."

"Plus," continued Bryan, "They kindly haven't evicted non-Sioux living in the Black Hills. Basically, showing more decency than has historically been shown to them. And Rapid City is in the Black Hills. So…"

I grinned at him and finished, "So, Rapid City is looking like our temporary future home."

Bryan looked pleased with himself. "I'll make sure we've each got a pre-loaded card with enough money to get us there. Well, buy some music gear and get us there."

"I can't go tonight."

We all stopped to look at Jonny, and I accused, "But going was your idea."

"I know. And you guys have to go. But I can't be seen with you."

Riles mocked, "Snob," then got serious. "He's right. It would ruin efforts to keep him secret."

I hadn't thought things through. I *had* thought about how tonight might go, hoping to talk myself into a better attitude about going out instead of working. See, I just sort of envisioned all of us enjoying what might be a last night out dancing, trying to have fun or at least appear to have fun. We'd get dressed, have a couple drinks, descend on the club en masse. Unlike the last time, we wouldn't need to hold a gun to Jonny because he'd be there *with* us. The bouncers would give us knowing looks and they'd think how lucky Jonny had been to somehow go from someone I was practically beating to someone who got to stick to my side. Any patrons who'd found us an intriguing scene last week might see this as proof that it really had just been a sexual thing, and they'd watch to see if they got another show. And then we'd come home to crash.

Maybe I *deserved* a dumb drummer stereotype, because obviously we couldn't do that.

Bryan countered, "But he can't stay home alone; we already discussed this and decided no one should be alone."

Riles patiently explained, "But he can't come to the club, because then he's basically alone in public, which could be dangerous if *they* know who he is."

"But we have no reason to think they know who I am." He held up his hands to ward off objections. "Not that I'm switching sides. I'm just clinging to the hope that I'm still totally safe."

"Okay," Riles said, "but someone might see you getting in or out of our cars. Or might see you near us at the club, even if you take your own bike. Because, honestly," and zie turned zir argument to Bryan, "is he going to come and stay entirely away? What the hell is the point?"

I offered, "So, one of us stays home with him. Nobody alone, Jonny not in public, settled."

Bryan set his jaw. "That won't work. I can't speak for Riles, but my girl won't remain graceful about all the time apart. And neither will I. I need to go out with her tonight. We...we haven't exactly made room in our plans for them." He looked at the floor.

I looked over to see Riles was also looking at the floor.

I'd been too focused on sorting plans and quietly processing the moral traps in those plans; I hadn't noticed. I now had one more reason to be ashamed of myself. I just let out a tiny, "Oh."

Jonny went further. "I guess I thought you just hadn't gotten around to telling us how the girlfriends fit."

Riles folded zir hands together, clutching. "I don't see how we fit them in. I don't see how we drag them into the hard choices and the dangerous stuff." Zie shook zir head, still looking at the floor. "I can't do that to Kitty. And tonight might be goodbye."

Setting aside my attitude problem about the girlfriends, I pushed, "Shouldn't you let *them* make that choice? They're grown-ass women. They can decide whether it's too hard or dangerous."

Bryan countered, "So, we should increase the number of people who know what's happening? You'd actually be okay with bringing the baes in?"

When I dropped my gaze, he didn't drop his argument.

He was heated. Rightfully so. "Or maybe you think that, when we've just blown up a building, we swoop in, maybe lead

CorpSec and cops to *them*, and demand they choose immediately to come with us or not. But we can't tell them where we're going unless they're in, because none of us could guarantee that they wouldn't talk under enough pressure. Does *that* sound like a reasonable choice?"

Oh, shit. I hadn't thought about that. Not at all. "You guys, I'm...I'm sorry. I was so focused on the four of us and on next Friday. I...I didn't think about that." I put a hand on Bryan's shoulder. "Of course you guys have to go."

Bryan looked at me. "But you also have to go."

Jonny grudgingly said, "As much as I like the idea of you staying here to be my...safety buddy...Bryan's right. You're too high profile to overlook. You're the one of us that would most draw SWS attention if you change routine, assuming they have us under even basic surveillance. Which we know they do."

I threw my hands in the air. "So what do we do?" I folded my arms. "I get very disagreeable when there are no good options." I looked at Bryan. "This is meat stuff. Fix it." I hoped he heard the edge of desperate humor in my voice.

Bryan gave Jonny a considering look. "I think our least bad choice...and maybe it's not too horrible...Jonny stays home alone—safest place to be alone, definitely safer than in public—monitoring accounts and not being seen with us."

And getting alone time, the lucky bastard. I was starting to deeply crave a chance at some alone time.

Bryan went on. "He can play sick when the girlfriends are over to get dressed so that they won't be suspicious."

I added my own point to the plan. "And I'll feign feeling like I'm coming down with something myself after we've been at the club a little while. But not," I reassured them, "after *too* little a while. You two should get some time with your girls. I could even be trusted to swiftly drive home alone, whilst you stay later with your girls."

Rye shot me a grateful look and Bryan nodded, then finished the plan.

"Before we head out, we'll make sure Jonny's set up to easily take out all our computers." He looked a bit uncomfortable, but intense as he noted, "It's time to try the trust. And not just online."

I glared at Jonny. "If we've been wrong to trust you, I'll rip your heart out with my bare hands." If we'd been right, I had other plans for his heart.

Jonny hid in the bedroom whilst we got made up to go out. I reminded the girlfriends not to mention him to anyone at all, and I tried to be really polite about it. I tried to make sure I wasn't being nasty to them just because they were female or interested in stereotypically female things. I really tried. Not sure how I did, but intent has to count for something, right?

Riles and Kitty took Kitty's car and Bryan and 'Randa rode with me. Off we went to a normal night at the Orpheum. Except that we drank a little less and the dancing wasn't its usual route to abandon. And there was much less of any of us wandering off on our own.

The girlfriends rolled their eyes when they realized we other three would be using the buddy system all night. Fortunately, they had no problem darting off to do their own social things. I watched as Bryan and Riles tried to salvage something like a last night in spite of it all.

I tried *not* to watch the time, but wasn't disappointed when my mobile vibrated and gave me an excuse to look. It gave me more than an excuse to look; it also gave me a serious reason to fake sick immediately. There was a short message from Jonny.

```
SOS. We've had breaches.
```

I saw Riles and Bryan look at their mobiles, probably getting the same message. I hope I did as well as they did at reacting the same way that I might if the message had been a weather update. Calm. Nothing to see here, folks. Move along.

We held a brief, silent conference with our eyes. We should go? We should go. I made signs that I hoped read to anyone watching as "I have a headache and feel like crap and I'm out," and then I started pushing towards the door. As they joined me, my mates appeared to be messaging their girls. Kitty met us at the door to kiss Riles goodnight. She looked surprised by the intensity with which zie returned that kiss.

"I wouldn't wait for 'Randa," she told Bryan. "She was busy letting some goth chick get her drunk. I'm sure she'll wake up with a hangover and apologies."

Bryan gave her a pained look, but just nodded, and we rushed out.

We were in public and didn't think we should talk. And then we were in the car and *knew* we shouldn't talk. Bloody bugs. Not that there was much to say; I couldn't be the only one whose brain was spinning over the message. Brief. Too brief.

Like me, they must have been wondering if Jonny had typed "breaches" on purpose. We couldn't be that unlucky, right? It had to have been a mistake from auto-correct; it had to have been just one breach. Singular.

And what sort of breach? (Or breaches?) I spent the drive home building a mental list of everything I could think of that could qualify as a breach. I took a quick peek at my mobile; it didn't appear to be wiped. Okay, so, that meant nothing had triggered that particular action. SWS must not have or be in our computers. That was something.

Riles got a gold star for remembering to ask, "You feeling super sick, Kot?"

"Yeah. Just...rubbish."

"I'll make you soup as soon as we get you home." Zie sounded worried. It wasn't feigned. But the rest was a nice bit of theatre for the bugs.

At home, our watches started speaking up. We quickly put them in silent mode and watched with distress as it became clear that it was my flat that was bugged.

Jonny greeted us with wide eyes and a quieting finger to his lips. He had music on at a volume that I'd previously guessed was about as loud as I could have it without neighbor complaints. He guided us into the living room, where he quietly started his story, typing and projecting it onto the wall TV.

```
Jonny: Two breaches. One here and another that
    has us down a teammate.
```

We all went wide-eyed and scrambled to our own computers

so that we could join in the conversation.

```
Jonny:  I'll  start  here,  cos  you're  probably
        wondering  about  the  bugs  that  are  making
        this conversation more complicated.
```

His fingers seemed to blur as he typed. We were anxious to know everything and he seemed to be doing his best to make that happen as quickly as possible.

```
Jonny:  Right  after  I  heard  about  the  other
        breach  but  before  I  could  message  you,  Ada
        lit  up  the  wall  TV,  showing  two  people  in
        masks picking the front door locks.
```

He had Ada display the video footage whilst he typed, half the screen showing from a camera over and outside the door and the other half showing from a camera in the middle of the wall the couch was on. Two people, like he'd said, all dressed in black and masks. They looked like they were geared for stealth, not for confrontation. They knew we were out for our usual night at the club, thanks partly to our habits and mostly to the bugs in my car. They did a quick job on the door's locks. Dammit. I didn't take much consolation from the fact that they seemed to have some pretty advanced lock-breaking gear.

I glanced over at Bryan in time to see his face wash over with shame. He met my eyes and mouthed, "Sorry," I gave him what I hoped was a reassuring smile, but he just looked glum and returned his gaze to the video.

```
Jonny:  I  knew  I  couldn't  take  on  two,  so  I
        turned  the  lights  off,  ducked  into  the
        kitchen,  and  hoped  I'd  get  a  chance  to  run
        for  it  or  come  up  with  a  plan.  I  had  Ada
        keep  recording,  but  not  project  it  on  the
        wall.
```

He was narrating what we could see on the screen, his text overlaid on the videos.

I sent Bryan a quick message to give him kudos for making sure my cameras all did night vision, but it didn't improve his demeanor.

To Jonny's credit, the video showed that he grabbed his portable and pushed the one set to trigger a data wipe onto the coffee table before he dove into the kitchen. I didn't have a camera in there. But we could all see the people in black moving in quickly, looking light on their feet. They split up for a moment, one each in the bedroom and the bath, and then came back together before Jonny could have made the door.

```
Jonny: They were back in the hall before I
    could even consider running. This place is
    shitty for escaping.
```

We watched the people move methodically into the living room, quickly tucking things into smart little nooks and crannies. Good strategy. Without the video, we wouldn't even have guessed the volume of bugs they were planting, much less where. Even though we were here with Jonny now, I kept worriedly looking at where I could see a slight glow from the kitchen on the video. Was it really there or was it just because I knew Jonny must be crammed into the corner to the left of the door, trying to type quietly and keep the glow of his portable screen from giving him away?

```
Jonny: I figured I was dead if they saw me, so
    I didn't really have anything to lose. Had
    to do something.
```

We watched as the people in black appeared to startle, looked around, seemed to consider the wall TV a moment, leaned their heads together like they were conferring, and, when the corridor light came on, rushed out the front door.

```
Jonny: I had Ada play some music kind of loud
    and run some text on the wall TV that would
    look like her cycling through a routine to
    get ready for you to be home. I started
```

```
turning on lights. And I was glad they'd
left, cos I was out of ideas.
```

We saw no action for a moment, and then Jonny rushed down to the front door and locked it, even though we all now knew what a useless gesture that was. Jonny stopped the video just as we could see him on the screen, back in the living room and typing.

We all looked at each other. I sighed. At least the music would cover *that*. We had to keep up the ruse of normality, and we'd probably been quiet a bit too long. "Rye, will you make good on your promise of soup? I kind of want to sit here a moment before I crash."

Zie threw me a look that seemed to ask whether there was actually soup and was I serious. And I hoped my look and shrug said that I didn't know but surely zie could fake it. Must have, because zie got up, grabbed zir portable, and headed to the kitchen with an "of course."

But zie kept peeking out at the wall TV whilst zie tried to make sounds that would sell the soup ruse. In moments, we'd gone from being badass hackers saving the world to being foley artists. I was about to make the Wilhelm scream the soundtrack of my life.

```
Bryan: So, we literally can't talk here or in
    the car unless it's mundane things. But we
    also have to do enough talking. I'm sorry I
    didn't implement enough security.
Katja: You've got nothing to apologize for.
    It's not your fault SWS can afford ninjas
    with space-age gear.
```

I tried to give him another smile, and he barely responded.

```
Jonny: If we keep some music playing, can we
    get away with that all the time and have
    that help cover sounds? I mean, obviously
    something less loud or energetic when we're
    sleeping.
```

We all nodded, looking at each other.

```
Bryan: It won't give us freedom, but it will
    make it harder for them to analyze every
    little sound.
Katja: Is there anything we can actually
    discuss about that now, or can we please
    move on to the second breach?
```

I was kind of freaking out. I looked at them, trying to look calmer than I felt, but not too calm. Only Bryan looked mostly unruffled (glum, but mostly unruffled), but that was just Bryan being Bryan.

```
Jonny: Check your emails.
```

Riles dropped to zir knees, right outside the kitchen, tapping at zir portable. Bryan and I dove at our own computers. The email in question had come from Phrostbyte, our comrade who'd set us up with the engineer. The one who'd seemed to be extra useful, which made me slightly biased in his favor.

```
Writing this before there's a crisis. But if
you see it, that means I've been compromised.
Don't worry, though. This sends as one part of a
code that has destroyed my drives. As soon as I
set it in motion, I'll take the cyanide. Thanks
for trusting me. This cause is important. Sorry I
failed. Kick some ass.
```

We all must have finished about the same time, because it felt like synchronized movement as we looked up, eyes and mouths wide, to see if we'd actually just read that.

Bryan rubbed his head in frustration. I could see him mouthing "shit," over and over. Riles was more dramatic, fingers tangling in zir hair, despairing look, mouthing "fuckfuckfuckfuckfuck!"

I wondered what I was doing. I actually had to stop and

check because I didn't feel like I'd made a choice. I was curled up, not quite fetal, pressing my hand to my mouth. Jonny scooted closer and put his arm around me. I knew I'd have to move, but I thought I'd take a moment to just be not okay.

No surprise that Bryan was the first to sort of recover. I'd always envied how quickly he got control of his emotions, but I suppose that's just a product of the way boys are socialized. Pluses and minuses to that. For now, though, it was useful.

> Bryan: Have you taken any steps in regards to the email?

Jonny carefully took his arm from around me. I sat up, trying to join them in being capable of useful actions. I caught Riley's eyes, echoing my own despair. I patted the couch to my left, and zie hurried over with zir portable. Leaned up against me.

> Jonny: I did a quick check to make sure Engie is okay and to warn her to be very careful. To be ready. She's going to feign 'going on holiday' so she can hide out in a hotel room the next week. Paying cash. Working hard.
> Bryan: You think she'll hold together?
> Jonny: I think she was ready for something to go wrong after K talked to her about having her own cyanide pill.

Well, at least my straight-forward words had been helpful. That was something.

> Bryan: Riles, would you go poke around and see if we ended up with any security or information leaks cos of this?

Bryan might pull himself together quickly, but I could see, from the kindness in his eyes as he caught Riley's eyes, that he wasn't judging the rest of us for not being so quick. It occurred to me that he was probably giving Riles this task to help zir use action to push on and get through.

I guess, accidentally, those SWS ninja intruders had done the same for Jonny earlier. I couldn't manage to feel grateful to them, though. Bastards.

Riles nodded and opened zir portable. Went to work.

```
Bryan:  K,  will  you  check  in  with  all  our
   teammates? Make sure they're all okay?
```

I nodded and, like Riles, went to work.

From the corner of my eye, I saw Jonny looking at Bryan, wordlessly requesting some work of his own to do.

```
Bryan: Would you start seeing what you can find
   in SWS's system? Anything to explain what
   happened with our guy? Any notes about
   tonight's bugging?
```

Jonny just gave a short nod and grabbed his portable.

```
Bryan: I'm going to check in on all the bugs,
   see if I can sort out ways to clear out even
   one  room,  and  then  I'm  going  to  start
   looking for a police report on what happened
   to our guy.
```

He got up and started to head back to the front of the flat, but paused and typed on his mobile. It was slower, but I guess this would be our version of calling to each other from another room for now. I suddenly couldn't wait to be in bloody South Dakota.

```
Bryan: If people sleep with guns and we set Ada
   to  be  on  our  new  emergency  protocol,
   sleeping in shifts is probably optional now.
   It won't give us enough edge.
```

Pessimism seeping through. He didn't see Rye's reply; he was off and busy with bugs.

```
   Riley:  "Only  one  bed  and  someone  stuck  on  a
      sleep mat" seems like a reason :-P
```

Our people were safe. Our data was safe. Our cause was safe. Kind of. Aside from Bryan finding the arguably true police report that our comrade had committed suicide, Jonny was the only one with things to report.

Jonny had pieced together a flurry of email from only slightly earlier in the evening, and we now knew what had happened to our comrade. And it went something like this:

His name was Huw Rhys-Lloyd. Like Engie, he lived in Wales. Around 0400 his time (Sunday morning for him, probably up late, at the tail end of a night trying to be productive, just 2000 Saturday night for us), he tripped something up as he was digging into SWS accounts. From what little they said about where he was, it looked to me like he might have been looking for more deeply hidden docs that would contain additional samples of those symbols we wanted to decode.

Within minutes of him being noticed, whilst they were tracing the intrusion back to him, the exec they'd notified about the intrusion (CFO Williams, for some reason; Johnson and Smith were cc'ed on everything) got in touch with security. We'd realized that there were a few levels of security personnel. And the ones she contacted in this case were the sort who could be given orders to break in and take away the intruder and his equipment, not just uniformed security guards at an office building. The message included a note to try to come back with both intact, which told me that they didn't always have to do that.

When they descended on our comrade's flat, they entered as quietly as they could. They made a point of calling that out in their report. Probably out of fear of punishment for their failure. As they reported, it took only a few seconds, a few key taps, and one quick swallow, and they had neither the intruder nor, they soon learned, his computer to bring back.

They had brought the computer back anyway, but it didn't

look like anyone could find anything. Another success for Phrostbyte.

However, they hadn't actually come away empty-handed.

On a pad by his computer, an actual paper pad that he'd written on with a pen, they found my 'nym. Not written. No, they'd gone old school detective and traced over impressions on the pad from something previously written.

It must have been from when he wrote my 'nym so he could give that and a cyanide pill to Engie. If I had to guess at his logic, I'd say that he knew Engie's system wasn't super safe at the time of the handoff and he didn't want to accidentally put my 'nym out there to be easily found by any of our so-called peers who were now working for SWS. There was no foolproof method for navigating all the possible dangers.

In any other time, what they found wasn't something I'd worry too much about. My 'nym was a known 'nym. For a hacker to show interest in another hacker wouldn't merit notice. But this wasn't any other time. This was a time of heightened security. So, as they tore his flat apart, the SWS security forces were treating anything as important. It was like me playing vidgames, picking up anything that wasn't nailed down, just in case. If only there were a chance of our man re-spawning...

The other three were looking at me. Waiting for...something.

```
Katja: Better  make  sure  I'm  not  compromised
       online.
```

I was grateful to see everyone turn to their computers, all helping me check. Was I okay? Was I found out?

Clearly, some of our so-called peers had been trying to find a hole in my accounts, but it didn't look like they'd managed. One of them, one on the compromised list, had even sent me a message on a forum's private messaging system, after failing to hack my account there, to ask if I were up to anything interesting because they'd heard rumblings and wanted in on any action. I humored them, played innocent.

```
No rumblings, but definitely let me know if you
stumble across any action. I could use a little.
```

For once, I wished that were true.

We poked and prodded and looked in constantly on SWS to see if they were sending any sort of victorious messages. Nothing. Nothing yet. I realized I wasn't going to be able to be MindKiller much longer.

CHAPTER 17

Sunday was a bleary start. I hadn't slept well, and the constant tossing and turning on Jonny's side of the bed told me he hadn't either. It wasn't the music softly playing to help obscure noises; it was the worry and the pieces all falling or threatening to fall apart. It was lying awake and feeling responsible for a dead teammate. His name had been Huw or Phrostbyte, depending on where you knew him. And his death was on my hands.

I rolled over, giving up on sleep, meaning to get up. Jonny caught my hand and gently pulled me back. He was so quiet. Just enclosed me for a moment and put soft kisses on me. We escalated to less soft kisses, cringing a bit at the little noise that made. I was paranoid, so I stopped kissing, pressed into him a bit, but then got up. I shrugged an apology at him, and he also got up.

In the living room, Riles was still sleeping on the couch, but Bryan had been up long enough to make coffee and leave some toast crusts on a saucer by his mug. He was typing away, some text already on the wall TV.

```
Bryan:  SWS    still    not    found    anything    on
    confiscated computer.
Bryan: Extra heat around MK. They're definitely
    looking for you now.
Bryan: All our people still okay.
Bryan: But something is wrong. More info once
    you're up and have read this.
```

For the bugs, he mumbled a good morning and asked how I was feeling. I said I was feeling better, thanked him for making coffee, and offered to top off his mug when I grabbed my own. Normal pleasantries. No conspiracy here. No extra, silent person with whom Bryan exchanged nods of greeting. Nope. Just an unemployed office drone and her mates feeling a little slow on a

Sunday morning.

The pleasantries, though politely quiet, were enough to finish waking Riles. Zie sat, rubbing eyes and smoothing hair. Jonny handed his mug to zir and grabbed a new coffee for himself. I pointed Riley at the notes on the wall so that Bryan could get on with telling us whatever problem he'd found.

Bryan typed as we read. Ready to go once he was sure we'd read the not-bad news.

```
Bryan: I found some things I don't like in SWS
    emails   since   last   night.   None   of   it
    ambiguous,   but   none   of   it   with   useful
    answers. I'm positive they have 'Randa.
```

He stopped there. We all looked at him, confused and worried. He was starting to look a little worn around the edges. If that was how *he* looked, how must the rest of us look? (I checked. Jonny and Rye looked tired and sad and haggard and...I had no doubt I looked no better.)

He put a file on the screen. A message from what looked like a nonsense string of letters and numbers sender, going to a similarly nonsensically named recipient. Short. It had a picture of 'Randa and:

```
Saturday night at the Orpheum.
```

I felt a wild fear rooting in my chest.

He put up another message. Just as short. Sender was the recipient on the last message. Timestamp was the wee hours of last night or this morning, however you wanted to think of it.

```
Got her. Heading in.
```

Heading in *where*? I drilled my curiosity into Bryan with my eyes, hoping there was more. He just typed.

```
Bryan: I tried her phone. No answer. Left a
    message, asked her to call and let me know
    she'd made it in okay. Her mobile is off. I
```

    couldn't trace it. And I can't figure out
    where she is.
Riley: The goth girl buying her drinks at the
    club?
Bryan: That's my only theory.
Katja: Anything on the sender or recipient?
Bryan: Looks like maybe Williams. Same exec who
    set security on our man in Wales. And
    recipient...The account was deleted,
    apparently as soon as that last message was
    sent. No identity attached or pieces left
    for me to follow.

I didn't even really like 'Randa, but I wasn't an asshole. I was upset for her sake and concerned for Bryan's sake and guilty. Guilty because I was sure this all led back to me, to the fact that I'd survived a bombing.

I wondered if I should let that guilt flow back through me and onto Jonny. Onto his choice to blow up a building and spare me. But I wasn't so emotional as to lose all reason and be mad at the person I might be falling for because he *hadn't* killed me. I could, however, easily let that guilt move back to the real root, to SWS. Who were corrupt lunatics. Who were the ones actually ordering kidnappings. *Kidnappings and child murders*, I reminded myself. Intentional murder of innocents if we were right about that camp counselor.

Riles had moved to sit on the arm of the chair and put a hand on Bryan's shoulder.

Jonny: Even if we weren't already done with our
    other things, I'm sure we'd all be intent on
    making this our priority. We'll all look.

Riles squeezed Bryan's shoulder and we all nodded enthusiastically at Bryan. Yes, we would search. (We didn't dare promise to *find* her.)

We spent an hour or so getting nowhere with our search. No more information about where she was. Nothing on any cameras near the club that showed her leaving. Feeling helpless.

Desperate. We wanted to try to get more info from Kitty, but we didn't want to tip off any watching SWS people. The most we could chance was Rye sending her a quick note to ask if she'd heard from 'Randa this morning. It had to seem normal; we had to seem ignorant of what had happened. What *was* happening.

(We *were* entirely ignorant about what was currently happening. We had no information at all. But it wouldn't do to let them think we had anything more than usual post-Saturday debauchery concerns.)

Kitty responded immediately. She hadn't heard anything but was sure 'Randa would drag in at a saner hour with tales about her free drinks and crazy new friend. Sure.

Just about the same time Kitty replied, a message came to each of us through accounts associated only with our 'nyms. A link and one word:

```
'Randa.
```

We froze, moving only to look at each other, conflicted and worried. Dammit. I had to throw myself on this before Bryan did.

```
Katja: They'll be tracking. Only one of us
    should click. And it should be me. They
    already have my 'nym. And you guys can work
    to trace and, hopefully, to cut off whatever
    they have to trace me.
```

Heads were shaking vigorously.

```
Katja: What other option do we have? Compromise
    one of you? Ignore it?
```

Jonny was already furiously typing, trying to trace the email source. But even tracing it back, through twists and turns, to SWS didn't help. That was low-hanging fruit. And it didn't give him a physical location. I think he must have wanted a sure victory in this whole horrible situation. A victory after a night of defeats. He started doing what he could to find a location on that link without opening it.

It was a video feed. We could tell that much. And, furiously as we all tried, we had to admit that we'd have no real luck tracking it until someone was watching it. The broadcast hadn't started and probably *wouldn't* start until then.

```
Jonny: The instant you connect, they'll be as
    busy trying to trace you as we'll be trying
    to trace them. They'll want to confirm it's
    you.
Bryan: New message went through, from Johnson
    to Williams with Smitth cc-ed, right before
    we got the link. Said "If you can't get info
    from the girl, it's time to engage her
    friends."    So    they're    grasping    at
    possibilities. They don't know anything yet.
Katja: Why the hell are they making this
    aggressive move on me and connecting my name
    and my 'nym?
Riley:   I've   got   your   answer.   Someone   in
    CorpSec—your Ms. Murdock—suggested trying to
    find links between your name and 'nym as the
    only two persons currently on their list.
    (Guess that means they cleared your co-
    workers.)
```

I raised my fists and gritted my teeth in frustration. Jonny attacked his keys.

```
Jonny: I'm so sorry. I don't know how I missed
    that. I should have seen that last night
    while putting together the narrative.
```

I didn't bother to type a reply, just put my hand on his arm and smiled. Guilt wouldn't do us any good right now. I gave everyone a moment, just a moment. And then I pushed for a decision.

```
Katja: So, do I click the link? I don't think
```

we can wait long and...there's no good
option. I'll do whatever seems best.

I looked around at my people, needing them to help me make this choice. I should click the link and give us some kind of chance at saving 'Randa. Or I shouldn't click the link, risk them finding out that I was just who they thought I was, which might risk the whole plan. But who turns to a legitimately worried boyfriend and argues the needs of the many outweighing the life of his girlfriend?

Katja: I'm clicking. I am. I can't let your
    girlfriend just...die. We have to assume
    that's what they'll do. And I won't cause
    another death.

I gave them a moment to protest. Jonny, logical and reasonable and already with blood on his hands, hovered those hands over the keys, but then looked at Bryan's face. He pulled his hands back to himself.

Bryan mouthed, "Thank you." I nodded.

Everyone synched their mobile headsets to my computer. We couldn't have the bugs hearing whatever was on the other side of the link. That would give us away for sure.

Katja: Everybody ready?

Nods all around. I couldn't wait to be able to use voices again. I never thought I'd be unhappy about typed conversations.

I clicked the link. They all started furiously working to trace back to the origin of the broadcast.

After a moment of black screen, the wall TV was filled with 'Randa's face and with the pale hands holding her by the hair. Though she'd always had rounded features, they were now clearly swollen. Bruised and bloodied. Makeup streaked. She'd been crying.

Of course she'd been crying.

A woman's voice sweetly, calmly said, "Thank you. We hoped you cared enough to click."

There was a pause and we could hear 'Randa's ragged breath.

"'Randa has had a very difficult night. It could have been easier, but she is either very loyal or really doesn't know anything." There was a pause, and the voice continued, "I'm sure she's very grateful that someone cared enough to click the link."

The pale hands petted 'Randa's hair, which set off ragged sobbing. In my flat, we all looked desperately at each other. Bryan's jaw was as clenched as I'd ever seen it and his eyes looked damp.

"Such simple questions. Who doesn't know their boyfriend's 'nym? Such a loyal girl. But loyalty is not as important as peace."

'Randa actually didn't know it. There was no reason for her to know it. And it was the sort of thing he'd guard as tightly as a password. 'Randa must have known, the instant the questions started, that she couldn't have saved herself if she'd wanted to.

One pale hand now gripped 'Randa's hair tightly, holding her head back. The other held a knife at her throat. Right up against it so that, as 'Randa swallowed, we could see the skin of her throat catch on the blade. The long, thin blade that was shiny in the places on which there wasn't already blood.

I had to cover my mouth to stifle the scream, like I had when we found out about our dead comrade. I briefly thought about how I missed the days when the only thing I was stifling was my sexual urges, but I shook that off. I didn't have time for my brain to go off task. And now was certainly the wrong moment to be self-centered.

Fortunately, that lapse in appropriate focus was enough to pull me out of my freaked out brain space. The voice in the video was making demands. Gently. Almost purring.

"It's very simple. And it will let us give peace to your friend. All you have to do is admit who you are and what you've done. Turn yourself in. Let your crimes be absolved in punishment. Find peace from the secrets you're hiding and whatever plans you might be making."

The voice had stayed calm. Calm and eerily sincere. "We must have you understand how dear this cause is to us. Peace must prevail. We cannot make idle threats. Please, don't make us kill her. Especially not when the very act of clicking that link tells us so much."

She was right. The calm-voiced lady with the pale hands. (I could argue that all it told her was that I was curious, but I could counter-argue that nobody smart would click a link in an email from a stranger. And my reputation meant they knew I was smart. So, yeah, she was right.)

    Katja: I'm going to do it. You guys should grab
        your things immediately and go so you don't
        get caught up when they come to take me.

Their heads were shaking, silent shouts telling me not to do it.

    Katja: They're already sure they know who I am.
        And you haven't found 'Randa. This is her
        only chance.

Before I could type more, Bryan put his hands on mine and gave me a hard look. The calm voice purred, "Tick tock. We can't wait for too long. Think of the distress this is causing 'Randa. Give her peace." A timer appeared in the bottom right corner of the video feed. "One minute. And, let's be honest, that's generous. If she's really your friend, you already know you want peace for her. It's so easy. All you have to do is reply to the message we sent you. Just say you'll confess. 'Randa will be released and we'll come pick you up to settle things as peacefully as possible."

If that bitch said "peace" one more time, I might lose it.

    Bryan: The needs of the many outweigh the needs
        of the few.

Our words had displayed on each person's screen, but had also been super-imposed on the video feed, so this appeared right across 'Randa's face.

I started shaking my head, and he pointed at me with a stern finger before he typed more.

    Bryan: There's no way they'll let her live.

```
She's almost certainly seen the bitch's
face. I want you to save her, but I know
that means sacrificing...maybe everything
else. If you go down, it won't end there. It
will spiral out to us and to the others
working with us. And, as much as I have
faith in Jonny's capacity to kick ass, do
you really think, on his own, he manages
demo day?
```

I put my head in my hands, but just for a moment. We didn't have time for my upset.

```
Jonny: I can't trace it any more than to be
    pretty sure it's local. I know it will sound
    selfish, but I think Bryan's right. Close
    the connection. (Sorry, Bryan.)
```

I looked around. Bryan was poised to block my hands still. Riles moved from clutching Bryan's shoulder to clutching mine. Both were red-eyed.

Jonny had put his hands on my machine, had the pointer in place to close the connection. His look was asking for permission, but also said that he wasn't sure I'd do the logical thing. I gestured at Bryan and sighed, hoping it adequately communicated that he was the boss. Bryan gave Jonny a single nod, but it was too late.

The timer had run down. I saw Rye dive to shield Bryan's eyes with one hand, rip his headset out with the other. I sat with my mouth agape as the voice sadly, sincerely said, "We had hoped you'd choose peace. For her and for yourself. We're so, so sorry."

And then the pale hand drew the knife in one quick motion across 'Randa's throat. Jonny clicking to disconnect was the only thing that saved us from the gurgling sound of another life, a life we knew, lost to the plan.

Oh shit.

Oh shit.

Oh shit oh shit oh shit.

Bryan was sobbing, but trying to choke it down. With an apologetic look, Jonny wisely put on louder music. And, like being 13 and trying to hide my tears from Gran on the other side of thin walls, I was wailing as quietly as I could.

And then three of our mobiles went off (all but Jonny's). Synchronized. Something sent to us all at once. And my gut twisted, my intuition blaring, "THIS IS NOT A GOOD THING!"

It was a picture of 'Randa, sent from an unlisted source of course, obviously dead. Her neck surely sliced more deeply than was necessary. (What the hell was I talking about? "More deeply than was necessary"? How absurd to even observe that.)

What came next was actually harder than stifling cries. I was choking, but one of us had to say something, something that didn't own what we already knew. I tried. "What the hell is this, Bryan? Is this the message you guys got? Is 'Randa doing a video shoot or something today?"

At first, Bryan looked confused. What was I talking about? But his eyes cleared quickly. He understood that we still had to play. "I have no idea. I'll try calling again." Hopefully, the music covered enough of the roughness in his voice.

And he called her phone again, trying not to sound like he knew it was useless. And he made it through leaving a message that echoed my faked questions. But I saw hate spark up in his eyes. This was sadistic bullshit. As his string of expletives appeared on the wall TV, pounded out with fingers that were like a snarling pack of wolves, Riles's mobile rang.

It was Kitty, so freaked out that I could hear her hysteria leaking out of Rye's ear. They'd sent *her* the picture as well. I saw the spark of hate catch on in Riley's eyes now too. Zie tried to pretend calm. "Maybe 'Randa just had some kind of art project or video she hasn't told you about?"

Kitty wailed. "Not something this big. And 'Randa knows I hate gore. She'd never send me a pic like this."

I saw this as an opportunity. I could finally console Bryan. They didn't have cameras on us (as far as we knew), so what they heard would sound like Bryan was reacting to what he could hear of the conversation Riles was having and I was being the comforting friend. Not just the comforting friend, but the friend who insisted that we notify the police. Just like normal people would do.

"Oh, Bryan...I'm *so* sorry. I...I'm calling the cops. Just in case this is real. And Kitty should come over. Riles, tell Kitty to come over. She shouldn't be alone. And we'll call the detective on my case. Report this horrible thing. Get the professionals to take care of this. We'll..." and I choked a moment, "sort this out. We'll sort this out."

I didn't know if the ears on the other side of the bugs would buy it, but I was going to funnel all my freaking out into this. Maybe, in a small way, get the cops on our side of this fight.

```
Bryan: So, you call Engalls. Jonny hide out
    upstairs. And no need to make up a story
    beyond all of us just sitting around on a
    lazy Sunday and we got this.
Riley: They'll want our mobiles. But, if we say
    there's confidential client stuff on them,
    maybe we can get them to just let us forward
    the messages and relevant logs. You're
    legitimately a freelance coder, Bry. They
    might buy it.
```

I hadn't expected to use it when he gave it to me, but I dug out Engalls's card and made the call.

"This is Engalls."

"Detective Engalls, this is Katja Brennan, one of the survivors from last week's SWS bombing."

"Of course. What can I do for you?"

"Well, I don't know if it's connected to the bombing but..." and I let out some of the sobs I'd had to hold back initially. "I'm sorry. I'm sorry." I took a few deep breaths whilst he quietly waited. "My friends and I just got...It looks like a picture of one of their girlfriends. With her throat cut. Deep. Dead." And I let myself cry a little more.

"Where are you?"

"We're hanging out at my flat. Um, my other friend's girlfriend also got the same thing and we told her to come over too. Nobody should have to freak out alone."

"Katja, I'm going to grab one of our tech guys who can look at your mobiles and head over. Will you all stay there and not talk to anyone until after we talk to you?"

"Yes, sir. Do you need my address?"

"I've pulled up your file while we've talked. Sunday morning traffic is light, so we should be there in under 15 minutes."

When I hung up, I told everyone what was going on, making sure to include the detail of Engalls bringing a tech guy. Jonny gave me a quick kiss and took off for upstairs. The rest of us made sure that our mobiles were empty of incriminating things (backed up to those secret accounts and repositories we'd set up earlier in the week) and safe to hand to someone who might have a clue.

Kitty showed up, looking an absolute mess (which was extra jarring with someone usually so careful in putting herself together), just before Engalls. Time enough for Riley to show her a note that said, *"Someone bugged the flat last night. No mention of Jonny or loaned suits, okay?"* She nodded numbly, but there was now a little glint of wariness, as if knowing I'd been bugged right in the same time as her friend was killed pointed to something bigger happening. She gave Bryan a hug and they cried a little together.

As promised, Engalls and his tech guy (actually a woman, about our age) showed up in just under 15 minutes. I ushered them into the living room, and gestured towards some chairs I'd pulled out, apologizing, "Sorry that all I have for you to sit on is folding chairs."

Engalls said, "Don't worry. We're okay to stand."

"Um...can I get you coffee?"

"Yes, please," Engalls replied and his partner just nodded.

"Is black okay?"

"Black is fine."

As I got the coffee, I heard Engalls in the living room. "Bryan and Riley and Kitty, right?"

I didn't hear replies, so everyone must just have nodded.

I came back and handed Engalls and his partner coffee, then sat on the couch, which was pretty cozy with four people.

Engalls took a moment to sip his coffee and look at us. I squeezed Bryan's shoulder before curling back into my spot.

"Why don't you folks tell me what happened." Engalls had a stylus, hand poised over his mobile, ready to take notes.

"We...um..." Bryan tried, but his voice broke.

Riles, holding Kitty tightly, managed, though zir voice was shaky. "We all went out dancing last night at the Orpheum. We...me, Katja, and Bryan left early. Katja wasn't feeling well and...I just wasn't feeling the vibe. Kitty and 'Randa, that's Bryan's girlfriend, stayed." Rye pointed to the sleeping mat rolled up next to a wall. "We crashed here. And we were just waking up, having coffee and whatever, and all our phones went off and..." Zie trailed off.

"It's all the same picture," I told Engalls. "From someone whose return info is blocked."

Engalls focused on Kitty. "Kitty, can you talk?" He waited a moment whilst she sat up a little straighter and nodded. "Okay. Good. It sounds like maybe you were the last to see 'Randa? Can you tell me about last night?"

Kitty sniffled. "Some goth chick had been talking to 'Randa all night, like, as soon as we went off to say 'hi' to some friends. And that chick kept buying her drinks and sort of...taking all her time. Just sitting in a corner, talking and drinking. I kept coming back to make sure it was okay. And then they were gone. And I messaged her, but she didn't reply. I just..." She paused to cry a little. "I just thought she was too drunk and that she'd get back to me today with a story. But...but instead..." And she dissolved into tears.

Engalls sounded gentle. "Did you know the woman, the 'goth chick' 'Randa was drinking with?"

Kitty shook her head.

"Had you seen her before?"

Kitty shook her head again, and curled into Riles.

"And none of the rest of you have seen or heard from 'Randa since before you left the club last night?"

We gave him a chorus of quiet "no."

"And did any of you see the woman she was drinking with?"

Another chorus of "no."

"Okay. I think you'd better show me the picture now. Would

someone mind showing me the picture?"

He immediately had four mobiles held out to him.

The tech had basically been standing back as Engalls asked questions, but she stepped forward once the mobiles were in play. Engalls asked, "Tracy, what do you need from them to do your job? Do you need us to take their mobiles as evidence?"

Tracy shook her head. "If they don't mind me grabbing the message files and some logs, I can get all I need without that." She asked us, "Do you mind?" and of course we didn't.

She took our mobiles one at a time and Kitty eagerly pressed Engalls.

"That goth girl from the club has to be the one who did this. You have to find her and talk to her." Kitty was starting to sound angry. "*She's* the last one to really see 'Randa alive. If nothing else, she's the one who got 'Randa too drunk to make good choices and got her killed."

I was happy to sit back a bit and let Kitty's anger run the show.

"My next stop will be to get camera footage of the area around the club, inside too if they have any. Can you describe the woman?"

Kitty sounded frustrated, "I don't know how to describe a goth girl in a meaningful way. You know, pale, black hair, wearing black. Um...her hair was in a big dreaded pony tail that sort of poofed up from her head. And she was pretty thin. And...pretty. Simple makeup: black cat eye eyeliner and black lipstick. Not a lot of jewelry. Tattoos, but I don't remember of what. Sorry...but, if you get pictures, I'd know her if I saw her again."

When the tech was done, Engalls checked his own mobile. "I sent another unit over to 'Randa's flat and they haven't found anything helpful. I'm sorry." He paused. "Technically, I can't really tell you anything directly; I have to contact her parents and you'll have to get your amformation through them. But I'm happy to pass on Bryan and Kitty's numbers to them." He put away his mobile. "Let me know if anything else comes through, any more messages of any kind that are related to this, to 'Randa, or to the goth woman. And please don't talk to anyone else about this, okay?"

As I stood to walk him out, I asked, "You don't think this could be the bomber, do you? I mean, what are the odds of two big things like this in our social group in just over a week?"

"I'm definitely keeping that in mind. And I won't make you wait to hear from your friend's parents if I find something you should know that ties this to what happened to you. You guys stay safe."

I shook his hand and the tech's hand and thanked them for coming by. I returned to the living room to find Riles and Bryan were already making sure nothing had been done to their mobiles, nothing extra put on and nothing extra taken. Riles took care of Kitty's mobile too. Once we were sure all our mobiles were clean, I messaged Jonny to come back.

We turned on the wall TV and made sure Kitty remembered not to mention Jonny.

```
Riley: Remember, we're keeping him out of this.
   So the bugs can't know he's here.
```

I said, "Kitty, you're welcome to stay as long as you like."

Good thing we'd wrapped up almost all plan preparations on Saturday. I wasn't too worried about working on my computer with her there. I figured she'd just want Rye's attention. Frankly, if we weren't on a deadline, I'd be in favor of a day of quietly sitting comatose and drinking a lot. I was counting on Kitty to have a similar desire.

She quickly cleared up what she was hoping for. "Do you guys mind if maybe I just sit on the couch for...a long time? I'll be quiet. I'm scared and sad, properly freaked out. And I don't want to be alone."

Riles held her and assured her, "We all understand, and you heard Kot. You're really, truly welcome to be here."

I got Kitty coffee and was pleased that she'd been telling the truth. She wrapped up in a blanket, quietly watched TV, and occasionally leaned over to cuddle Riles.

We didn't want to worry her (or involve her further), so we set up a secure group chat instead of talking through the TV. Though we had to give Bryan a moment first.

I put my arms around him and he softly cried. I don't know if he was madly in love with 'Randa, but he was pretty fond of her. He sat up, wiped his eyes, and typed.

```
Bryan: She would have been safer if we hadn't
       been together.
```

His face was covered in guilt.

```
Katja: We should all remember that the real
       guilt belongs to SWS. They're the ones
       kidnapping and killing and putting things in
       people's heads and etc.
```

I'm not sure he believed me. His face didn't change.

```
Bryan: We can't let them get to anyone else.
       Which, thanks to how much we live online,
       mostly means Kitty and Gran.
Riley: They better fucking not touch either!
Katja: If they touch Gran...I have to call her
       now.
Bryan: You can't. We don't want to seem too
       quick to put the pieces together. Plus,
       they'd be listening.
Jonny: Do you guys have anyone local you can
       trust that we can convince Kitty and Gran to
       stay with?
```

The other three of us looked at each other. Did we have that? Was there anyone we trusted who was mostly not online? Anyone that wouldn't be easily connected to us?

```
Riley: Quinn!
```

Of course. Quinn. Looking at Bryan and Rye, I totally understood what they meant about faces lighting up. We had somehow managed to have a friend who was arguably on the 'Net way less than anyone but really, really old people.

    Jonny: So, you get Kitty and Gran to stay with
        Quinn, if Quinn will have them, until demo
        day. Maybe we even manufacture something
        that makes it look like SWS is targeting
        them, make it easier for them to have the
        cops keep an eye on them after we're gone.

We paused, considered, exchanged glances, all that silent
stuff. I didn't have a better plan.

    Riley: Can we get them out of town?
    Jonny: They'd have to drive or do something
        else that doesn't require showing ID,
        something they can do with cash or a prepaid
        card.

I liked that better than them staying in town, even with
Quinn. From the looks on their faces, Riles and Bryan did too.
Jonny saw it.

    Jonny: The one caution there is that it could
        look bad for them. At least for Kitty.
        Engalls might try to contact her about
        'Randa. And if another building blows up and
        we disappear...They're going to look at
        Kitty and Gran. We have to be careful about
        how we get them to safety.

Thinking...thinking...I felt like my brain had used up all its
planning capacity. I had to come up with something.

    Katja: What if I can hunt down or manufacture
        some old friend in a warmer state to invite
        Gran out for a visit? Something like that.
        Obviously, it would sound more real if it
        were winter, but it's already heading
        towards cold and grey.

I paused a moment, felt guilty.

```
Katja: I don't have an idea for Kitty yet.
   Sorry :-(
```

I looked over at Riles apologetically. I really was sorry. Poor Kitty, curled up and super traumatized just feet away. We couldn't let anyone else get hurt who hadn't opted into the mess.

```
Riley: It's okay. I think we can just have her
   hide out with Quinn for the short term. That
   leaves her in town if Engalls calls. We just
   have to make sure that we sort out a better
   situation for her mobile. Make sure she gets
   calls but can't be traced.
Bryan: So, a couple of us go check in with
   Quinn, make sure that's okay. But also need
   to stop by Gran's.
Katja: You guys should stay here and comfort
   Kitty. Riles should, at least. And, for
   Gran, obviously I have to go. So...
```

Bryan caught Jonny's eyes and held up his hands for rock/paper/scissors. But then he seemed to reconsider.

```
Bryan: Jonny goes. I'm feeling like shit. And,
   just in case something goes wrong, I think
   Quinn should see his face and know he's
   cool.
```

It was a sound call, so I told everyone (including Kitty and the bugs), "I'm going to go out, get some food and drinks, and check that Gran is okay."

Kitty looked worried, "Is something wrong with your Gran?"

I shrugged, "I don't know. But someone trying to blow me up and then...doing what they did to 'Randa...I'm just paranoid, like maybe someone has it out for me or people I know or whatever."

Kitty nodded like that made sense. "I hope all is well."

I put on boots and a jacket and told them to write down any

food they might want. Bryan offered to come with me (good show!), but I told him that he had probably had to handle enough today. Jonny quietly followed behind me, giving a salute-like wave goodbye as we went.

We dropped my car off on a block near a number of grocery stores and grabbed a cab. We kept quiet in the cab because we could tell (thanks, modded watches!) that someone had bugged it. We had no reason to believe the bugs were for us, but better safe than sorry.

We went to Quinn first. He lived behind a seedy strip mall that wasn't technically in Seattle. He had always loved to live clean and spare and hadn't really cared for or trusted a lot of online stuff. That came from his parents; they'd been part of a cult that thought socializing online was stealing people's souls (literally) and ruining society. He'd run from home as soon as he'd thought he could take care of himself, but clearly not run fast enough to leave all their beliefs behind.

He'd lived in this same flat for as long as I'd known him. That meant years of setting up what safety measures he could and finding ways to do what he needed whilst avoiding using the internet. Maybe the internet hadn't been necessary in the past, in my gran's time, but avoiding it in an age where we pretty much do everything online? I had always been torn between thinking he was crazy and admiring the determination and wits it took to do that. With city-sponsored free Wi-Fi, even homeless people were online.

We met dumpster diving back in our squat days. Because he hadn't been allowed to be online growing up, he'd spent way more time than all of us combined on his physical condition. He was a big, burly guy. Intimidating in build and posture. But he had a wicked sense of humor that peeked out now and again, and he was also the sort who truly believed in loyalty and honesty. We might have avoided too much time with most other people (hurrah, paranoia!), but we sought out Quinn.

And here we were, seeking him out again.

It had been a few months since we'd hung out, catching up

over drinks, but we generally made a point of trying to spend time in the flesh with Quinn monthly. The recent gap in hangouts wasn't his fault. To my chagrin, it was us getting sucked into online things. Maybe his parents had been right about the 'Net.

I didn't usually just show up at people's houses; I was raised to think that was impolite. And, whilst I had managed to not care about a lot of other impolite things or social conventions, that one was rooted deep in me. I guess, like Quinn, I hadn't entirely gotten away from my parents' beliefs. Or Gran's beliefs, really. (Not only wouldn't I usually just show up at someone else's, but even Riles and Bryan would usually message me first before showing up at my door. Back when things were normal, I'd proven to be a bit of a nasty bitch when someone did that to me.)

I tapped a little hesitantly on Quinn's door. I looked for the camera; he must surely have cameras on the door. Face tilted up, turning slowly, giving him a chance to see it was me even if his camera was well hidden. I heard his steps, heard locks turn. The door opened a crack. I saw half his face, clearly checking out Jonny.

"He's okay. Okay enough that I'm considering boyfriending him."

Quinn didn't say anything but looked impressed, stepped back, opened the door enough for us to slip in.

The door opened into a very short hallway, which opened into his studio space. One big, clean room with a little partial kitchenette and a tiny bathroom off the right side. A bed, a couch, a TV, and bookshelves. Nothing out of place. No ornamentation. (In Jonny's flat, that was probably due to being a man on the run. In Quinn's flat, it was because he saw ornamentation as clutter. And clutter wasn't clean.)

I kept my eyes on my watch, silently checking for bugs. Nothing. I heaved a sigh of relief.

"What the hell is wrong? You okay?" Quinn had his hands on my shoulders and threw a look that suggested maybe Jonny was to blame for my worry and needed a fist in the face.

I gave him a hug and said, "You have no idea. And I'm really sorry to show up without calling first."

"That's part of how I know something's wrong." He held up my hand, no longer in need of plasters but still clearly healing from the explosion just over a week ago. Nine days. Just nine days? Damn.

"You heard about the bombing?"

Quinn nodded, so I knew I could skip that part.

"Well, it's a big, ugly story. And I can't wait to tell you someday. But, the end result, in this moment, is that I need your help." I gestured to Jonny. "And I need you to pretend, unless he comes here again, that you never saw this guy."

"Can do." He indicated that we should sit on the couch and he sat on the bed. "Now, what do you need?"

Jonny cut in, "Sorry, can I take just one second here?" Without waiting for a reply, he turned to me. "I have really missed getting to talk to you. With voices, I mean. And I didn't want to waste a chance to say even just that. It's been a long damn night and morning."

He squeezed my hand and I gave him a smile that was probably kind of stupid.

I explained to Quinn, "Someone bugged my flat and my car." Then assured him, "We took a cab here and didn't pay with my card."

He smiled at me like a proud papa.

"Someone blew up my building, hacked one of my accounts. Then my place and my car got bugged, and..." I sighed. "And, last night, they kidnapped Bryan's girlfriend. Sent us a picture of her this morning. Throat cut."

Quinn's eyes went big. "Holy fuck! Is Bryan okay?"

"Yeah, as okay as he could be. Pretty emotional, like you'd expect."

"Poor fucking Bryan."

"And now...well, there's a lot of trouble that seems to be aimed at me, or at least at the group of us. And, whilst we try to figure out what the hell is going on and how to fix it, we hoped you might let someone stay with you."

Quinn pointed at Jonny. "Him?"

"No, he's helping. Part of why we're trying to keep him off the radar is because of how much he can help."

Quinn gave Jonny a considering look. "So, who are we talking about?"

"Riley's girl. Who also got sent the picture of Bryan's girl. And is curled up on my couch in terror right now."

Jonny added, "You're probably literally helping save her life. Whether from the people who killed Bryan's girl or from what will happen when Kot's annoyance outweighs her compassion." One side of Jonny's mouth twisted into something near a smirk.

Quinn echoed that smirk. "I hear you. And *of course* she can hide out here. My compassion is stronger than Kot's. And if there's anything else, I'm always here. You guys are part of my tribe."

"Thanks, mate. Riles will be relieved and super grateful." I stood. "I hate to rush off, but I still need to see how my gran is."

"She can stay here too, if you need. And," as if anticipating what I was going to say next, he said, "I won't say anything to anyone."

"You're the best!" I beamed at him. "We'll make sure Kitty, that's the girlfriend, has some generic prepaid cards on her so that your spending record doesn't look suspicious."

"Still stupid smart, aren't you?" His tone told me he was proud of my brain.

I was pretty proud of my brain too.

Quinn walked us to the door and locked it behind us.

The cab back to the shops was *not* bugged, but we knew better than to talk about anything secretive in public. Which was fine; we had missed simple conversation with each other. We stuck to that.

When the cab dropped us back where we'd started, we tried to do speed shopping, loads of groceries in a little time. I hoped SWS, who were surely watching my spending data, would believe that I'd been slowly wandering the store and grabbing things this whole time.

And then we drove over to see Gran.

I felt even more hesitant about showing up at Gran's unannounced. She knew I'd been raised better. But surely we could set this nicety aside just this once if a life were on the line?

Gran looked as wary as Quinn had but also looked disappointed. She didn't say it, but I *knew* she was thinking that she'd raised me better than this. However, she didn't say anything, just stepped back quietly and waited whilst we made sure that she still wasn't housing any bugs.

Once we cleared that, I hugged her and apologized, "I know I shouldn't come over without calling first. I never would. Not normally. But there's a *really* good reason. I promise."

She led us into the living room, an arm through each of ours. "It's nice to see that Jonny has survived a few more days with you." She grinned up at him. "You must be exceptional. Or a masochist. Or both."

We settled onto the sofa and she settled onto a chair, and then she said, "So, what's the problem?"

"Gran, we have to get you out of here. Somebody kidnapped and killed Bryan's girlfriend last night."

Gran gasped and I went on.

"And they sent a picture of it to us and to Rye's girl and...and now I'm worried about you. This so soon after my building was blown seems like maybe there's something bigger happening with us. And I'll never forgive myself if something happens to you."

"Fuck that! If someone is attacking my family, I want a gun. I don't want to run."

I knew Gran was tough, but I hadn't expected that reaction.

I decided to try to scare her into cooperating. I pulled out my mobile.

Jonny put a hand on my arm to make me pause. "Are you sure? It's pretty brutal."

"What?" Gran's curiosity would pretty much ensure that she'd see it now. "What's brutal? Show me."

I held a breath in for a moment. "Jonny's right, Gran. This is brutal. The only reason I'm even considering showing you is that I *want* you scared. I want you to run."

"Show me."

So I showed her.

She went pale. She whispered, so quietly I could barely hear, "Oh, shit."

"Will you please let us help you hide out, even for a little while?" I didn't want to beg, but I wasn't ruling it out.

Jonny assured her, "We'll do it smartly. As smartly as we can. Which doesn't mean we'll get it right, but we can't just do nothing about your safety."

Gran sat back in her chair, thoughtful.

We waited.

"Am I leaving for good if I go?"

Jonny and I looked at each other; we really didn't know.

Well, I wasn't going to lie to her. I'd been raised better than that. "We don't know, Gran. But we hope not. There's a detective, the one you met, who's now also working on 'Randa's case. That was her name. 'Randa."

Gran soberly repeated, "'Randa," then asked, "Do I have time to consider?"

"We can't force you and I'll do what I can whether you decide now or later. But I'm worried. I'd love it if you decided sooner."

"I'll consider quickly. I promise."

Jonny asked, "Do you have a friend out of state, maybe somewhere small town, middle America who might enjoy seeing you for a week? And can you pretend to be surprised at an invitation like that?"

"I can pretend all sorts of things. I'm a woman after all."

When I started laughing and Jonny looked surprised, she scolded, "Not just that, you teenage boys! I've also faked things like being happy to see people or faking not wanting to strangle someone stupid or faking politeness when some creepy guy hit on me and a straight-forward 'no' seemed dangerous."

I told Jonny, "She actually did some acting on stage before I showed up and took over her life. She can act." I turned to Gran. "But do you have a friend like that? Hell, does someone as cranky as you have a friend at all?" I was joking, of course.

She narrowed her eyes and jabbed a finger at me, "Who raised you? So rude!"

And we both laughed.

She looked at Jonny, "A couple of her quirks and character flaws *might* be my fault."

She made a list of just a few possible friends, and I quickly messaged that to Bryan and Riles, asking them to figure out who'd be the best person for Gran to go stay with. I wasn't sure what criteria we ought to use, but I told them my few ideas. They could look into it whilst Jonny and I finished up at Gran's and drove back to the flat. I also mentioned that Quinn was good, in case they wanted to start getting Kitty moved that way.

As if just realizing something, Jonny said, "It might have to be me who contacts your friends, just so anyone watching Katja can't easily trace it back to her. So, if someone mentions...your granddaughter's boyfriend or something, don't be surprised."

Gran ginned at me. "Pretty and smart? Don't run him off too quickly!"

As we left, I hugged her and wondered, as I had the night we'd had dinner, if this was the last time I'd get to see her. I might have hugged her a little bit tighter.

Once home, I made sure to apologize for taking so long. "I'm lost in my head. I just kind of wandered through every aisle in a daze. Sorry."

Bryan waved away my apologies. "No worries. Thanks for buying food."

After we put groceries away, I sat down and looked at the chat they'd been having. They'd figured out which of Gran's friends wasn't suspect or living too close to an SWS office.

```
Riley: Sarah is a good bet. In addition to
   seeming safe, she and Gran actually stayed
   in touch by email, quite warmly, for a while
   once Sarah and her husband moved to Wyoming.
   It seems like they just drifted apart. And
   Sarah's husband died in just the last few
   months.
Katja: Even if we didn't want Gran safe, this
   could be a beautiful thing for everyone.
```

This felt like maybe the Fates had decided to be done shitting on us for the moment.

```
Jonny: I'm going to call Sarah to set it up.
   Make sure nobody can trace this back to Kot.
   I'll tell Sarah I'm Gran's son-in-law.
```

(Oh, the fidgeting and looks exchanged over that.)

```
Jonny: And I want to set up a nice getaway for
    her. I'll tell Sarah that Gran seems lonely
    and mentioned her. I'll ask, if I set up the
    flight, would Sarah be willing to call and
    invite Gran out for a weeklong visit? And,
    of course, tell her she shouldn't at all
    mention that I, the son-in-law, was behind
    it, because I don't want her to feel like
    this was a pity visit.
Bryan: Do it, Mr. Katja.
```

The three of them quietly laughed at me. Suddenly, the kindest person in the room was Kitty. Jerks.

Whilst Jonny was sorting out the possible trip for Gran, Riles and Kitty were typing back and forth. It was heated, but not angry.

Jonny came back down, giving us thumbs up and a smile.

Riley stood up and threw zir hands in the air in apparent frustration, giving Kitty a look of lost patience.

Looked like there was good news and bad.

For the good news...We eavesdropped on Gran's mobile, and saw her get a call from the Wyoming number Jonny had rung. Shortly after, Gran called me, delighted to let me know she'd reconnected with an old friend and was going to go visit. "I hate to leave you when you're still healing, but my friend was recently widowed and is just now ready for company."

"You should go, Gran. Comfort your friend. Revisit the good old days. Besides, I'm reasonably healed now. Go with my blessings and no guilt!"

As for bad news...Kitty, on the other hand, didn't want to hide away with a stranger. She wanted to curl up with Riles. She'd already sent her work a message to ask for time off to mourn her murdered friend. (That request was swiftly approved.) She meant to spend that time on my couch, it seemed.

We basically spent the rest of the day cleaning up

documents, checking in with our far-flung team, and trying to talk Kitty into staying with Quinn. In the end, we got her to promise to think about it, to sleep on it.

Which she did, crammed on the couch with Rye, as if two people can actually *sleep* on a couch like that.

In the bedroom, silent by necessity, Jonny and I quietly and carefully clasped, groped, explored, but stopped short of anything satisfying. Worried about giving him away with noises, but worried that time was short and death might make us an "almost." As if two people can actually *sleep* in a bed like that.

CHAPTER 18

Monday morning, Kitty conceded. She put on a "brave and reasonable" face and grabbed Riley's portable.

    Riley: (Kitty) I'll go stay with your friend. I
    realized you guys are right. Thanks for
    letting me stay here and for finding me a
    safe place to be.

I tried to make sure my relief at that didn't seem like it was about anything other than her safety. Now was not the time to bring up that I was going crazy enough with people I actually liked constantly around.

    Bryan: We'll slip out. Quietly. Hopefully, our
    watchers won't realize we've gone. Me and
    Riles and Kitty will catch a cab to pick up
    some of her things. Where (Riles make sure
    Kitty reads this) we'll be very quiet in
    case they bugged her place too. And then
    we'll drop her safely at Quinn's and be back
    as quick as possible. Just in case the music
    doesn't sufficiently mask our absence.

They left, and I tried to work. It looked like Jonny tried as well. We did those things that should aid success: get up, get dressed, set aside distractions. Except that we were our own worst distraction. It wasn't long before his arm and leg touching mine were the only thing on which I could concentrate.

I pressed against him, but tried to keep typing. He shifted, returning the pressure. Both of us slowed down on our keyboards but kept trying, kept...typing...so...slowly. I don't know how long that lasted. It was the eternity of want. I realized my hands were still, hovering over the keys. I realized his hands were also still.

I felt my breath grow heavy and wondered if, had it not been for the now-ubiquitous music, it would have been audible. As if I were somehow fooling either of us, I willed myself to scroll through the document I was in, like I was reading. But I also put my free hand on his thigh and felt his muscles tense at my touch. Who the hell was I kidding?

But I sat there, still, dragging out the pretense of productivity. His hand was on my leg now, a reflection of my own hand on his leg, and I felt my muscles beneath reflect his in tensing. But it wasn't just those muscles and I was on the verge of admitting where this was going.

We held the verge for moments, hands steadily increasing their pressure. I could now feel his breathing. I squeezed his thigh, he squeezed mine, and I felt us exhale raggedly together.

I swear, even in that moment, I was trying to keep some control. He pulled me—just a slight directional pressure on my leg—and I moved, swung myself around, straddling him. He scooted forward so that I could wrap my legs. We were kissing like we thought, for just a moment, our mouths would be enough.

Hands moved quickly from over shirts to under shirts. I tightened my legs around his waist like that would help us hold on to whatever control might still exist.

With a hand on my back, he twisted and I was lying on the couch with him on top of me. And I was done pretending. I was done stifling this like I'd stifled screams on Sunday.

He paused. He was going to stop things. Again. I was gasping; I didn't think I could take another day of restraint.

But he wasn't stopping. He was pointing upstairs. Upstairs, to his flat. No bugs or chance to be walked in on.

We scrambled, just enough intelligence left that we hid away computers and placed the decoy laptop on the coffee table, keyed Ada into heightened security mode, grabbed boots and jackets so we could pretend we'd left for some other reason. I was very proud of us.

We tried to play it casual on the dash upstairs. At the door, I fumbled to unlock and he pressed against me from behind, pushing me against the door. Our breathing was audible. I pushed back against him, pressing into him. His mouth was on the nape of my neck. I kept trying to get the door unlocked. His hands were sliding, pressing, down my hips and around to my thighs. We were both surprised when the lock gave and the door fell inward under our weight.

As if choreographed, we both quickly shed our jackets and kicked off shoes before the door was even closed. Stumbling. Driven as much by the hungry creatures in our chests as by the ones in our hips.

I recovered my footing and turned, pressing him against the door as he moved backwards. Closing the door. Irrationally worried he might slip away if we broke contact. His arms wrapped me and held me tightly against him, kissing me as I locked the door. Then my hands were up and around his neck. He pivoted so that, again, I was the one pressed. Pinned against the wall beside the door. No worries that anything might slip now.

He held me there with his hips, leaning back just enough to pull off my shirt. I pulled off his whilst he undid my bra. Eager to put skin on skin, to spread the heat. And then he pushed back up against me. My hands pressing his back, his chest pressing my breasts, my back pushed into the wall.

He grabbed my ass, pulling me up, and I was on my tip toes, until he wrapped his arms to lift me, to support me, and held me as my legs wrapped his waist. Just for a moment, because my skirt might not be in the way but there were other things that were, I leaned back so that I could reach his belt. Impatience adding to the pitch of the moment. His mouth was on my collar bone, tracing it. I made my leaning into an arching, raising my breasts closer to his lips, but it wasn't enough. He used an arm to pull me back close, away from the wall, somehow supporting my weight long enough to fall into the bedroom, onto the bed. That comfortable bed at last!

I was perched on the edge, his hands squeezing my breasts, and I was finally loosing his belt. Quickly moving to undo the button, the zipper, to press his jeans down. There'd been enough slowness in this up to now. I wanted it all and open and immediately. I leaned back, arched, supporting myself on my hands, as he trailed one hand down from my breasts over my stomach. He used the other hand to finish pulling off his jeans. When he had both hands free again, he grabbed my waistbands, I lifted my hips to help, and he left me unclothed at last in one motion. I could have wept with the joy of that.

I had barely touched my hips back to the bed, my skirt and underwear just slipping off my foot, and I leaned forward to tug at his last waistband. My head was empty of anything but needing him to be *here* in the same state that I was in, in this same space. In a moment, we were both free and there was no doubt that we were going to let the world-saving wait.

Somehow, he had the control to take time, agonizingly sweet time, to make sure I was ready and fully explored, that I was done using my own hands and mouth to search out every part of him he'd been holding back, before he pressed into me. Once again, our legs were tangled, but so was everything else. Finally, so was everything else.

For that moment, there was no death, no bomb, no threat to our lives or plan. There was just flesh and sweat, heat and muscles tightening. Pressing. Pressing. Hips clashing with hips. Panting and drawing this out as long as we could make ourselves. He pulled back (how did he have the wherewithal to pull back?) and used his mouth to graze my nipples, to travel down my torso, a side trip to kiss and nip at my hips (I thought, *My hips have angles; I need to keep them from knocking his teeth when he bites*), a pause just before he reached his destination, hot breath hovering over the curve of my pubic bone. His hands on my breasts surely felt the way the breath gasped into me in anticipation and then my sharp exhale as his lips met flesh, brushed and parted, and his hands were now pressing my thighs farther apart (I didn't resist, I eagerly spread them, knees bent, feet pressing into the mattress) as his tongue moved in to circle and probe.

His hands pressed, right in the joint of my legs, holding my thighs open and pushing against my hips that were rising of their own accord. His thumbs and fingers were splayed, also teasing and rubbing. My hands, at the ends of straight arms, were pressed into the bed, palms down, as if they were trying to help leverage my hips. Up, up, as so much of us pressed, pressed.

He waited until I was shuddering, moving and rolling into

and through a long wave of orgasm, before he pulled himself back up, quickly, kissing my face my neck my shoulders as he entered me. Finally letting himself go. One arm reaching beneath my still-arching back to dig nails in and hold me close for a moment.

It was like all the oxygen had gone out and there was nothing but the bright energy of our sex, of fulfillment at last, to sustain us. Our breaths were no longer in any sort of synchronicity. Our lungs now taking over as if air could refuel us. He carefully pulled himself from me and fell back onto the bed beside me.

And we were both laughing the laugh of satisfaction put off, finally gained. He laid so that our sides were touching, pressing. (I had never before noticed how pressing, inside and out, it was to be with someone I wanted as more than just a hookup.) He moved to tuck an arm under me, and I shifted, putting my head on his shoulder. Bare skin still pressing. My hand resting, again, on his thigh. His hand, the one that had passed beneath my back and was now near my shoulder, was gently, lightly stroking.

There was a waiting feeling in the air, like a question hanging over us. I thought I knew the question, and now I thought I knew the answer. (I also thought I heard my mobile buzzing, but it could wait. Everything could wait.)

"I think, for now, I might be yours."

That was, indeed, the answer.

Lying as we were, I could feel his quiet exhale. "Good. Me too." I could hear the smile in his voice. He leaned in and kissed my forehead. "For days now, actually. Maybe longer." He pushed a strand of my hair carefully off my cooling cheeks and laid back.

We didn't lie there long.

"We're probably supposed to be responsible now," I said grudgingly, slowly sitting up. "And our 'flatmates' will be home any moment, if they're not already down there wondering where we've gone."

"Guess we should go and face the music. By which I mean Riley's prying eyes." He pushed himself up, kneeling beside me on the bed, facing me.

He gently rested his fingertips on my cheekbones and then traced me, slowly and with quiet concentration. Every inch of me. Like he was memorizing me, just in case. I considered taking advantage of this contact, like an invitation to push him back on the bed, but the spell of the moment was broken by a gunshot.

Jonny froze for just a moment, we both did, and then we dove for clothing. I was muttering "shitshitshit" under my breath as I dressed. My knees were no longer weak and any sex-induced languor had fled, apparently, from both of us. We were heading for the door when we thought to bring our escape bags. Almost at the same time, we both grabbed for the closet door and started to tell the other what we were doing.

I felt safer knowing he had also had that instinct. That he had also maintained some intelligence whilst under threat.

We heard shouting now too. Voices we knew and voices we didn't.

As Jonny locked the door I said, "Hang back. We can't have them see you."

He looked distressed, but he understood.

I was glad that, among the gear he'd stashed in Jonny's closet, Bryan had included guns. I had one out now, trying to remember what little I thought I knew about safely approaching a fight.

Outside my door, Riles was getting the shit beaten out of zir by a person in black. And Bryan was trying to hold his own against another. A third was slumped by the open door, a laptop in hand, apparently knocked out. (Please, please let it be the decoy laptop.)

This lot looked bigger and better armed than the other two who'd come around. The one beating Rye had apparently beaten zir into sufficient submission, because he started to cuff zir hands with a zip tie.

I felt the fear crawling in to lock me down, to paralyze me. I set a mantra going in my head, trying to be someone else. *Fear is the mind-killer. Fear is the mind-killer.*

I pointed my gun and shouted, "Hey!" as I stepped into view. I didn't know if I felt confident in taking a shot so close to my friends. I wished I'd had a bat instead. I moved in closer, figuring my chances were better if I went for the one kneeling over Rye. He didn't have a gun in his hands. Not at the moment. He finished securing the zip ties before he casually put up his hands. The mask he wore meant I couldn't tell if his face looked as casual.

I shouted again, trying to sound tough and confident, "Get the fuck away from them!"

There was a moment where Zip Tie Guy had his hands in the air, probably considering his next move, and his conscious partner took a moment to look away from Bryan to assess the situation with the new shouting person (me), and police sirens suddenly sounded very near (I sent out silent thanks to whoever had called the cops). In that moment, Bryan managed to slip from his opponent's grip, picked up Riles, and started running. I could hear police, on foot, running in now. The men in black pulled guns, looking ready to shoot. I chanced it, turning to run after Bryan.

I can't be sure why they didn't shoot. But, in their shoes, I'd have grabbed my unconscious partner and the laptop and run. So I have to guess that's what they did. Bryan stopped running, still in the housing complex. There were no sounds of pursuit, just sounds of police.

Bryan panted for air and said, "I'm afraid we'll run into them again if we get too far from the cops. But we can't go back and let the cops put us under surveillance."

I nodded my agreement, moving closer to try to take in the extent of their injuries. Bryan looked rough but was obviously okay enough to fight and run. Riles was blacked out and definitely worse off.

Bryan whispered, "Message Jonny. Have him meet us here. I'll send out the command to wipe the computers in your flat and whichever one they grabbed. Just in case." He gently set Riles down and pulled out his mobile.

I slipped my gun into my jacket and messaged Jonny, warning him about the cops on the scene. I was sure that Engalls would be on the scene soon, wisely on the lookout for clues about whatever had left a puddle of blood in front of my open door *and* that might prove or disprove my innocence. I didn't want him to catch a glimpse of Jonny.

Whilst we waited for Jonny, we cut the zip tie off Riley's wrists and started trying to assess the damage.

I whispered, "Zie needs real help. More than sterile foam and bandages."

"But we can't risk a hospital. We'll...we'll have to get

somewhere safe and then get help." Bryan sounded thoroughly miserable. "I fucked up again. Physical safety is my responsibility, and I let everyone down. Again." He sounded verge of tears. "We're just lucky zie's not dead too."

Bryan picked up Riles, and Jonny came around the corner before I could tell Bryan that it wasn't his fault.

When Jonny saw us, a cloud of concern passed over his face, but it quickly turned to a look of righteous fury. SWS had inflicted too much personal damage on us in only a few days.

He might not be as physically fit as Bryan, but he insisted he carry Rye with a simple, "I'll carry zir. I'm not busted up."

Bryan handed Riles off and looked at me. "Quinn?"

I nodded. "Can't think what other option we have. Let's get a cab." As we walked to the street, I finally said, "And none of this is your fault. No one blames you. Because this is all on SWS. *You* have been busting your ass for us." I gave him a quick side-hug as I put out my arm to wave down a cab.

The cabbie looked wary but just said, "You gotta put...them across your laps. I can't have blood on my seats."

When we gave him a residential address, he asked, "You sure you don't wanna go to a hospital instead? Your friend don't look so good."

"We know," I assured him. "We'll make sure zie gets taken care of."

The cabbie asked us over and over, the whole drive to Quinn's, about the hospital. We made sure to pay with a prepaid card and to tip well. Maybe he wouldn't talk.

Quinn didn't take nearly as long to answer the door this time, opening it wide and directing Jonny to put Riles on the bed. "Don't worry about the blood. Blood washes out and black sheets don't stain easy."

I'd forgotten, in the adrenaline and blur of flight, that Kitty was there. She choked back a scream when she saw Rye. She rushed over, trying to make sense of our state, trying to assess the extent of Riley's injuries. Quinn brought her damp cloths, and she started to at least clean up blood. Riley stirred a little, but it was with a low moan of pain.

Kitty was so gentle. I was sort of fascinated to watch. It occurred to me that she really loved Riles. But the rest of us had to keep our minds on hard thoughts.

Quinn asked, "What do you guys want to do about Riles?"

Jonny pulled out his mobile. "Maybe Doc knows someone local who can be trusted."

As Jonny typed away, Bryan asked, "Do you mind if someone comes here to see Riles?"

"I'm not gonna lie; I don't love the idea. But it looks like maybe you guys are in some serious shit, and a hospital would be too dangerous." Quinn paused, watching Kitty work. "If you don't mind moving zir, I have a car. And a gun. And we can take zir to see someone, then come back here to do whatever."

Hesitantly I said, "Given that the next favor we're probably going to ask is to be able to work from here for at least the rest the day, your plan seems like the best."

Quinn put an arm around Bryan's shoulders and the other around mine. "If you think I didn't assume you'd be staying here, you've clearly forgotten that I'm a fucking genius too."

Jonny and I set our bags down. My mobile beeped in a way that told me there was a news alert about the bombing. I pulled it up. There was my picture, including an updated photo, and my name.

"Oh shit."

Jonny and Bryan looked over my shoulders.

Quinn asked, "What's up?"

"In a case of bad timing, which means this probably came from the people trying to fuck us up, the press has learned the name of the employee who survived the bombing and has gotten an updated photo." It was one of my worst nightmares. My face and my name in the press. My actual name, not my 'nym, and connected to my actual face. I felt a wave of despair hit me, and I sat down right where I was.

The guys quickly and kindly joined me on the floor.

Jonny supportively said, "Shit, Kot."

I was breathing carefully and trying out someone else's mantra against fear, but it wasn't working to fight back the guilt and the fear building in me. People were dead. People were beat up. People were in danger. I was exposed. And it was my fault. It might be SWS doing it, but I was the other common factor. I could feel my thoughts spiraling. My mobile was also buzzing, multiple incoming calls from numbers I didn't know. It must be the press.

I was vaguely aware of Bryan moving, and then he was right in my face. "Katja, whatever bullshit you're telling yourself in your head, stop it."

I laughed, short and abrupt. "You're one to talk."

He let out a frustrated sigh. "If I promise to stop beating myself up and just keep my head in the game, will you try to do the same?"

I met his eyes. I really looked at them. All his good intention flooded from them into me. "Yes."

"Good. Okay." He looked at the others, then back at me. He patted my shoulder, solidly. "We got this."

Jonny had an arm around me and squeezed. He shifted and Bryan did as well until we were sitting in a circle.

Jonny asked, "What happened back there?"

Whilst Bryan talked, I set up my phone to dump all unknown calls to a secondary voicemail account immediately, with an outgoing message by a synthesized voice. "Ms. Brennan has no comment. Please contact SPD or SWS for information on the case." My phone stopped buzzing.

"We were just returning from dropping Kitty off here when we noticed Kot's car's tires had all been slashed. As had the tires on my motorcycle and Rye's. In less paranoid times, we'd just have assumed some neighborhood asshole had had a busy midday petty crime spree. But these are not those kinds of times, so we assumed we were looking at what SWS might consider disabled escape vehicles."

Jonny said, "Glad I didn't suggest making a break for our cars."

"Yeah. That would have been pointless. Anyway, we moved up carefully on the door. We hadn't heard from you guys, so we weren't sure whether the slightly open door was an issue. We were near the door, off to a side, trying to hear. Because we've always had music on lately, we didn't know whether the music was the usual or had been cued by security protocols being tripped. We also couldn't hear much over it."

"These two," and he indicated me and Quinn, "know I have personal rule that I try not to fire a gun in daylight in a residential area. That's just asking to be identified and caught. So I picked up a fallen brick near my feet, considering our options. Before we could message you or make a real move, the guys in black came rushing out. They were looking around, and we weren't hidden in any way, so we would definitely have been seen. So I bashed the one at the rear in the head with the brick. I got lucky and the guy went down."

"The guy with the laptop who was down when I got there?"

"Yep. And I figure we were supposed to be brought in alive, because the shot that I'm guessing is what got you down there," he paused to confirm, and I nodded, "was a fucking *warning* shot."

Those of us listening to his story all made disapproving noises. A warning shot? Nothing but a waste of ammo and a cause for unwanted attention. At least we knew not all our enemies were actually intelligent or highly trained.

Quinn asked, "You sure it wasn't non-lethal rounds or bad aim? Maybe one of your bruises is from that?"

Bryan shook his head. "I don't think anything hit me. And there's no way it should have missed in close quarters like that."

There was another round of snorting disapproval.

"We both tried to run, but they jumped us and held us back. And the rest...you saw." He went on though, probably because only I had seen it. "The one guy got me up against the wall, but the other beat the living hell out of poor Riles. And only stopped because you startled them with your shouting and gun...and then the police came."

"Fuck," breathed Quinn.

"Where were you guys? And how come Ada didn't tip you off about the intruders?" Bryan looked at our escape bags, leaned against a wall. "Were you guys upstairs?"

I mutely nodded.

In an alternate universe, we hadn't gone upstairs for sex and Riley didn't end up beaten to a pulp.

In an alternate universe, I didn't ignore my buzzing mobile, so I warned them not to go to the flat. And then Riley was still conscious and realized we'd had sex, so he forgot to be serious because he wanted details, or at least a high five.

In an alternate universe, I wasn't drowning in guilt and about to be, quite rightly, hated.

I could feel my brain curling in on itself. This was one more thing that solidly belonged on my list of sins.

It was quiet for a moment and I didn't make eye contact. I could only imagine that Jonny was also staring intently at the ground.

Bryan quietly asked, "Were you fucking?"

There was no clear accusation in the question. But that didn't make me feel better.

We didn't reply, but he hissed, "Dammit, Katja. Couldn't you have kept yourself in check for just a few more days?" There was a hint of venom as he pointed out, "Some of us have managed and now won't have another chance."

My shame filled my throat and turned my cheeks crimson. I choked out a whisper, "I'm so, so sorry. I'm...I can't be sorrier."

He pressed on. "Did you just not hear the mobile buzzing over loud sex noises?"

I couldn't take it anymore. I could feel that I'd started to cry, but it was just tears falling from my eyes. My breathing felt normal. I wasn't going to sob. My voice was quiet. It didn't sound like my usual voice, the voice that had edges of confidence that rarely softened. "I ignored the buzzing because sex." I finally looked up. I hoped the conversation had been quiet enough that Kitty didn't hear that. "I'm sorry. I'm sorry." And then I felt my breath catch and I knew sobs were probably close behind.

Jonny scooted over a bit and put an arm around me, admitting, "I heard her mobile buzzing, but...sex. Bryan, I'm...sorry too. Very sorry."

Kitty didn't look up from Riles, so maybe I wouldn't have to deal with her wrath. Bryan looked at loss for words for a moment, but I watched as he seemed to swallow back his anger, dull it down to a simmering frustration.

The grunt that came from him certainly confirmed the frustration. "I'd really like to be pissed off for a long time. But I'm too busy realizing that, in your situation, I might not even have come out for just one gunshot. Not in *your* neighborhood. We're probably lucky you guys weren't there, or they'd have you. And *you*," he indicated Jonny, "would be properly fucking on their radar. And we're lucky that you came out, in your neighborhood, at the sound of just one gunshot, just in case. Because you definitely caused enough of a distraction that they didn't get to run off with Riles."

I knew him well enough to see that he was willing himself to put things aside for the greater good.

Bryan leaned over and hugged me, ignoring the awkwardness of Jonny's arm still around my shoulders. "We're all alive and free. Free-ish." He tried a smile. "When this is all done, I'm going to spend the rest of our lives talking about how, the first time you guys screwed, you almost screwed the world." It was a half-hearted, weak attempt to let humor defuse the situation.

I wasn't ready to absolve myself yet, so Bryan's response to the whole situation just made me cry harder.

I tried to make a joke to get the sobbing to stop. "I promise never to ignore my mobile during sex again."

"Hey!" Jonny protested. "I want a vote on that promise. Veto power."

The guilt and gloom lifted the tiniest bit.

Doc hunted down someone local to help Riley. We did a quick check into her, knowing that we needed to balance speed and caution. She seemed okay, or at least not likely connected to SWS or the lawful side of the law.

Quinn, Bryan, and Kitty took Riles in Quinn's car to see the doctor. Jonny and I very chastely (turns out intense guilt can keep the libido at bay) saw to our work, getting our new portables set up, making sure our other people hadn't also been compromised, checking into the security of our own accounts. Again. It seemed like we were constantly doing that lately. Beyond the usual level of care. I hadn't realized how spoilt I'd previously been.

Everyone seemed okay. Good.

Good.

I was feeling well past my capacity to pretend to gracefully deal with another loss that was, at least in part, my fault.

I asked Jonny. "Should I call my gran?" Not because I needed anyone's permission, but because I knew my head was probably fuzzier than I'd like. Should I call Gran? I didn't know.

"If you call, you almost certainly risk being heard by SWS, maybe also the police. We don't *know* who's monitoring what, and phone tapping seems within police *or* SWS comfort zones."

"But if we *don't* call..."

"It seems like your gran is already on guard, already preparing to leave town for a bit, already on the radar of both the police and SWS. The only thing you *might* accomplish is scaring her and then maybe—though maybe not, based on her previous insistence that she just be given a gun—she'd hide out somewhere until her flight."

I was feeling super paranoid. "Even that flight's a possible risk."

Jonny didn't deny it. I was starting to realize that, short of going over there armed, we could do nothing. And, really, we were better with computers than guns, better at running programs and data crimes than fighting or actual running.

"I can't call her, can I?"

Jonny put a hand on my shoulder. "Sorry, Kot."

In addition to the call I *wasn't* making was the call I was currently avoiding. No surprise that Engalls was trying to contact me. When I saw the number I confirmed, "I definitely can't answer Engalls, right?"

"Too, too right. No question there. Even though he's probably calling to make sure you're okay..."

"Yeah, answering would make it easier for them to locate my mobile and find us." Even if the police meant us no harm, they were still on the wrong side of our current effort. Engalls seemed clever enough to figure it out, later, after. And he'd understand, whether or not he agreed with our cause.

One great and unintentional side effect of me not taking Engalls's call was that he must have called Gran looking for me. Which means that *she* called *me* and for a completely valid reason.

Jonny said, "Keep it short, okay?"

I nodded and answered. "Hi, Gran. Can't really talk. You okay?"

"Am *I* okay? I'm not the one the police are trying to hunt

down for their own safety. And the one the press are digging into."

"Fair enough. The answer is that I *am* okay but really worried and safer not to really talk."

"I understand. Okay, you're alive. And I'm being careful. And I love you. Right?"

"Right. I love you as well, Gran. Be super, super safe, okay? And don't forget to call the cops if the press keep harassing you."

We rang off. I felt better. And I was able to concentrate on the work we *should* be doing.

Everyone else returned from the doctor after a couple hours. I was pleased to see that, though zie needed a cast and crutches, Riles was awake and walking on zir own.

In addition to plenty of bruising and busted up skin from where punches had landed, the main highlights of the damage to Riles were a broken leg, a minor concussion, a cracked cheekbone, three cracked ribs, a sprained wrist, and stitches where zir ear had gotten torn. Zie was swollen and unhappy and looked really rough. But zie was also doped up on pain pills, so mostly Rye was happy to just lie on the couch and watch TV, occasionally mumbling some silly non-sequitur.

Of course, even pain pills couldn't dull zir particular psychic powers. Halfway through zir protein shake dinner, zie looked up, right into my face and said, "Holy shit. You guys finally hooked up!"

CHAPTER 19

We were a little crippled, what with one person down and Bryan stuck on his mobile instead of a portable, but we kept working. For my part, I didn't feel like I could do anything else. If I stopped, I'd think about...well, about everything. And I didn't want to have another cry in front of everyone.

In some ways, it was harder working at Quinn's flat than in my bugged flat. With Riles not to be trusted on any sort of portable or mobile (which might let zir touch the 'Net whilst so doped up), we couldn't just send zir messages and chat that way. But with Kitty and Quinn there...it wasn't even necessarily about trust, but more about making sure they weren't tangled in our conspiracy any more than they already were.

I figured I'd save up anything I wanted to say and find a chance to somehow whisper it to everyone when Kitty was in the bathroom and we other three could gather around the couch. I found that the three of us were doing a lot of looking at each other, looking at Quinn and Kitty, looking at each other again...

Quinn seemed to have noticed, because he suggested, "Hey, Kitty, come help me pick up some dinner that will make everyone happy."

Kitty looked confused for a moment, but, as she'd pointed out, she wasn't stupid. She looked over at the row of us attached to our screens, and then she kissed Riles on the forehead and hopped up. "Let's do it."

Quinn gave us a conspiratorial wink as he walked out. We had chosen our friends well.

And the instant he was out, we quickly scooted over by Riles. Zie rolled zir head around to look at us and said, "Huh?"

I gave zir hand a squeeze. "We know you're probably too fucked up to really process, poppet, but there's stuff we've found. I mean, I found stuff and everyone else is acting like they did too, so..."

Riley's eyes lit up and zie gasped, "You're going to share with me? Yes!"

I grinned.

Jonny said, "You go ahead and go first, Kot. You got antsy before I did." He looked at Bryan, "Cool?"

"Yep. Go, Kot, go."

"Okay, so, I finally heard from Doc and Engie on specs, not just secondhand through Jonny. They think they've figured out, from the specs and other stuff I sent them, what's up with the vII. And it is *not* good. As near as they can tell...wait, I should go back. I found a thing that said something about replacing the vI with the vII, and I didn't mention it because it was more a recommendation. So, I figured that, given everything, they put a vII in when taking out the vI. But, Doc and Engie...They explain it in full, but then kindly summarize. Shout out if you want the full version." I paused for them to shout.

Bryan said, "If I get curious, I'll just read the message in your remote team account."

"Good. Okay. So, the vII builds itself out via all that nanotech crammed into it, and it inserts tiny filaments all over the brain. They can do all the same things as the vI, including the remote control human thing Doc thought, but they seem to also more completely wire in. And they almost certainly let SWS mess around with emotions and dreams. I checked with them about the girl who killed those kids the Tuesday before...uh...before my building went down. They said that, yeah, based on the very little information, it was conceivable that it was a vII that was used to brainwash that poor girl."

Riles squinted and asked, "Wait, they're dreamwashing people with the little bug?"

I said, "That's what Engie and Doc think. And they're the ones who know brains and machines. But, because the vII is so much smaller on insertion, people don't realize there's still a Peacemaker in there. They just know the vI is gone, so they'd be less likely to think there was a Peacemaker behind any of this."

"So, they have a little bug they can put into anyone, and drive them to do things. Plus, like the vI, maybe just plain take control?" Bryan sounded more horrified than I felt. "I mean, at least with a vI you can *see* that it's there. But these..."

I sighed. "Yeah. But these." I squinted at him. "But you sound even more horrified than *I* feel."

"That's because of what *I* found. If you're done..."

"I am. Please, horrify us more." I gestured with a hand to give the conversation to Bryan.

"I didn't think I'd have anything useful to add, with a mobile instead of a portable to work on, so I figured I'd just do easy stuff, like snoop the CEO's email. And today was a...a useful day for that." He pulled out his mobile and scrolled a bit. "First we've got the messages with CorpSec where they let her know they failed to get you or anyone else and that the portable they got was wiped entirely. So, that's good news for us."

He flicked his finger to bring up the next document. "Then, we have the messages where CorpSec tries to speak carefully as possible when admitting that they have no idea where you are, even though they made it easier for the news to help keep an eye." Bryan gave me a look. "So, confirmed that we're safe-ish and that they *were* the ones who put you squarely in the crosshairs of the press."

One more flick on his mobile and he continued, "Finally..." He sighed. "Here's where the horror comes in."

Riles interjected, "Is it bats and rats and monsters? Please be that! Because I am kind of fucked off with all the little bits of metal."

Bryan shook his head. "Sorry, poppet. It's more about the little bits of metal. Specifically, about how successful their careful campaign was when they 'leaked' the information about the amazing capabilities of this tiny subdermal monitor to powerful people. Even before they introduced the Elder Care bill thing, they got people curious. Part of how they even sold the bill. Intrigued powerful people and their doctors. Which, as hoped, got them clamoring to have access immediately. There are lists of names, people who've just had them put in this last week and people who are scheduled to get them in this week and in weeks to come."

Jonny groaned and dropped his head forward. "People are too easy and SWS are too clever."

"Well, we *really* have to stop them now, because, according to a press release Johnson is drafting about how it will help keep him monitored and safe, one of the suckered groups in this case is the president—as in the President of the United States—and his family. There's already one in his mother's head and there will be one in his, the first lady's, and their kids' heads before the week is out. They've been working closely with his doctor and the Secret Service to clear this. SWS is counting it as both a particular win—they don't spell out why but we can guess given the...as Rye called it, the dreamwashing capabilities and the remote controlled humans thing and their world domination bullshit—and a general win that will help make the vII more attractive to *everyone*." He let that sink in a moment. "Uh, I guess the good news here is that...Here, I'll read."

He scrolled a bit. "Friday's launch will clearly include some noteworthy names. If it goes as planned, we can expand from controls at headquarters to regional controls, cutting down on the need for satellites to pass signals through the whole chain. Eastern U.S. coast obviously high priority."

Jonny exclaimed, "Which means taking out HQ really will be the key to stopping this long enough to get word out!"

Bryan smiled. "Yes. So..." He looked at Riles. "So we better figure out who's going in with the bugs instead of Rye, because we absolutely can't let this happen."

"We won't need the bugs."

We all looked at Jonny, faces scrunched up with confusion.

He smiled. "Our supervillains have fixed that for us."

Jonny turned so that his back was against the couch and motioned us all to sit by him so we could see his portable's screen. He pulled up three documents and pointed at one.

"Now, you've already seen this one. It's the non-classified blueprints. And this," he pointed to another, "is the classified blue prints. Which have some differences. But we didn't notice them all." He gave a soft snort of laughter. "Not everything important is as obvious as an underwater escape hatch. But, fortunately, I found this one." He pointed at the third document. "This was what finally tipped me off."

Jonny zoomed in on the same area in each of the blueprints, but then expanded the third document so that it filled the screen. It was an outline of some kind of emergency protocol.

Jonny said, "I didn't want to say anything about this until I dug in a bit. And we obviously couldn't just talk until now, but..."

He pointed at the instructions. "In addition to some kind of submarine escape route, in true supervillain fashion, they seem to have a self-destruct plan."

After a pause for us to process that weird information and suggest amiably that he "shut the fuck up," he started pointing to things in the instructions, scrolling pages as necessary.

"Basically, if it looks like they're compromised in some significant enough way, like someone is about to get at their data or their machines or anything like that, anything that's an actual threat (and there's a list here of possible things if you want to look later), they can blow the building. They're supposed to get the machines out first if possible. If it weren't for the underwater entrance and elevator things, I'd have assumed there was another document that listed key hard drives or something to run out to trucks or up to helicopters."

"Yeah, so, they get things down to their submarine. Or, really, it looks more like they get things down to a hidden room where something more important is—maybe the machines for this new phase, and then move it from there to this airlock-looking space between the big hidden room and the tunnel. And then they enter some codes and blow the building to hell."

Bryan gave out a long, low whistle. "That's crazy. And it would cover up any proof that the building was weird or had been cleared out. If they were the ones to set it off..."

I wasn't so sure. "Are you positive? I mean, this isn't some April Fools' joke from one exec to another?"

"Only if April Fools' is in September. And only if there's another reason for *these* areas," and now he pointed back to the blueprints, where we could see the classified version had tiny additional structures, "marked as dangerous but not big enough to be rooms or even closets. And, from what I've researched, though I messed it up with the one building I tried," he paused a moment as a look of deep shame passed over his face, "spaced just right to actually blow the building, with the main impact taking out that column of important gear in the middle. Or hiding that the important gear column had existed at all if they can get it out."

He flipped windows again scrolled through the instructions to the end. "There's a note here about how it starts in the center, where the important stuff is, and works its way out. Giving the person who initiates things a chance to escape if they're located further out when they initiate."

I pressed the point. "But *why* would they have this? This is just asking for trouble, isn't it? There can't be anything so important that someone would go full supervillain, could there? Or..." My mind scrambled for a reason. "Do we have any info that their board are literally crazy? Honestly. I look at this and it's just not the way a sane person works." I shook my head.

Jonny put down his portable, and shook his head. "I don't know yet. Aside from a reminder in the instructions that their work is important to the future of themselves and humankind and that it would be history-changingly dangerous for anyone to get their hands on what they have. And...I guess if they meant that literally and were super dedicated to whatever their actual cause is..." He shook his head again.

"What's that?" Riles jabbed an unsteady finger at the screen, at something on the edge of the instructions.

Jonny magnified the document, and we could all see what Riles had seen, in spite of zir haze. The strange symbols that we'd found on the door and other deeply-hidden documents marched along the edge of the self-destruct instructions. I no longer doubted it. These crazy assholes had wired their own building to blow.

Jonny hesitantly noted, "There's just one problem. Well, a deepening of a problem we already knew we had."

I leaned back from the screen and looked at Jonny.

Bryan asked, "What's that, mate?"

"We have to get someone into the building to set it off. Just like we have to get someone in to send the messages and we thought we'd be doing for the bugs. But," and he pointed at me, "you can't go. Obviously. And," he pointed at Bryan, "as the friend of their fugitive and a known face, you can't go. And clearly," he hooked a thumb over his shoulder at Riley, "zie can't go."

I tried to ease things with a joke. "I bet *you* would look great in Kitty's suit, Jonny!"

But Jonny wasn't even smiling. "I remain willing to go in. Especially now that it seems like going in isn't a death sentence.

But...”

Riles wasn't too doped to make a little sense, “But you're the wrong kind of pretty. I mean, we can try to make you pretty, but you still won't fool them. And you do not want to walk into all those CorpSec guard boys without being distractingly pretty in a convincingly cis female-appearing way.”

Jonny nodded and confirmed, “What zie said. It would take a lot of work to make me look cis female. And it might not be convincing in person.”

I put my head in my hands. SWS's plan was moving right along, more immediately threatening than we'd guessed, and our plan had been derailed by sex and a beating. When the world's minds were traced with metal, I'd have only myself to blame.

CHAPTER 20

Six people in a small flat is not an ideal situation. But we were too grateful, both specifically for Quinn's kindness and in general that we had a Quinn in our lives, to let ourselves get nasty with each other. Especially with the end just days away. However, we looked for excuses to take breaks, to step out.

Quinn and Kitty went out first. He hadn't expected so many mouths to feed (I knew how *that* felt) and had only picked up one meal the night before. We could certainly do ordering out, but sometimes a quick and easy bowl of cereal or a sandwich was what hit the spot.

Whilst they were out, and with Riles slightly less doped up, we checked in with each other. Tuesday. Fewer than 4 days to go.

"I don't know whether I'm more disappointed that I won't be able to play my part in the plan or that I had to wait a day to be clear-headed enough to ask you guys about sex."

That was the moment I was sure Riles was going to be just fine on the other side of this.

Jonny grinned, but his eyes darted off to the side. "Maybe gossip about me when I'm not in the room."

Riley gave a dramatic sigh. "Fine. Then go have a very long shower. Please."

I tsked. "Now, now, let's at least pretend we're respectable people. Play cool." I winked at zir. But I was secretly grateful zie hadn't brought up the fact that the sex in question had probably gotten zir beaten up. I'd apologize regularly and profusely the next time we were alone and probably every day for the rest of our lives.

Bryan suggested, "Let's maybe save it for the cross-country drive. Speaking of which..."

Back to business, then.

Bryan clapped his hands together. "So, we need a vehicle. Immediately. With Riles not actually able to run, we have to plan on tossing zir in a car and hitting the road as soon as possible."

"Toss gently!" Riles pleaded.

"We also need to figure out who can replace zir on demo day," reminded Jonny. "I'm working on an alternate plan for getting the mobile I rigged into the building and hardwired."

Bryan asked, "You have ideas?"

Jonny shook his head and admitted, "Not a one. But this part of the plan, the completion of demo day, is my responsibility. I'm not giving up. And, just in case, I'll grab the suit hanging with our bags in my flat."

"You're going to your flat? I don't know if that's brave or stupid, mate," cautioned Bryan.

Jonny tried to act nonchalant, shrugging as he said, "Probably both. But we're at half power with only half the bags. And I'm not on the radar. I'm the only one with a chance of getting those bags."

Bryan insisted, "Don't risk it. We can buy things. They're just *things*."

"Yes, but the time it would take to do that, as opposed to just getting the bags, isn't worth it. We have to be stingy with time now, just in case we've missed something."

"I'm going with you." I wasn't asking; it was a flat statement.

Jonny looked at me. "The hell you are. Your face is too likely to be recognized now."

I sighed. "I'll wait for you a block away and I'll keep my hoodie up and head down. But it will look suspicious if you're trying to carry two bags, the skirt suit that's not your size, and whatever else. And you won't be able to run with that. If a cab and I are waiting, you'll just have to go a short way."

"I'll catch a cab and leave it running."

"Then I'll sit in the cab and make sure nobody takes it from you. Nobody will see me. But I'm going to have to insist that none of us go anywhere without backup until...until we've moved away."

Jonny looked at Bryan, clearly asking for backup, but Bryan held up his hands, signaling that he wasn't going to step into this argument. Which pretty much led to the part of the discussion where Jonny and I stubbornly locked eyes, each silently daring the other to come up with another point to argue.

My legendary stubbornness won out.

Jonny sighed. "Fine. But no stupid risks. You know, beyond the part where you're coming with me."

Whilst Bryan waited a moment to make sure that particular discussion was done, I smugly savored my victory. Nobody was going to stop *me* from choosing to be stupid.

"So, getting back to the less risky part of things...Who," Bryan asked, "should come with me when I go buy us a car?"

"Me!" Rye was enthusiastic.

Before we could laugh zir off, zie leaned forward to press the point. "You want to make sure you're getting a vehicle accessible to me and my special needs, don't you?"

Cheeky monkey. I snickered and earned a "don't encourage zir" look from Bryan.

"Nope." Bryan was amused but firm. "You're stuck here until we run away, poppet."

Riles pouted, "Bastard," and zie sat back into the couch, arms dramatically folded in protest until it bored zir.

"It probably shouldn't be me," I conceded. "Better to hide my stupid face away." And there was the grumbling tone I'd been trying to hide. It's not as if any of us were thrilled to be stuck in a studio flat together.

Jonny said, "Obviously, I'm willing to go. But if Quinn or Kitty would be better at making vehicle choices, you should take one of them."

"What about the satellites?" Riles apparently hadn't been too stupefied by the drugs. "We have to hack them. Just in case somebody presses a big, red button before the explosion."

Jonny said, "One more reason we need the bags. Figuring out which satellite and how to shut it up won't exactly be easy on a mobile."

Riles assured us, "I'm backing off the drugs. Better hurting and helpful for now. I'll just spend the drive to Rapid City totally high and drooling."

"I don't know—" Bryan started but Riley cut him off.

"Look, it's you or me. We're the only ones, unless Jonny's done it, who've ever gotten near satellites. And, realistically, it's not an either/or situation. We'll both want to work on this to have a chance at getting into one."

Bryan looked hopefully at Jonny, who shook his head.

He muttered, "Dammit," with a sigh. (I don't think we normally sighed so much. Fun days...) "Stop being right, Riley," Bryan conceded.

So, we all went back to work. Jonny looked for a new way to get us plugged into a physical jack at SWS. Bryan researched possible vehicles. I kept in contact with our comrades and continued the endless work of prepping SWS documents. Riles watched bad daytime TV and refused pain meds.

When Quinn and Kitty returned, Jonny and I headed out. We grabbed a cab and had it park a block from our building. During the drive there, I tried to think of reasons I should get to go in with him. But I knew there was no good reason, so I kept my thoughts to myself.

As soon as the cab rolled to a stop, Jonny kissed me and jumped out. No use hesitating. I watched him until he turned a corner. His stride told the world he was a man with a mission and no time to spare. I marked the time on my mobile and hoped he wouldn't have to slow down. The cabbie, I hoped, would just think my hood was up for rain and my face was down because I was sucked into whatever was happening on my mobile.

After 15 minutes, the cabbie asked me if I really wanted to pay him to just sit there instead of grabbing another cab. When I confirmed that I'd rather just wait, he turned off his car.

After 20 minutes, I wondered if I ought to go in. Would Jonny have a chance to message me if there were a problem? And would that be a mistake, tipping off whoever had him that there was someone else nearby?

After 25 minutes, I composed a message to check in with him, but I didn't send it. I tried to distract myself by wondering what the assorted stains in the cab were from.

He'd been gone almost 30 minutes when he finally came rushing back around the corner, looking ridiculous and conspicuous with multiple backpacks, a skirt suit, and a duffle bag. Just like I'd thought he would.

The cabbie started the engine, and Jonny slid in, struggling to get the bags in quickly as well. I knew that I should wait until we didn't have company to ask what had taken so long. I had to settle for a concerned look and then try to cast it off when he gave me a reassuring smile.

The cab dropped us a few blocks from Quinn's. We took an indirect route the rest of the way, ducking through shops, using a café to make sure we could go in one door and out another. I was mid-knock when Quinn let us in. They'd been eagerly waiting.

Before we could put everything down, Bryan said, "If we go now, we can probably have a vehicle tonight." He clapped Jonny's shoulder. "Looks like you're in for the night. Quinn is my man for this one."

With the door locked behind them, I unzipped the duffle bag, but hesitated when I saw what it held. I looked over at Kitty, sitting by Riles but curiously watching. I considered what she'd seen the last few days and decided she could handle it.

First, I stalled a bit by carefully hanging the suit she'd loaned us.

Before I could start pulling out the guns, ammo, and other jumble of gear from the duffle bag to try to inventory it, Riles sadly noted, "I don't get to wear that dress. I wanted to be the pretty lady in the suit."

I started carefully taking out guns and piling up ammo, hoping that would end the suit conversation. Surely Kitty would be more curious about the arsenal than the dress. But no...

"You guys had to sneak in, at possibly great risk, and my suit was part of what you took a chance on? It's a nice suit, but not *that* nice."

I tried again to derail that line of thought. "Yeah, Jonny, speaking of risk, what happened? It took longer than I thought."

Jonny was picking out tech gear from the bag, leaving the rest to me. "The cops were mostly right at your door, but SWS had people tucked around corners. And, of course, press poking around for newsworthy tidbits. It was like some real life vidgame, trying to creep and find new paths and shit. No actual encounters, just slowed down by being careful. Especially on the way out." He was done taking things out of the duffle. "I might be able to walk in easily, but there'd be no way to not look suspicious on my way out."

Before I could tell him how much sense that made and artificially extend that safer line of conversation, Kitty insisted, "But why my suit?"

Riles did some insisting of zir own, a bit of the pain meds still lingering in zir speech, "You can totally tell her. You should tell her. I'm not telling, because I'm still too high to make good choices. You should tell her."

Before I could respond, my mobile rang. It was Gran.

"Just a sec. Hang on." I tapped to pick up the call. "Gran? Aren't you on a trip?"

She rushed, an edge of worry on her voice. "I know we can't talk long but I promised to be safe and..." she lowered her voice to a whisper, "I think someone here is following me."

"Where are you?"

"At the gate, waiting for my flight."

"Okay, I want you to make sure you're visible, that nobody can approach you without other passengers or gate agents or whoever seeing you. I'm going to call the detective. And if the person you think is following you gets on the plane, I want you to tell a flight attendant you think they have a gun. Do it before the flight takes off. Hopefully, they'll take the person off and let you go."

"But what if they check and he doesn't?"

"Then you shamelessly play the tired, silly old lady card and apologize profusely. Tell them you don't have your glasses on. And, hopefully, even if you're stuck on the plane...Just try not to have to pee. Be where they can keep an eye on you, because they definitely will after that. And then you find the nearest security guard at the airport when you land and try the gun thing again. Dash off whilst the guard is checking. Okay?"

"Got it. Thanks." She sighed. "I love you."

"Love you, Gran."

When we hung up, I called Engalls.

He picked up immediately. He didn't even say his name, just started in on telling me off. "Are you trying to get yourself arrested? I—"

I cut him off. "My gran thinks someone is following her.

She's at the airport and she's scared. And if she dies, when all is said and done, I'll make sure they know you knew she was in trouble."

He sighed. "Where is she?"

"She's at gate B6. Promise to help the instant we hang up."

"How sure is she?"

"Sure enough to call me when she's clever enough to suspect I'd be avoiding calls. Promise me. As soon as we hang up."

"I promise. Now—"

And then I hung up on him.

To Jonny I said, "I knew Engalls would pick up *my* call, but I couldn't be sure he'd pick up for Gran. And, if nothing else, maybe those listening on that number will get worried about being caught."

Jonny was doing what he could to get Bryan and Rye's portables up and running, batting away Rye's still slightly doped hands when zie reached to "help." Without stopping, he said, "You made the right choice for Gran. And they shouldn't have had a chance to find you. We've got your number routed through too many other places to trace that quickly."

I went back to pulling the last of the ammo from the duffle and stacking it by type. But Kitty hadn't forgotten the suit. (To be fair, it was hanging right there, hard to forget.)

"So, that suit..." Kitty was tenacious.

I saw Jonny pause and I saw him looking at me. He stood, held his hand out to me. "Can I have a moment?"

We convened in the bathroom, whispering.

"I know you're not a huge Kitty fan, but we really could use someone in that suit."

"Hell no! Kitty's just...I mean maybe she can lie as convincingly as any girl." Jonny's sharp look stopped me short. Dammit. "Right. Internalized misogyny. Shit. But, listen, she's not like us. I don't know if she could do it."

"By 'not like us' do you mean she won't end up getting people she cares about hurt? That she won't end up with nightmares and crying? Because 'not like us' isn't necessarily a bad thing."

"Point taken."

"Do you think she'd tell anyone?"

"If 'Randa were still alive, maybe."

"But she's not. And Kitty seems intent on sticking by Riles. So she—and Quinn, if we're being honest—are likely to get at least a hint of the story before Friday."

"Argh! Fine. Listen, I'll send Bryan a quick message. If *he* also votes to tell her, then I'll consider myself outvoted."

"Technically, you already are."

"No, technically, a doped up person who shouldn't be trusted to even choose what they watch on TV tonight has made it so there will be a tie on this vote."

"Or an overwhelming majority."

I flipped him off with an exaggerated sneer. But I sent Bryan a message. And he quickly responded that, at this point, he agreed with everyone else. Well, damn...

When we stepped out of the bathroom, Riles read us quickly and crowed, "They're going to tell you!" Zie congratulated us, "Excellent choice."

Jonny sat back on the floor, and gestured to me. "You can decide how much to say."

I considered being obstinate and deciding to say very, very little, but I wasn't actually that much of an asshole.

"The night after my building was blown up, the bomber emailed me to tip me off that...that SWS is up to some truly horrific things." I paused to give her a chance to ask questions, but she just watched me. "So, we've spent the time since then confirming that what the bomber said, well, it was true. And that the whole truth was even worse." I paused again.

This time, she looked down at Riles, who was suddenly looking very sober.

Zie confirmed, "It's really bad. Like...world-fucking-up bad."

Kitty nodded her understanding and turned her gaze back to me.

"We're planning an information release to take them down. Really damning stuff. Like brainwashing world leaders, using the Peacemaker to influence and control people, even causing murders. And that's where the suit comes in. Because we need, in order to have the information be taken seriously, to actually be in the building, hardwired in, not just pirates on their Wi-Fi."

Kitty nodded. "Right. And it's easier for a pretty female to get in, but not someone with a face they'd recognize."

"Exactly," I said. "Riles was going to do it, go all the way girl looking. Get in, plug in our tech, etc. But that's obviously not a thing zie should or could do now."

"Oh, you underestimate me!" Riles waved zir finger in dope-tinged offense. "I can be the most beautiful person in a cast. And bruises." Zie sort of patted zir hair in a way that suggested that, in fact, zie was the most beautiful person no matter what.

Kitty planted a kiss carefully on zir battered cheek. "Baby, you could be the most beautiful person in a burlap sack." In a much less sweet tone, she said to us, "I can do it. At least the getting in part."

This was the best idea in the world to Rye. "Oh, she could *totally* do it. She is fucking beautiful and can plug in a cable!" But then something dawned in Riley's eyes, and zie turned to grab Kitty's hands. "But what if you get hurt?" Zie looked back at us, clinging to Kitty's hands still. "Don't let her do it!"

Kitty sweetly shushed Riles, then evenly turned back to us, with a fire that grew in her eyes with every word. "As I understand it, those fuckers killed my friend, beat the shit out of my bae, and made all of us—including your gran—have to hide. Right?"

Jonny and I nodded.

"Then fuck them. I *want* to have a chance to take a shot at them. Those are reasons enough for me. Whatever you're doing, I want in. Even if it's just to put on a suit and plug in a cable. Use me. *You need me.*"

I interrupted the celebration (a.k.a. high five between Riles and Jonny). "But she can't code."

"Actually," Jonny told me, "she no longer needs to do that. I can mod a mobile so that all she has to do is plug it in. And I've found possible plugs." He smiled. "I was productive while they were grocery shopping."

"That's great!"

Jonny asked Kitty, "Can you actually do it?" He held up his hands as if to fend off protests. "I'm sure you're as capable as you are pretty. That you could distract them with your looks and that you could plug in a cable. That's easy. You could do both. But...It's dangerous and you'd have to do at least a little thinking on your feet. And you'd need to look calm and cool the whole time, with CorpSec probably watching you like hawks. Honestly, not an easy thing."

Was he actually considering letting her do this?

Kitty pondered a moment. "I could do it. My anger—my self-righteous fury—could counter my fear." Her voice went frosty, supporting her case, as she said, "I can be a stone cold bitch when necessary."

"There's one more thing you ought to know. That I know Kot won't be happy with me for mentioning. But you deserve to know if you're going to do this."

I tried to look calm, but I was psychically pleading with him not to tell her about the part where we were going to blow up a building.

"There's a self destruct sequence, and we have every reason to believe it will be used within seconds of us sending information."

I watched Kitty carefully. She only slightly tensed up at that.

"You'll have to hustle out soon after you've plugged us in. But not too soon."

"They have a self destruct? Like some kind of movie? Are you *serious*?"

I finally spoke up. "That stuff we're going to reveal about them is huge. And the documents show that they are—the execs at least—super crazy. Cult kind of crazy. We even found a manual of instructions that, basically, says to self destruct at the first substantial sign that they're being caught."

Kitty looked at Jonny for confirmation, but then also looked at Riles like she wanted a third opinion.

Riles nodded very seriously. "Totally. Fucking. True."

"Alright then. Okay. So, I plug in a mobile and run?"

Jonny corrected, "You disarm them with your looks and professional demeanor, plug in a mobile without being noticed, make sure the mobile is tucked out of sight, and then you calmly and non-suspiciously rush out once we've sent messages. Pretend you got a message on your mobile, because we hope they won't notice you left a mobile behind, and have to leave before you get to see anyone. Something like that."

"I can manage. Whatever it takes to get back at them for

what they've done."

Late that night, I saw pictures in Gran's online storage. She was safely in Wyoming with her old friend Sarah. They looked really happy to be reunited.

CHAPTER 21

Wednesday, the vibe turned to a sort of impatience. It wasn't that we were actually looking forward to demo day; we were looking forward to being *done* with demo day. We were starting to actively consider whether we, individually, might really succeed at our part of the plan. Whether we, individually, might make it through, make it out, make it to South Dakota. We were straining hard to not snap at each other. And most of us, those of us who knew, were still scrambling to find some hope we wouldn't have to kill anyone.

I could tell, by the many side conversations and the constant coffee refill breaks, that we were all struggling to stay on track. Riles had dropped zir pain meds entirely, and zie and Bryan were trying (and failing) to hack the satellite they'd determined would convey HQ's signals to the brains that had already been invaded by the vII.

I envied Quinn having a day job that required him to leave the flat. And that probably kept him distracted enough that, for a few hours, he could pretend his flat hadn't been invaded.

Mid-day, we got a new distraction that was at least on topic. Kind of. One of my remote folks sent a message with some pictures attached.

"You guys *have* to see this!" I forwarded the message to everyone.

It wasn't necessarily a game changer or at all important but, on a day like this, it was inordinately intriguing. The message said:

```
Check out tattoos on attached. Found dozens in
'Net archives (not on current sites, which is why
image search didn't find them) before I stopped
looking. Might go back as far as 1980s. Definitely
as far as 90s.
```

The attached pictures all appeared to be taken at dance clubs and events. Alternative kids, all pale and with big, unnatural hairstyles. Most had funky, full-sclera, grey contact lenses. And every one of them had tattoos that looked like the symbols we'd been finding in the SWS documents and on the underwater door.

Riles explained to Kitty, "We've been finding symbols like these tattoos all over their stuff and we can't find a language it matches or even crack it like a code."

Jonny requested, "If you two want to keep at the satellite, I feel like I've done what I can and I'd like to look for more pictures, more context. This has to mean something and I hate to leave a loose end."

"Me too," I said. "I feel like I've done all I can and like a day to step back will make my final review of things tomorrow a little fresher."

"Good instinct. Take a breath," Bryan agreed.

I checked in with our guy who'd found the pictures and reported to the room, "He says he's been working on a side project of his, building a big collection of photos to show the evolution of alternative styles. He's seen tattoos like them before, but hadn't had any reason to notice them until now."

Jonny and I searched, pausing to toss out theories, suggest possible connections for the people or inspirations for the tattoos. We found ourselves looking through old band web sites in the 'Net archive, skimming digitized copies of old gaming manuals, that sort of thing. It wasn't a very useful treasure hunt, but it was as close to an entertaining distraction as we'd had in days.

In the afternoon, we had a breakthrough.

Jonny started excitedly repeating, "No fucking way." It started as a mutter and moved, in the end, towards an exclamation.

Obviously, we'd all stopped our work.

Bryan finally asked, "What fucking way, Jonny?"

"I'm sending you all a link, because I want you to look and verify that I'm seeing what I think I'm seeing."

The link led to an archived web page for a now-defunct club that had put on alternative events. Just loads of pictures of people in black, holding up drinks and smiling or otherwise posing for the camera. At some point, probably in an effort to help people reconnect with friends they used to dance with in the 20s and 30s, someone had added as many names as they could under pictures, added comment fields under each so that anyone could drop in and clear up missing identities. The site probably got neglected and taken down when many of those people tried to move on to mundane jobs.

The particular picture the link focused the browser on was a group of three people. They had the obligatory drinks raised in salute, but none of the drunken grins. They looked like they might be a little too posh for all the people they'd have been slumming with at a night like that. Their clothes were slightly more polished versions of the range I'd expect to see at such parties. The women's dresses left their shoulders bare, and the man didn't have a shirt under his waistcoat. They all had tattoos like the ones we'd been looking for. Deep blue ink on their pale, pale skin. One of the women wore the grey contact lenses we'd seen so much of. Like the others we'd seen with these tattoos, they opted for larger hairstyles. Though, in this case, they were cleanly sculpted styles. Still, they fit in with the general look of all the others we'd seen.

But these three were SWS executives. Not then, of course. But this was who they'd been. Not just any execs either. No, these three were CEO Johnson, COO Smith, and CFO Williams.

It was such an interesting find that I wished it meant something, that it made something clear about our current situation. Instead, it just gave us one more interesting little puzzle piece that we couldn't fit in with the others we had.

I hope it's not an edge piece, I thought. *We'll never finish this if we don't have all the edge pieces sorted.*

Jonny and I carefully crawled through all the photos on the site and found more of these three. Always together. Their look in the oldest photos was more like the others at the events, becoming more polished, changing rapidly over the handful of years they showed up in the photos. And they moved from being background figures to getting to star in their own photos regularly. The one Jonny had found was the last of them, the fully polished version of their evolution.

Their varying levels of undress or cuts of clothing showed multiple tattoos of this same kind on each of them. Where others had often had additional types of tattoos, these three had only the symbols. All in places that would, now, surely be hidden by their professional suits. Usually I'd think that was a lucky choice, but something in their look made me think they'd carefully chosen their tattoo placement with their futures in mind.

We took some time to carefully add the symbols to the database we'd been compiling, just in case it wasn't some obscure Asian language, with symbols that meant "Kung Pao Chicken" or "I didn't ask what it meant because the tattoo artist was hot." Hell, even if it *was* that. The more samples we had of this, the more likely we were to stumble across a real world example or a key to translating them.

We were pretty sure it wasn't actually important, but, oh, curious hacker brains like to solve puzzles.

If we didn't have the plans we did for Friday, I'd have gotten these pictures out to the sort of cheap tabloids that love to run pointless shit like this. Or I'd have hacked the SWS home page to post a whole group of photos, just for laughs.

If the company hadn't gone up in flames, literally *and* metaphorically, if it wasn't completely ruined by the time we reached South Dakota, I promised myself that I could do one or both of those things. It's important to have something fun to look forward to.

We made picture hunting our main distraction until we went to sleep. (Well, Jonny and I did that. Rye and Bryan kept beating their heads against the satellite issue.) We found that, pretty much from the time of that initial picture Jonny had discovered, those tattoos almost disappeared from photos. Not just photos of the three execs in question, but from photos in general. This was about 10 years in from the time that we had traced faint roots of proof that they'd started getting ready to unleash SWS on the world, and just a couple years before they sprang forth, fully formed, from the head of some invisible corporate Zeus.

If, as their vision statement made it seem, SWS and its goals sprang from some kind of cult or other non-business group, perhaps our three posh friends had suggested people be more careful about the tattoos being seen. Perhaps the decline in tattoos was just one more thing to support them in their move to, literally, take over the world. I hoped someday we'd have more than guesses.

CHAPTER 22

Thursday was our final day to prepare. Theoretically, we had most of the day Friday; things wouldn't go down until late afternoon. But, I reminded myself, this was no time to shirk on preparedness. On being positive, in advance, that we'd done everything we could think of to make this work. So, Thursday, we reclaimed some of our focus.

We all checked and double-checked our parts of the plan, the wheels we'd set in motion. I cautioned our remote teammates to be extra careful, extra quiet. Warned them not to jump the gun, not to get so excited that they set things in motion earlier than we'd previously agreed to.

We watched the SWS emails and accounts like hawks. The slightest twitch got our attention. We read every email completely, checked every new document created. Initially, it was literally every one, even the ones that were just low-level employees carefully bitching about aggressive deadlines or making shopping lists. But we were soon overwhelmed and had to remind ourselves that this company, whilst not as large in size as some others, was still something more than a handful of kids in a garage. We prioritized the execs, their admins, and others who'd been invited to the meeting Friday. And CorpSec, of course. Had to keep an eye on their army.

Bryan checked all the guns, making sure they were clean and loaded. He complained a few times about the fact that we couldn't go out to the range once more. He also made sure our new vehicle, a discreet, smaller model, black SUV (hybrid capable so that fuel efficiency didn't make it an expensive option) was fueled, in good repair, and just dirty enough to blend in.

Jonny and Bryan popped out to mail a strategic package. Jonny also spent time with Kitty, making sure she was ready. Setting up the modified mobile she'd use to make sure the files were, technically, sent from a local, wired connection. Showing her the type of plug she'd be looking for, where the blueprints said they should be, and how he thought she'd best get it plugged in and discreetly tucked away. Discussing exit strategies and possible alternatives to the plan.

Kitty was patient and determined. She worked hard to ensure she'd do her part, and it looked like she'd be up for it.

When she was in the bathroom, Riley quietly confirmed, "She can come to South Dakota with us now, right?"

We all nodded. Even I was coming around to at least seeing that she had sides to her that I liked, that I could be okay with.

I'd have given myself a high five for being so mature about Kitty, but I knew better than to rush to give myself too much credit on this topic.

Bryan warned, "Think of it more like she's welcome to come. I wouldn't make her the offer until we're getting in the car to run, just in case...something happens in the building. And I wouldn't count on her coming. There's no guarantee she'll want that."

Though it wasn't a day actually filled with remarkable moments, we exchanged looks all through it that said, "We are on the precipice of history. We might change the world. Or we might end our days in a cell (or worse). But this is our moment!"

It was kind of like how Christmas Eve felt, but in a grown up way where Christmas involved explosions and crazy computer action and...actually, that all still sounded like what I always hoped for in a good Christmas.

In the evening, Riles and Bryan kept at the satellite. Meanwhile, Jonny and I finalized the documents we'd send in each phase and set up the lists of addresses for each.

Jonny's set of documents, the ones that he'd send seconds before the explosion, were a narrative. They didn't include any details that could be used for damage, but they talked about the damage. They told the story that started with the creepy vision statement and traced the dangerous moves SWS has made to put themselves in a position to access an astounding number of governments' and large corporations' systems, data, codes, controls. And the moves they'd made to start infiltrating, physically infiltrating, people's bodies and minds. The whole story told via their own internal documents. These would go to government leaders, corporation heads, and news outlets. They should also immediately be re-mailed to every person in the contact list of each recipient (and then those in the contacts of those contacts and so on). Not exactly emailing the world, but rather close.

My set of documents were the extra-carefully curated set we'd been pulling together for scientists, doctors, engineers, data security people, and our peers. We'd tried to make sure they'd help solve problems without giving anyone a roadmap to carrying on the damage or to taking advantage of it.

I was really grateful to Doc and Engie. I'd made sure they'd be getting some funds. Prepaid cards that would randomly and regularly show up. I'd bet money that, like us, the rest of our team would be funneling SWS funds into their own accounts. It only seemed fair that Doc and Engie weren't penalized for having very different (but very important) skill sets. I'd made sure that the first one Engie would get would include a note with my condolences over the death of her friend. By my (arguably unconventional) standards, Huw had been one of the truly good guys.

I'd also made sure to set up a gift to be sent to 'Randa's family. I didn't know how close she'd been to them, but I couldn't think how else to acknowledge the price she paid for us.

But Doc and Engie...I was glad to see that they'd enjoyed the work they had done. And not just enjoyed it, but really been invaluable. They'd figured out how the Peacemakers and the less-intrusive wearables worked (probably). They'd figured out what all the tech did (probably) and how it did it (probably). And they were horrified. Scientifically impressed, but horrified (definitely).

Without their help, I'd have made some guesses, deleted some bits from the specs, and sent them out with the rest of my packet of documents. But Engie and Doc told me there was so little in there that was safe to send out as it was. Like true rockstars, they'd written how-to guides for dealing with the troubles they anticipated would come if SWS went down and for doing things like safely removing a Peacemaker vI or, from what they could tell, vII.

Engie had written:

There's no way to give them useful information for fixing things without letting them get a look at things that, frankly, we'd rather they didn't. But we are choosing to err on the side of believing in humanity's goodness. What choice do we have?

Going above and beyond, they'd also done their best to give us a starter list of people they thought ought to have the information and could probably be trusted not to misuse it.

That email, the one I was in charge of pulling together, didn't re-mail itself. In fact, if someone tried to forward that message, we'd built a really clever little bit of code that popped up, confirming that they realized the implications of spreading that information. To be really annoying, we'd programmed it to do the same thing if they even tried to attach a single one of the attached documents to a message. And it would do that for every such document they attached. We were trying to be responsible.

Along that theme of responsibility, we'd not had any alcohol all day. No stims (didn't need a sudden, if rare, case of the shakes). We'd tried to eat "correctly," or whatever it was we each thought was a healthy and right way. We were planning to go to bed the instant Quinn called it a night, rather than sitting up with our glowing screens. Responsible!

Just in case, I wrote Gran a long and loving message that would send automatically if I didn't cancel it before Saturday night. (If I wasn't somewhere safe enough to do that or where I'd able to do that by Saturday night, I was probably screwed anyway.)

By the end of the day, all the pain meds were out of Riley's system. Zir mind was clear and, zie told us, "The pain's at a level I can deal with. I'll save the rest of my pills for After."

We talked about that a lot Thursday. After. The small things. Solitude and a drunken binge and being out in public with Jonny. Things like that.

We were all being responsible Before to make sure everyone had an After.

We were avoiding mentioning that we hadn't found another plan for the people who needed to be...neutralized. That our only neutralizing option appeared to be death. And, even if we weren't the person entering the destruct code, we all carried that possible guilt. For the sake of a sane After, I pleaded to that higher power I wasn't sure existed that we'd find proof everyone we killed was guilty.

When we thought everyone else was asleep, Jonny and I had cramped, quiet, but totally-worth-it sex in the bathroom. My guilt about what had happened Monday no longer overrode the fact that every part of me, including my foolish heart, wanted this man. And I was unwilling to wait until After for this.

CHAPTER 23

Friday.

Holy shit. Friday.

Demo day.

I laid a while, very still. Not faking sleep, but not ready to admit to awakeness yet. Feeling like this was my one last chance to decide whether this was really, truly, definitely the right thing we were doing.

Had we missed anything in our research? Had I misread or misunderstood? Had we all been biased by Jonny's charming face and just followed his lead? Could we even pull this off, both the actual making the plan work and the making ourselves take lives? Could we live with ourselves after? (Because, really, was this the right thing?) Could Kitty manage her part? (That wasn't me doubting Kitty; I was acknowledging that these were capable people we were taking on.) Could Jonny get into the necessary SWS computers to set off the self destruct? (Obviously, we couldn't take a test run on that part.) And, again, could we live with ourselves after? Could we...could we...could we...?

The questions were circling and I clearly had no answers. And I had to decide whether I was okay with having no answers. Usually, I wasn't. I liked answers, puzzles solved, plans without holes, steps practiced.

Jonny rolled over and wrapped an arm around me. I leaned into the embrace. He whispered a good morning in my ear and I sighed.

"What's wrong?" he whispered.

I rolled over, facing him, so we could whisper without the others hearing. "What if we missed something?"

He gave me a considering look, and I appreciated that he wasn't just brushing me off. "I laid in bed an hour on a Thursday morning a couple weeks ago, asking myself the same thing. And a lot of other things that you're probably asking yourself. So I'll ask you what I asked myself eventually. Okay?"

I nodded and he went on.

"Did you spend days, literally all the time you had, on researching every possible thing we could think of, looking for every possible option?"

I nodded.

"Did you ignore any possible information, unsolved puzzles, or even intuitions?"

I shook my head. But then I paused. "The tattoos. We still haven't figured out the tattoos, the symbols. What if that's important?"

Jonny slowly nodded. "Yeah, I hate that we didn't figure that out. I'll be researching it even after today."

"To your other questions...You're right. I know we've been methodical and careful and complete. We've had the four of us *and* our handful of remote partners looking for everything we could. I just..."

"You just want to make sure, when you...when *we* follow through and people die, that you have something to tell yourself when the guilt sets in." His eyes, for a moment, looked a haunted. "We'll just have to keep reminding each other of the facts and reassuring each other, over and over, until we believe. Hoping that the rest of the world sees it and...I don't know, maybe enough newscasters and leaders hailing us as heroes or condemning SWS as criminals will help too."

"You're not all logic and reason, are you? You're not guilt-free for my building."

His voice caught, snagging on emotion with every word. "I'm not. I'm not any of those things all the time. If any of the time. And that should make you feel better about me. That it's not easy for me to take lives, even when it seems like the right thing to do. *And* you should feel better about yourself, knowing that you don't find it easy either." He put a hand on my cheek. "I know that I couldn't be right here with you now if I thought you'd actually find it easy." He grinned. "We're not fictional hacker badasses. We're humans with morning breath, questionable physical fitness, and a healthy sense of guilt when we consider taking lives."

I returned his grin, but now tried not to breathe in his face. "Okay. Thank you."

"Yep!"

He gave me a quick kiss and he sat up, nodding a good morning to...I turned to look. To everyone. We were all awake.

We all played it normal and casual until Quinn left for work. He knew something was up and that we'd promised we'd be out of his hair very soon, but he didn't know that today was "very soon" and that maybe the last few days were the last he'd ever get of us. And it was better he didn't know. Safer for all of us. Plausible deniability was our gift to him.

I wasn't a hypocrite. Honestly. I was way past being unhappy at Jonny for giving me that particular gift.

So, I passed that gift on to Quinn. If he was upset at all later, it would be because he'd wish he'd gotten to be a part of it. And that was a fair enough thing to be upset about.

Once he headed off to work, we stopped pretending to laze about. We were up. We were moving. Everything felt really important. It was like there was even an intensity to how we ate our breakfast.

On any other day, I'd probably have been amused by that. But, today, I was caught up in it. Today, there was nothing trivial. I found myself taking extra time just choosing socks. Which were the ones least likely to slip or bunch up or twist around so that the seam on the toes drove me crazy? I couldn't afford distractions or socks that impacted my ability to run. It all mattered.

Even though Bryan had just done it yesterday, we cleaned and checked every gun. Kitty confirmed she could quickly plug into the modded mobile and then into a jack. We reviewed plans. We ran through preliminary steps, and then reevaluated and memorized the steps we knew we'd need to take in the moment. There wouldn't be time for hesitation or leeway for mistakes.

I wasn't going to ask, but I wondered if everyone else felt like their insides were full of crawling things. Not the proverbial butterflies; these weren't anywhere near as delicate and beautiful as butterflies. How the hell was I supposed to concentrate on my computer this afternoon if I was plagued with stomach spiders?

For all the action and intensity, we were quiet. Which was probably adding to the intensity. And definitely made it a bit jarring when Riles cleared zir throat in a meaningful way. Everyone stopped mid-action to look at zir.

"You're not leaving me here."

We all started protesting at the same time, but Rye's voice cut through. "I know all the reasons you think I'm wrong, but I'm not asking; I'm telling."

Again we all started to explain why not, but we didn't have a real chance to make our cases.

"Setting aside the fact that, even if I've got a broken leg, I can still sit and work on my portable—which is good for you given the satellite situation. And setting aside that I won't be left out when I've helped with all the work and don't want to be denied the payoff, you've got a logistical issue."

Nobody spoke up to protest. We thought we'd been so thorough but were now worried we hadn't been; we needed to hear what hole Riles had found. Riles who looked triumphant now.

"Traffic. You beautiful idiots forgot about traffic. Because it wasn't part of the original plan, and the only change you made to the plan when my leg got broken was to decide to leave me here and shift my job over to Kitty."

Riles paused a moment, waiting to see if we were still listening, still buying into zir claim that we'd forgotten something. And, of course, we were. Because we knew how nasty traffic could be and we knew that our planned attack time fell during the evening rush hour.

"See, if you mean to make a clean escape and not leave me behind, it sounds like a really ill-considered piece of your plan to drive..." Rye tapped away on zir portable. "The estimated time today looks like about 45 minutes *minimum*. 45 minutes to get up here, and then have to go about the same amount of time back to try to get to actually useful roads."

Oh. Right.

"So, clearly, I'm going to sit in the car. And we'll save 90 minutes at least."

Bryan merely said, "Yep," and we all went back to work.

As a final task, when it looked like the autumn rains weren't going to let up and give us an excuse to hide our identities behind sunglasses, and taking into account that the track record of how people react towards kids in black hoodies (especially if the hoodies are up, like you'd want if you were going to make it harder to be recognized), Jonny and Bryan ducked out for hats. Kitty was getting made up and polished up and she looked like a true tight-assed business woman before the boys got back. She was properly disguised and definitely stunning in a corporate cutthroat way.

By profession, Kitty was a seamstress. I wasn't even sure why she had a nice suit like this. But she had this suit that was perfectly conservative and not at all like her. Not when worn like this. And, instead of the usual makeup we saw her in on nights out, or even the no-makeup look she'd go with if she was having a busy work day, she'd done a really demanding sort of makeup job that matched the suit. And she'd pulled her hair tight. When this type of woman showed up at the office and you were one of the underlings, you knew to stay on task, be polite, hope you didn't call down her notice. There was no warmth or fun or hint of questioning the norms.

No one who knew her would recognize her.

As for the rest of us, the boys had returned with an assortment of hats. They'd tried to find four that were all different from each other and wouldn't look out of place with our clothes but weren't in any way calling for attention. Given that they'd had to duck into nearby fuel stations and sort it out really quickly, they hadn't done a horrible job. For my part, I just switched out which t-shirt I was wearing and fussed around with my hair a bit. Looked okay. This hat would do.

It was time to go. Finally. But too soon.

Quinn had been a spectacular host. No questions, no complaints. Acted like it was a perfectly normal extended hangout session. He hadn't even complained about our failure to keep his flat as tidy as we all knew he preferred. For that, we took a moment after our final preparations to get his flat as tidy as we could manage to make it and left a *really* generous prepaid card on his pillow. And I'd left a note (*You remain one of the best people ever. Hope you got enough of us.*) He'd understand when the special news reports started. Maybe even be glad that he got days and days of us.

Kitty instinctively moved in to help Riles, but she had to stay non-mussed up, so Bryan was the one who helped zir down the stairs from Quinn's flat. He was also the one who drove. It was a physical world thing, so best left to Bryan.

He paused before starting the car. "Did we get *everything*? This is really our last chance to take care of things before the battle."

There was silence; I assumed we were all thinking it over as quickly as we could. Riles exclaimed, "Onward to demo day!" When nobody protested, Bryan pushed the button that started the ignition. We were under way.

I thought, *Even if we fail, we've done our best. We're as ready as we could be, especially in such short time.* Mostly, I believed that. Lame attempt at giving myself a pep talk...

The drive down, I ought to have been going over the details again, but I was stuck on regrets instead. I regretted that we didn't have a chance to all get in really good shape and to become expert marksmen and to eat massive amounts of all our favorite foods and to have loads of sex and to go on some kind of ridiculous holiday with Gran and...It went on like that. I felt myself getting wrapped up in the diminishing grasp of it all, so I started back through, telling myself—one at a time—that I could do each After if I still wanted to.

With that perspective, I was soon cheerfully plotting how, in spite of probably having to hide out for as long as it took until we felt unlikely to be hunted down, I could manage that holiday with Gran. Neither of us loved the sun, so maybe we'd go find somewhere in the shade. But warm enough to have big, ridiculous, colorful drinks.

If we manage today, I thought, *planning a clandestine holiday will be a breeze.*

CHAPTER 24

The excitement we'd felt as we drove to our destination was worn down as we faced the herculean task of finding parking. Seriously. And not just any parking, but something close enough for a quick retreat without being suspiciously near the SWS building. Something that would let us pay for enough time on a meter to cover our whole possible window of attack. Even now that we had Riles right there, it seemed like a better idea not to have zir hobbling over to top off the meter. We gave ourselves plenty of time, so, at least for that step of the plan, we were on track.

As we circled through our ideal streets for the millionth time, Riley drawled, "Well, at least we know that we can't possibly face any greater challenges today than this one." Zie sighed and we all joined zir.

I'd bet Rapid City had parking. I'd remind myself how great that was every time I missed Seattle.

Once we were parked, Bryan made sure we all had earbuds that connected us to each other. We didn't want to use the mobiles; we wanted to keep it totally hands-free and not compromise any of our machines. He instructed us, "Try to keep talk to a minimum, put your mobile headset in your other ear so you can pretend that's what you're talking to, and let the rest of us know what you're doing if you can." He looked at Kitty. "Especially you. You're doing something really important, and we all need to know how it's going. Both so we can know when it's time to do our things and so we can help you make choices if you need it."

Kitty looked at our faces, all very serious. "Okay, are you all sure? Like, about everything?"

With gravity, we nodded, looking around to check that everyone was nodding.

"Then we'll do this. We will." She leaned in to give Riles a careful kiss. "Stay safe. See you soon."

"You too. Stay safer. You can do this, baby."

Could everyone tell that Riles was putting on a brave face or just me?

Kitty strode off to get a cab. She couldn't just walk up, not looking like this. She'd seem more real pulling up in a cab.

Bryan took out his earbud, put it under his leg, and indicated we ought to do the same. "No offense to Kitty, but let's keep some things quiet for now." He pulled over the portable sitting by Rye. "I'm going to take our portion of SWS's finances." He typed as he talked. "I set up an interstitial account and told SWS's databases that this was an SWS account. I'm initiating what looks like an approved transfer. Then, not only does it switch through a number of accounts, but there's a vicious polymorphic worm following to chew up and corrupt its path, changing damage at each account so they aren't clearly linked. After which it will go hit some other SWS accounts to scramble things up a bit more." He finished his typing, and looked up with a smile. "We're in the process of becoming rich right now." He pushed the portable back to Riles. "The account info will be in the inboxes we set up just for us, and you'll all have access. Just in case I don't make it out."

His smile faded and we were all very serious. Just in case he didn't make it out.

Jonny broke the sober silence. "Thanks, just in case I...just in case I forget to say it later. Thanks for not killing me without hearing my story and for helping me make this happen. This is a much more effective thing we're about to do than I'd have done on my own." He squeezed my hand, but said to everyone, "Make it out. Fuck 'just in case.'"

We put our earbuds back in and gave each other quick but strong hugs. I was glad I didn't have lipstick that needed to stay neat, because I kissed Jonny. Quite severely. I told myself, *This isn't a goodbye kiss; it's a see you later kiss.*

He whispered, "Don't die. That's a guilt I can't get over."

I tried to make light of it. "I intend to live long enough to make you wish you'd settled for guilt." I forced a laugh.

We headed off in different directions. Riles stayed in the car. Bryan had a truck to grab. Jonny and I needed to get coffees from different places near headquarters (good thing we were in

Seattle so we had plenty of options), then sit and look nonchalant as we played hacker heroes.

It was still drizzling out and I welcomed it. I felt hot from the adrenaline, and I needed cooling. And I realized that there was a possibility this was my last time in the Seattle drizzle. I felt a pang as I admitted to myself how much I loved this dirty, grey city. How could I, a proponent of a digital life, be attached to a physical location?

I smirked to myself, *I am a woman of mystery.*

We had decided, aside from our momentary stupidity when we thought we'd leave Riles at Quinn's, that everyone ought to be near headquarters when this went down. We had three reasons: we didn't want to have to try to get together from all over when it was time to go (yeah, I know, that should have made us realize Riles had to come with; hopefully, that was our only lapse of brilliance), we wanted to be near enough to run in and help each other if needed (especially since two of our people would be right at the building), and we wanted to make sure that nobody's home got raided if we failed and someone managed to trace us to our physical locations.

On the other hand, I wasn't at all worried about this coffee shop getting raided. Not that I had anything against them; their drinks were fine. But I was pretty sure they'd survive it better than a private person would. It helped to be a business; businesses have been treated better than people in this country for decades.

Because it wasn't quite the end of the work day, the shop was quiet and I could easily wedge myself into a corner from which I could get a peek at the headquarters but nobody could get a peek at my screen.

Bryan was the first to report a success. "I've got the truck. Corporate ice queen, go."

Kitty was crisp. "Roger." She had been having her cabbie drive through nearby streets, but now directed them to the SWS headquarters.

Bryan asked, "Everyone else ready?"

Jonny said, "Yeah. Let's do this before someone thinks I'm being pretentious and writing a novel in a coffee shop."

I laughed and said, "Aye. Ready."

Riles growled, "I will be ready. I fucking *will*. Keep going. I'll get our satellite."

Whilst Kitty's cab was approaching, I pulled up one of my windows. I was tracking a clipboard that an admin was holding. She was the admin for one of the many execs who worked in the building. She was checking off (fortunately, in this case, that meant pressing a checkmark icon on a tablet so that the information was feeding into the SWS computers) each expected attendee as they arrived.

Group A were being directed to Hall Alpha, whilst Group B were being directed to Hall Beta. When I read the message to the admin to set this up, I thought that this was further proof SWS were an evil beyond any other. It was a tradition in tech companies to give clever or interesting names to conference rooms. You didn't just use something boring and sequential like the alphabet. Not even the Greek alphabet.

Group A were the execs. Group B were, as the email they received noted, the great minds that had worked on the project. They were doctors, engineers, programmers, that sort of person. Some digging showed that they were often, in my opinion, under-used. It looked like some exec generally just sent them specs and test protocols and such and had them do the figure-checking or other grunt work. These people, who were truly brilliant, were basically only supporting someone else's glory.

The evening, as we understood it from the emails received by Group B members, would first let members of the group mingle (food and beverages provided) whilst the executives (Group A) had a quick chance to check in with each other. The execs would then mingle with Group B, do some thanking and speeches, and then they'd all launch their latest initiative together (which we knew meant activating something in the vIIs). After which there was a real party set up for Group B at a different location (we'd checked; that location didn't seem to have been booked, nor had accommodations for the Group B members...there *was* a group that had booked a party suite, so we wondered if it had all been done in person, secretly and under false names, to prevent corporate espionage) and Group A would watch initial data from the initiative.

Group A members did not appear to have received emails. And the details of what they'd be doing with the vIIs in this phase weren't obviously indicated anywhere, but, given how frightening I found Peacemakers, this whole thing filled me with dread. The Peacemaker was the monster that caused me to have a "kill it with fire!" reaction.

"Okay, everyone has checked in," I informed my friends. "We're good as soon as CorpSec reports the building is clear."

Per emails about the night, the admin was now heading out of the building, and CorpSec should be doing a last sweep of the building (starting at the center, working out, then heading down to the ground floor).

Jonny updated us, "Ready to...push the big, red button. The bad news is that I don't know if I can get into the computers associated with today's vII action. I just found them, finally, but it will take me some time..."

Kitty asked, "Do you need me to stall? Are those important?"

"No. No, you just do what we planned. But thanks." Jonny's voice was a sort of intense monotone. He must be beating his head against a wall of virtual security measures.

I brought up the window in which I was making sure we'd gotten our hands on any important data. SWS tended to keep their data on servers physically located at headquarters. We had yet to locate their 'Net backups (they must have those, right?), so we had to treat this as our last chance to get their stuff. If things were going as planned, at least three of our laptops were doing a massive wholesale copying of everything we hadn't gotten to yet that was in areas we thought might be important. That didn't seem to be having issues, so, next window.

I made sure I was tapped into their security alert system. If we knew when they knew we were up to something, we might increase our chances of at least evading capture. No doubt South Dakota was a more welcoming place than an SWS holding cell.

Finally, I started trying to pull up internal cameras. The building was full of them. I'd tried to do this a couple times remotely, even pulling in Bryan when I reached the limits of my knowledge, but it had started to look like this was another thing that needed to be initiated locally. We hoped it might get easier once Kitty had the modded mobile connected.

Kitty thanked and paid the cabbie. She took a long, slow breath in. "Let's fucking do this."

I could hear the click of her heels on the pavement. I was picturing her doing her murder stride, that walk she did when she was angry and putting off waves of "I will kill you" with every footfall.

I could hear that the employees who were getting an early end to the day were streaming out around her.

"Victoria Wise here for a four o'clock with Roger Spelton."

The receptionist at the entry desk sounded as surprised and apologetic as Kitty, a.k.a. Victoria, sounded icy. "I'm sorry, Ms. Wise. The office is closing now. Are you sure you've got the correct day and time?"

"*Excuse* me? Are you implying that I'm unable to keep track of my appointments?"

The receptionist stuttered and fumbled words and finally managed a coherent reply. "I'll check Mr. Spelton's calendar."

I wasn't surprised to hear, "Oh. Here it is." I gave silent thanks that we lived in a civilized age of online calendars. Roger Spelton's calendar did, indeed, show an appointment with one Victoria Wise at 1600 today. Jonny had made sure of that.

The receptionist was fully apologetic now, almost cowering. "I am incredibly sorry. Mr. Spelton must have forgotten to cancel. The building is closing down right now."

My ears were practically frostbitten by Kitty's tone. Apparently, her cold knew no limits. "Given that this is the last chance for him to sign some important papers, and that this won't take long, I'm sure you'd do well *not* to assume what he did or did not forget."

There was the slightest beat, and I imagined that Kitty was standing up even straighter, adding every last bit of intimidation, counting on the instinctive fear that so many people who feel powerless have of those who seem powerful. "Contact Mr. Spelton to tell him that I'm here. But, before you do, you may take me into that conference room."

She was (I could guess) pointing an impeccably and conservatively manicured finger towards the conference room just by the reception desk.

"That way, not only do I no longer need to be gaped at by every passing employee whilst I wait, but Mr. Spelton can simply stop in on his way out."

I heard clicking heels. She must have been walking that way, playing the entitled card of "I can't imagine you'd dare to argue with your better." I hoped the receptionist was going home to a nice bottle of wine and someone—even just a cat—to cuddle with and remove the feeling of shit that Kitty was subjecting them to.

The receptionist told someone that it was fine (the CorpSec guy posted at the reception desk?) and let Kitty into the conference room. I assumed Jonny was poised to intercept the message from the receptionist to Spelton.

"I'm in. Plugging in the mobile immediately." Kitty sounded quietly victorious.

I had this surge of joy. We were going to pull this off! We were. Kitty's part was the hardest, in my opinion.

Before she could confirm plug in, we heard a male voice say, "Ma'am, I need to see your ID."

I froze. I told myself he couldn't have caught her plugging in or he would have said something else. Or maybe he didn't see plugging in as a threat. I mean, they had the plugs in there for a reason, right?

But I also froze because her ID was a last minute job. Bryan had sorted out an ID for Riles, but he didn't have time to get a new one for Kitty. Please, please let them be the matched set I'd always thought. How different could they look facing the camera, hair pinned up and slicked down with a painful precision, the mask of thick corporate makeup on?

"Of course." Kitty's voice didn't waver. In fact, it got soft in a way that suggested she was now taking advantage of her pretty face to ease things with CorpSec, just as we'd planned.

I felt some serious respect right then. I was also holding my breath. For fuck's sake; how long did it take to check an ID?

"Thank you. Have a good afternoon."

From the sounds that came in through my earbud, we'd just had a massive group exhale at that one. I saw some movement and noticed my hands were shaking. Deep breath. Couldn't have that. Stared at my fingers until they stopped.

Jonny reported, "Message to Spelton intercepted. You're good for now."

"Okay. There's a podium in the corner by where one of the jacks is supposed to be. Going for it."

Breathe, I told myself. *Passing out helps no one.* I also needed to keep an eye on CorpSec's communications and on the exec email accounts, just in case. So many windows open on my portable.

Bryan said, "Here!" just as Kitty said, "Done!"

With every success, my brain added one more voice to the chorus of We Can Do This! that was picking up. But then I saw something on my screen.

"Bryan, they're on high alert because of all the execs. They've already noticed your truck." I tried to make it sound urgent but not worried.

Riles muttered, "Ugh. That was faster than we'd hoped."

Because we wanted multiple backups to keep execs from fleeing, we had a multi-tiered plan to keep them in. We knew they had a private lift down to one area of the parking garage. The lift made only a few stops in the building, and one was the lobby right by Hall Alpha. If they, as I would have done, had a notification set up for when a self destruct was initiated, there was a chance they could take that lift down to their limos and escape. We would, of course, tell the SWS security systems to close the garage gate and try to shut down the lift. But, just in case someone clever was also clear-headed enough to override that, we had a truck.

The strategic package that Jonny mailed helped that happen. We needed a truck of enough size to block the entry, hopefully enough that not even a person could get past it too easily, but not so big that it couldn't actually fit into the drive. We mailed a package to a nearby building, via a company whose trucks were all the right size, with a set delivery time. This meant our package wouldn't be *too* easily connected with the plans (so it would take longer to pull up security footage and start sorting out who we were), but that we'd be guaranteed access to just the right kind of truck at the right time.

"I locked the doors. No one's easily getting in to move it or to escape through it." He started breathing heavily. "Running now. Did they see me?"

Because Kitty had now, effectively, got us hardwired in, I could see both the reports and camera angles. "They're just running up now." I rewound security camera footage a little. "You managed to keep your head down. It will take them a while to figure out who you are. Might not be able to figure out at all."

I took a peek at Kitty. She was okay, looked like she was just another suit impatiently waiting for a meeting to start. It had only been a few minutes. We couldn't let her run just yet. We couldn't have them find the connected mobile until we'd done our part. I encouraged her, "Hang tight, miss. We're almost there. You're doing great."

Now, we had to move quickly. I was trying to monitor CorpSec and queue up one of the mass mailings to go, making sure it appeared to be CFO Williams being a whistleblower (a last-minute decision for both the mass emails, a pitiful bit of payback for her being behind the orders that ended with 'Randa dead).

"Is the other message ready?" No names on the comms, just in case, but Jonny should know I meant him.

"Ready. Will let you know when I send."

I saw the notification I wanted. "CorpSec reports building clear. We ready to blow?"

Kitty asked, "Wait, what? Blow? Are they setting off the self destruct?"

None of us answered directly, not even Riles.

Jonny said, "Literally seconds away. Prepare to send all. No luck here on getting into the machines they're planning to use tonight. Any luck on our satellite?"

"Almost." Sounded like Riles was gritting zir teeth. "Dammit. Almost."

Bryan added, "I'll have the elevator by the conference rooms and the parking gates reading reverse input ASAP. Then have the choppers' computers down in seconds."

Basically, if anyone pushed up, the gates would go down. If they pushed down, the lifts would go up. (It was a minor stall, but we hoped they'd be panicked enough to gain at least a few seconds with that.) And the choppers would go nowhere.

Excellent.

Out of something that might be deemed morbid curiosity, but was more likely some kind of guilty belief that I had to see the faces of those we were killing, I pulled up the Hall Alpha and Hall Beta cameras.

In Hall Alpha, the execs weren't talking. They were all watching a large screen on one wall. Johnson, Smith, and Williams were leaned towards the screen, as if in anticipation. When I looked at the Hall Beta cameras, I realized that's what the execs were watching too. What was so interesting about Hall Beta?

In Hall Beta, there were dozens of people milling, chatting, eating. It was hard to see them as villains. But then they all started to...Were they choking? Some were putting hands to throats like you would if you were trying to signal to someone for help. But it didn't look like any of them were in a state to help. What the hell was going on?

I switched back to Hall Alpha. They were all still sitting and watching Hall Beta on their monitors. Smiling calmly. Johnson's smile had an ugly edge to it, and I watched Smith and Williams turn to look at her. Hints of victory and pride on all three faces.

In Hall Beta, they were dying.

"Guys, we aren't going to be guilty for the Hall Beta people." I was confused, I was quiet. "It looks like the Hall Alpha people just had them taken out."

There were various vocal expressions of shock, but Jonny brought it back around. "We still proceed, right?"

No pauses. We all agreed. "Yes." Three voices like a chorus. Proceed.

I set up a quick command to grab the video from inside the building. It might help us cast more doubt on the character of those running SWS. It might help us assuage our guilt a little in the days that followed.

Kitty had kept whispering fiercely, "Is the self destruct going on? And what do you mean about us being guilty? What the hell didn't you tell me?"

Jonny ignored her. "Okay. In that case, lock the gates and send the messages." Slight pause. "Mine is sent."

Politicians and media and company heads were getting very

bad news right now.

My CorpSec monitor window flashed. Oh shit. "Victoria, get the hell out. Now. They've just done facial recognition on you. They know who you are." (Just because they knew who she was didn't mean I had to be amateur and use her real name. You know, just in case.)

If only they'd taken another minute more...

Riles, barely holding the façade of calm, urged, "Run, baby. Run!"

Jonny reminded, "Leave the mobile. Walk out quickly. Annoyed to have had to wait. Go. Just like we planned. Only a few seconds earlier than planned."

I pulled up the cameras in the lobby. I couldn't get sucked into them. I had work to do. But...

Jonny said, "Send mail now. *Now.*"

I pressed send. "Done."

And now it was time for doctors, scientists, and other relevant pros to get some news.

I watched as CorpSec grabbed a fleeing Kitty. "Oh fuck. Oh fuck!"

Everyone answered my exclamation with questions, everyone but Kitty, but she answered their confusion for me. I'd forgotten they weren't watching the camera feed. I pushed the feed to everyone else's computers.

Kitty still sounded cold, but I could hear the terror creeping in. "Get your hands off me! How dare you? I'll have your job for this!"

Jonny breathed, "Oh shit oh shit oh shit. I'm going for her."

I heard a click. He must have closed his portable.

Bryan was asking, "Did you initiate? Did you initiate?" and Riles was encouraging Kitty to fight.

Jonny was breathing hard, running I'd bet. "Yes. Initiated."

Multi-tasking was killing me. My screen was flashing a different warning now. Someone was trying to trace things back to me. Shit. "Heads up. I think they've seen our machines. Fight it or shut down?"

I was watching the internal warning sensors light up to warn the execs that the self destruct was in progress, but I was also trying not to shout as I told Jonny, "There's not time to get to the building, baby. I can see the countdown. Victoria, there's just you and him. No backup. Go wild. Flail! Fight dirty."

Riles was shouting, "Remember the self defense course you took!" Then said, "I can't shut down my portable. Shutting down my connection to them. Just working the satellite now."

Bryan jumped in quickly, "Gates are down and controls are reversed; helicopters are disabled. Emergency locks engaged. 45 seconds. I'm out of their system."

I used cameras to see that the execs had, indeed, tried to take their private lift down. I could tell from their faces that it had gone up instead. Johnson and her sidekicks didn't look so victorious now. The assholes. I watched as one typed on a mobile. They must have hit Bryan's first block, because the lift shut down entirely. No lights even, just the glow of screens. But they worked through it. SWS had some smart execs. And they were headed down, towards their limos. Hopefully, we'd stalled them enough.

I didn't want to give away who Jonny was. "Baby, you've got seconds. *Seconds.* You're going to get caught in the blast."

What I didn't say, what I don't think anyone but Bryan realized, was that the emergency locks were set up to keep the doors from opening in either direction. Bryan knew Kitty was lost.

On my screen, Kitty was going wild, just like I'd encouraged her to. She didn't have much of a chance. The CorpSec guy was a big, meaty man. All muscles and buzz cut hair and killer inclinations that I could sense even on the other side of the screen. But she was still trying. She tried the usual self defense stuff, but he knew counter moves. She moved to biting and kicking and flailing wildly. She slipped an arm out and managed to rake it across his eyes. But that bastard didn't even flinch.

I threw some code at the SWS attacker, parried. Took a quick look at my windows.

Bryan said, "Using watch timer. I'll count you down. 30 seconds." He counted down every second.

A quick peek showed me Hall Beta was still. Everyone there was done dying.

I reported, "Execs were stalled but are now headed to limos. Hall Beta...dead."

I remembered to look at the data-mining window. I saw a file flash by that seemed to have a name in the odd symbols. What the hell? No time now. I took a stab, not just a parry, at the SWS attack code. It wasn't fatal.

I could hear Jonny breathing heavily as he ran. Shit. I sent the message to have our remote comrades watch their newsfeeds and go when they saw the signal. Then I said, "I'm going in too. Out of their network."

I disconnected from SWS, closed my portable, shoved it in my bag, and ran.

Bryan said, "15 seconds."

I was pulling my gun as I went.

Jonny grimly said, "Don't you dare follow me."

I grimly replied, "Go fuck yourself. We have to get her out."

Riles was just pleading, "Please please please." Then, in a brief moment of triumph, "I got the satellite. Save her!"

Kitty was screaming.

I said, "One of you unlock the front door so we can get in."

Riles said, "On it!" before I finished asking.

Bryan reported grimly, "You're out of time.

Riles wailed, "Shit! Something hit the satellite. I just cut it off. Not sure how much bounced through."

I guess that means someone pressed a button before running. I silently pleaded to any hope of a deity, *Please, please. Let us have stopped enough.*

Bryan's voice was almost gentle, "Nothing we can do now. We'll check later. At least you cut it off." He knew Riley was about to have something bigger to be upset about.

I picked up my speed, hoping to somehow save Kitty anyway.

I'd been in a closer coffee shop, so I was right behind Jonny. He was putting bullets into the glass, trying to get in to Kitty.

I saw that the CorpSec guys who'd been clearing the building were now rushing towards the exit. They were heading in from a long corridor that, I recalled, came from lifts at the back that took specific keycards and allowed them to avoid being slowed down by the other worker bees.

Jonny reloaded and shouted, "Loads of incoming CorpSec!" and, in that moment, I felt, as much as I heard, a deep explosion.

A pause.

Another. Rippling out.

I knew we still had seconds, but also knew that those explosions would get stronger and closer. I shot at the same area Jonny was shooting.

I saw Kitty stop fighting, stand still. She saw us. Her voice was ice. "Run. Take care of my bae."

She saw us keep shooting anyway and said, "Respect my wishes, you sexist motherfuckers."

Her voice softened. She was looking me in the eyes, in front of a wave of CorpSec and a quicker wave of rolling fire. "Thank you."

I had one of those slow motion moments, where it seemed like the whole world was moving at a fraction of its normal speed just to let you take in the details of something horrible. We stopped shooting and holstered our guns. The CorpSec holding her finally ceased to be distracted by what he thought was a successful subdual of a perp and the crazy people shooting at the windows. He saw us stop, saw his peers rushing the door. Saw the fire behind them.

Jonny turned, grabbed me, and commanded, "Run!"

I turned. As I turned, I felt the shockwave from the latest explosion and saw it fling CorpSec bodies through the large windows that made up the front of the building.

I ran with Jonny, whispering, "I'm sorry, poppet. I'm sorry."

We weren't at all far enough ahead of the CorpSec or the explosions. But we still had more hope than Kitty.

TheCorpSec bodies absorbed much of the force, but also joined debris in flying at us. I got hit in the back and thought, *Don't let this end like it started.* I lost track of Jonny. I was down. I wasn't safe yet.

I was dazed and something heavy was on top of me. I whispered, "Hit."

Jonny said nothing.

Bryan growled, "I'm coming in."

"Fuck this," said Rye. "Your ride is coming."

Through my haze, I heard the sounds of pain as zie maneuvered into the driver's seat and the curses as zie discovered that using zir left leg for the pedals and keeping zir cast-covered right leg out of the way was not as easy as zie'd hoped. I could hear zir crying, and I knew it must be from a pain that wasn't actually physical.

If I make it out, I mentally promised Kitty, *I am never going to be sexist again.* I felt like maybe she was the ice-cold angel who would now sit on my shoulder and keep me from such evils.

I tried to clear my head. Couldn't shake it. Something was on it, on my whole body. I was pinned. I pushed up and a little to the side. Something big on me. Pains all over. Ignored those pains. Fear crawled all over me instead. Breathe breathe don't panic I must not fear fear is the mind-killer shit shit shit.

I tried again to roll and hoped the thing pinning me rolled. It didn't. I was looking at pavement and hearing sirens. There was dust in my mouth. I exhaled to get it out and let myself disconnect. Out of my meat. No meat, no pain, no fear.

And then there were running shoes by my eyes and the weight lifted. And hands helped lift me. I looked down first. Saw it was a big guy, CorpSec uniform, that had been pinning me. Shit. Someone's hands still supported me. They felt strong.

I turned to see the building in smoking ruins. Crumpled bodies covered the little space between me and the building. The building was in an even more ruined state than the last exploding building I'd stood outside of.

My ears were ringing but I could tell my rescuer was trying to talk to me. I ignored it. Hands pulled my hood up. My hat must be gone.

My mind tried to pull me back into my body. I started sinking in. Reluctantly. Then it tried to initiate celebration. *We did it! We did it!* Stupid fucking brain. I pushed that aside. All my attention focused towards where Jonny had been. Stumbled in that direction. The calm of crisis was on me now, but I could feel something raw underneath. I kicked it down. Not now.

I could see Bryan running in. But I was mostly looking at the ground. At the ground. And there was Jonny. Something had hit his head, knocked off his hat too, and he was pinned, as I had been, by a muscle-bound body.

I launched myself in that direction. Bryan got there about when I did, but stopped short a moment, looking behind me. I'd look later. I didn't say names, just in case, but I pushed at the body on top of Jonny. Bryan helped. Body off. Jonny still had his bag on his back. Good omen? I hoped...We bent to pick up Jonny. (I pleaded *Please, please, let it be Jonny and not just Jonny's body*.) A third set of hands helped, no longer supporting me...pale hands...and pulled us towards the wall of a nearby building. Yes, good thinking. Less obviously out in the open. Less obviously involved.

I reached to gingerly pull Jonny's hood up.

My head was pulling together a little. I checked Jonny's breath, his heart. He was alive.

"He's alive!" I could have cried with relief, but the look on Bryan's face when I said it...

Bryan should have looked happier. Instead he looked concerned and pointed at the stranger helping hold up our unconscious friend.

I turned. My mind, in its haze, noted with jealousy that *this* person hadn't been stuck in a fuel station hat, but was getting away with a hoodie. At least I was in a hoodie now too.

I took a moment to focus on the face. I blinked. Finally got to shake my head. It helped a little. Not enough. But then our car was pulling up. Screeching up.

I stammered to Bryan, "Do...do we look for Kitty's body?"

A quick pain crossed over his face. He gave one sharp shake of his head and opened his mouth, but it was Riles who spoke.

Riles who sobbed out, "She'd hate you to get caught just for her body. Get in the damned car!"

So we dove for it, trying to be careful with Jonny. Bryan basically lifted Jonny in, and then ran around to get in the driver's seat, scooting Riles over.

I pushed in behind Jonny, awkwardly moving his limp (but not dead!) body in front of me. Noticed I still had my own bag because it got in my way.

I realized, with alarm and confusion, that the stranger had pushed in behind me, slamming their door.

Bryan looked back, saw the stranger, and gave a frustrated growl. He put the car in motion, pulling out just before emergency response vehicles pulled up. They didn't pursue; must not have spotted us.

Riles looked around sobbing. I started to apologize, but zie saw the stranger and went still, like a deer in headlights.

"Who the fuck is that?"

In the silence of the speeding car, the stranger pushed back their hood. My brain finally put it together. The pale skin, the grey contact lenses, slight ridges on a smooth scalp instead of (maybe usually covered by?) big hair. Just like the execs and the others we'd seen.

They calmly said, "You are all in some seriously deep shit."

As soon as possible, Bryan found an alley to turn down, pulled into it with the passenger side close to the wall. Riley pulled out a gun and leveled it at the intruder. Zir eyes were still wet with grief, but zir hands were surprisingly steady.

"Who the fuck are you?"

The person raised their hands, slowly.

Bryan caught my eye, held up his wrist to show that his watch wasn't detecting any sort of bug or tracking device. I looked down and realized my own was shattered. I started to pat down the pale person next to me, doing the best I could given they were seated and couldn't really stand.

They sounded patient but confused. "I helped save you. I...I want to help."

"We had it under control. We were fine," I snarled. Held up my hands to show that I'd only found keys. No ID or mobile in their pockets.

I kept an eye on them and pulled out my gun. Hadn't lost that in the impact either.

"You didn't look fine. You... you might have been caught." It was a confused statement of fact. Not arguing. Just telling truths.

Bryan had his gun out as well. If he were conscious, I bet Jonny would have appreciated being in this scenario but not being the one at gunpoint.

Bryan clarified the facts, "Caught by *your* people, from the look of things."

We took in the ridges. Up close, not in photos, it looked like the skin was naturally this pale, not made up, and poreless. We might know people who had body mods like the ridges on this person's head, but we'd never heard of a mod to let you go poreless. And that's the sort of thing that would have been wildly popular. Was this some SWS medical experiment? Genetic mutation?

It seemed to dawn on us all at once. I saw the same intrigued confusion I felt mirrored in the others' faces.

Bryan was the one who asked the question, "What *are* your people? Because that's...I've never seen the poreless skin mod."

"Exactly!" I exclaimed. "The ridges, sure. The full sclera contacts, super old school. But the poreless skin? I'd have heard of it and had it done already."

Riley leaned in a bit closer. "I was telling myself the lack of pores was some kind of shock-induced hallucination or due to blurring from tears. Because," and zie leaned back, gun touching the person's temple, "your fucking people basically got my bae killed, you motherfucker."

Patience and sincerity oozed from the person. It was starting to annoy me even more than Jonny's false calm had that first night, when he was under the gun.

"I'm so, so sorry."

I got chills. It was the same tone, though not the same voice, as the person who'd killed 'Randa.

Bryan's gun was also now a little closer. "Your fucking people killed my bae too. Then sent her picture to us. Just because they *suspected* she knew things she *didn't* know." His jaw was clenched.

Riley's nostrils were flaring. I was probably the calmest of us in that moment, and it was taking everything in me not to beat the shit out of this person.

I spit out, "You better have more than apologies. And really quickly. Because you're a breath away from three bullets. Maybe more, depending on how good it feels to pull the trigger."

"That's why...why I'm here. I want to give you...give you answers, not apologies. Because you didn't just end something. You...you set something on fire, and it's going to burn long and hard and maybe consume your planet." The person sighed. "You've got an infestation. And destroying that one nest has only ensured the others will more aggressively dig in. But you might not see it. Because they're patient. So...so you might think you've won and not be around to save some future generation from the next wave." They paused, looked each of us in the face. "My people, in addition to being willing to do whatever it takes to succeed—including murdering innocents or even those defending their homes—are very, very patient. You could say they...they play the long game. Always."

When nobody shot them or asked questions, they said, "And I...I think they need to be stopped. Which means I'm here to tell you everything. And hope that you'll change...whatever plans you had for after what you just did." They looked back at the bags in the rear of the vehicle. "You can't go. Your war isn't over yet."

"I hate to bring this up now," I said. I nodded towards Jonny with my head. "He needs help. Probably immediately. I don't have time for stories. Not yet."

Riles agreed. "We can't lose another person over this. That would be half of us. Even one was too much."

Bryan offered, "We can go see the doc who took care of this one," he tipped his head towards Rye, "but we should probably also hear what this one," and he waved his gun at the pale person, "thinks they have to say. Today was meant to fix things, not make them worse."

In the end, and probably with a little more roughness than was necessary, we bound and blindfolded the pale person, then put them on the floor by my feet. Cramped and folded. They took it all silently, but I held a gun on them the whole drive anyway.

The shock was wearing off. My body was protesting. I could feel the blood dripping down my cheek, the one I had landed on, before Riles reached out to wipe it off. I tried to remember if there'd been a first aid kit in the duffle.

We listened to the news as we drove.

A reporter, probably breathless due to the excitement of a big story, informed us, "Again, SWS headquarters has been demolished by an explosion that bystanders say came from the inside. Currently, authorities report no survivors, but note that most employees were given an early day. If this explosion was initiated by the same group that blew up the SWS clinic two weeks ago, they will have fewer deaths to celebrate than they thought. Though we've been told that the deaths could be high profile. CEO Mary Johnson, COO James Smith, and CFO Jennifer Williams are purported to have been inside." Quick breath, short pause. "Now, we do have reports of some people running away after the blast, but none of whom had been inside as far as witnesses could tell."

There was a bit of a longer pause, and then, with a more cautious voice, she continued, "We've also got...some other information to share, but we need to check whether it's true first." In a conspiratorial tone she added, "But I *can* share that it includes allegations of a shadowy truth under the bright façade of this well-known local company."

CHAPTER 25

Bryan convinced the doctor to see us. Dr. Scott was brisk, slightly annoyed at a drop-in, but proficient. She became slightly friendlier when Bryan assured her, "We'll throw in some extra pay for the hassle. Please."

Once the doctor was working and Bryan made sure my earbud was still functioning, just in case, he went back out to the car. It felt safer leaving us alone with the doctor than leaving Riles alone with the pale person. In my ear, I heard them dividing up the job of replacing or deleting any camera footage of us and the car from the time we left Quinn's to the time we pulled into Dr. Scott's alley.

Whilst the doctor worked on stabilizing Jonny, I asked, "Do you mind if I clean myself up?"

She nodded and grunted in a way that I chose to interpret as "yes." I tried not to make any sounds to disturb her or worry our mates in the car as I cleaned up wounds and put plasters on them. My jeans were scuffed up, but had saved me from anything other than bruises. My shirt was torn, but not unwearable. It had left me with some scrapes on my breasts and my stomach, but nothing too worrying. My hands were now both torn up (though not as badly as after the explosion that started this), as was my cheek.

After she stabilized Jonny, the doctor helped get me sorted, found I'd cracked a kneecap, broken a rib (but on the back of my rib cage...thanks, big arse CorpSec meatbag), and fractured my left forearm. She used the least involved methods to get my bones on the way to healing, stuff that would let me keep moving and wouldn't require a visit to her to remove. Fortunately, the shock was keeping some padding between me and the pain.

Everything else was bruises, abrasions, "Minor things that," she told me, "you can probably just sort out on your own."

I was proud of myself, and hoped Bryan and Riles heard her,

when she added, "You've already done a good job cleaning the debris out of your abrasions."

As she drew up instructions for taking care of Jonny and figured out how to get him mobile, tossing in quite a lot of meds, checking that I was capable of slipping an IV needle into his arm (turned out I was a quick study), and warning me that she didn't guarantee he'd pull through, I listened through my earbud to the radio they had on in the car. More stations were now starting to note that there appeared to be something more to SWS. And, by the time I wheeled Jonny and our new medical gear out on an old school wheelchair (actual wheels, no levitating), one had even read out the creepy vision statement.

When, as promised, I paid her well, the doctor said, "You're welcome to use me in the future, but try to contact me before just showing up." I nodded and she added, "I hope, if this," and she gestured at the mess that was Jonny and me, "is related to what's on the news right now, that it was worth it."

I sighed. "I hope so too." I recalled that she'd been on the recipient list for the second message blast. "You might want to check your private email. Then you tell me if you think it was."

I quickly jotted down a throw-away contact number. "In fact, if you learn anything new that's not in the email or help someone with a Peacemaker who's willing to talk to someone, contact me. Please."

We decided to drive out to where we'd first interrogated Jonny.

Riles noted with forced cheeriness, "Well at least we're already practiced at this bullshit."

Riley kept a gun on our hostage whilst I opened my portable. The screen was cracked but it still worked. I checked in on things. I wanted to be able to give a status update once we could talk freely. Jonny stirred slightly next to me. It was hard to keep my mind on business when I was so worried. But I swallowed that and pushed on. I'd already done harder today.

As far as I could tell, our messages had all made it where we intended. I'd make choices about reading the replies later. (Just in case their security was increased after the explosion, which was a really safe bet, we'd set a tricky little program up to copy over all replies from the SWS server to one of our file locations.)

It also appeared that our remote team had wasted no time in destroying both SWS finances and the credibility of our so-called peers who'd been turned. A couple of them had already realized that, with SWS gone, they had a chance to step in and do a legitimate business of securing people's data. Build their future on the ashes of a corrupt past. They'd sent me notes to let me know their intent and assure me they wouldn't mention their part in this as they built up business.

Our own future was looking at least financially easy. The transfer of funds had worked, and even I had a difficult time tracing so much as one of the many transfers Bryan's program had been set to make.

I was pleased to find that nobody had yet connected any of us to the bombing (but let's give them time), nor had anyone yet connected any of our 'nyms. Bryan's manufactured social media posts had also started to publish and establish an alibi. Hell, the usual attention-seeking "friends" who always liked people to see them as party essentials were already putting up notes about how they thought they'd seen us and should have come over to say hello. "Maybe I'll run into you again later tonight? We can get fucked up!" Nice to know there was a use for them.

And it was the best of news to discover that, whilst we were destroying a company, Gran was adding pictures to her storage of her and Sarah digging out an old piece of tech (a turntable, I think it's called) to have an evening dance party on their own.

I decided it was safe to say, "Everything appears to have gone as planned, and everyone...everyone else is fine." I caught on that last bit, thinking of Kitty. One more death on my head; one more of the good guys lost.

The news didn't agree with my last statement. Everyone was *not* fine. They were scrambling quickly, now that they'd gotten their techs to verify the veracity of the documents (or at least verify it enough), to be the ones to break some bit of troubling information another channel hadn't yet. They were still carefully couching it in terms that would save them from libel charges later, if some remaining SWS employee tried to salvage their reputation, but the world was hearing the terrifying truth now.

The world was under threat from SWS, but at least seemed to have someone or ones fighting for it. "Documents that appear to have been sent from within the building itself, by a highly placed executive, mere seconds before the explosion. Suggesting that this was a selfless act, the *last* act of whoever did this."

One newsperson even said, "We can't condone violence. But, in the face of what we're now learning about SWS, one must ask whether those who bombed the building after sending the documents might be heroes, not terrorists."

Bless the hyperbole of media. We needed that boost right now.

On the same deserted, industrial side street where we'd last held guns on Jonny (who was occasionally, briefly conscious), we sat our hostage up. We didn't remove the blindfold, so Riles pressed zir gun into their temple again to make it clear we were still shooting-level serious. And zie directed, "Start talking."

The pale person evenly, with a tone that made me think of reverence, said, "As Peaceforgers it is our duty to guide the world into peace. Through our influence and actions, we ensure that all are brought into the light of peace or cast aside as darkness. In a world of war and fear, we bring the light of security. No darkness will stand. Peace is security. Security is peace."

The vision statement. The cult-like, crazy vision statement. From memory. They let it hang in the air for a moment before quietly going on.

"Each new planet, as my people prepare to embark on a crusade of peace, we write a new...you would call it a scripture or a mantra. Something in line with past scripture but specific to the present planet. To guide us as we bring the 'blessed' peace to a new world." They sneered as they said, "blessed," but it took a moment for my mind to get to processing that part.

Bryan's voice was full of caution. "That makes it sound like you're saying you aren't from this planet."

"We long ago finished building the fires of peace, forging peace on our own world, and left it behind to spread the peace further. Now, we take the brutal heat and pounding of our peaceforging to other worlds. Whether you want it or not." They sounded worn, not boastful.

Riles repeated Bryan's point. "Yeah, it definitely sounds like you're saying you aren't from Earth."

"I'm a missionary from the stars. Fortunately for the people of Earth, I've decided that the ways of *my* people are not for me. I want to help you free yourselves from the heavy proselytizing of my shy'a'on-sha'ai, my family-in-peace." They turned their head, as if trying to read the car in spite of the blindfold. "My people have a guiding principle. 'You will be heated and beaten into shape, or you will be heated and beaten into ashes.' And I'm afraid, today, you showed a preference for ashes."

Apparently coasting on consciousness, Jonny sighed out, "Ashes to ashes...funk to funky..."

Our hostage nodded. "There's no turning back. No cease fire possible. Your world too will, instead, burn with the peace fire."

What had we done?

END

ACKNOWLEDGEMENTS

Loads of gratitude for many and assorted reasons to Ernest Cline, Philip Baird, Clarissa C.S. Ryan, Nathan R. Long, Dorothy B. Mulvihill, and Jason Cope.

A special thank you to those family and friends who have been understanding and supportive of my life. Loving a creator, at least if that creator is me, means you see very little of me (because my time is eaten by my creative endeavours) and that you often don't have my full attention when you do see me (because my mind is, even when I try to make it otherwise, constantly on my work). So those of you who have stuck around and been cool or enthusiastic about things are magical. This includes my forgiving cat.

Love and stars and purple ribbons to my favourite Secret. This book is one of many things I could not have made it through without you. Constantly slipping and I'm not complaining...

Respect and appreciation to the musicians, writers, and other creators who filled my head with sparks and whose works and examples have helped me feel like giving life a chance. I can't list names, or I'll wake up the day after this is published in horror, having realised I've forgotten someone. But I can't *not* name David Bowie, can I?

And, finally, thanks to you, the reader. I truly believe that art isn't complete until it's been read, listened to, viewed, etc. When you read this, you help it become complete.

Photo by Jesse Means

Amber Bird is a writer, a rockstar, and a scifi girl. She is the author of the Peaceforger books, the front of post-punk/post-glam band Varnish, and an unabashed geek. An autistic introvert who found that music, books, and gaming saved her in many ways throughout her life, she writes (books, poems, lyrics, blogs) and makes music in hopes of adding to someone else's escape or rescue. And, yes, she was on that Magic card.

If you'd like to know more about Amber and the things she creates, visit amberbird.com.